Praise for Evie Wyld's

THE BASS ROCK

"Like Sarah Waters and Attica Locke, Hannah Kent and Celeste Ng, Evie Wyld writes novels that are fast-paced page-turners with meticulously crafted narratives. . . . Wyld entertains while she provokes." —*Chicago Review of Books*

"Riveting. . . . Powerful. . . . Like any good gothic novel, there is a dark old house full of noises and things that go bump in the night." —*The Brooklyn Rail*

"A haunting survival tale that lingers long after the last page." —*Kirkus Reviews*

"Vivid and gripping." —*The Irish Times*

"Tremendous. . . . A powerful and beautifully written narrative of male violence and the three women who endured it." —William Boyd, *The Daily Telegraph* (London)

"Wyld is unhesitatingly brave in her writing. . . . Her prose shines, even as it devours." —*Financial Times*

"A multilayered masterpiece; vivid, chilling, leaping jubilantly through space and time, it's a jaw-dropping novel that confirms Wyld as one of our most gifted young writers." —*The Observer* (London)

"Wyld's skillfully woven narrative will keep you turning towards a final, unexpected twist." —*Evening Standard* (London)

ALSO BY EVIE WYLD

After the Fire, a Still Small Voice
All the Birds, Singing
Everything Is Teeth (with Joe Sumner)

Evie Wyld

THE BASS ROCK

Evie Wyld's debut novel, *After the Fire, a Still Small Voice*, was shortlisted for the International IMPAC Dublin Literary Award and was awarded the John Llewellyn Rhys Prize. Her second novel, *All the Birds, Singing*, won the Miles Franklin Literary Award, the Encore Award, and the European Union Prize for Literature and was shortlisted for the Costa Novel Award. She is also the author of the graphic novel *Everything Is Teeth*. In 2013 she was named as one of *Granta*'s Best of Young British Novelists. She lives in London.

www.eviewyld.com

THE BASS ROCK

Evie Wyld

VINTAGE BOOKS

A DIVISION OF PENGUIN RANDOM HOUSE LLC

NEW YORK

For the Wylds

FIRST VINTAGE BOOKS EDITION, AUGUST 2021

Copyright © 2020 by Evie Wyld

The Library of Congress has cataloged
the Pantheon edition as follows:
Name: Wyld, Evie, author.
Title: The Bass Rock / Evie Wyld.
Description: First United States edition. |
New York : Pantheon Books, 2020.
Identifier: LCCN 2019059637
Classification: PR6123.Y43 B37 2020 | DDC 823/.92—dc23
LC record available at https://lccn.loc.gov/2019059637

Vintage Books Trade Paperback ISBN: 978-0-525-43270-8
eBook ISBN: 978-1-101-87189-8

www.vintagebooks.com

Printed in the United States of America
10 9 8 7 6 5 4 3 2 1

I was six and just the two of us, my mother and I, took Booey for a walk along the beach where she and Dad grew up, the shore a mix of black rock and pale cold sand. It was always cold—even in summer we wore wool jumpers and our noses ran and became scorched with wiping on our sleeves. But this was November, and the wind made the dog walk close to us, her ears flat, her eyes squinted. I could see the top layer of sand skittering away, so that it looked like a giant bed sheet billowing.

We were looking for cowrie shells among the debris of the tideline. I had two digging into my palm, white like the throat of a herring gull. My mother had a keener eye and held six. I felt the pull of victory slackening.

Resting in a rock pool was a black suitcase, bulging at the sides. The zip had split and where the teeth no longer held together I saw two fingers tipped with red nails and one grey knuckle where a third finger should have been. The stump of the finger, like the miniature plaster ham I had from my dolls' house. The colour had been sucked from the knuckle by seawater, leaving just a cool grey and the white of the bone. It was the bone, I suppose, that made it so much like the tiny ham. I moved my arm to swat something away from my face and, as I did, flies rose from the suitcase in a cloud, thick and heavy.

Behind me, my mother—"Another one!" she called. "I've found another one!"—and then the smell, like a dead cat in the chimney in summer, a smell so tall and so broad that you can't see over or around it.

1

My mother walked up behind me. "What's . . ."

I kept looking at the fingers and trying to understand, my mother pulling me by the arm. "Come away, come away," she said, and spitting over and over on to the sand, "don't look, come away." But the more I looked the more I saw, and peeking through the gaps between the white fingers was an eye that seemed to look back at me, that seemed to know something about me and to ask a question and give an answer. In the memory, which is a child's memory and unreliable, the eye blinks.

The Lamb

I

The small supermarket in Musselburgh is open until 10 p.m. and the staff look offended by me as I walk in at 9:35. I imagine how I must appear after eight hours in the car. I splashed my face with water in a service station near Durham and my hair has dried strangely. I am unkempt enough to present as a shoplifter.

I have parked towards the back of the supermarket by the cash machines, to remind myself to get some on the way out because the shops nearer the house prefer not to accept cards.

I spend a long time at the herbs. There's fresh ginger and the chillies and I wonder how I would go about making something with them. I put some lemon thyme in my trolley instead. Perhaps I will roast a chicken tomorrow. Or a couple of thighs. I'm not a good cook—I like thighs because when I forget them they don't dry out.

I always overdo it on the fruit—but it's hard not to feel excited. They have all different colours of plum from Kenya—yellow, orange, purple, red and black—and I put a carton of each in my trolley. That's thirty plums for me to eat in a week, which is only a little over four a day and feels like something I could accomplish. Two in the morning, two at night. If I were the kind of person who could preserve things, I'd preserve

5

a jar of each variety and just have them to look at. But they would grow a film of mould, like the time I made chilli olive oil and the bottle went black. I am missing some fundamental element of preservation. I suspect it's cleanliness. I move on, and though I try to think of something new and interesting to cook, by the time I get to the frozen aisle, I have spaghetti, tinned tomatoes and tinned clams. A box of eggs I will never use and some sliced brown bread and the herbs. None of it I want to eat tonight. But it is at least food that suggests a certain seriousness. I am the sort of woman who is here to work. Who is doing her family a favour, not the other way round. I am no longer the person who failed every day last June to get out of bed before midday. Who stopped going to work and seeing her friends and answering the phone, and had to be driven by her sister to the hospital when the breath stopped coming in and going out, and who could only make one long lowing noise. I did not spend seven days in a room with no edges, with a sign on the door that said *No Cutlery Whatsoever (including teaspoons!)*.

The tannoy announces that the store will be closing in five minutes and it feels a message to me in particular.

There is a woman in the frozen aisle, which I am only in because it marks the completion of my shopping trip. She has no trolley or basket even; she's looking at the choc ices. She picks out a box of four expensive mint ones that have a woman's mouth large and rude on the front cracking through the chocolate.

She has an unlit cigarette in her mouth, ready to go, big curly hair that has been teased and sprayed and she's wearing pink lipstick. She smiles at me, and says, "Late-night ice cream?" and I feel so flustered I go red and then I laugh too

6

loudly and just say, "Plums." She smiles back and turns to leave. I'll be hearing myself saying *plums* all night.

At the end of the frozen aisle is a display of Mr. Freeze's Jubbly orange ice lollies. When we were kids, Dad, in his best moods, when he wanted nothing more than to make Katherine and me laugh, would sing a song from the advert that was on TV when he was young, *lovely jubbly, lovely jubbly orange drink*. Why that was the thing that made us laugh the most is hard to pinpoint, but I think it had more to do with him wanting us to laugh, than the song itself. Even so, I am standing still because, like so many small things discovered every day, I am faced with never hearing that song in his voice again. I have forgotten the fucking chicken thighs and so I speed back to the meat fridge and all the nice chicken is gone, there's only the stuff that has had an awful life and tastes of fish. I put a tin of sardines in my trolley, put the herbs back on the shelf. Pre-sliced Swiss cheese, a bar of chocolate and some celery, just for show.

There is only one till left open, a small queue of us trying to project that shopping this late is not usual for us. I flick through a magazine. There's a moody image of a man thumbing his upper lip to show off either his cufflinks or his watch. He wrinkles his forehead in a way that is supposed to be sexy. And then opposite him, a pale stick of a girl with hair parted down the middle, lips painted into a red bow, a puppet at rest. She stares off into the distance, sad. She's there to be looked at by the man with the cufflinks and the wrinkled brow, but she is not there to look back.

My mother's voice in my head—*Why do all these women want to look like deer in the headlights? Why do all these men want to look like they laugh too loudly in public?*

I am glad that the time spent thinking about how other people will respond or not respond to my body and face has passed. I'm older than my mother somehow because at least she participated in her life at my age—she had a husband and children and then lost part of that and now lives as it seems she always meant to, alone and with her work. She's been working on poisonous fungi of France for nine months now. The only framed picture in my flat is one she gave me as a moving-in present three years ago, a fly agaric with a stag beetle meandering past it, for scale. It leans unhung in my bedroom. There is probably a house spider nestling behind it. My mother has found being alone a new beginning. Her house is tidy. She eats what she wants, when she wants: nothing for a day and then a dressed crab at eleven at night, or a bowl of frozen peas, uncooked, which she eats like peanuts for breakfast. I admire the singleness that she has embraced since Dad died. I think I could aspire to that, but without having to be widowed first.

Sometimes, though, it would be nice to fuck and to be fucked.

I look now and again online at single men and women, older than me, I always go older, not because I am looking for someone mature or experienced, but because the young have filters on their profiles to get rid of the elderly, which, at close to forty, I have become all of a sudden.

There have been a few matches: Steven from Harringay, fifty-six; Philip from Clapton, forty-nine; Isabella from Hampstead, sixty-two. And if they don't have filters, like Marco, Tooting, thirty-six, it is possibly because of some sort of fetish. My phone was low on memory, and so I deleted the app, I did it while my sister watched so that she could throw back her head and cluck in an exasperated way.

The woman at the till says "Good evening," as if she is booking me in at a police station.

I am walking to my car with my small bag of food, when I see the woman with the ice creams is there, just outside the sliding doors. She is eating one and drumming her long fingernails on the packet with the other hand. My car is the only one in the car park. She must be waiting for someone to pick her up. I try not to catch her eye. "Hey!" she calls. I smile but don't make eye contact—is she going to try to engage me in conversation again? Should I explain the plums?

"Hey!" she says again. "Good to see you, hen! How are you?" She seems to think we know each other.

Perhaps she wants money. Suddenly I feel very alone in the car park—the security guard has started to put the shutters down, and I glance back at him but he's not looking.

"Um, sorry, I'm not sure I know you," I say and start to walk quickly to the car—I won't get cash out tonight.

"Yes," she hisses, trotting to keep up with me, "but pretend that you do, there's a man hiding behind your car." I stop and she bumps into me. I can't see anyone by the car from where we're standing, but the cash machines are lit brightly, which means everything around them is a deeper dark.

"I got you an ice cream," she says, in the loud voice. She hands me one from her box. I take it automatically.

"What do we do? We should get the security guard." As I whisper the light at the front of the supermarket goes out.

I still don't see anyone there, and have a sudden and bad feeling. Who goes shopping that late at night, no car, just to buy choc ices? It's not normal behaviour. Get to your car, I think, shake this woman off, give back her ice cream, which is making the whole situation much more difficult to navigate, physically and mentally. I push the button to pop open my boot, and the woman says, "It's been so long, I haven't seen ye since school—what've ye been up to?"

I open my mouth in confusion and as I fumble for an answer, remembering as I do that it doesn't matter, we didn't go to school together, a figure rises up out of the dark from the passenger side of my car, and all I can see is that his hand is in the pocket of his jacket and he is wearing dark clothes and is away from us quickly without running. I stand there watching him go, my heart beating in my throat. I have the terrible feeling that I might cry.

"Feckin creep," she says, and opens another ice cream.

"Should we tell someone?" I say.

"Tell them what? There's a man being creepy? There are men being creepy all over the place, hen. Believe me."

"Um, look, thanks so much, I'm sorry, I didn't know what was going on."

"Hey, no drama," she says.

"Here's your ice cream back," I say.

"Ha!" she says. "You keep it, hen—I got two more right here." She bites into the new one and the chocolate cracks loudly. "So, take care," she says and turns to walk down the pathway towards the main road.

"Wait. What if he comes back?" I say. "Can I give you a lift somewhere?" It is unlike me to offer a lift at any time of day, let alone in the dark, to a complete stranger, but it is out of my mouth before I can stop it.

The woman turns round, smiles.

"You know what? That'd be great."

Inside the car, I wonder what I am doing.

"You mind?" she asks, gesturing to her ice cream.

"Not at all."

We drive out of the car park and up the hill. "I always have to have ice cream when I'm stoned, you know."

She directs me, and tells me where she is from, and I forget immediately what she says.

"It's pretty shitty," she says, "but then I'm from a pretty shitty part of it."

I nod. I can't think of a single question. There are no street lamps as we head towards the coast, and my high beams haven't worked in years. I expect to see something slinking after us, its eyes lit red in the headlights. She seems completely unaffected by the incident in the car park. I feel as homesick as an eleven-year-old.

"What do you do?" she asks.

"Freelance stuff." I try to make cleaning out my great-aunt and grandmother's house sound like a job. "Archival stuff, mostly. I'm just up for the weekends, about to start a new project." I clear my throat for a long time.

"Cool!" she says. "Art?"

"Yes. And other stuff."

I have said stuff too many times.

"That's cool. I like art, me."

There is a long, long silence.

"How did you get into that?"

"I did my degree in history of art," which is almost true, I did the first year anyway, and it was so long ago that any influence it might have had on the direction my life has gone in feels only tangential. "My mother's a botanical artist, so that sort of thing is in the family." Except that it's not really. I almost tell her my father has just died, to try and gain some ground, as though it happened that morning and actually it's incredible that I'm buggering on, but no one accepts that now

11

that two years have passed. *It's time to move on*, they may not say it but you see it on their faces.

"Like, plants and that?"

"Yes, well, fungi really."

"Oh aye," she says. And then the silence is back.

I realise too late that I should ask what she does; the silence has ended that strand of conversation. A light rain begins to fall.

"I'm Maggie. Not short for anything. Just Maggie," she says.

"Viv. For Viviane."

"I've never met a Viviane before," she says like it genuinely surprises her. I feel the need to elaborate.

"My mother said she liked the name because it sounds sharp."

"Ha!" she says. "My mother thought Maggie sounded like a fluffy chick."

I have nowhere to go, nothing to say. I wish I could stop bringing up my mother.

On the coastal road, by the golf course, she tells me to stop.

"I walk from here. Nice stroll under the stars."

"Are you sure?"

She puts out her hand and we shake like we've completed some kind of business.

"See y'around, hen." There are no other cars on the road, and I watch her disappear down the slope towards the beach, her gait loose and comfortable like she walks to music. Somewhere, out in the darkness, I can hear waves breaking against the Bass Rock though I cannot see it.

II

At the butcher's Ruth bought stewing steak. She planned to make a pie. She'd been able to smell all day the meat pudding Betty had left for them—popular, it seemed, in Scotland, it had appeared insidiously on her dinner table at least four times in the five weeks since they'd arrived. It made the spirits sink in the same way that fish pie had back home. The thought of it sitting in its steamer turned Ruth's stomach. She would make a basic steak pie with potatoes and runner beans. One of the few supper recipes that she kept in the back of her appointments diary. Perhaps she would also make a Victoria sponge for the boys. Would they like that, or would it seem like a bribe?

It was, she decided, possible to think too much about this sort of thing.

The day was bright with the remnants of late summer, too cold not to wear a hat, but the sun warmed her back so much that she felt rather damp by the time she had walked the length of the high street, and so she stood a while on the concrete steps of the outdoor pool, watching the swimmers, their limbs glowing white under the water. One woman moved so slowly there seemed barely any momentum. She ducked her floral-capped head under the water and came up, spraying wet breath. Other swimmers more dedicated to movement

13

swam around her. *She is enjoying being weightless*, thought Ruth. *She doesn't care about going forward.* A baby gull stood hunched on the top step watching the swimmers too. It cried and paddled its feet in disgust. Ruth looked at it. "They do it for fun," she told it, and it angled its head to give her the benefit of one marble-black eye.

At the post office was a letter from Alice. Ruth bought a postcard of the pool and the Pavilion with the steep side of the Law looking unfriendly behind it. When she'd first seen it, the severity of its incline had felt unnatural, and the whale-bones on top seemed signifiers of some kind of awful paganism. But as she had become used to it, she thought more about the people who carried the bones up there, and what a feeling, in the end, of triumph they must've felt each day, seeing them up there glinting in the daylight. In the postcard, however, the Law was badly served and lumpen in black and white, the whalebones on top of the hill barely visible; despite this, she liked the idea of being able to place a cross on the window she was sitting beside as she wrote it. They recognised her at the Pavilion by now, and the serving girl nodded hello and escorted her to a table which had a view of the pool. She watched for the floating woman, but she was gone, or, perhaps, sunk. There was still the unmistakable glance here and there of ladies wondering about her. It wouldn't be long, she knew, before she would have to make allies, or else risk appearing aloof. But she had always been slow to warm up, and she viewed befriending Betty the housemaid as the more urgent task, as Peter had several dozen complaints about her cooking, which would have to be handled in a delicate way.

Alice's stationery was tasteful and curated. A pattern of willow on the lining of the envelope, white crisp writing paper with an ornate watermark. Letters from Alice were small parcels to be unwrapped and to keep and look at for years to come. Surreptitiously, after she'd given her order—a pot of tea in a silver teapot and a finger of shortbread—she sniffed the envelope. It could have been Alice's expensive hand cream, but it could just as easily have been that she had perfumed the letter with the coral-and-brass atomiser that sat on her desk. Ruth pictured her wearing a gossamer robe and heels while she wrote. The content, however, did not live up to the packaging.

Darling Puss,

Such bad luck, dear old Ludwig is dead, probably rat poison, though of course he was ancient and, poor thing, almost completely blind last I saw him. Spoke to Father at the weekend, who is beside *himself. They didn't want to bother you with the news, Mother thinks you're dealing with "enough death in your marriage at the moment," at which I roll my eyes on your behalf. I knew you'd want to know.*

Father wants a grave marker, but they are at loggerheads about what to put on the stone—Mother is for "Albert," Father stamps his foot and shouts that the war is over, and that he shall bury his friend under his proper name. Mother fears vandals, though I'm not sure how many of those live in Much Hadham. Antony of course would have whisked the body away for burial at sea.

Anyway, so sorry to be the bearer of sad news, Puss, do hope you keep well in all other ways.

Mark and my 5th anniversary this weekend—can you even conceive of it? Wish you could be here, have a "wee dram" for us.

London is hell.

All my love,

Alice

15

Ruth refolded the letter and carefully housed it back in its envelope. She pressed it flat on the white linen tablecloth and weighed it down with the salt cellar. Out of the window she looked past the pool and the harbour, and there in the dark water she noted the floral swimming cap again, bobbing out in the open sea this time. Or perhaps it was just a sun-pinked buoy. On clear days like these the Bass Rock looked close enough to swim around, though she had received a humour-less lecture from more than one local for exclaiming this in public. She drank her tea without milk and slipped the short-bread into her pocket so as not to draw attention to herself as a wastrel. She counted out money, leaving extra to make up for going without saying goodbye and thank you; she tied her red handkerchief over her hair as she went, the clouds outside threatening spit. She couldn't bring herself to get back into her overcoat. The gentle skit of the harbour boats and their sails connecting with their masts was louder than it had been earlier—the wind had picked up. The cries of seagulls were incessant.

On the way home, she stopped at the bridleway that veered off through the trees and towards the beach. Underneath the trees it was dark, and the wind didn't penetrate there. A pinprick of light—a dove—landed in the topmost branch of a fir, and the whole tree swayed like the dove was made of lead. Ruth left the stewing steak and her coat hanging over on the fence and walked towards the dove, feeling her heart throb, not out of fear but as if it were being pulled towards the blackness of the trees, out of her chest. Butterflies, white and blue and black, that should have been long dead coasted the still air. "Tell me something," she said to them or to the dove or to the trees—she wasn't sure—"tell me what to do next." Silence. "Tell me *something* at least. One tiny thing."

But the dove didn't even cock his head to look at her and the trees were just trees. She wondered if she had gone mad again, and started when she saw, curled in the bracken, a sleeping fox. Or perhaps it was dead. The earth around it was scuffed and disturbed, but no blood about him. His fur grey, not orange like the foxes at hunts or in pictures. Not dead; she caught the rise and fall of its little ribs.

When she returned to the fence, the meat and her overcoat were gone. She felt foolish. The walk home was cold, the brightness of the afternoon had given way to the usual damp wind, and Ruth wrapped her arms around herself and walked as close to a run as she could. Her home was not yet a natural one—she still found as she rounded the corner of the golf course and looked up at the house that it didn't quite sit with her correctly as *home*. It felt like something belonging to a grand relative. It was too big, which she'd pointed out to Peter when they first saw it, it was too big for a couple and two children at boarding school. And the space—the servants' quarters were the same size if not larger than Peter's cottage in Dummer. And the empty ballroom with the unplayed piano as big as the flat in Kensington she had rented before Peter came along. She'd meant to get the piano tuned, but there was no one in North Berwick who could do it, the man who used to service it had died, Betty had said, and so they'd really have to look to Edinburgh to find a new one. She'd blushed rather, after saying, "Well, who does everyone else use to tune their pianos?" Betty had looked at her and she was aware, as she had been hundreds of times, how easily it could have been another woman standing there, doing the things she was doing. She wished she could say, "Just tell me how *she* would do it and I'll do it like her."

She came in the back door, so that she wouldn't be seen without her coat, and had to squeeze past the old retriever Booey who lay like a draught excluder against the door. She patted him in apology and walked briskly to the tallboy and turned out the pockets of her skirt for keys and change purse. Even through her gloves her fingers were solid ice, and she touched them for a moment to her face to warm them up. In the mirror she noted how the skin of her cheeks reddened from the cold and the salt wind, and her hair, once she unwrapped it from the scarf, had gone out of shape and no longer complimented her long face. In fact she looked horsey and ruddy. She stabbed at her hair a little and applied a small amount of lipstick that she kept in the drawer of the tallboy along with her cigarettes. She looked no better, though perhaps she looked a touch more purposeful.

Peter and the boys were having late-afternoon tea in the kitchen. On the counter, a large Victoria sponge made the day before by Betty. She'd known, of course—Betty always made sure to tell Ruth what was available for the children—it just had slipped her mind. She would bake some apples then— hardly the height of sophistication. Ugly to look at, but she felt the need to contribute in some small way to the evening meal, even if it was only to prolong it after the wretched meat pudding.

"Darling," Peter said, kissing her cheek, "how was your morning?"

"Fine," she said, leaving the letter from Alice in its envelope on the counter. "Though the butcher was closed, I'm afraid— we'll have to eat what Betty's left us."

"How perfectly ghastly. Will you have some cake with us?" he asked. "It seems the one real talent Betty has, we ought to make the most of it."

"Oh, stop it, darling—we're just not yet used to Scottish food. They have different traditions up here," she said, pouring herself a glass of water to quell the thought of dinner.

"You would say that—you're afraid of her." Peter made a face at the boys. Michael laughed, but Christopher had recently become too mature to. She smoothed down her jumper over the waistband of her skirt. She felt a little sick.

"You know perfectly well that's absolute tripe and so I shall ignore you." She addressed the boys: "And how was your day?"

Michael with his mouth full: "We saw a shark."

Ruth flicked her eyes to Peter's.

"He's quite right. It's washed up on Milsey Bay—poor creature must've got stuck when the tide went out."

"It was dead," said Michael.

"Big, was it?" Ruth poured another glass of water, the first being rather too tepid and not having the calming effect on her stomach she had hoped for.

"Very," said Peter.

"We asked a fisherman what kind of shark it was and he said a basking shark." It was the most Christopher had spoken to her since the move. She smiled.

"Did it have great big teeth?"

"No," said Christopher, "because it's not that kind of a shark." Peter raised his eyebrows slightly over the boy's head and Ruth sat down next to him.

"Perhaps I will have a small piece of cake after all," she said. "And maybe sometime tomorrow you boys might show me where this shark is—it sounds absolutely disgusting."

"There was a seagull eating its eye," volunteered Michael.

With the boys long in bed, Ruth climbed the staircase to the top of the house and quietly opened the door to their room.

It would be Michael's first term boarding—he ought to have started in the previous year, but the raw chest had kept him at home. Christopher had been boarding these past two years, since the wedding. Things were calmer now, by the sea. Like the wind swept certain moods and memories away with it, so one could be feeling rather black and then find oneself stood at the line of foam left by the waves and wonder what the blackness had been about. She just needed to become an ounce more settled, get stuck into a project. Maybe the painting. There was the lightest sense of movement in the boys' room. She could see by moonlight the seal-like bumps of the sleeping children. The window was open a crack, a breeze moving through delousing them of their bad dreams. She shut the door again quietly and stood outside their room listening for a moment. Just the whisper of song came from the room, unfamiliar to her, and then gone. A trick of the golf course, it brought sounds unfiltered by trees from far away. Ruth left the landing and walked down the outer strip of the staircase, so as not to make a noise—the staircase did creak terribly if one was careless—and joined Peter in the drawing room for a nightcap.

"The boys were very happy today," he said, looking up from the drinks cabinet. He handed her a brandy, poured himself a whisky. "I think they're beginning to get the point of the place—I told you, all they needed was some good sea air." He took a drink from his glass, and heaved a loud sigh of contentment. "It's done us all the world of good."

"Yes, you're right." She smiled, raised her glass to him and drank. The summer holidays had seemed like an eternity when they'd first arrived, plenty of time to get settled, to all get used to this next part of their lives together. But still nothing felt settled.

"I'm certain that boarding will be fruitful for Michael—he's got a little too much of me in him sometimes, I'm afraid." Peter smiled back over his drink.

"How do you mean?"

"I caught him going through the pockets of one of your coats this morning."

"What was he looking for?"

"Money, I imagine. Now that we live somewhere with a sweet shop in walking distance. I once took a pound note out of Father's money clip. I got found out because I tried to get a quarter of bullseyes from our grocer's and he couldn't break it, and he told my mother when she was next in." Peter laughed one loud bark. "I got the thrashing of my young life."

"You didn't hurt Michael?"

"He received a gentle cuff around the head and a stern bollocking. I haven't really the stomach for anything else these days. Saw a boy shot in Greece for stealing grapes—rather puts things into perspective." He let out a small and unconvincing laugh. "But he'll need to stop all that when he's boarding. For now, though, a good idea to lock away your valuables."

Ruth wondered whether Michael would have made it out with just a gentle cuff from Peter if he had behaved in the same way before the war. It had shaped men so entirely. Or else melted them away.

She wished one of them had a birthday out of term time so that she would have a reason to arrange a picnic. A picnic for no good reason felt like an oversell. It would be bad parenting. She had seen a picture of Elspeth on a picnic blanket with the boys, Michael just a bulb-headed baby, Christopher with those same black eyes like an otter's. Three creatures on a blanket, in love.

"I saw a letter from Alice on the counter—all well in London?"

"Oh yes, quite well. It'll be the anniversary party this weekend."

Peter looked up. "I expect you'll be feeling rather beastly not going?"

"Oh. No. Not really. The idea of all those people, and Mother and Father, and all that noise. It's never appealed very much. Anyway, it's not even their actual anniversary." Since they had celebrated their real anniversary with a month and a half in Kenya, and since Alice was not willing to miss the opportunity to throw a party, they had quite boldly taken to telling everyone it was their anniversary when it was not. It was at times a little irritating, Alice's confidence that everyone would play along. And yet they did, Ruth had received not even one aggravated phone call from her mother.

"Quite—couldn't imagine a worse time—all those opinions flying around and the chaps making off-colour jokes." Peter was referring to a party Alice had thrown for them when they became engaged where someone had brought along a carton of marijuana cigarettes.

"Yes. Very pleased to have an out." She wondered for a moment if that might be true, and thought it might be. It was sometimes a little hard to tell. There was a hard kernel of something inside that felt wretched.

"Yes, all is quite quite well. Though Ludwig has died." The moment it came out of her mouth she felt a tiresome constriction of her throat.

"The dog?"

"Yes."

"Mmm. Old?"

"Yes. Also, rat poison."

Peter moved behind her and put his hand on the back of her neck. "It's been a rather bad day for the animal kingdom," he said.

"Well," she said, finding she was holding back tears, "he was only a dog."

"Quite. Though I'm only a man. A shark is only a shark." He went to stand at the bay window though it was dark outside and there was nothing to see. Through the glass could be heard the waves breaking on the beach. She rested her hand on her stomach, and hoped the tide would not take the shark away before Christopher and Michael had a chance to show it to her.

The next morning, before the rest of the household awoke, Ruth stood at the back door and surveyed the garden. She didn't like to smoke in front of the children, or even Peter. It felt like something left over from another part of her life, leaning on the balcony at Kensington, dropping ash on the shoppers below.

Weeds were starting to grow in the damp spaces between the bricks of the garden path. The air was a different beast today, you felt the lick of it cold on your bare arms the moment you were out of the sun. There had been a phone call to Alice late the previous evening, to congratulate on the false anniversary. Wood, you were supposed to give for five years. Peter and she were only up to cotton. Both flimsy materials when you looked at it. Alice had spent the phone call happily recalling her and Mark's wedding day, which had passed in quite a different tone for Ruth, everyone dutifully taking their turn in speaking to her, as the maid of honor. She had relived it that night in bed, while Peter slept.

During the speeches her brother's name had been used like punctuation. Ludwig had cavorted in the roses, ignoring the guests and getting on with his own business. He had taken to eating the snapdragons, which passed through him nearly whole so that he left colourful little deposits upon the lawn, upsetting Nanny monstrously. It would have been bliss to take Ludwig and leave through the front gate, to walk down to the pond and unlock her feet, to lie smoking and speaking to Antony in her head. Instead, Ruth had worked her face up into a smile and aimed it at the family doctor with the clouded eye, who said loudly, "And don't you look handsome!" so that she noticed a sideways glance and a blush from the young woman who stood next to him.

"Kind of you to say," she'd said, and excused herself and found a spot not too far from Alice and Mark, who was showing people how he might fit his two hands around his wife's waist. Alice's dark hair curled so serenely at her temples that it looked painted there. She leaned towards Ruth. "Darling girl, if you can get to my bedroom, find my cigarettes in the top dresser drawer and we'll steal away for a moment. I'm absolutely trounced."

But on entering the house, Ruth was given a tray of curried eggs by Nanny and ordered to distribute them among the guests.

"We've paid help for that," said Ruth, wherein Nanny had fixed her with a shiny black eye.

Now that Alice was married and Antony was no more, she had thought, as she walked the garden path with her tray, moving among the guests not waiting long enough for any one of them to see what she was offering, let alone pick one up, Ruth would have to start buying her own cigarettes—and for that she would need her own money. These were the hateful little thoughts she found herself thinking since Antony's death; they took her unawares, and made her bite the inside of her cheeks with shame. It was more than that, she knew, she just could not put a name to it.

Ludwig's bark sounded and for a second there was a dip in the welter of conversation on the lawn, while all eyes turned to the dachshund, who pointed his long nose at a wagtail peering down from the top of the white fence. "Oh, Albert!" said Ruth's mother loudly.

Ludwig performed a small dance at the base of the fence, his ears turning themselves pink-way out. The clamour rose again and Ruth looked at the wagtail. "Hello, Antony," she said to it, and then wondered what had gone wrong to produce that kind of nonsense, that her dead brother had come to the wedding reception disguised as a small bird. Aunt Josephine had been stood not too far away, and had given her a look of great compassion, Ruth had thought, but later it turned out that Aunt Josephine had reported it back to her mother and, combined with her behaviour later that year, it had been used to install Ruth for a fortnight in the sanatorium in Deal, which had been humiliating and alarming, and where she had learned a thing or two about pretending.

They couldn't see the shark yet, but they could smell it.

"They used to catch whales on this beach," Christopher was telling her, "and then, they'd turn them into perfume. The fisherman told me."

The smell of the dead shark made this seem unlikely, but the interest in the boy's face was too great for Ruth to wonder about it aloud.

Michael lagged behind, dragging a stick along the beach. He'd done so all the way from where they had left the golf course, half a mile or so behind, so that they were followed by a long black snake.

"Do sharks and whales interest you much, Christopher?"

The boy considered it a while.

"I've never really given them much of a thought. But now I've seen one and now we live here, and they live just there . . . I didn't know they were so big. It's funny there are so many big things right under the water that we can't see."

"I suppose so," said Ruth.

First the smell and then the noise—the sound of gulls calling each other to the feast. They rounded the corner towards Milsey Bay. Three golfers stood at the clifftop, one with a box camera, looking down and talking more than she'd been led to believe golfers talked. The excitement was not enough to get the golfers down off the cliff—they waved their clubs, speculating confidently about the manner in which such a revolting spectacle had come about.

As they crossed over the dune and reached the peak, the bay became visible, with the Bass Rock looming behind it. On clear days with a low tide it appeared so close that it might have beached itself on the sand, as if it were unmoored and went where it pleased. She did not much like the rock; Fidra and Craigleith she saw as charming additions, punctuation in the grey North Sea, but something about the Bass Rock was so misshapen, like the head of a dreadfully handicapped child. She often found herself drifting if she stared at it for too long, unable to look away, like the captivation she felt sometimes looking at her own face in the mirror, as if to look closely would be to understand it.

The shark was under a blanket of seagulls and the birds lifted all at once, crying out when Michael ran at them waving his stick and shouting "Yah! Yah!" as though urging on a horse. The shark an enormous black crescent, gunmetal against the sand. A huge cumbersome trunk, desperately heavy upon the earth. Its gills loose and intimately fleshy. Behind the shark stood a white-haired man wearing a long coat that matched in colour the shark's skin, and a clerical collar. His hair was wild, parted at the side by the wind; he smiled broadly, showing widely spaced teeth, his hands clasped behind his back. Once the birds had cleared, the four of them stood around the dead shark in silence. The golfers on the clifftop had disappeared just like the birds, and there was only the rush of wind between them.

The man broke the quiet by raising his hand and calling in a strong accent that was perhaps Welsh, "You must be the Mrs. Hamilton from the big house?"

"Yes," she called back. She did not feel like circumnavigating the shark to reach the other side. "Ruth Hamilton. These are my"—she tried not to pause but it felt so much a test of them all that she struggled for the correct word—"boys. Christopher and Michael." The boys looked up at the man, unsmiling. The man walked to the shark's snout, which was lapped by waves. He waited until there was a break and quickly darted around it, to come to their side. Close up he was not as old as she had first thought, and though he was not excessively tall, he was broad-shouldered and stood with his feet planted far apart, as though he might take a giant leap in seven-league boots.

"Reverend Jon Brown," he said, extending his hand. She shook it, and then he had a good look at the boys, shaking their hands and making sounds of approval while they looked over his shoulder at the shark.

"Good, good," he said, "not many children around here, need a bit of invigoration in these parts. Bit of hijinks and japery. Will they be starting at St. Augustine in the new term?"

"They'll be boarding at Fort Gregory."

"Ah! I give the sermon there regularly. Splendid—they'll get on just fine. Splendid, splendid. How long have you been ensconced?"

"Five weeks now."

"I've been meaning to drop by and introduce myself—I'm an old friend of your Betty, you see, me and her go way back."

"I'll remember you to her."

"Yes, do." He licked his lips and showed his teeth, which were on the grey side of white. "I haven't seen you at the Sunday service yet?" It was of course what all of this had been leading up to. He smiled warmly but did not allow her the comfort of glancing away. He moved his fists to his hips and looked like a buccaneer.

Ruth willed herself not to flush.

"With the move and everything, we've been so busy. Perhaps we'll come next week."

"Good," he said and moved his gaze to Christopher. "I was thinking of doing my sermon centred around this shark. You like sharks, my boy?"

Christopher nodded, looked again over Reverend Jon Brown's shoulder. Michael turned and ran down to the shoreline, began a new task of drawing with his stick all the way round the animal.

"Something about these great big powerful monsters, ending up eaten by small white birds," he said, "there's something there. That's why I came down to see it for myself—inspiration, you know." He looked back at Ruth.

"Of course," Ruth said, because a response was called for.

"Anyhow, it's a delight to meet you all, and I'll come by sometime soon and meet Mr. Hamilton. I'll be in touch with Betty, will I, to find a time that suits you all?"

Peter would not enjoy the visit. There was too much to explain, it was all too intimate. "Of course," she said again and he tipped a pretend cap at her, nodded to Christopher who nodded back.

"Must be off—I've got a cream tea owing to myself," and then he started up the dune towards town. Michael had stopped his line drawing and poked in the shark's mouth with a look of horror and delight.

"Michael," she called.

"It stinks!" he said, joyful. She walked down to him.

"Please don't do that—what if you get some of it on yourself? Do you want to be the one who explains that to Betty?" Slowly the seagulls began to return, as though only the Reverend Jon Brown had any power over them. One had planted itself on the shark's tail and began a particularly invasive exploration of what might have been its private regions.

"Shall we go somewhere less revolting, do you think? How about a crumpet in town? Or we could find a scone—Reverend Brown has put me in the mood for one." Standing there with bile rising and the fish stench clogging her nose, she imagined nothing so unpleasant as cramming down a scone and its cream, but the returning gulls had started to give her a creeping feeling. She looked to Christopher for a response and found he was staring off in the direction Reverend Jon Brown had gone in, and he seemed like a boy lost at sea or among the stars.

III

"They've a girl in the pig house. They mean to burn her."

The Widow Clements has come banging at the door in her nightdress, a thin line of red across her cheekbone. My father does not wake in the disturbance—the drink has done for him. Cook puts a shawl around the woman's shoulders and pushes her to sit, stokes the fire up again, but the woman is tearful and wrings her hands.

"Get himself, boy," says Cook.

Father lies face down on his bed, his nightshirt has flapped up over his rear end. The sight of his buttocks is almost enough to send me straight out of the room again, great grey boulders with a dark and haired crack, a diseased bear. The room smells strongly of wine and some other dirt I do not like to name, and my father snores in snaps and shudders. I prod him rough between the shoulder blades and he stirs and turns over.

"Father, wake up." He opens one eye and then goes back under.

"The Widow Clements is hurt. She says there's a witch to burn." At the widow's name both eyes open. He blinks, trying to make sense of what he sees. A sob comes from the fireside in the next room. He blinks again and sits up, runs a hand over his face as if trying to pull the skin off.

"What?" he says, but does not wait for my reply, the widow is crying loudly now. "Pass my breeks." For a moment he is the man he was before Agnes and Mother died. He is broad and strong. My heart thumps to see it.

I leave him to dress and come out to find the widow's cheek has bled down her face. Cook tries to dab at it with the edge of her nightgown but she flinches away. When she sees Father in the doorway she stands and holds her arms out to him like a child. Father looks at Cook and me and I see that something has already passed between the Widow Clements and Father. He accepts her embrace, firmly sits her down and wipes his thumb along the bone of her jaw where the redness gathers.

"What happened, Charlotte?" he asks, and all is confirmed in her name. This is not something for now, I will think on it later and decide what it means. "They say they have a witch. They mean to burn her."

"Who says they have a witch?"

"The Browning twins caught her in the woods. They have her in the pig shed. She's just a girl." My father stands and is out the door without leaving instruction. I follow.

"Stay here, Joseph," he says, but I do not, I hang back a little so he will not see me in the dark.

The Brownings' pig shed is not far—just the end of the runnel our cottage rests on—but it is a mudded route, and I have to tread carefully to stay upright. I see my father fall twice, but he scrambles upwards without putting a break in his stride.

A dim light comes from inside and he disappears through the low doorway. I watch through an open hatch in the wall: the scene is hard to make out. I see at first no girl, no witch.

31

"What in the name of hell is this?"

Several men, those who remember my father as he was, slink away, afraid, but the younger men stay. They know him only as a drunk and a fool. Something on the floor moves and lets out a sound, low and awful like a cow calving. A girl lies with her dress nothing more than a rag about her armpits. Two men—one half of the Browning twins and someone I do not recognise—stand on her wrists, and the other Browning stands up from the girl's body, his shirt untucked and pulling up his breeks. She is hard to make out for being coated in the mud. Grits of colour, the whites of her eyes, the red of her open mouth. It is not easy to tell if she is alive. Her body stained black with dirt and shining in the lamplight. I should turn my eyes away.

My father strides towards her, and three men go to hold him back. He throws them off like nothing.

"She has bewitched me!" shouts the Browning twin, holding up his breeks. My father catches him under the chin with his fist and Browning's head snaps backwards and he loses his legs from under him. The remaining men back away a little, and my father picks up the girl, pulling her dress down as he goes, though it is torn and clings to her with wet mud. He holds her over his shoulder so that his arms can be free. "If she is dead, I will come back and take your ears."

"Put her back," says a voice, and out of the shadows comes the other Browning with a pitchfork. Father stands still. I know he will not put her back. The man advances so the fork is pointed at Father's face. Father takes a step, so that the prongs meet his throat. One thrust from Browning and his throat will burst. He looks him in the eye. Browning lowers the pitchfork and Father turns and walks out of the pig house, the girl a bag of bones on his shoulder. I feel a swell of pride—there he is, my father the hero. I have missed him.

"It was the witch made me do it—tell him!" squeals the Browning twin with the hurt jaw.

"She has bewitched the men as well as the land," yells the other, looking for support among the small crowd. But my father is gone and there is no explaining himself.

Browning stands forlorn with his arms at his sides. "She is ours to burn," he says, quietly.

In the morning we sit hunched around the fire, while Cook attends to the girl in her own room. Cook comes out occasionally to announce, "She's washed," or, "She's taken some oats," or, "She's sleeping." We have not slept, each noise in the night the sound of the Brownings setting the cottage alight.

Father sits with his hands in his lap, thinking. I am certain we think the same things. The village is not what it was. Their relief of having someone to blame. There was a need for it, in these times.

It is four years and some months after we laid Mother in the ground, and since then Cook has fed us, even at breakfast—her two chickens and their eggs kept us after the barley failed, but one stopped laying and so she killed it to make a stew. The meat, when she had plucked and cleaned the bird, had taken on some kind of rot. That was the first—it started at our house. Before long it was everywhere, in all the meat, the colour of it dark and oily. The smell is sweet and foul—when your nose first catches it, you think you've found a meadow lily, and then like a finger behind the eyeball, the smell scratches in. And if you handle the spoiled meat, it stays about your skin so that others smell it too, and avoid your company altogether.

One morning, opening up the egg boiled by Cook, I found a black baby chick, like a fully formed crow bird, and it had stained all the inside of its shell.

It is like a memory of something dreadful in childhood, something from the woods. And even in all that, the people are starving and so some have eaten the black flesh, and those few who tried it, gone in the most terrible fits of screaming and vomiting mud. I have seen farmers standing in fields of dead cattle with clay from the ground stuffed up their noses. I have seen folk take their children into the woods and return alone or not at all, their cottages lying quiet and dark, and no one checking, because the fight to stay alive yourself has become more than the need to care for others. And now the girl comes, and we are the ones to save her—the rot started in our home and it will take more than the dwindling respect the villagers have for Father to convince them it shouldn't end with us.

There is a hammering at the door, my father's old friend, the miller Fergus. He looks behind him before entering, like he fears being seen here.

"There's a meeting's happened," he tells my father, "and it looks bad for you. There's a few of us stood up, but those Brownings have the ear of the village."

"They can't do anything about it—I'm their priest." My father raises his voice, as though trying to convince himself of it.

"Ah, Callum," says Fergus, "not for a long time now." And no one corrects him.

When Agnes was found in the woods, Father prayed and spoke and was wise. When Mother died, mad and screaming like birds were sewn under the skin, that strength left him. Only I remained to be wise for, and I was not enough.

The girl comes out of Cook's room and the light has started to go from the sky. She walks with a limp and she has a line where the flesh has split from her nostril to her top lip. She is unlike any person I have seen before, her hair is red and, not only that, her lips are near-purple, from bruises or the cold, or if that is their natural colour, I cannot tell. I am unable to look away from her bare feet, though her toenails are outlined darkly, the skin is a white that you only see on the breasts of birds. It is hard not to see Agnes in her, or the woman she could have grown into.

Cook puts her hands on the girl's shoulders. "This is Sarah. She's been lost from her mother and sister this past winter."

The girl's eyes are wide and brown. I cannot tell her age, though I know from what I saw last night in the mud that she is older than her face would have you believe.

She speaks little, answers the questions my father asks her with nods of her head and one- or two-word answers. Her voice sounds as if from far away, and she is hard to understand.

Father puts a blanket around her shoulders, watches as she warms her hands by the fire.

We all watch as she eats a bowl of porridge soup, Cook with an unhidden softness. It is some time before I recognise Sarah wears one of Mother's old dresses. There is a cold stone that fixes in my stomach at this noticing. Is the natural way of things. Agnes's clothes would have been too small, Cook's too big. My small red-cheeked mother's, just right.

Cook bosses Sarah back to bed after the soup, and she looks grateful for it. We are perhaps watching too hard.

Father sits holding his hands in front of him, facing the fire. His eyes are watery.

"Joseph," he says, after some time, "do you feel it?"

"Feel what?" He doesn't answer.

I am silent. I do feel something.

"We must keep her safe," he says. "We must keep her safe. It is the second chance."

Ruth had slept badly, waking throughout the night, too hot or too cold, with the smell of the school in her nose, like thick mud and flowers left to rot in their water. And now she could not get the smell out of her nostrils, even with the car window down. It had given her a headache. Michael had looked pale and unconvincing as he and Christopher waved from the steps of their new school, the nurse standing grimly behind them in case there was a scene. They have each other, she thought, but knew that in reality once Peter and Ruth had driven out of sight, they would be separated and into their own age groups.

Come the Christmas holidays, they will be bolder, stronger, more resilient, the head had told them proudly over ginger snaps. What they hadn't asked was what methods were used to produce this resilience. Ruth buried the thought. The head was war-aged and was missing the ring finger on his left hand. He wore a black prosthetic instead, which attached with a band around his wrist. It was rather elegant. So strange, she always thought, how a bullet could take out just a finger or it could take the whole person. After Antony had died, she had taken the bullet casing her father kept as a paperweight and studied it. How absurd that the human body could not survive with such a small hole through it, such an unassuming object. A great disappointment. It was not long before conversation in the head's office had turned to the war. She was relieved to find the man had not been in Normandy—a small part of her held a horror that she would one day meet someone who had been there and held Antony as his life melted into the mud. That flower smell, too long in the vase.

They had taken a drive along the coast in the afternoon. Peter, who drove with both hands gripping the steering wheel, like he might at any moment leap over the top of it, had been quiet since dropping off the boys.

"Do you feel sad leaving them?" she asked, and he changed gear as they dipped over a hillock in the road.

"I try not to think of it," he said. "Listen, now that the boys are back at school, there's rather a lot of work I need to catch up on. Would you mind terribly if I caught the London train tomorrow? I think a week there ought to get me back on track. It's just, I know that it means missing your birthday."

"Of course." She had planned on using the journey to bring up the loss she had had last week, but now it felt like she'd be using it, when really it was nothing like that. And it wasn't a baby yet anyway, just a collection of things clumped together and hanging on to her. A chick clotting in its shell. She had only known what it was by its timing and because Alice once confided in her that she had had three, so she knew when the cramps came they were something more than her monthlies. But to bring it up now would be unnecessary, and Peter would feel he had to stay and comfort her, take her to the doctor, demand answers. And in truth she was fine. A little tired. Next time she would know to be softer with herself, sleep longer, or at least lie longer in bed. "My parents will keep me occupied, I'm sure."

"Oh damn," he said and gave the steering wheel an unconvincing smack. "I had quite forgotten they were coming. What day do they arrive?"

Ruth smiled. It was easier, really, to keep them separate. That way there was no chance of crossed wires. "You know perfectly well they arrive on Wednesday and go home on Friday." He threw a glance at her to gauge her reaction, saw she was smiling, and so he put a hand on her knee.

"Blast it, I think I shall probably miss them."

With Peter gone she would have a few days of quiet to get to grips with her newly empty home, to finally feel like she was running it, to rest and be well. It was a good plan, even if Peter did not know why. She hummed a little tune to show that she really was all right about it and not sulking.

"You're not the worst, you know that?" He squeezed her knee and then his hand started to move upwards.

"Reverend Jon Brown is still very keen to meet you at church, darling," she said, hoping for some kind of leverage. He snorted and placed his hand back on the steering wheel.

"Yes, well, you'll have to make my apologies for me," he said. "Any thoughts about what your reverend's place was in the war?" It was his go-to question if he disliked the idea of someone. It was because usually the person in question had not been engaged in combat while their wife died of pneumonia. Though he never really made it as far as saying that outright.

"Well, I didn't ask him, obviously. But I think perhaps he's too old." Peter snorted again.

And so she closed her eyes and a memory came to her, a happy one of sitting on the back of Antony's motorbike with one arm around her brother's waist, holding Ludwig as a whelp with the other, bunched up in her dress. It did not seem that long ago, and yet now only the motorbike was left, covered over with a dust sheet in her father's shed. She was left too, she supposed. Though she was not quite as she had imagined she would be.

Having kissed Peter goodbye at the door, the telephone rang. Her mother.

"Darling Puss, is that you? You have a terrible cold, I can tell." Ruth had only answered the phone with the words *Hamilton Residence*.

"Not the best night's sleep, that's all. Is everything all right?" It wasn't like her mother to ring. Usually she waved in the background of one of Alice's letters.

"Oh, quite all right, darling, quite all right. I was just calling to say this Wednesday is looking rather hopeless—Dad's got his gout back, and really the journey is rather arduous, you understand, don't you? I expect you'd rather have the place to yourself anyway, on your birthday, nice to have an opportunity for quiet."

Ruth held, for a moment, the space between her eyebrows and then smiled to make her voice sound pleased. Betty had gone over the various meals with her just last night, confirming that salmon and partridge had been acquired from a game-keeper who was a personal friend, for the birthday dinner, and a pineapple was on its way on the sleeper train from Fortnum's.

"Of course, Mummy."

"How are the children?"

Ruth imagined her mother used *the children* to refer to Christopher and Michael because she could not be bothered to retain the information that they were boys and that they had names. *You'll soon have your own*, her mother had said, patting her indulgently in front of Christopher on their wedding day. She jerked suddenly at the memory.

"They're quite well."

"I expect it's a great relief to have them away at school. Anyhow, Dad sends his love, we saw Alice at the weekend, she's put on a little weight, but it *does* suit her. She's talking of getting another cat, I can't fathom why, I tell her there's no replacement for your own children, but she doesn't listen." Alice had never told their mother about her losses. It would have involved months of overbearing concern.

Ruth looked at herself in the mirror that hung above the telephone, and opened the second drawer of the adjacent tallboy to take out a packet of cigarettes and a tin box of mints to freshen her breath afterwards. Tucked in with the cigarettes was a book of matches from the restaurant Alice had taken her to when last she visited London. It felt an age ago. She struck a match in the silence, cradling the handpiece between her shoulder and ear.

"Well, darling, we're expected at the Winslows' and so I must off and pack—do look after yourself and keep warm, won't you? I hear the weather where you are is absolutely macabre. Bye-bye, Puss darling."

"Goodbye, Mummy. Love to Dad." Her mother had hung up the telephone efficiently as soon as Ruth had said *goodbye*.

Her mother had never been a woman good at lying—not because she fluffed her lines, or worried too much, but because she seemed to care not at all that her lie be found out. The Winslows were a three-hour drive west from her parents'. They were old friends and excellent hosts who held expansive dinner parties, planned well in advance. Her parents would have known for some time that they had no intention of coming to Scotland for her birthday. Gout or no. She mustn't let on to Peter if he telephoned, or there'd be some dreadful scene about coming home for company on her birthday.

Ruth blew smoke into the mirror. When it cleared, she stared at her face until it changed into a series of shapes and shadows and then disappeared altogether. If only Antony could be here, taking up space, mixing drinks, instead of churned into the soil somewhere across the sea.

It was for the best, they'd only complain about the cold, the wind, *the dark, fathomless house*. Her parents were the sort who were always cold, and her mother point-blank refused to wear thermals because she thought them manly. And they'd only enquire into her health in a pointed way that questioned why she was not yet vast with her *own* child. Last time her mother had actually pressed her hands to Ruth's stomach to feel if there was something rattling around in there and, when she found there was not, made some comment about *too much haggis*.

She walked to the back door and opened it, the crispness of the day a satisfaction against the warmth of the cigarette. She stepped out and surprised Betty, who also had a cigarette tweezered between her dark fingertips. It ought to have been awkward, but Betty only nodded at her. Ruth leaned against the stone wall nearby.

"It's a smoking day," she said. Ruth noticed Betty had taken off her indoor shoes and stood barefoot. Considering her calloused hands, her feet were surprisingly white and well tended.

"Aye. The sun's got an edge to it today." She had come to the end of her cigarette, and Ruth watched as she pincered it out with her fingers like one would the wick of a candle.

"Will you have another with me?" Ruth asked, holding up her packet. Betty did not reply, but took one and lit it with her own rather smart-looking pocket lighter. Ruth blew smoke out of her nose.

"When we dropped the boys off, their school had this smell—I just can't get rid of it, like rotten potatoes or something, quite deathly."

"Aye—well, it's stinkhorn season. They get them in the woods up there."

"Oh, really?"

They were silent a while, appreciating the patterns their smoke made in the cold air.

"Sorry, Betty. What is a stinkhorn?"

The woman smiled. "A filthy mushroom, smells like rot. Looks like a man's engorged member." She waved her cigarette.

"Ah, right." More silence.

"Betty, I'm terribly sorry for the late notice. That was my mother on the telephone. They won't be joining us this week after all."

Betty inhaled sharply through her teeth and let out an impressive smoke ring.

"That's no bother for me, madam. I'll cancel a few things, the rest can freeze. No Mr. Hamilton either?"

Ruth shook her head. "I've decided to ignore it this year. One gets rather tired with relentlessly reminding oneself year after year that one was born and is alive. I can't bear the fuss of it," she said and tried to gauge if she felt that might be true. It very well might.

A herring gull landed on the garden wall, above the raspberries, and eyed the late fruit with the scrutiny of a seasoned shopper.

"I didn't much like my own mother, thinking back," Betty said as though they had been mid-conversation about it. "I

EVIE WYLD

don't think you're allowed to realise these things until they're dead and gone."

Ruth looked at Betty properly now, and saw the woman had been crying.

"Oh, good God, Betty, has your mother died?"

"Aye," she said, and smiled. "But that's not what the tears are for. It makes you reflect on things in your life, is all."

"Dear me, I'm so sorry." Ruth felt a fool for thinking herself stoic about a cancelled birthday party, as though she were nine years old. "You must take the day off and be with your sister—take the week off, it's only me here, really." Betty's younger sister was *resting* at Landbrooke, which was what Ruth's mother would have called *a madhouse* for Betty's sister, but a *sanatorium* for her own daughter.

"That's kind of you, madam, it really is. But there's no love lost between Mother and I. To be honest, the tears are more for Mary. It's my niece's birthday this week, always sends her into a flap."

"Mary has a daughter?"

Betty sucked air noisily through her nose. "Aye. Bernadette. Eleven years old tomorrow. She stays mainly with our aunt in Musselburgh."

"This sounds terribly difficult for you, Betty." The gull stretched its neck down to try to reach the berries—it was not far enough, and it resettled itself on the wall and tilted its head the other way, as though a different eye on the situation might be of some assistance. "I hope I'm not prying—the child's father?"

"One of the mysteries of our time," said Betty. She pulled so hard on her cigarette that it burnt down halfway. "I was thinking, madam, if you wouldn't mind me bringing her round one or two days now and again. Bernadette. She's bright and

44

quite helpful. My aunt is getting frail. It's not much of a life for her down there."

"Of course, Betty. I'll talk to Mr. Hamilton, I'm sure if we can help in some way . . ."

Betty smiled, an openness about her face strange to behold and rather lovely. "That'd be pure gift, madam," she said, and turned her gaze back towards the sky, empty of birds, empty of clouds, just the hard blue of the start of autumn. "A pure gift."

They stood in silence a moment. Ruth felt the wind raise up her hair, saw Betty's eyes narrow in thought.

"Your sister in London, are you close?"

Ruth shrugged. "We get on—we're very different. But I suppose when you come from the same origins, there's an unspoken affinity. I was close with my brother but he went in the war."

Betty turned to look at Ruth like she hadn't seen her properly before.

"Ah now, there's a hard thing."

Ruth nodded.

The gull sounded off, made Ruth think of Rumpelstiltskin, pummelled its feet in rage and launched itself from the wall, berryless. Betty smiled, her tears gone, only the lightest softening about her hard face.

The house had a habit of growing around her as the sun began to lower, especially with Peter away. Betty had retired to her wing with Booey, and Ruth poured herself a sherry and went looking for direction. The spare room at the top of the house, next to the boys' bedroom, was filled with unpacked boxes. She planned eventually to put a cot in it. She tried to picture it but nothing would come, and so she went instead to the boys' room.

The room was pristine and unlike her own as a child, which Nanny had refused to enter. Their beds were immaculately turned down. It wasn't Betty's doing—it was something that Christopher had taught Michael from school. The hospital corners.

On Michael's bedside table was the small bear that he had until now kept with him always, either in his coat pocket or trailing by a threadbare paw. His body must now feel it was missing something. A handful of tin soldiers arranged around the bear, guarding it. She opened his bedside drawer. Three books of matches, partly used, several small rolls of coloured thread, a nail file, two pencil stubs and a bright red lipstick in a gold case. There was a dried catkin, an acorn, a pressed buttercup, and a list in an unfamiliar hand. *Bank, tailor (£4), bread, salmon, toothpowder.* The remains of his mother. Perhaps he had not been searching for pennies in her coat pockets, but had imagined the coat had belonged to Elspeth. Indeed, Ruth had inherited two warm overcoats. She had been relieved when the one that went missing from the fence had been her own.

She sat on Michael's bed and ran a hand over the pillow. Months after Antony went missing, she had panicked suddenly at her inability to remember his face. Looking at his photograph didn't help. His face existed in movement and noise, the person photographed, just a play of light and shadow on paper and nothing more. She had taken a pair of scissors to the inlay of one of his jackets, cut out a square and stroked it under her pillow at night, pretending he lay next to her and Ludwig, who pined and made her cross and then made her sorry again.

On Christopher's side, a photograph of him and Elspeth shortly before she became sick. Her arm flung easily around his small shoulders, his face open in joy. Around the photograph, collections of things, neatly ordered. Cowrie and winkle shells, a small stone with a hole in it, three jay feathers brought from the garden of the Dummer house laid in descending size, white sea glass and a piece of willow-print china the width of a penny. New objects, collected in the new place. Ruth's breath disturbed the feathers and they scattered on the polished tabletop. She pushed them back into place, knowing as she did it that the feathers were important, and knowing also that Christopher stood behind her watching. She steeled herself with a broad smile, turned with his name on her lips. But he wasn't there, of course. He was miles away, thinking of something completely other.

The sun had almost gone from the sky while she had been in the boys' room. From the landing, through the stairwell window, she had a perfect view to the beach. She watched the last orange gleam on the horizon, thought, as she always did in moments of beauty, of her brother's last breaths, the seconds before and the seconds after. From the corner of her vision, she caught movement, turned, expecting to see Betty, embarrassed to have been found in the dark with a sherry glass in her hand. Nothing again but the soft fluttering of a crane fly thrumming at the window. She moved to check the bathroom, the only door that was ajar, and inside she imagined she saw a figure standing in the corner, but all was gone as soon as she pulled the light cord.

On the morning of Ruth's birthday, Betty had laid the breakfast table ornately, and there was toast on the rack as well as two boiled eggs and a covered dish on the hotplate smelling of bacon.

"Betty, thank you," she said, "but really, there's no need to trouble yourself with Peter and the boys gone. Especially given your mother."

"Madam," she said, an answer that suggested neither yes nor no. "Happy birthday, by the way." She planted a thin vase with a single branch of heather in front of Ruth's plate.

"Oh, that's lovely, thank you." It was not the first time she had spoken to Betty about toning down her attentions. But it had never made the slightest difference.

"For protection," said Betty, as if it were obvious. She wrapped a scarf around her head. "If it's all all right with you, madam, I will be off now to see Mary."

"Of course. And thank you so much."

Betty gave a tight smile and left the room, her efficient footsteps sounding down the hallway and out the back door. She never used the front.

The house fell silent and Ruth looked at the long runway of the dining table and tried to imagine herself comfortable. There was a lace doily under the butter dish, which was silver. The butter itself had been curled somehow into the shape of a seashell. She pictured Betty sitting with the butter, thinking to herself how Ruth would eat one of these curls for her breakfast, and so shaping that one curl into a conch, and laying it with its tiny silver knife on the silver plate. She cut the butter in two and it crunched with salt. She scraped it on to her toast and lay the toast on her plate.

There was a creak from upstairs, and another, as if someone had walked through her bedroom. She stayed very still, the butter knife in her hand. The door to the dining room opened slowly.

Booey's cow-like head appeared between her knees and she yelped. She held her wrist to the bridge of her nose.

"I forgot you, old dog. I'm so sorry," she said, putting down the knife and taking hold of both of his ears. She gave them a rumple. Booey's breath was mackerel and he smiled with his black gums, panted happily, producing a filthy steam. Ruth picked up a rasher of bacon and gave it to him, and his chops made a hollow sound. He rested his chin on Ruth's knee and looked up at her beseechingly with clouded eyes. She put the plate of bacon on the floor and ate her toast.

When he'd finished, Booey gave her a glance over his shoulder in thanks and swayed off slowly to the kitchen to lay with his back against the Aga. Ruth poured herself tea and floated a slice of lemon on top. What would she do with her birthday? The noise came again from upstairs and she listened, held her breath. The wind perhaps. Softly she pushed back her chair and left the dining room. Booey already snored in the warmth of the kitchen as she walked past it, into the hallway, where she looked up the stairs. One, two, three creaks. The house settling? She started up the stairs very quietly. Reaching the top, she trod lightly off the runner and found the door to her bedroom closed. She had left it open out of habit, her father never liked any door closed in his house unless one was dressing. But Betty could have shut it—she was much more the door-closed type.

The sooner Ruth looked inside, the sooner her fast heart and sense of dread would be revealed as childish nonsense. She opened the door. The room was empty. She did not see the girl standing by the window. She did not see her red hair and white face and the dark hollows of her eyes, or the rags she was dressed in, her bare angular feet and the bones of her hands protruding out like sticks. But she could imagine a girl just like her, one she had never seen before; she could imagine her strongly but knew her eyes could not see her. Just like she knew there was no reason at all that she could not move, that it was some trick of her brain preventing her from doing so. There was a feeling of all the furniture in the room, the bed, the chairs, the dressing table and the curtains, being pulled off the floor by some magnetism, all held—not floating but stuck, for the time being—to the ceiling. It was not, of course, but that was the impression Ruth had. And the smell again of rotting flowers, the dead breath of it.

A loud bang came from downstairs and she turned her head. There, she knew she could move, and when she looked back the room was empty and the furniture sat on the floor where it always had.

At the back door was a man holding his cap in his hand. "Good morning to you, madam, Betty asked that this be sent up to you from the train." He handed over the box that had rested at his feet. Inside, a large pineapple.

I

The instant coffee is the kind with milk already dried into it. The estate agent must've left it. I'm not an expert but I think it might be disgusting. I cannot get out of bed without a coffee, as much as it makes me sound like a person with lifestyle choices. It's a question of lying there and thinking things through. It is not enough to get out of bed because the bladder is full, because that is not really getting up—if I get out of bed just to pee, I will end up back in bed, or sitting on the sofa, using the cushions for warmth. It is a false start. But if I can picture the best version of a coffee, a large pot of it, not burnt with impatience or over-stewed, then I can bring myself to go about the procedure, the small creation, and then, having poured a cup, I find I can wander over and stare at something I need to get done for the day.

This morning I am going through boxes of pictures that used to hang on the walls.

There is a very amateurish watercolour of a shark or a whale washed up on the beach. I think probably shark, because of the attention paid to the face, which has been gone over many times and looks rather anxious. There are four small figures around it, barely more than single brushstrokes, and in the background a badly shaped Bass Rock. Mrs. Hamilton painted a lot, and never really seemed to improve. I come across stacks of watercolour paper, each one as imperfect as the last. It was where Mum started as a girl. She told me that after Mrs. Hamilton's husband left her, she and Mrs. Hamilton would sit side by side on the beach with their easels, Mrs. Hamilton trying and failing to fit everything into her picture, Mum focusing instead on something small—a mermaid's purse, or a cowrie. The companionship is so at odds with the woman I knew, moving through her giant empty house like an old fox, seeking out the quiet spots where she could drink and smoke undisturbed. She never painted in the days I knew her. We didn't often see her other than on special occasions, a birthday or once when we were there at Christmas, and we all would gather in the dining room and eat orange-and-carrot soup in dread silence for the noise it made. Or if I passed her on the stairs and she tried to seem less drunk than she was by giving me a nod, and saying something like "Very good," as though I had completed some task she had asked of me. Mrs. Hamilton, never "Grandma," and certainly not "Granny," is the only grandparent my sister and I have known, though Dad told me that as a baby I was introduced to his and Uncle Christopher's father once, at a train station. As a teenager, I wondered aloud if we referred to our grandmother as Mrs. Hamilton out of some reticence to acknowledge those other grandparents, estranged, dead or mad. I was told to *Please stop being so boring* about it by Mum.

Mum was always quick to remind us we'd have grown up eating offal and stewed prunes in Blyth had Mrs. Hamilton not stepped in and sent her to school in London, but we never saw that generosity for ourselves. The warmest I ever saw her was when she rubbed the ears of one of her Booey dogs before whispering into them, so that the dog flapped his tail and dust rose from the sofa cushions.

"She saved all of our lives," Mum would say, as though that explained everything or indeed anything about Mrs. Hamilton. If we persisted in our questioning she would leave the room on some errand or other.

Several pictures from the boxes in the ballroom that I've unpacked have produced a glimmer of memory from childhood. I never paid much attention to the pictures in the house then—I wasn't interested in the cobwebby landscapes, I drew pineapples and dogs. I coloured them in with highlighter, taking care to stay within the thick black outline, and thought they were fabulous. Katherine, three years younger, would set up an actual still life—a vase of dried flowers or some oranges and a green bottle—and she'd sit and ponder over her drawing. She used pastels, she blew the dust away with a serious puff, wore an old wax jacket from the cupboard so as not to mark her clothes. She rolled her eyes at my turquoise pineapple, my purple dog. I thought her drawings were a waste of colour, the ones on the wall a waste of paper.

I recognise one of the watercolours. *Lothian landscape with Tantallon Castle in background*, it says on the back. There is no mention of what is going on in the foreground. Tantallon Castle is a small sand-brown affair just before the cliffs. Normally, when you see it painted, it is from the sea, and it looks vast and imposing and stormy. Here it looks inconsequential. In the foreground, a dark hole in the ground, a cave with a tree growing over the top of it, its coiled roots snakey and fat and its leaved branches flattened by wind. The mouth of the cave is not black, it is dark but in a way that invites you to squint your eyes to peer inside, expecting to see something there. This hung over Aunt Bet's bed, over the bed my mother shared with her on cold nights. I put it in the stack for the saleroom.

*

53

I stop for lunch late, make my way into the kitchen, which smells the same—shortening and the old fat of a thousand roast dinners, Brasso and hot Fairy liquid. Those awful meat puddings Bet used to make us until Katherine announced she was vegetarian, the moment I felt most affection towards her as a child. Probably, the thing I feel most affection for now we are grown.

The large rusted fridge is gone. Instead, a small beer fridge, brand new, has been installed and the estate agent has filled it with fancy green bottles of mineral water. It will take more than mineral water to convince someone the house is a modern oasis. It will likely be bought sight unseen, in any case—an American billionaire looking for a holiday home by the golf course, who'll hire a contractor to gut the place and straighten it out by painting everything bright white or buttercup yellow. They will install a tap that produces already boiling water, and several flat-screen televisions. They will somehow fix the Wi-Fi and the problem of telephone service.

Most of the furniture—the old sofas, the writing table, the piano, the matching chaises longues Katherine and I used to read our comics on—has gone to the auction house at Musselburgh. The estate agent has moved in what she refers to as "a neutral piece," which is a grey sofa. I have taken a few bottles out of her fridge so that I can squeeze in Swiss cheese and celery and chocolate, and I take a slice of cheese and four squares of chocolate now. I wrap the cheese around the chocolate. The ghosts of Aunt Bet and Mrs. Hamilton look on appalled.

The kitchen table remains, its yellow-vinyl-cushioned chairs, a split in each seat that pinched the backs of your thighs if you sat on them with shorts. Funny, that memory—so strong and yet I could count on one hand the number of warm days we spent at North Berwick. The shorts would have been worn along with a thick scratchy fisherman's jumper and hat. The estate agent requests the broken seats be kept hidden underneath the table.

On the first-floor landing, a view across the golf course and to the sea. The Bass Rock looks far away, but I remember it peering over my shoulder while I crept up on limpets in the rock pools. You used to feel it leaning into the outdoor swimming pool in town, like it should cast a shadow over us.

Here and there, personal items have been overlooked. On the landing at the window, hidden by a large curtain tassel, is a silver-framed photograph. In it, Mrs. Hamilton is still what you would call handsome, and she sits on the sofa with Uncle Christopher and Dad before he grew his hair long but, guessing by his smile, after he was regularly stoned.

Mrs. Hamilton has her hands behind her head, rather dangerously—you can just make out the lit tip of a cigarette in close proximity to what would have been strongly set hair. A yellow puppy—Booey IV, the one that ended himself by eating half a kilo of butter—sleeps across her knees. The woman's mouth is closed tight and she gazes into the middle distance. Uncle Christopher looks directly and unsmilingly at the camera, he has a full beard and a side parting. He looks like D. H. Lawrence, and it feels wrong that the photograph is colour. I never knew him with hair that black. In my first memories of him, it had mostly gone. Dad sits on the floor in front of them, his face blurred as though someone called him just as the shutter opened. I put the photograph down and place the tassel in front of it again so it's hidden. There should be something remaining of the people who once lived here, once the place is sold.

Leading off from the landing is Mrs. Hamilton's bedroom and an office. It always felt an obscene intrusion of privacy looking in her bedroom. I passed the door often as a child, after Aunt Bet's quarters were closed off to save the heat, when Katherine and I slept together upstairs in Dad and Uncle Christopher's old room. There were plenty of rooms to choose from but Mum was firm that we share. *There's nothing here that'll hurt you, but there's plenty that can scare you.* Mrs. Hamilton scared me. Listening at her door I used to hear her talk to herself, leaving long pauses for someone to answer. Inside, her bed is made up, and I have to remind myself that I'm not trespassing. There are pictures on the wall in here that will need cataloguing. Something that is almost, but not quite, a Stubbs; two elegant daguerreotypes, one of a large woman in a high-necked blouse, one of a collie dog. A well-trained dog to sit still for so long. Or stuffed, perhaps. There are more of Mrs. Hamilton's amateur watercolours on the walls of her bedroom. The Bass Rock, starfish and seagulls. It will be hard to know what to do with those ones. The estate agent has asked me to leave behind anything that might "appear appropriate for a neutral seaside-home feel." She sent along a "mood board" of what she means—wooden seagulls on sticks, mounted driftwood, a white-and-red-striped jug. Perhaps these bad paintings can be hers.

Aunt Bet was old by the time I knew her, with the body of a cabin boy; every piece of flesh on her earned its place. Her biceps stood out like tangerines. Looking back now, standing in front of the neatly made bed, it seems probable she and Mrs. Hamilton were lovers. Maybe just companions by the end, mostly silent around each other, but always there, in the corner of the other's life.

I lift up the corner of the duvet, compelled by a practical curiosity about death. Did somebody make the bed after

Mrs. Hamilton's death, or did Mrs. Hamilton make it before she took the gin from the cabinet and the car keys from the hook by the door? There is no sheet under the duvet, and the mattress is stained—a dreadful dark colour has pooled and then overwhelmed the material. It has run down the side, so the light blue stripes of ticking are black. I let the duvet fall back. Who knows what other illnesses Mrs. Hamilton battled. You could bleed a lot if you drank too much. But she didn't die at home. She died alone in the woods in January. They found her with a cigarette between her fingers, a nearly empty gin bottle next to her. Well, there's a comfort.

I take myself outside to check my messages in the garden. To get a signal, you have to climb on the bench next to the raspberry bushes, now just brown stumps tangled in a green netting, and pull yourself up to sit on the wall. Three golfers look suspiciously at me and I wave. None of them wave back. It's not part of the game, waving at women.

My phone buzzes. It's Katherine.

Have left Dom. Dinner when you get back?

Typical. There is no way of answering satisfactorily.

R U OK?

I wouldn't usually revert to text abbreviations, but have found the best way of dealing with my sister is to get my disappointing sloppiness out of the way first. Her news does not come completely out of the blue. Katherine doesn't like to surprise people, she has been dropping hints over these past six months that all is not well at home. Conversations about children, mostly, how she thinks she might like a child but she wonders if Dom is up to it. He is not—that much should have been clear immediately on meeting him. But Katherine does not want children. She just needs a good excuse. She is very much not unstable or having a breakdown—that is my department. Her one moment of recklessness was marrying Dom, whom she met on holiday and who needed a visa. Dom, whose ambition was to kayak from his home town in Nova Scotia to Cuba and write a book about it. In six years he had developed a way of talking about the trip that suggested things were just on the verge of happening, or would be if only *the suits in charge* would *pull their heads out of their asses* and fund his trip. Who the suits were and how much expense was involved in kayaking was never pinned down. I did not like Dom, and I had not liked him long before there was anything between us. But our mother thought of him as a lost soul, and so pretended to find him fascinating. They ended up drinking together at family gatherings, and you had the feeling my mother was agreeing with him that our family were a bunch of pompous bores, that he was the special one. She sensed he needed that.

Fine. Wednesday? Yours?

I send a yellow thumbs up. I feel her disapproval in the three dots indicating she is typing a reply that never arrives.

Back inside, I see that the drinks cabinet is still in its place in the living room. It used to house miniature cans of R Whites lemonade, which Mrs. Hamilton kept to relieve her indigestion in the mornings. I find an open bottle of whisky. I will replace it before I leave, though who would notice now, I can't imagine. It is not yet three o'clock, so I add a little water from the kitchen tap. Not something Aunt Bet would have approved of, but it makes me feel sensible. Once I take a break from work I find it hard to start up again. Perhaps a drink will focus me. Too late anyway if it doesn't.

In my memory, Aunt Bet sat mainly in an ancient bath chair in the ballroom. She'd have our mother take the wicker basket of colouring pens out of the bureau and she'd tell me to sit on the floor at her feet and draw. We passed the longest mornings in silence there, contented. She used to say, "You just get on with your drawings, girl, I'll keep watch," and we'd do exactly that. She would stare out the window like she was waiting for someone to drag themselves up out of the sea. I drew my pineapples, my dogs, naming each one once it was finished in exchange for a nod of the head, as if I'd drawn something that had long been lost to her, and it was a relief to see it finally on the page. She might touch the lines with her small hands, askance and swollen, and not the same colour as the rest of her, like the blood stopped flowing at her wrist.

I am standing with my forehead just touching the glass of the windowpane when I hear the front door open. I put down the glass, pick it up again and put it inside the drinks cabinet, then walk briskly into the hallway breathing through my nose, like someone with lots going on and endlessly hassled by the small requests of other people—which is to say, I impersonate my sister. I stand for a few seconds in the hallway, confused because there is no one there. Then the sound of a drawer closing and behind me, by the back door, is a man putting something into his mouth.

"Viv, darling." With the light behind him, it's hard to see a face but I recognise the beaky features of our family. Uncle Christopher steps out of the shadows, balder than he was when I last saw him, thinner too. There's a weathering to the skin of his face—he is not from a generation comfortable with sun cream, and the snow up in the Highlands reflects the sun. The Christmas I turned sixteen we spent in his small stone bothy with the rainwater running in underneath the front door, making its way through the house and disappearing into the grate underneath the fire. Katherine swept at it with a broom, on the verge of tears, on the verge of puberty. I pretended to love it, didn't step over the stream but walked through it in socks. Wet sleeping bags and porridge made with water.

"Hi, good to see you." I start forward and we exchange cheek kisses, and I hope he can't smell the drink on me, though I can smell it on him, through peppermint.

"I was just stealing one of Mum's mints—I don't suppose she'll mind. Now, how are you? I'm so pleased you're able to do this, it really is so kind."

"Oh—I'm so happy to. I feel embarrassed taking money for it."

"Nonsense, we'd only be paying someone else lots more to do it." Both of these statements are lies. I would not have done it for nothing, and I am being paid more, hourly, than my sister makes, and that was the primary reason for taking it. And I'm fairly sure that the reason the work was offered to me was because Christopher knows about last year's spell in the hospital.

"Well." My hands hang in front of me and I clap them like a trained seal. I have forgotten how to be around him, our contact has been patchy since Dad died.

"Good, good. And how are you finding the old place? I used to have a bad night's sleep here when I was a child. But then I suppose you're not a child any more, are you?"

"No, I'm nearly forty actually." It is supposed to sound funny but I'm anxious that it sounds like I'm showing off or, worse, reprimanding him for not knowing how old I am.

"Of course, of course!" he says. "Well, in that case, we must celebrate your coming of age with a drink!" He moves past me and as he does so he clasps my elbows and gives them a little squeeze. I am relieved to see he hasn't taken it in the wrong way. He goes into the living room and straight to the cabinet. I squirm when he opens it, and he pulls out the half-filled glass and tuts.

"Deborah. No wonder it hasn't sold yet." But he says it smiling and it occurs to me he is trying to put me at ease, and that he knows the estate agent has done nothing.

"Do you know her well? The estate agent?"

"My sister. Half sister. I can't really give it to anyone else, she'll cause havoc."

Somehow this information makes everything much more embarrassing. I have heard of Deborah, though never met her. I wonder if she will report back to him about my movements. I wonder what she knows about me, and then feel ashamed of my own thoughts.

He pours us two new glasses, hands me mine and we chink. He closes his eyes as he swallows.

"Your grandmother would very much approve of having you here."

It seems unlikely. "Mrs. Hamilton? You think?"

"Oh yes. She liked you enormously. Very hard to tell with that one, she was quite a fishy character in the end, wasn't she? I expect you and Katherine were terrified of her."

"I didn't really know her," I say, which seems polite and non-committal.

He smiles. "Not exactly a granny off a box of shortbread."

In the light from the window I can see how very thin he is. "Tell me, how is your sister?"

"She's OK. I think she's going to divorce her husband."

"The American?"

"Canadian."

"Well. That's probably a good thing. If I were a woman I would give men a wide berth. I have always rather fancied the idea of being a lesbian." He says it wistfully, as though he had simply taken the wrong career path.

"And how is your mother?"

"Mum's fine—she's exactly the same."

He smiles. "Perfection." He drains his drink, and his eye is drawn to a brown-and-white pottery dog on the mantelpiece. It's one of those ugly squashed-face ones that are usually in pairs in fancy houses.

"Funny, we never found out what happened to the other one of these—would have been worth a fortune if we had both. Our father decided your dad or I had smashed it, but if we did I really don't remember. I just remember there was this huge to-do about it, and both of us being accused." He turns to me, his eyes bright. "Nothing worse than being accused of something as a child when you didn't do it. I don't suppose you want it, do you? Looks rather bereft here on its own."

He passes the dog to me, and I take it because it feels rude not to accept. Christopher has never seen my flat and so he won't know that it is not a place for valuable pottery.

"Listen, I wanted to drop by and give you some money, and also ask a further favour if I may."

"Oh?"

He takes an envelope out of his pocket and starts rifling through fifty-pound notes.

"It may well be on the market for some time, the way Deborah carries on, and it's always good to have a bit of a presence about the place . . . I wondered what you thought about house-sitting for a while—staying on once you've finished the inventory? I'd feel so much more settled if I thought there was someone here looking after the place."

He stops counting the money out and looks up at me.

"I don't expect you to stay here all the time, and of course, I'd pay you extra for it—and any travel. Is it a total nightmare coming up from London? Because if it is I can always get Aunt Pauline to come by—she's about because Uncle John has been having a few turns."

"No, no, it's fine. Yes, of course. I'd like that." I don't know yet if I like the idea or not, but I know it is my job and not that of distant and old relatives. I already have that sinking feeling of failing and I have only been up twice. The first time, I drove up and down in the early hours of morning when the roads were empty, and then slept all day, was awake all night and then had a two-day migraine. But it is money for just hanging around, which is what I do anyway.

"Great," he says. He puts the money back in its envelope and hands the whole lot to me, closes my fingers over it. He pats my hand twice. There has definitely been a discussion with my mother. I wonder if perhaps she has supplemented the amount in the envelope.

I drive back to London that evening. I've never slept well at night, and I like to pretend I'm on the run. Witness protection or fleeing nuclear holocaust. I sing difficult songs on the motorway, I sing Dolly Parton and Jimmy Somerville, and there's no one to hear me as I fail to hit the notes. When I run out of energy for singing, I listen to the radio. None of the news is good. *A fashion designer has killed himself out of grief for his mother.* I change the station. A very unsettling thing that way round—the other way round makes more sense, a mother killing herself out of grief for her son. That I can get behind, and it is the reason, or one of the reasons, I have never wanted kids.

I find a music station that plays a song from the tape we used to have in the car when Katherine and I were young. *Bonedigger, bonedigger, dogs in the moonlight*, the long journey to Uncle Christopher's house, the quiet between our parents, Katherine maturely ignoring my efforts to irritate her by crunching through Polo mints like it was my job. Christmas evening, after venison and red cabbage, which I ate only because Katherine did not eat meat, I was given wine along with everyone else. Katherine was offered but declined, saying, "I'm only just thirteen?" Long after Mum and Katherine and I had gone to bed, there were raised voices from Dad and then Christopher, mouth lazy with drink, hissing, *You're just so fucking generous, Michael, aren't you?* And then the sound of the car door opening, and the tape playing long into the night. And when we left two days later, Mum sat in the car with her arms crossed, and Christopher and Dad held each other briefly to say goodbye, and there was a redness in both men's eyes.

I turn the radio off. It is near to midnight. I imagine a wolfman running alongside the car. I used to do this on the drive to Scotland when I was a kid. When you look into the scrub at the side of the road, when you peer into the dark, it's easy to see them, waiting to race you, willing you to break down. London is warm and comfortable, street lights and rain-wet pavement. Everyone is sleeping, the wolves have turned to foxes.

The girl lies with dirt in her mouth, naked from the waist down. To find her, a dog is needed, and a man with it. She has walked further from the village than she intended. No one comes.

Instead a jackdaw comes from its roost where it sees from the forest to the great rock in the sea, where it maybe saw the violence and waited, thinking in its bird's brain how this is the nature of man and soon it will be over and soon there will be meat.

It settles on the ground, ruffles its feathers, walks around the girl, it shows some respect. Then little careful movements, it touches her with its beak, fluffs away, then back again. It is careful. The eyes are still good, the tongue, once shaken of dirt. The soft paunches of face. More birds come, and ants too, in the hair, in the moist parts, blowflies and their meaty babies, beetles, their prickled feet, gossipy little men, buttinsky, fussbudget, intermeddler. The small things of the forest make it their business to know the girl, before the larger things come at night, the foxes, the buzzards, a red stoat that eats from the web between index finger and thumb. It is a relief, to be picked clean, to be rid of the worst of the flesh.

The hole in the ground is not big enough to contain her, especially once the swelling comes, she pops out of it, the loose earth dances from her stomach.

Still no one comes. She needs a dog hunting a deer to come with the men of the village. The dog will find her and bark and the men will enter the forest. They will lift her body up and take her back to the village. There will be shouts of anger and sadness, of revenge, and those that say she brought it upon herself walking so far from the village alone.

A fox takes away a section of leg, a hand, mostly dry now, but still some meat remains. Another tries for an arm, but when the girl moves, he dances away, frippityfrip, the girl's shawl still holds together the top sections of her.

Her small breasts underneath it gone now altogether, sunk, retreated, dried up and disintegrated. The snow comes, and in the spring, the rain, the girl is clean bones in a hole in the ground. The jackdaw's eggs hatch, the babies call for meat. And still the men do not come.

The Sisters

I

I sleep until midday when my doorbell chimes. I do not answer it. I hardly ever answer the doorbell, because no one I know ever rings it. The person knocks loudly. I roll out of bed, and kick over a glass of water onto the book I've left face down and splayed on the floor. I pick it up, but having no obvious surface to rest it on, I put it down again, to the side of the water. I put on my dressing gown, which has been lying for several days in a damp heap on the floor, having been used to mop up a previous water spill, and I try to pat down my hair, which has dried in a way that makes it look like a slipped wig. I walk as quietly as I can to the door and look through the spyhole. It's a delivery man.

"Sorry," I say, attempting to appear a convincing human, "I work nights." I wonder if he can see the lie steaming off me. He just presents me with his little machine to sign. I do it with my finger and we both notice that my fingernail is not clean. He won't believe I'm a doctor or a nurse then. Could be blood from a long surgery. He hands me a parcel and turns to leave. "You can go back to bed now," he says.

I close the door and look at the parcel while I carry it into the kitchen—it feels important to have some sense of what it is before I open it. There's a small tickle at my neck, and I shrug my shoulder. I glance up at the mirror. There's a house

69

spider the size of a mouse on my shoulder, and I yelp and drop the parcel and throw off the dressing gown. The spider lands on its back, flips over and scurries into the darkness of the sleeve. I yell wordlessly, then catch myself again in the mirror. Naked, mouth open, hair nest. I will have to get that spider. I will have to clean my flat and get the spiders out of it. I go back to bed, and from there stare at the wet book that has swollen now to twice its original size. I have lost my place, but that doesn't matter. I used to read. Now my eyes just meander over a page of text and make no sense of it, send no images to my brain. I close my eyes. In my sleep spiders burrow into my ears, knit their webs behind my eyeballs.

At six o'clock, I wake and remember Katherine was going to come for dinner. But I haven't been in touch, and neither has she. The dressing gown remains on the floor in the kitchen and I inch around it cautiously. I never opened the parcel. I pick it up and it feels like whatever is inside may be broken. I pull out a small wooden box—one of the brass hinges has shattered, and so the lid hangs off. Inside it, five little brown pebbles. There's a note.

Viviane,
 It's just a trinket box, but Mum was very fond of it, and I thought you might like it. The rocks—very old rabbit's teeth I think!
 Much love,
 Christopher
 x

It's a perplexingly boring gift. He must have sent it before we met yesterday, which all seems a bit unnecessary. I put it on the mantelpiece, along with the brown-and-white dog, a postcard that has been there so long I can't remember who sent it, and a dirty fork.

"Well," I say, "that'll do lovely for my trinkets." I open the bin to put the jiffy bag in, but the bin is full, and smells, so I drop it on the floor next to it instead.

I'm hungry and I stand in the light of the fridge until the fridge alarm begins to beep, but still I can't think what to do. In a moment, once I have gathered myself, I will sort out the spider, I will take out the bin, and I will also clean the sink, which has a greasy rim around it.

In the freezer I find a bag of large green prawns suffering acutely from freezer burn. I defrost them in cold water and keep an eye on my phone. In the cupboard there is a bulb of garlic with green shoots coming out the top, and spaghetti, though not linguine, which is what Katherine would make it with, because that is considered the more correct shape with which to serve seafood. The dust of chilli flakes in a jar. I keep half an eye on the phone, waiting for her to cancel. I would like her to cancel. I won't navigate these waters well tonight. I would quite like to eat the prawns by myself on the sofa and maybe watch a cookery programme. There is what my sister would think a wholly unacceptable bottle of opened sweet white wine in the fridge, and I drink a glass of it, wondering if I ought to go to the shop for a salad. I definitely need to go to the shop for wine, whether or not Katherine comes.

I put my shoes on and decide that if she hasn't texted by the time I'm home again, she's not coming. My hair has evened out a little—it is nest-like on both sides now, so it looks deliberate. The money Christopher gave me is still in its envelope. I counted it when he left—£2,000, more than twice what we'd agreed—and I had thought to speak to Mum about it and ask how to give some back, but have not yet got around to doing that. I will not ever get around to doing that because I want, quite badly, to keep the money.

With the envelope in my pocket I go to the more expensive shop, rather than the Co-op, and I wait in line with a basket holding a punnet of plums (I left the others in North Berwick, and they will have rotted by the time I'm back), a loaf of sourdough and two bottles of wine that cost £22 each. The queue is long, and the man in front of me has got a jiggly leg. I spot a bottle of wine for £15. I could leave the queue and swap them, but I don't want it to look like I'm in the expensive shop trying to buy the cheap wine. What am I here for, why didn't I go next door and buy my staple Fat Man's Creek, at £5.99? What if in trying to swap bottles I knock one to the floor and it breaks and the man behind the till has to behave like it's fine and it's not? What if I try and rejoin the queue and someone objects? Or if I don't rejoin the queue and someone tells me to go back to my original spot? I strongly feel I ought to have stuck with Fat Man's. The leg jiggler in front of me is holding a can of coconut water and a bag of buffalo mozzarella. He turns to me and gives me a friendly eye roll, because the woman being served is taking a long time to decide on the flavour of ice cream she wants, is asking if she can try the bergamot and tarragon, and the man behind the till is very politely explaining that unfortunately if he lets her try it then he'll be left with a tub he can't sell, and the woman is unreasonably put out by this.

I raise my eyebrows in return.

"It's worth it for this cheese, though," he says not that quietly. I smile.

"I'm Vincent," he says.

"Oh. Viv."

"Wow. Double Vs. You don't get that very often."

I look determinedly at the till. I have clearly hit some milestone in my life that signals a desire for people in shops to talk to me. Perhaps it is time to get a haircut.

He looks like he's borrowed his mum's coat.

"I see you've gone for the twenty-two-pound option," he says.

"Yes."

"It's my birthday next week."

I raise my eyebrows again and nod. This is getting out of control.

"Last year for my birthday I got a tattoo, an actual tattoo, on my actual shoulder." He's doing a loud whisper, like the information is not for the others queuing. I feel like other people are frowning at me for not being friendly back.

"What is the tattoo of?" I ask, but he is already taking off his coat and unbuttoning his shirt to show me, right there in the shop, and I start laughing out of surprise. Completely without embarrassment he exposes a haired shoulder, not muscled and smooth but also not overly flabby or hairy. Just a bit. I can smell his own smell through deodorant—he gives his armpit a sniff.

"Shit, sorry, I must stink," he says, unbothered by it, "I forgot to put deodorant on this morning, so I had to do it in the pharmacy on my way into work—I think I missed the actual armpit." What it must be to move through life without caring what it thinks of you. I remember a group of girls at school buying another girl a roll-on deodorant. Her shame that her body had betrayed her. Them patrolling the playground, arm in arm.

He shrugs down his shirt and shows me the tattoo: a small dog. No one seems offended by his naked top half but no one finds it funny either.

"I wanted a wolf," he says, "that's my spirit animal, but the tattooist ended up making it look more like a Jack Russell, and so really it's a dog now."

"It's good," I say, because I have to say something. It is not at all good.

"It's not at all good," he says. "Oh shit—I'm so sorry, I actually just got my tits out at you." There is not an ounce of concern in his voice. "What are you doing now?" he asks, buttoning up his shirt.

"Um." I look at my basket of things. "Cooking dinner. I think."

"I'm going for a drink. You should come. I'm amazing when I'm drinking." Is this how people used to meet? How did anyone ever fuck anyone else? Perhaps he is not British. Perhaps he is on meth.

"I've got lots of work on."

It is Vincent's turn at the till, and he puts down his drink and his cheese, pays in pound coins and tells the man behind the till to keep the change, which is 2p.

"Great," he says, turning towards me as I put my basket on the counter. "Hoopers—I'll be there from about eight."

"Yes," I say because no feels stuck up. "I'll see how things look."

"Great, see you then," he says and speeds up to a trot as though I had been delaying him. As he heads out the door, he waves without looking back at me, and I raise my hand too, which is pointless.

The people behind me in the queue shift and clear their throats, clearly embarrassed because a scene from a romantic comedy has played out in front of them but without the requisite level of attractiveness in casting, and I turn back to the counter and fumble with my envelope of money.

Still no word from Katherine. I put the punnet of plums on the table, along with the wine, which has almost torn through a hole in the paper bag. I will get around to emptying the recycling, which is overflowing, and then I will put the ripped bag in there.

I have another shower, because if I am clean that's half the job done. The dressing gown remains on the floor. I put on a skirt and tights and a soft shirt. I want to look as though I have been doing work things all day.

I boil a pot of salted water, drop the prawns in and watch them turn orange. I take them out and put them in a bowl, and while they cool I cut the heel off the sourdough bread and find some malt vinegar. Still nothing from Katherine. I open a bottle of wine, drink a glass while I take off my skirt, which is uncomfortable, and sit in my shirt and tights on the sofa. There is a hole in the toe of my tights and a ladder that starts just above the knee. I get up and reset the washing machine because I left a load in while I was away and the room smells neglected. I refill my wine and flip through the colour supplement of last week's newspaper. By the end of it, I have no memory of what I have looked at. On my phone I look up symptoms of early-onset dementia, which I feel gratified to discover includes *loss of ability to do everyday tasks*, and then I follow a link to a list of foods that prevent dementia. Then I look up how to pronounce *cruciferous*. I have a patch of eczema on my shin that I have had for most of my life, but if every day I tend to it with ointment, and if I don't drink too much, or eat too much sugar, or scratch it, it goes away. It's now the size of a pin feather, and it is a regular throbbing itch that accompanies me always. In the hospital, they put a gel sticker over it and bandaged it which made everything soften, and smoothed it out. If I eat the cruciferous vegetables and cream the disgusting leg I would feel better and I would look better and I would be better. I scratch my leg through my tights until I feel the satisfactory glow of broken skin.

I sit and watch the dust float above the lamp on the kitchen table. There's no movement from the dressing gown. I cannot decide whether going for a drink with a man you meet in a shop is the sort of thing a mad person does or the opposite. I wonder what Maggie from the supermarket would do. Some kind of positive action is needed. Some forward momentum. Saying yes to life. Maggie would do it, wouldn't she? Vincent would play the lead in a film where he is misunderstood and charming and eventually the victor. I would not play anything in the film. My sister could nicely play the stuck-up bitch who softens to a computer-playing nerd who makes fart jokes. In fact that may have been her thinking with Dom. Maggie could play the free spirit, who actually has great sadness about the death of her mother, or better, *daddy issues*. Maggie, in a film in which Vincent is the lead man, would crack and you would see that her life is lived only out of fear of death. Katherine would eventually concede that sitting in her pants eating processed cheese and watching *Die Hard* is something she has been missing all this time. *Thank you, Vincent, thank you.* I am in a different film that did not get the funding.

The prawns are cooled and I squeeze off their heads and their tails, unwrap their bouncy bodies. I bite into one as I'm peeling—I haven't deveined them, but I'm sure I've eaten worse things than prawn shit in my time. The inner flesh of the prawn is the whitest thing. Prawn-white—it could be a Farrow & Ball colour. Imagine having skin like that.

I eat the rest of that prawn and put the others on the buttered heel of bread, sprinkle over too much vinegar, and sit on the sofa with my plate. When I pick up my phone there is a message from Katherine, she says she's on her way over, should she bring anything. I turn off the lights and eat my sandwich and drink my wine with just the light of the orange street lamp outside my window. I decide it is a ridiculous thing to do, not to mention dangerous. At 8:15, I put my skirt back on, rinse my prawn fingers and make my way to the pub.

Hoopers is empty of customers, apart from Vincent, who is reading a paper with an almost finished pint of Guinness in front of him. He does not look up when I come in, and I have to approach him and clear my throat.

"Hi," I say, and he looks up, a wrinkle of confusion on his face.

"Oh! It's you! Hi!" he says.

"Well, I was just passing, so . . ."

"Well, yes," he says. "I told you to come here." There is a silence.

"So, I'm going to get a drink—do you . . . ?" I gesture to his drink, and think he will say no, or think he might insist on buying me a drink, but he says, simply, "Same again," and I am at the bar and he returns to his paper.

I take the drinks over—I wish I wasn't already drunk. He is sitting on the banquette, and the other seat is a stool, so I lower myself onto it. It feels lower than average. He hasn't even put the paper down. He holds on to it one, two, three, four long beats, then folds it and puts it to one side, letting out a deep breath.

"Sorry," he says, "fucking state of everything."

He does not say thank you for the drink, but says *cheers* instead.

"What were you reading about?"

"Oh"—he wipes foam from his moustache—"to be honest, I was just trying to look busy and intense until you got here, in the hope it would impress you. I'm not great at making stuff up, gives me a rash," he says. He puts down his drink, makes eye contact finally and smiles at the look on my face. "Did it work?"

I take a long drink, put down my glass.

"So a wolf, then?"

"A wolf?"

"Your spirit animal?"

"Ha. I was just trying to make conversation. It's just a badly drawn dog, but I find when I'm stressed I tend to let my mouth run away with me. I told you, I'm not great at making stuff up."

"Oh. Were you stressed?"

"I was hungry. I wanted to eat the cheese I was buying. I went home, I put the whole ball of mozzarella on a plate with some salt on, and I ate the whole thing just like that."

"Oh—I went home and ate some prawns. In a similar way."

"See?" he says, like we have revealed something fundamental about human existence. He picks up his drink, brings it close to his mouth and looks at a point above my head then says, almost to himself, "That's what it's all about."

It is not the feeling of drunkenness that I am used to, of a water balloon under the skin of my chest.

For an evening I am the woman I thought I was going to be, bookish and funny. I tell him stories about my family, about the job I have been sent to do, about Mrs. Hamilton. I exaggerate her until she becomes a character. The aloof, acerbic posh woman. I do a voice. I talk about my job as if I am casually competent at it and as if it is a real job. I am generous about my family, their need of me. Vincent looks disappointed when I say I will be spending more time in Scotland, and I notice it. I imagine myself exercising for health, visiting a dermatologist. I make him laugh by telling him about the time Dad took me for a champagne breakfast in Piccadilly to celebrate getting my period.

When the pub shuts, we stand in the cold air outside. Our breath comes white, measuring the space between us. Vincent gets his phone out and asks for my number. He doesn't try to kiss me when he leaves, just hugs me, chuckling to himself. I thought he would have tried to kiss me, and try to look like the thought had not occurred to me.

A fine-with-not-being-kissed face.

He does not offer to walk me back, which is also fine, but disappears down the street whistling. I think about those quiet moments drinking champagne with Dad, when he started to realise that taking his fourteen-year-old daughter to breakfast on this occasion was perhaps not what was expected of him. "That's OK," he said eventually over the silence. "Let's celebrate something else?" And he scanned the newspapers hung on the wall for customers to read. "How about we toast Torvill and Dean?"

I am back inside my flat in the dark, laughing about it. And seamlessly I am crying about it, which is just how it is when I drink gin after beer.

II

There was apparently no way of shaming Peter into coming to the service on Sunday.

"It will make it so awkward when next we see the reverend. And this is a small town, people like to know that everybody believes the same thing, everyone points in the same direction." Ruth was sitting at her dressing-room mirror, fastening her hair to her head with grips so that it wouldn't blow around on the walk to St. Baldred's.

"We don't all believe the same thing, though, do we?" he said. It made her feel tense when he spoke about his lack of faith. It was as though he was staying behind on an island, blithely drinking gin under a palm tree, while she and most of the people they knew left on a boat. It was the moment before the pineapple arrived that had made her feel more inclined to go, though she hadn't told Peter about it, of course. She couldn't imagine that his reaction would be anything short of sending her straight to Landbrooke to join Betty's sister.

"My dear, you go ahead and sit in a freezing church and bore yourself stupid. Fill your boots. I, meanwhile, will read my paper and eat my toast and drink my tea."

In darker moments Ruth considered it an act of infidelity. That the death of Elspeth could turn him against God, but his love for her couldn't turn him back the other way. It had very little to do with how she felt about God.

He had arrived late on Saturday night, a day and a half later than he had intended. He had also arrived a little drunk, which only bothered Ruth because he fell asleep before they really had a chance to talk, let alone anything else. She had worn the short silk kimono her sister had given her for her wedding night. She had planned on getting up to greet him, but in the end she kept it concealed underneath the counterpane as he staggered in pulling off his tie and talking about how exhausted he was. Truthfully, she had been rather irritated, and felt reluctant in the morning to perform as he expected her to, but he was not put off. She had found herself watching out of the window while the day began, giving him the occasional encouraging smile when she thought it was called for. One wasn't supposed to find one's husband's attentions irritating.

Betty had been largely absent during the day in the week after her mother's death, and Ruth had found herself wandering North Berwick like a stray. Despite asking Betty to refrain from going overboard, she would wake to an unnecessarily ornate breakfast which she deposited mostly inside the dog, and then she would go from room to room, the feeling of purpose that she had on waking slowly ebbing away. She looked often at the room she had meant for a nursery which was full of boxes, and decided that perhaps turning it into a nursery was a bad idea. Because at some point she may have to give up and turn it into something else, and that would mark something she didn't much like to think about. Each time her monthlies arrived, she had the feeling of having failed at something fundamental. She would take a walk along the golf course to the sand, and see the rock hunkering down under its white coating of gannet mess. There *was* a feeling, though, of something forgotten, something out of reach, a nagging disorder or wrongness. She would visit the Pavilion and drink her tea and then loiter over a paper. She had vivid dreams about a baby that she had forgotten she had birthed. In the dreams she was walking by the rocks when she remembered the baby was alone, cold and starving. In the seconds after waking she felt as clearly as she ever had that she didn't want her own baby, grown from her roots and gristle, her heart in another person's body, walking away from her. It was never meant to take. She found that, because she couldn't put into words her feelings of wrongness, she couldn't present these ideas to God, and she had after several days stopped praying. Which made it all the more important to get to church today, to try to grasp hold of some of those loose threads.

"Before you go . . ." Peter stretched out his arm to reach a small box on his bedside table. He shook it at her as if she were a child and the box contained a chocolate. She found herself slightly irked, but that was just how it was after a separation— you had to get used to one another again. And she had missed having someone to talk to, to set her thoughts in order.

"Happy birthday, darling. Sorry I wasn't here for it."

Inside was not a necklace or ring or even a bracelet. It was a brooch. It looked rather like something her mother might wear to pin a scarf to her shoulder, on a day that she wanted to convey a sense of *jauntiness*. It was a small dog in pewter, a terrier of some kind, with emeralds for eyes and a diamanté collar. It was conclusively ugly.

"Oh!" said Ruth and tried to take it out of the box in a way that conveyed that it was absurdly beautiful and delicate. It was not without difficulty that she said, "I just love it."

"Come here, let me pin it to you," said Peter in an indulging tone. He placed it a little too low on her pullover, so that it dangled. She turned to the mirror to look at it.

"It's the same one, isn't it?" he said.

Ruth panicked and thought hard of what on earth he might be talking about. "I love it," she said again, instead.

"The dog," he said, nodding, attempting to make her nod with him. "Your dog—with the poison—he was that kind of dog. Am I wrong?"

"Oh!" The fact of his wrongness, of the ugliness of the brooch, was swept away, and she felt touched by his effort.

"Oh, it's perfect. Thank you, darling." She stroked it and watched herself stroking it in the mirror. There was a pause.

"It's the wrong sort of dog, isn't it?" He sounded so dreadfully miserable about it.

"It's the perfect dog, I love it. I'll call it Ludwig."

"You're sure? I just . . . I saw it and I thought instantly of you."

For a second, looking at her reflection and hearing those words, she thought she might burst out laughing, but managed instead to lean back and kiss him on the lips.

"This last week, a beast has washed up among us. A kraken, if you will." Here Reverend Jon Brown looked up, smiling, and he winked at the congregation.

"Many of you will have been down to see, or will have been told of the great shark washed up on Milsey Bay. Perhaps the rest of you have smelled it."

There was a murmur of acknowledgement, some rather unnecessary chortling from a man in the front row.

"Now, I went down to see the shark after our service last Sunday, and stood about watching the waves lap at its snout, the birds pick at its eyes, and I thought, *Magnificent creature. Why are you here? On land just as feckless as any of us, wandering the earth in search of God.* Perhaps it was that search which brought the shark to the land. And then I thought of how open to interpretation nature is."

Ruth thought of the boys, how naked their wonder had been. Their letters had arrived, small and bare, addressed to Peter but he had left them on the table, so she read them. They did not seem to miss home, but they were probably told not to write about that sort of thing. She wondered if someone read their letters before they were sent, like Antony's in the army. That peculiar feeling that someone else had shaped the words and thoughts to be more universally palatable.

A man coughed and was shushed by his wife. The man held up his palms, *What would you have me do, choke to death?* And the woman shook her head, *I'm not listening to you, I'm tired of listening to you.* The man settled back against the pew and the woman stayed so still and so straight it seemed she might lift off the seat and float in irritation to the ceiling of the church.

"Perhaps," Reverend Jon Brown went on, "she heard the church bells chiming and she thought, *I'm tired. Tired of eating and swimming.* And doing those things a shark does. And she thought, *That is where I'll find my peace. Up there with the two-legged hairy folk.* And she lumbered her great body up on to the sand, and there she died, drowning in the air, as the birds appeared and picked at her, taunted her, and the sun rose and burnt her wet skin.

"A shark, tired of being a shark, dies. But what does she then become? Like Our Lord Jesus Christ on the cross, perhaps, but for whom does this shark sacrifice herself?"

Along from the man with the cough and his wife, Ruth recognised the back of Betty's head, badgery hair garlanded with a green scarf today. Ruth started a little in her seat when she saw the woman next to Betty had turned and was staring right at her, her chin dipped to her chest, a lug of dark red hair under a blue scarf. A slow smile drifted across the woman's face. This was Mary then. Ruth attempted a smile back, but just then Betty caught her sister looking and sharply turned Mary's face back to Reverend Jon Brown. Ruth could tell from the shape of Mary's face that she still wore the smile.

"Or perhaps it was some other thing the shark was attracted by, perhaps a sort of spell drew over her and she sleep-swam to the bay and only knew far too late what she had done.

"Perhaps, the dead shark marks a traveller. Think of Jonah and the whale. Perhaps this shark beached herself in order that another crawl out of her belly, to tread the earth, to fall in among us. Perhaps this soul is here out of kindness, but what a mode of delivery. A shark, this violent, unscrupulous fish—not a whale like Jonah, but a toothed hell creature."

It made Ruth smile—she imagined she could get Christopher to school Reverend Jon Brown on shark species when he returned for Christmas. The sermon sounded to Ruth muddled and in some places quite stupid, like the reverend had nothing really to say, but thought he ought to work the shark in somehow. Were it not for his tuneful voice, she doubted anyone would pay much attention at all.

A movement caught Ruth's eye, streaking down from the pulpit and behind stone pillars—a cat? She narrowed her eyes to make it out in the dark. Close to the wall, a small fox, panting. It pressed itself to the stone, wild black eye, tongue lolling, its ribs beating in and out and in and out, sharp white teeth, its tail held straight out behind it like a dart. No one else seemed to have noticed. The fox cub shook its head, refluffed itself, raised one black foot.

My child.

Before Ruth could examine the thought, something clasped on to her ankle and she made a deep sound of fright, not overly loud but enough that most of the congregation turned their heads to look at her. There was nothing beneath her pew, and nowhere for a child to hide down there. It must have been a twitch of her own that had made it feel as if a small hand had wrapped fast around her ankle. She was very hot, and coughed into her fist twice to try to give the impression that was what had caused the sound. She gave an apologetic smile to her neighbours without looking at them and focused with a frown on Reverend Jon Brown, who was sending around the collection box, saying, "Round she comes, and remember, 'Those who trust in their riches will fall, but the righteous will thrive like a green leaf.'"

The fox was gone, and she wondered if it had been there at all.

"And speaking of generosity," said Reverend Jon Brown, "I'd like to take a moment to remember Mrs. Andrea Whitekirk, who has left this earth for finer places. Many of you will recall Andrea's fine suet puddings and her excellent eye for detail at the harvest festival and winter picnic celebrations up at the big house." Again, Ruth felt faces turn towards her. "Andrea leaves behind her beloved Elizabeth and Mary, hard workers, warriors for Christ, and joins her husband Declan at the feet of almighty God. And so let us pray for the children left behind."

Heads bowed, some knelt on cushions. The wife of the coughing man knelt and then all but pulled him down to kneel next to her. Betty and Mary remained sitting bolt upright during the brief muttered prayer.

"I wonder, Mrs. Hamilton," the reverend said, clasping Ruth's hand in both of his as she tried to file out with the rest of the congregation, "if I might have your ear about something? You could wait for me by the gates and I'll walk you back— I'm lunching at the marina today."

"Of course," Ruth said, feeling immediately that she was going to be reprimanded.

She watched him saying goodbye to the last of the gathered, saw him touch Mary on the arm, as Betty, linked to her sister at the elbow, smiled in a toothy way that Ruth hadn't seen before. He touched a lot, a strong hand on an arm, a palm cupping a child's face, a pat of an elderly woman's back. He left the curate to take charge of whatever needed doing inside the church, with an elegant gesture in the air and a hand clapped on the young man's shoulder. The curate turned and disappeared back inside, his large ears glowing red.

"Mrs. Hamilton," he said, coming towards her, "where's Mr. Hamilton?"

"Oh." She considered lying. "I'm afraid he's not really one for church."

"I expect half of my congregation are not really ones for church—but they come anyway for how it looks. I admire your husband for his clarity of mind."

She wasn't sure how to take it. "You wanted to talk to me about something?"

They had started down the lane that led to the seafront, and white gulls drifted between rooftops, looking pretty against the clear blue of the sky.

"It's just that, well, you've been settled in the house a good while now, haven't you?" Settled was a word that implied a lot of things that Ruth didn't feel just then, but she nodded anyway. There was an edge to his question, the meaning behind which Ruth was unsure. She thought of the unseen girl in her bedroom and quickly flicked the image away.

"Everything is quite comfortable, thank you, Reverend."

"Have you met many people, made many friends in the town?"

"No, I don't suppose I've—"

"I know you frequent the Pavilion, and you have your walks along the seafront, but wouldn't you be happier with more than that? A friend's table to sit at, perhaps? Someone to while away the dark with?"

"I have a husband."

"Of course. Then someone to sit next to at the Sunday service."

It wasn't a secret that she went often to the Pavilion, but it did feel uncomfortable to have it remarked upon. Did people say she went too frequently? It wasn't every day. She liked to watch the swimmers. She felt angry at the thought of someone finding that worthy of reporting to The Church.

"I really can't see what business it is of anyone's where I drink my tea or who I sit next to in church." She tried to sound light-hearted about it, added a smile on at the end to show she wasn't as irritated as she felt. A breeze picked up as they left the shelter of the high street and walked out past the harbour. Ruth gathered her collar at her neck, but the reverend let his jacket flap open, pushed out his chest at the cold air.

"Absolutely, and it's only that you keep to yourself that raises so much interest about you. Which brings me to my question."

He turned to her as though he was asking for her hand in marriage. "Would you be kind enough to host on your beach this year's winter picnic?"

"Winter picnic?"

"We have one at the start of December every year. Historically it has taken place on the beach just forward of your house— which I realise is private property. The dunes offer some protection against icy blasts. The previous owner, Mrs. Beech, used to throw the picnic to welcome the children back for the Christmas holidays. We have a bonfire and baked potatoes and games and everyone has quite the time of it."

"What would I need to do?"

"Your Betty knows what's needed—her mother used to cater a good number of winter picnics—Mrs. Whitekirk used to provide such a spread. It just involves food for about thirty people and perhaps the odd bottle of drink. Mrs. Cleaver supplies us with rugs to sit on and the Allens bring wickets and bat and ball. A friend at the harbour gives us the use of his passenger boat—I don't know if you know this, but I'm a very keen skipper; in my previous life I sailed all over the Irish Sea. I take the children off to see seals and puffins, and everyone else stays on the land to drink brandy. It's extremely jolly. And really it's a simple affair to organise and very much looked forward to. We've held it elsewhere these past few years since poor Mr. Beech left us. But I think now is the right time to exorcise those old ghosts."

"Ghosts?"

Reverend Jon Brown smiled warmly. "Turn of phrase, of course. So, what do you think? It'll be a way of introducing yourself and you'd be doing the whole town a wondrous turn."

"I suppose I can ask Mr. Hamilton what he thinks, but I can't imagine he'd object." She hadn't been aware of many other children in the town. It would be good for the boys if nothing else.

"That's wonderful news, really, wonderful news. Everyone will be so excited." He turned again to look at Ruth and his eyes were shining and wet with enthusiasm. The wind blew the neck of her coat open. "Oh!" he said, touching her brooch, "Greyfriars Bobby. That's a good one."

"A gift from my husband. He was away in London over my birthday, surprised me with it this morning." She didn't want him to think she had chosen the brooch herself.

"Edinburgh," he said.

"I beg your pardon?"

"That would be Edinburgh he'd have picked this up for you, I know the place too: Clark's, in the old town. I have an aunt lives in America who bought nearly the exact same one. Though I think hers hadn't the green eyes." He looked cheerfully at Ruth. "Course you know the story—the dog's master died, and the little scrap spent the rest of its life sitting on the grave. Teaches us a few things about loyalty and dedication, I can tell you, that little dog. I did a sermon on it once, went down rather well, perhaps I'll dig it up—so to speak. I like using the animal kingdom as examples; they're following their nature always, aren't they?"

Betty had put the lamb on before she left for church, and by the time Ruth returned home all there was left to do was carve, which Peter did while she removed some of the armoury of her hairgrips.

"And how was church?" he asked, making no attempt to hide his amusement. For a moment she felt anger at his derision, but then she exhaled and conceded.

"Perfectly ghastly. I'm afraid I've been roped into throwing a picnic."

"A picnic?" He paused, arranged the slices of meat on the platter and looked out the window where a gull was being blown smartly across the golf course. "In winter?"

"Apparently it's a thing they do here."

Peter shook his head. "Scots," he said. "Always trying to prove they are hardier than the rest of us." He put the platter on the table and sat down.

"Well, actually, he's Welsh."

"They have the same problem, I'm sure." Peter eyed the covered bowls on the table nervously. "Betty's gone again, feels like she's barely here."

"Oh—her mother died at the start of last week—I suppose there's lots to sort out—and her sister is up at the sanatorium, so I imagine that's very difficult."

"Really?" He looked up, perhaps holding a moment's thought for Betty and her mother. "Poor old girl," he said, and Ruth saw him twitch bodily as though shaking something off.

"I suspect she was rather old. And they didn't get along," Ruth said as some kind of consolation.

Peter transferred lamb and then leeks onto his plate. "Oh, how dreary—is that swede?" he said. And then, picking up the lid of a tureen, "It's the blasted boiled potato, again. We must speak to her about roast potatoes. As soon as her grieving period is over, of course."

"I wanted to ask you something about Betty."

Peter looked sharply up at her. "Oh Christ, you don't want rid of her, do you? I can't bear firing staff, and she's been with the house forever—boiled potatoes are not the end of the world," he said, as though it had been her who'd brought them up.

"No, darling. I just wondered—Betty's niece, she needs a place to stay. Betty asked if she could come for a visit, but I thought we could offer that she stay on. She could help Betty perhaps, and there's plenty of space in her quarters. Would that be a problem?"

Peter gave the meat on the end of his fork a sniff, a look of sadness coming over him before he placed it in his mouth.

"How old is this niece?" he asked with his mouth full.

"Ten, I believe."

"You don't think it might . . . distract the boys?"

"I think everyone is too young for that. Besides, they'd only see her in holidays."

"Well"—Peter's attention was now on the watery gravy—"perhaps she'll be more use in the kitchen than Betty. So long as we don't have to pay her anything, I can't see the harm. I say, when you give Betty the news, would you also request beef next Sunday, with Yorkshire pudding? All this wet food is giving me trench foot."

When, that evening, Ruth told Betty her niece could stay with them on a permanent basis if she liked, Betty reached out her cold small hand and held Ruth's for quite a time without speaking.

"She'll be nothing but a credit to the household, I can promise you that, madam," she said. Her eyes were not wet, but there was something stronger there.

"I'm sure she will," said Ruth. Betty drew breath to say something else and must have noticed that she was still holding Ruth's hand, which she let go of, smoothing her apron down the sides of herself. "It'll just be so good to have her here where I can keep an eye on her. She's had a difficult time of it."

Ruth smiled. If she was completely honest with herself, she would welcome another body in the house, especially while the boys were away. "And, Betty, Mr. Hamilton is very keen on roast potatoes, and we were thinking maybe beef next Sunday?"

"We'll do the works, madam," said Betty and swept herself away into the kitchen where Ruth could hear her breathing loudly for several moments.

Ruth brushed her hair, watchful in the mirror. It was a little uncomfortable how much she could affect another person's life, without it really impacting hers at all. What would have happened had her mother not telephoned to cancel their visit, had she not gone outside and found Betty in an unusually sad and talkative mood? How was one to notice these things without them being set in front of one's face?

III

The girl does not leave her room the whole day, though I hear her cough and turn over in her bed. That night I sit staring into the fire. I think of leaving this house, this village. Of leaving Mother and Agnes in the ground, alone. The choice when it comes will be to give up the girl or leave. Father will choose the girl. I see him turning it over in his mind. He has a brightness in his eyes, he speaks of redemption and grace, but all I can think of are her bare legs underneath Mother's dress.

I went into the village during the day and tried not to see the shaking heads, spitting into the mud. If I were fully grown, the damage I would visit on them. The crack of a stick on their skulls. I stopped at the hayloft and sat a while in the dark. Agnes and I had played games there, the air thick with dust when the light came through it. When I stopped playing games with her she had felt hurt, not knowing what had changed. I never told her why, only said that we were becoming too old.

I look up. The girl is standing in the doorway, a blanket around her shoulders. She looks past me.

"I had a dream," she says.

I say nothing, just turn back to the fire.

94

"Shipwrecks."

She pulls a chair closer to the fire and it scrapes in the silence. I listen to see if anyone stirs, but the house is quiet.

"I saw them, the men, dragged down with their hearts filled of their love for life, for breath. The cold water, down their throats and gullets like thorns and filling the guts like stone."

She isn't looking at me. I glance sideways at her in the firelight. Her face is softened by it, she is very young and yet there is something wearied in her. The skin of her cheek is rough with windburn. The blanket has slipped from her shoulder, and there is a scar there the length of the top joint of my finger. I press my lips together because I would like to touch it.

"I was standing on the shore watching, but no one came back. Nothing at all for anyone to bury."

She looks at me for the first time.

"Are you a fox or a wolf?"

I say nothing.

"Foxes can smell death, they come trotting."

I cough into my hand. She sucks in air so that her whole body rises, then she lets it go and slumps a little.

"My mother made people well when they were ill." She speaks as though I have asked her to tell me a story. "She did not have a man. Men would come to her, if they had a boil that needed lancing, or a tooth that needed pulling. Like a dog with a sharpness in its paw. At first."

She is quiet for so long, I think she must have fallen asleep with her eyes open.

"But all those fat-arsed women of the village, jealous at their husbands finding their way to my mother, they said she was to blame for the storm and the ship going down. And they came for us. I hid in the corner of the field. Dug into the mud. I could hear them, first they shouted *Tell us your name, tell us your name, your real name. Tickle her, tickle her.* Over and over. Then it was not their words but the sound of them. Like men talking about how best to fix a plough.

"I waited till dark and then left. I do not know what happened to my sister."

I walk to the table and pour her a cup of hot water.

"Drink it hot."

I watch the movement of her throat as she drinks. She stands, makes a face that I cannot read.

When she is gone, the fire sinks back down into itself, darkening from the edges to its centre. It could all have been my imagining.

II

Ruth awoke at around three in the morning, with the sensation that someone had sat on the edge of the bed and then crawled over her. In the back of her throat a saltiness, which in her dream had been of drowning. She sat up and poured a glass of water to take the taste away. Peter was absent, presumably asleep on the chaise longue in his study, where she had found him more than once in recent weeks. When she had verified that the bed was empty but for her, and the feeling must have been one within a dream, she found she couldn't fall back to sleep. She worried about the nursery; how would it look to the boys if, on their return at Christmas, it was still a room filled with boxes from the old house? Wasn't it best to live without reminders of that past life, to make space for new life? If she made steps towards this new life, perhaps a baby would naturally come towards her. Ought she to have been pregnant by now? Ought she at least be seen to show willing?

She began as soon as the sun had risen. Mid-morning, Peter appeared at the door.

"What's all this?" he said cheerily. "Are you starting a white elephant stall?"

She thought she would say, *I'm clearing it for a nursery*, but what came out was, "I've decided I'd like a room of my own."

He nodded again. "Well, all right, Virginia, I'll come and fetch you for lunch, shall I?"

The photographs were the biggest undertaking. Every third one was of Elspeth. These she formed into a pile and tried hard not to look at them too closely. The woman had been extraordinary-looking in a way that suggested she was an extraordinary person. Ruth lingered a little over their wedding photograph, so different from the one on her nightstand, though at first glance so similar. Elspeth looked unfazed by the camera, she looked as though she had been caught mid-exclamation, whereas Ruth had stared hard into the lens, desperate to remember how one smiled. But the real difference lay in Peter. Fifteen years, two children, a war and a dead wife. All of it visible on his face, in the tension of his hand on a walking cane. The encased smile.

She found an album her parents had made for her with her initials on the front. Inside was a photograph of Nanny holding her as a baby, in front of the hospital. She had liked looking at the album as a child—it had given her a terrific feeling of self-importance.

The album documented a selection of birthdays and other milestones up until she was about fourteen, though there was one photograph, unglued in the back, of her looking morose and horse-like at Alice's wedding. The one she chose to extract from the album to find a frame for was of herself, Alice and Antony, lined up against the nursery wall in Kensington. She could not have been older than four, which made Antony around seven and Alice nine. Nanny must've taken it, the three of them absorbed by a small wooden box that Antony held. Alice had her hand on Antony's shoulder to better see what was inside, and Ruth's fingers clasped his shirt. All three of them smiling as though the contents of the box confirmed the existence of magic. Antony's face was lit as though the thing in the box glowed. Perhaps Nanny had set up the photograph to use as a Christmas card. She had no memory of it being taken, but she could feel the flannel of Antony's shirt in her fist.

At three, Peter came out of his study and knocked on the door frame. He whistled. "Goodness me. You're really getting things in order, aren't you, old lady? Come, come, lunchtime. I can hear the ham curling from here."

After lunch, which Betty always put out at twelve sharp, regardless of when they wanted it, they wrapped themselves in scarves and coats and crossed the golf course to the beach. The tide being low, they turned left to walk around the point and faced into the wind, which held the smell of tar. Peter had a small flask of brandy, and he passed it to her.

"How's work today?" she asked.

"Oh"—he made a sound of great weariness—"there's just so much to do. I expect I'll have to go back to London for a week or so before Christmas."

"I see."

He looked out towards Fidra. The sky was growing overcast. The lighthouse keeper would turn on his lamp early tonight.

"Yes, very boring altogether." Ruth passed his flask back, he drank again and then put it away. They linked arms.

"While tidying earlier I came across several photographs of Elspeth. I'm a little unsure of what to do with them." She kept her eyes trained on her feet so as not to trip over seaweed, and so she only felt a light tensing through Peter's body.

"I dare say I ought to keep them."

"Oh, of course, I wasn't suggesting—"

"No, quite, but perhaps I should put them away in a drawer for when the boys are older."

"Quite, of course." What she wanted to say was that she didn't mind him looking at them himself, but she could feel the discomfort it was causing him. "Betty's niece arrives next Sunday," she said instead.

"Ah yes. Remind me of her name?"

"Bernadette."

"Bernadette. Rather grand name. Or perhaps her father was named Bernard. Where is the father by the way?"

Ruth shrugged. "I get the feeling it's a bit of a sensitive area. Given Betty's sister's situation."

"Her situation?"

"She lives in an institution. I gather she's rather disturbed."

"Is she? Why didn't I know this?" There was an edge to his voice that made Ruth start. She *had* told him—could picture them at the dinner table.

He had seemed completely at ease about it.

"I did mention it, over lunch—it was lamb and boiled potatoes."

"I would have remembered. I'm only concerned for my children—what if this thing is passed down? Do we know why she ended up there? Can we find out?"

Ruth felt a rising panic about the idea of having to tell Betty that Bernadette in fact could not stay with them.

"Look, it's not anything like that—"

"Anything like what? I can't believe that you've invited this person to live with us, and it turns out she's a maniac." There was a tone to his voice she'd heard him use on the telephone with the office. It was a surprise to be on the receiving end of it. Perhaps she hadn't been clear. She found herself unable to speak, and after a period of silence, Peter sighed and ran a hand through his hair.

"I'm sorry, darling, I'm under a lot of pressure; I mustn't blame you."

It was again hard to speak, because the idea of him blaming her for the surplus of pressure was terrible. She placed a hand on his arm instead. She felt apologetic, but something else, too—*ruffled* might be the correct word.

Before she could think of the right words, Peter said, "Christ alive—I suppose that's your vicar friend."

Looking into the distance, Ruth was surprised to see a man stand up from the water's edge. She had at first taken the immobile black outline for a rock, but now the reverend was striding towards them, his hand already extending to shake Peter's, a broad smile on his face that showed teeth.

He started speaking when still too far away for the sound to reach them, and so began a soft jog in order that his voice could be heard.

"Well now, look at this—it's the mysterious Mr. Hamilton. Finally we meet," and then he was close enough to shake Peter's hand.

"Hello," said Peter very politely, not an ounce left of his previous mood.

"I can't tell you how pleased I am to see you."

"Oh, well, likewise, I'm sure."

The reverend turned to Ruth and gave her a nod and a smile.

"Are you fishing?" she asked.

"Fishing for what?"

"I mean, I noticed you were rather hunkered down over there. I wondered if you had a line hidden away?"

"Right, no. If you'll forgive me the eccentricity, I was only praying, I'm afraid. I like to come down and listen at the water's edge—listen for long enough and you hear Him talking back through the waves."

There was a long silence. Reverend Jon Brown began to laugh. "I do apologise, I tend to become rather exuberant after a long session by the water."

Ruth smiled and looked down. She inhaled sharply. "My God, your feet." He had no shoes on, the toes bright yellow and deep purple at their roots, the tops of his feet white and stark. "Are you all right?"

"My goodness, man," said Peter, laughing, "you really are an enthusiast."

Peter and Reverend Jon Brown laughed together for some time. When the laughter threatened to die down the reverend started it up again, until finally he bent over so that his hands were on his knees and let out a high-pitched groan. He was quite a few years older than Ruth had first imagined. The weathered rumples on the back of his neck attested to that. Peter shot her a look that made her bite her lip for fear she would start laughing too.

Reverend Jon Brown sprang up, sea spray flying from his hair, and he combed it back with his hands. "Oh dear me," he said, "I've been out here too long. It's just . . ." He held his arms out and gestured to the sky, the sea and the air.

"Quite," said Peter, smiling in a way that Ruth knew meant it was time to leave. "Oh, by the way, Reverend, while we've got you here: our girl Betty attends your service, I believe?"

"Indeed she does, God-fearing as they come is young Elizabeth."

"And her sister too?"

"Oh, Peter, I really don't think we can—"

Though Peter carried on. "It's just that we have Betty's niece coming to stay with us, and apparently my lovely wife mentioned this, I didn't hear her, but it seems Betty's sister is in an institution?"

Reverend Jon Brown nodded, his mouth a little open, eyes watchful.

"I didn't know that." He said it slowly and calmly, like the foam had washed out of him. "About you taking on Bernadette." There was a pause. He gave the impression that they ought to have first asked his permission. The reverend wiped his nose hard on his hand and sniffed violently. "Right. Right, that's very good of you. Betty didn't say."

"Oh, it's quite a recent plan. She's coming next Sunday." Ruth tried to gauge Peter's reaction to this. To say it out loud felt valuable. Peter looked unperturbed, and so that was encouraging.

"And I just wondered if you knew—if you would give us some indication of what the matter is with the mother? It's just I'm rather concerned for my boys, you see."

Ruth felt a hot bolt of shame as Peter asked the question, and also at the realisation that she wanted to know, too.

"I quite understand, Mr. Hamilton. You don't want young Bernadette walking in on you in the night and murdering you with a kitchen knife, that's quite understandable. No. I don't think she'll be up to anything much like that."

A little pink rose in Peter's face. "No, I didn't think—"

"Of course it's perfectly natural to want to protect your children, Mr. Hamilton. But the thing to remember about people is, the truer to their nature they get, the more the animal in them comes out, the more innocent they become, and so the closer to God they get. That Mary, she just came a little too close to her animal to be around people. But the pup's not to blame. Oh no." He seemed now to be talking to himself.

Ruth cleared her throat.

"Righto!" The reverend clapped his hands loud enough to startle both Ruth and Peter.

"Right, yes, of course," said Peter as though the man had talked complete sense and put his mind at rest.

"How are the boys, Mr. Hamilton? Full of stories of pitches and wickets, I imagine."

"Hmmm, yes, very much so."

"I'll be heading off now, I think," said the reverend. "I've got a bird in the oven back home and I intend to feast upon her." He started to walk backwards down the beach, waving and talking as he went. "Goodbye to you both. Mr. Hamilton, it has been a pleasure meeting you, and I look forward to seeing you one Sunday, or if not, at the winter picnic, which you are too kind to be hosting."

Once he was out of earshot, Peter took out the flask and drank.

"My God," he said, "the man's rabid."

"He doesn't appear to have even brought his shoes with him," said Ruth. There was no bundle of clothes anywhere along the beach. "I suppose we ought to head back, so that we're not just staring at him as he goes." But they stayed a moment longer. There was a curious lope to the way Reverend Jon Brown moved.

"What do you suppose his true animal is?"

"A very odd fish, I'd say," Ruth said, and they both laughed and Peter handed the flask to her and she took a swig, and then they turned for home, the disagreeable air of the previous conversation swept away into the sea.

"Do you suppose your vicar has a thing for grog, by any chance?"

"One can only hope."

It took four days to clear the room. She used the large cupboards in the bedroom to store the things that did not fit neatly within the house but she was too sentimental to abandon altogether. Once she'd finished, Ruth sat at the small desk she had had Betty help her lug up from the drawing room. She had positioned it by the window, and decided against hanging curtains. Curtains were for a nursery, to block out the light, a nursery was warm and sleepy. The unfiltered light of her study was brisk and unsentimental. She placed a sheet of paper in front of her and wondered what she was now supposed to do with it. She adjusted the angle of the photograph of herself, Antony and Alice, then flung open the window and let in the cold air. From the desk drawer she took a pencil. She held the pencil, squeezed a little too tightly, bent low to the paper, to draw or to write, she wasn't sure. Something in her vibrated. Something contracted. An urge just below the skin. A seagull shrieked away her thoughts as they came to her, and she stood up and closed the window firmly so that it rattled in its frame. The house was silent again, but still nothing came to her. Why should it?

She put the paper away, and took out the book she was reading, an Austen novel from her schooldays, but the words the characters spoke either enraged her or bored her, and several hours later she found herself staring out of the window towards the Bass Rock while the sky blackened around it. She looked up at the doorway, sensing Peter's presence, ready to spring into a justification of why she was sitting with her feet on the desk in the dark, but no one was there. And then it felt he had come into the room after all, and was just about to rest his hands on her shoulders, and she jumped a little in anticipation, but again no one was there.

Ruth turned on the lamp and brushed herself down as though she might have collected dust in the few hours of quiet stillness. What on earth she had been dwelling on she couldn't imagine. She looked at her room, neat and ready for something, and wondered if they ought to try again to have a baby instead. She felt the long blank passage from her throat to her gut.

I

If I am going to stay for any length of time, I have to find something proper to sleep on and under. My first thought was to sleep at the top of the house in Mrs. Hamilton's study, because sleeping in Dad's childhood bed feels too much like an endurance test of emotional problems. Deborah has tried to suggest a lady artist might paint in the study by setting up one of Mrs. Hamilton's easels by the tiny window, with a wonky lighthouse on canvas propped on it. I have a sudden memory of when I was small and found her slumped on her desk asleep, a cigarette burned right down to the filter in her fingers. And how she'd woken very suddenly and seen me there, and shouted *Get out!* And I close the door, my heart thumping, and turn my attention to bedding.

My sleeping bag is brittle-feeling and gritty with sand as though the last time I used it I'd gone for a swim and got into it wet. Deborah had expressed her distrust in an email exchange while I was in London, when I informed her I would be house-sitting on a more regular basis. She said that *unfortunately* she'd had to throw away my celery, as it touched the back of her fridge and was producing ice crystals, which made the fridge messy. *It is the little things*, she said in an email, *that make the big difference where prospective buyers are concerned.* She asked that I return the bedding, folded, to the wardrobe after using it, and that if I needed to run the washing machine, to please do so at night and be sure to remove any drying items before leaving the house. Her sort of buyers, apparently, didn't like the idea of any living occurring in a house they might like to purchase.

Of course.

And I know we have the mobile signal issue in that house, so I'd really rather know that all issues of cleanliness are taken care of at all times, because I can't always give you an indication of when I'm arriving.

I can check my messages if I climb the wall, I wrote back.

Even so, she had replied immediately.

Even so.

I wonder what I have done to appear so filthy to her. I suspect the uneaten celery has upset her more than she lets on.

The bedding, she said, was in the wardrobe in the master bedroom. There is the duvet on the double bed, which I have no intention of using, and two over-plumped pillows. There are three wardrobes in the room. The first two that I open are stacked with shoeboxes, inside of which I find Christmas decorations, children's toys, a threadbare teddy with orange eyes. For a moment it stops me from looking for anything else. I don't like the idea of Deborah finding it, and I put it in my pocket, it seems cruel to lock it away again.

In the third wardrobe I find yellow and pale pink waffle-weave counterpanes with horrible satin rims, which I remember rubbing against my nose as a child. There is a tablecloth that will do as a sheet, and there are still cushions on the grey sofa I can use as pillows.

I stand in the doorway of Dad and Christopher's room, twin beds side by side with their own bedside tables and lamps with yellow pleated shades that match the counterpanes I've pulled from the wardrobe. Katherine and I used to sleep in this room, with Mum and Dad next door in the study with its pull-out bed. I remember the sound of the wind as it whooped down the chimney breast. It never worried me then, but Katherine would sometimes get up and climb into my bed, allowing me a small moment of superiority, which in the morning she would explain away by saying she felt the cold more than I did, as though there was something uncouth about my not being cold.

I throw the counterpane on the bed and prop up the bear on the dresser. I'm not going to sleep with it, if that's what it's thinking. I've slept in the bed a hundred times before, just not since Dad died, and I can't stop seeing the imprint of his small child's body in this bed. I smooth the counterpane over it again and again but it always comes back.

On the wall, I continue trying to excuse myself to Katherine, without apologising or admitting that I did anything wrong in not staying in when she came round for dinner. I have tried saying I thought it was Thursday she was coming over, to which she replied by forwarding the text two above where it says *Wednesday*. I have also implied that I'm not feeling well, without specifying if I mean I have a cold or am having a breakdown. She does not reply. As I'm climbing off the wall, I notice a crow building a nest on the chimney pot. When we were small, Bet always had the fire on, the house needed drying out all the time. *The seawater gets into the bricks*, she used to say. *You'll smell seaweed if you don't have a fire on.* And at times it did smell of something salty, an ancient, mineral mud, not a bad smell exactly, just not the smell of a home.

Vincent messaged and suggested meeting when I'm back in London next week, going to see a film, but I'd rather just go for a drink. I only like the cinema alone. I don't want the conversation afterwards, when it's too late for dinner and too late really for a drink, and you have to say something pertinent about what you've just seen. I always get it wrong, say I loved the film when the other person hated it, or say I hated it when it's a transforming moment in the other person's life. In reality it is hardly ever either of those, it is just a story and a way of passing two hours in the dark without alarming anyone.

The crow takes off and flies to the top branches of the monkey puzzle tree. It yells at me from there.

"All right, I won't tell her," I say, but the crow carries on watching me. "Just don't blame me if she starts a fire and it roasts you."

Back inside, the lingering smell of the Booeys permeates the air. *Nothing like a wet dog drying in the heat.* Without a fire or the Aga, there is no blood flowing through the house. I know that before a potential buyer comes over, Deborah likes to arrive an hour ahead and set up heaters to blast the rooms. She has a spray that is meant to smell of coffee, but smells like a service station instead. The central heating just doesn't reach the bones of the house. In the kitchen, I boil the kettle and sit at the table with a mug of hot water. It tastes salty, and I pour it away down the sink. I take a bottle of Deborah's water from the fridge and twist off the top. I don't remember having drunk a single glass of water the whole day. I cook some pasta and throw in half a can of clams and some olive oil at the end. I stand with the half-full tin of clams for a moment, then push it into the space left by the water bottle. That should get her juices flowing.

If this were a film or a book, I would sit and eat my clam spaghetti in front of a fire, and I would read. But there is a crow nesting up there, and if I spill oil on the grey sofa I'll never sleep again. I haven't been able to read in months. So I eat the food, drink another glass of water and then go to the living room to fetch the whisky. Christopher has put the cork in hard and it won't be pulled out, so I search for a corkscrew in the cutlery drawer. The silverware is long gone. All that remains is a set of cheap utensils that could have been stolen from a school dining room. The next drawer houses a few items that I recognise as Betty's. I wonder if my mother would want them. Her worn dark red spectacles case, a whistle she used to wear and blow if she wanted us down at dinner, to save her voice. A little notebook that listed times and dates and weights, which she recorded with the seriousness of one noting down medication. And a glossy pamphlet in a Perspex sleeve that also held a bunch of receipts. The pamphlet is from the nursing home that I have seen signposted on the road to Musselburgh. The pamphlet reads in a curly font reserved for old people's homes: *Coping with the death of a loved one—the Landbrooke House guide.* I flip through it and inside is a form, filled out by Bet.

I never met my grandmother, Mary. I was only vaguely aware of her death, which, judging by the form, will have been twelve years ago in the summer. Mum is not cagey about her mother, but she is private. The story I know not to be the whole truth is that Mary was an epileptic and fell one too many times, that Landbrooke, when she first was admitted shortly after my mother was born, was not called a nursing home but something more sinister. Mum's father she knows nothing about. We are a muddled family—Mum and Dad nearly brother and sister, but no blood. The servant's daughter—sometimes Dad would tease Mum about it if she made a fish pie. The fact of their reconnection always amazed me. Mum was sent to school in London after our fabled grandfather left, and seven years later Uncle Christopher walked past her selling tights in the hypermarket. The three of them moved into a flat together and I don't know what happened there, other than whatever it was was disrupted by my arrival.

The pamphlet brings with it all of a sudden a memory of Dad in the hospice, husky and mustard yellow. I walk briskly around the kitchen table until the image is gone—I replace it with the image in a photograph I have of him, in sunglasses and a panama hat, smiling. Not much of his face is visible but it does the job. After he died, and I stayed those few strange days in the psychiatric wing, a doctor told me it can take a few years before your memory of them as sick dissipates and lets the old memories of before back through. They asked my mother to bring in a photograph of him, got me to look at it when the memories came. I dream of him before the sickness now, but in the dreams I always know there's something in the room with us, I just can't remember what it is. So embarrassing to have made such a spectacle of myself while my mother and sister were left to get on with everything, with the extra weight of me in hospital. And there's that rabbit hole again. I find a penknife and I use the tool to get stones out of horses' hooves to lever out the cork.

At four in the morning I am tired enough to sleep. I have not drunk an appalling amount, and that is something. It's not a good feeling turning out the lights and leaving the kitchen; the rest of the house gapes about me. I slide into bed, remembering once I'm in that I haven't brushed my teeth. I let myself off that particular chore. I switch off the light and, though the room is in absolute darkness, I get out of bed again and turn the bear to face the wall, because it stops me from sleeping.

The birds are drilling outside and the large curtainless window lets in white cold light. In the first moments of waking I am pleased to remember that I stayed at the house overnight, and slept, but I am quickly alarmed to find myself in Mrs. Hamilton's bedroom, under her quilt. I sit up, panicked, and pull back the covers. There is no longer any dark stain, Deborah must've replaced the mattress. That's good. But there's the small matter of waking up in the wrong room. Perhaps I was more drunk than I thought, perhaps I got into the wrong bed. The bear is in bed with me, and I am holding it in one hand.

When it is done, the three men look on the girl. There is not much to see, the darkness makes it so that blood is only another texture, and the sea air means that the smell of death is brushed away.

"I did not mean for her to die." The young one holds back the tears in his voice. The girl now seems to look a little like his mother. May have children herself. A sharp thought enters him. "What will happen to us?"

"Us?" says the short one. "I barely touched her." He takes a piece of cloth from under his coat and wipes his mouth again, as though after a good meal. The waves continue and the three men stand above the girl. White birds lift off the black rock, just visible on the edge of the darkness.

"Rome's eyes are cast elsewhere tonight," says the one with the high forehead. He bends down and picks up the girl under the armpits. She is not quite dead, and moans, and so he holds her under the water for just a little while. She does not struggle.

"There," he says, "we don't want more trouble. Help me move her further out, and the sea will take care of her as the tide comes in."

The young one takes off his coat and lifts the legs. He had felt tearful but something else overtakes him now, something like anger—a stupid decision to come at night to collect seaweed next to the camp. What was she expecting to find? They wade out, not too far, up to their hips. It is rocky, and some of the rocks are loose. The one with the high forehead prises four large stones, and places them on the girl's chest.

It is cold and the strange thing is that her body is warm, even underwater. The one with the high forehead grunts.

"That'll do," he says, "judging by the tideline it comes right up to the dunes—she will be swallowed up before morning."

He slaps the back of the young one. "Don't feel too bad. She made so much noise, there was no other way." The young one nods. There was no other way and he had only meant to quiet her, but she didn't understand that. Back on the sand the three look at the girl's basket of seaweed.

"Should we dispose of it?" asks the short one. They look a moment more.

"No," says the one with the high forehead. "No, there is nothing to say it is hers, and even if it is found by someone looking for her, they will only presume she is drowned."

"And the wound on her head?" asks the young one.

"Just the turning of a body on the rocks."

The three men adjust their cloaks and walk back to the camp, where the fires are low, and someone has caught a hare and roasts it, and the smell reminds the youngest one of home.

St. Baldred's

I

My mother breathes loudly and deliberately for several moments. She is completing a sudoku at her kitchen table. I have come over to deliver the few things of Betty's that I thought she might want, but I have arrived before she has finished her morning puzzles and she won't be distracted from them. I didn't manage to get to sleep in the night, so have been circling her house for about an hour, waiting for the cafe to open, with that rattly feeling that I need to talk to someone to prove that I can. It would not do to let myself in while she sleeps. That would give me away immediately, would make her worry. If I arrive with coffees I will have the cover of normalcy.

Nearly all the books, apart from those on a couple of shelves in the bedroom, are about mushrooms or lichen. Some have a certain amount of damp in them and need turning, but it would be a full-time job. Mum has grown immune to it and takes no notice of me picking up *Toadstools of the Outer Hebrides* between my thumb and index finger because it is covered in a black lichen-like mould.

"Mum, your mushroom books are growing mushrooms," I say and she makes no indication that she has heard me. She inhales noisily through her nose.

"I suppose Katherine and you aren't talking again?"

119

I shrug. "It's not that we're not talking, it's just that as usual she's making a slight misunderstanding into a commentary about what a terrible person I am."

Mum looks up briefly, just over her glasses. "Do *try* not to drive her mad, you know how she gets." I feel deep and unreasonable annoyance at this. "Darling, I've been meaning to say," she says, focusing again on the sudoku in the paper and rolling her pencil between her palms, "I do sometimes wonder if there's someone living up there."

"Up where?" I put the book down at a safe distance from my mug, imagine spores landing on the surface of my coffee.

"What I don't understand," she says, wiping a smear from her glasses as though it might help her to solve the sudoku, "is why . . ."

She does this. Starts a sentence out loud and carries it on in her own head. I will wait for the thing she doesn't understand to be uncovered but it will turn out not to be for me. A lot of my mother's life is internal these days.

"What?" I ask.

She looks up.

"Mmm?"

"What is it that you don't understand?" I try not to sound annoyed.

"Well, I don't know why . . . every time . . . ah. Aha!" She writes down a number in a box. "Got it, you little bastard." She looks up, peers at me over her glasses. "Sorry—I'm talking to myself."

"Yes."

"But," she says, "I don't know what's going on in the roof space. Sounds like a family of arseholes living up there."

I ring the pest control people while Mum unloads the dishwasher.

"Do we have any idea of what type of animal is making the noise?"

I want to tell them it's a family of arseholes.

"Probably squirrels—there's a large tree by the front of the house."

"Yes, well, sometimes the odd cat gets in, so, are we sure there haven't been any catlike sounds from up there? Have we opened up the roof space and looked ourselves?"

"We have," I lie.

"OK, well, we will have someone with you between four and six today."

"With us," I correct her.

"I beg your pardon, madam?"

"It's nothing. Thank you."

Mum comes into the kitchen as I hang up the phone.

"Four to six today. The pest man cometh."

She frowns. "You'll have to stay—I have an appointment about my hip at four thirty."

"What's wrong with your hip?"

"If I knew that I wouldn't need an appointment." She looks at me. "Well? Can you?"

I was meant to meet Vincent at five. We were going to have a look at a ceramics open studio—his suggestion. The cinema date had gone badly—the film was about a piano teacher who wanted her student to rape her. We'd agreed maybe not the cinema next time.

"OK?"

"Fine."

"Good." There is a distance of quiet air between us.

"How are you finding the old house up there, darling? On your own? Are you sleeping all right?"

I shrug. "I don't tend to sleep all right."

"No, of course. I used to see a little ghost there when I was young."

"What?"

"A girl."

"Mum."

"Are you sleepwalking?"

"Mum."

"Ah, you see. Don't worry, she's perfectly friendly, just a bit lonely I should think. I used to have a dream that I was following her down to the beach at night, and when I woke up, she'd be there and I'd have wandered all the way out of our quarters and to the top of the house!"

"Mum."

"Oh, darling, it's absolutely nothing to worry about. I actually thought you might like it. She used to hang around that top bathroom next to Christopher and Dad's room—the one you and Katherine shared. Christopher and Dad used to see her too, after all that beastly stuff at the boarding school. It's no wonder."

The school Dad and Christopher attended made the papers ten years ago after it was discovered to have been involved in what the press called a paedophile ring.

My mother had sniffed at the term. "I think that's rather a glamorous term for what went on there. They used to tell me about it in the holidays. We'd smash the shells of crabs in the rock pools while they talked about it. I've always felt terrible about those crabs." She stands, signalling that the conversation is done. I want it to continue.

"What was Mrs. Hamilton like when you were a kid?"

"Well, you know." She sighs. "She wasn't an easy woman, but really she saved us all. She was a lonely person, I think. So was Betty. I always rather felt I'd let her down."

"Let her down?"

"I think she wanted me to become something more spec-tacular, given I was the only child she really had any say in. She wasn't allowed to take the boys out of boarding school, because that was their father's lookout. So she put quite a lot of energy into me being happy."

"You are happy though."

"Yes, darling, of course, but I think she thought it might make her happy too. And I'm not sure, after all the effort she went to, that it did."

Mum starts to shuffle papers around on the kitchen table, which is a sign she is about to leave the conversation.

"Deborah's selling the house. Or trying to."

Mum looks up, rolls her eyes.

"Oh Christ—do you have much to do with her?"

"She sends me emails to let me know I'm very dirty."

"Yes, that sounds like her—she's one of those germ people, she always carried wet wipes, I seem to remember." My mother says this as though it is the very worst thing she can think of.

"Christopher is trying to look after her, I think."

"Soft fool," she says, though not unkindly.

"What's her story?"

"Well, I suppose it's that ghastly business with Mr. Hamilton. Your father couldn't bear her of course."

There's a long silence. I think about how a distant relation would talk about my life in thirty years' time. *Well, she house-sat for a time and then just stayed indoors mostly.*

"It's not great, is it?" I say out loud.

"It's not, no." Mum slaps her thighs loudly. "Come on then, you stupid old cow," she says to the dog, who lifts her narrow head to look at her. "Come on, I'll take you to the park and you can kill something." The dog drags herself out of the bed, yawns so that her tongue curls, and she stretches her toes, pointing them behind her like a dancer. She gives me a friendly nose and I thumb her warty cheek. Her muzzle has gone grey in the last six months and there's a wobble in her back legs that we don't speak about. Mum puts a hand on my head as she walks by. "I shouldn't have said anything about the ghost. Honestly, she's as harmless as air."

The dog sneezes. "Poo bags, keys, lead," says my mother and once she's heading down the stairs I call after her, "I don't believe in ghosts, so that's fine." But she doesn't hear or at least doesn't respond.

It is just like my mother to tell me about a ghost in the house in which I am staying, alone, and then to tell me that there's absolutely nothing to worry about. That is exactly her game.

"Eat some fruit," she calls from the front door. "Your sister still sends those ghastly boxes—there are more unripe pears and fucking kohlrabi than I know what to do with." She slams the door and I hear her thud down the stairs to the pavement. She is not light on her feet, steps deliberately every time. It is just like my mother to leave the house as soon as she has a visitor.

I text Vincent, ask if we can change it to a drink.

Thank god—I didn't realise ceramics meant bowls and mugs. What did you think it meant?

I don't know, just something more exciting. Maybe something to do with pastry actually.

The pest man arrives at five o'clock and is youngish with a West Country accent. He is enthusiastic about his job.

"I get to see some interesting places," he says brightly as I show him into my mother's bedroom.

124

"I bet you do," I say and immediately become worried that I've accidentally come on to him. He is up in the roof space, just his legs visible on the ladder, his large yellow sand boots. It would be strange to offer him tea because he will spend his time in the house balanced on a ladder, perhaps handling rat poison, and I hate making tea for people. The idea of leaving him alone in my mother's bedroom is not good. So I try to make conversation.

"What's the, er, strangest thing you've found in someone's roof space?"

He pops his face down so I can see it, says brightly, "Found a dead body once, that was pretty mad." He pops his head back up.

I feel an instant and robust warmth towards him. "Oh," I say. There are questions that I can't begin to formulate.

"Yeah—had to stay all day with the police, and it was October so had loads of work on. Animals start to cosy up in the autumn."

"Sure!" I say. I find that I am sitting on the bed, and I wonder how inappropriate that might be. He saw me when he poked his head down, and so it would be weird to move now. "I found a body once, too," I say, but I don't say it loud enough and he doesn't hear me.

"It's clean," he says, and for a moment I can't locate what we are talking about. He starts down the ladder, his torch in his hand. "Can't see any mess. But I'll lay a few traps, in case they've only just moved in."

I stand. "Great."

"I'll just run to the van and get them," he says, smiling. He has a dark freckle that overlaps his top lip.

"What had happened to the man you found?"

He shrugs like the question had never crossed his mind. "Woman. Not sure. She just died up there. All got to go sometime, isn't it?" And he ducks out of the room and pads down the stairs, whistling a familiar tune.

We have all got to go at some time. And it's not the deadness, really. It's being thrown away, the logistics of packing her away into a suitcase only marginally bigger than the hand-luggage allowance on a domestic flight. I sit back down on the bed. Her boyfriend killed her with a wire cord, stuffed her into a suitcase, set the suitcase on fire in their backyard and threw what was left into the sea. It was as easy as that to become dead. But there was a photograph and a name and all the story of that day and how she died and how her boyfriend hanged himself later, in his cell, and the child left behind.

The ladder is still leaning into the roof space. The black square of the hatch is bigger than I thought it would be. When it's closed it disappears as part of the ceiling, but now it feels like the house has grown. It feels bigger inside than it is on the outside. I climb the ladder slowly, listening for his footsteps on the stairs. The black is thick, as if it has been sealed up there. It smells of old damp photographs, the faintest scent of camphor. Without a torch I can see nothing. Not even the wind outside penetrates the space, no traffic noise, no house creak, no distant burglar alarm. But I have the feeling of the individual scales of my skin lifting, of every hair standing up like it is magnetised. I start back down, and nearly fall when I see he's there, holding the ladder.

"Oops," he says. "Careful there." He steadies me by placing a hand on my thigh, and I flush red.

"Sorry," I say, climbing down and trying to be brisk, but with the awful knowledge that he can see how red I've gone. "I just . . ."

"Oh, everyone's always curious," he says lightly, "everyone always wants to look—it's natural." He is standing very close and there is a sudden, unsettling intensity to him. Is he talking about something else? He has no smell about him at all, no aftershave, no deodorant, no sweat or coffee breath. No toothpaste, no washing detergent.

"I just wondered how big it was." Everything sounds like the start of a porno.

He smiles and the freckle lifts on his face. I sidestep so that I'm no longer between him and the ladder. I am careful to step away from and not towards the bed.

He holds up his two metal traps and the atmosphere may have never existed.

"Peanut butter is the most tasty thing to a squirrel—or a rat. So we'll get anyone passing through."

He climbs back up humming his tune.

"Now, if you hear the trap go off—it'll be like a loud thump—then ninety per cent of the time that's it, game over, they're very effective. But if you hear it go off, and then there's some scrabbling about, we might have to come and dispatch things ourselves. Obviously we'd rather that didn't happen—and honestly, ninety per cent of the time it comes down on the back of the neck and that's it. And it might not happen at night when you're in here, so if you don't hear anything, but there's a smell . . ."

He climbs back down, screwing the lid on a jar of peanut butter. He licks his finger. "Anyway, I'll be back in around a week to check them, but if you do hear anything, or smell anything, call me and I'll come round sooner." He smiles and I smile and I show him to the front door.

Before walking down the steps into the front garden, he turns and says, "It's been a pleasure meeting you," and for a second it is there again, enough that I close the door and lean against it and wonder what has happened. I can hear him whistling on the way to his van and I sing along, *Down deep in his soul, she can bring him such misery.*

I am twenty minutes late to meet Vincent, but then he is another ten. I am late because I haven't done any washing for a while and I had to go out to the high street and find something to wear. It was harder than I remembered. There was a time, I'm sure of it, when any old shit fitted just fine, and suddenly just a normal black T-shirt makes me look like I think too much of myself. *When*, I wonder, looking in the mirror of the changing room, *did my tits get weird?*

I end up choosing a top which is too big for me, because the smaller sizes highlight bad things I don't want to think about. It has a pattern—almost everything in the shop has a pattern. It is the kind of shop that only sells cropped trousers, and sneaks in a little embroidery here and there on something that should be perfectly ordinary. It is a shop for the mothers of children. Polka dots on every garment, even if it's in the lining of a jacket. I look like a virgin in my big top, I look outdoorsy and maybe even a bit Christian, but at least I don't smell of soup. It has a Scandinavian leaf pattern and a useless pocket on the breast.

"I think it's great," says Vincent once we are settled at a small table in the back of the pub, "that you can wear stuff like that."

"Like what?"

"You know," he says, "like young and old at the same time. I think that's very cool."

Vincent is wearing a T-shirt that has two howling wolves on it. At a guess I would say it was ironic, but I feel sometimes so confused by him, I can't say for sure.

We stay out late, drink fast. We kiss and he puts his change in the pocket on my chest, but I wake up alone. I don't recall what kind of kiss it was. It can't have been all that great if he's not here. There is a bubble of excitement which gets burst by the hangover and I take an antihistamine and a handful of Kalms and go back to bed for the day. When I wake again it is dark out, and I feel foggy, but know I need to get up to Scotland. I stand in the shower and let the water fall in my face. I should eat. I boil pasta, I eat it out of the pot with some olive oil and salt on it. I eat it too quickly and want to go back to bed, but instead I put my shoes on.

The drive up to Scotland is a silent one tonight. I don't feel like singing. I am not relishing sleeping again in the house. I am jumpy with a hangover, and will think about Mum's ghost; I imagine some horrifying Victorian child with blue circles under her eyes and a bent neck. It is cold exhaustion—hangovers have recently become long and insidious. I remember hangovers before guilt. Those days of waking at noon and eating a burger and watching TV, maybe with friends. Laughter about your bad behaviour the night before. Plans to get drunk again soon. Now there is a shake in my wrists and a feeling that someone has a hold of my head and is pushing it down to rest on the steering wheel, while they tell me every little loathsome thing about my behaviour the night before and how that marries up perfectly with the badness that seeps out of me. I am bad like a bad dog.

Every time I pass one of those signs *Tiredness can kill* I think about all the other things that can kill just as simply and comprehensively. If the pest man had kissed me I would have kissed him back, when Vincent kissed me I kissed him back. What was the difference? Dom once placed his hand on my lower back and pulled me towards him; when I avoided his mouth he mumbled into my neck, "I love what a fuck-up you are, it's so sexy you're such a mess. I bet you fuck like a beast." I stopped him talking by kissing him, and then made out that if only I wasn't his wife's sister then we'd be at it. He liked that. Sometimes I imagined explaining to Katherine what had happened. I only did it so he would stop and that would be the end of it. He only likes me because I'm another version of you. It's his varied diet he's always on about. Kombucha, turtle beans, a black girl, a white girl with red hair, sisters broken in entirely different ways.

When I reach the house I stand outside it in the dark for a few moments. I can hear the waves on the beach, the wind rattling the windows. I turn and look up at the stars, see how they frame the Law, and the moon lights up the whalebones, cold and white and beautiful.

I don't turn on any lights in the house, I climb the stairs and crawl under the duvet in Mrs. Hamilton's bed, and I am so grateful to feel the heaviness of sleep on my back, like someone lying on top of me. If there are dreams they leave me alone.

I am woken by Deborah rapping loudly on the open door of the bedroom, looking at me with horror.

"I emailed you—I have buyers coming in fifteen minutes." She turns and leaves and I hear her huffily scurrying about the place turning on heaters, spritzing the rooms that smell of damp and loudly putting the chairs under the table in the kitchen. When I come downstairs, she is striking matches in the sitting room.

"To give the sense of fire," she says, with a hand gesture like she expects me to be impressed. "Anyway. Did you remake the bed?"

"I did. I arrived late last night, I—" She sends a look up and down me. The meaning of the look is clear. I can see why my father didn't like her. She is very like a French teacher I had who made all the girls learn by heart, *Excusez-moi, madame, j'ai mes règles, s'il vous plaît, permettez-moi d'avoir une serviette hygiénique et de me diriger vers les toilettes.*

"That's fine. We'll be done in an hour." She does not want the details. She looks at me expectantly. She is waiting for me to leave. Obviously I am not the kind of person she wants them to imagine living here.

I drink a coffee in a cafe that calls itself the Pavilion, even though I remember the old Pavilion from before the outdoor pool was filled in, and it did not have photographs of young Italian couples amusing each other in roadside cafes while the elders look on. It didn't sell panini with the stripes painted on, and there were no inspirational words written around the picture rail. *Energy, Good times, Cappuccino, Laughter, Love.* And then, as though an outsider had burst into their meeting, *Bicycle.* The window next to me is framed by condensation. Dad walked into my bedroom once without knocking and saw what I'd been doing to my legs, and he shouted at me, like a dog barking at a car. And later on I heard him drunk on the phone, rabid, leaving a message on the school's answering machine, *What have you done to her you cunts,* and

I pretended not to know he had done this, and I moved schools and never had my period in France.

I hear Maggie before I see her. She has forced the young woman behind the counter to give her a high five and says "Livin' the dream" loudly so that everyone turns to look. The woman behind the counter turns away with a wide smile of discomfort. Maggie is wearing a grey air force jumpsuit with a black canvas bag over her shoulder. Her hair explodes from her head in a way that is suggestive of a lot of time spent having sex and almost none spent on styling her hair. She wears her sunglasses indoors and her trainers are red leather with their laces undone. Her lipstick is electric pink. Her outfit highlights that the rest of us are wearing Gore-tex and windbreakers and gilets. She is beautiful, and along with everyone else in the cafe, I hope she will go away.

And yet, when she turns to survey us while she waits for her takeaway coffee, I raise my hand. She sees me and instantly I flush because now everyone will think we are friends.

"Ah fucking hell, hen, how are you?!" Maggie almost shouts, eliciting a tut from a woman feeding her child a bun, and she pulls a chair from a nearby table, occupied by a man and his breakfast—she doesn't ask to take the chair, and there is a stool at my table, but instead she takes this high-backed chair and sits on it backwards like she's Arthur Fonzarelli. There is not an audible intake of breath, but there is the equivalent in silence. The man with his breakfast looks on in disbelief, though what can he say—he wasn't using the chair, it is not his chair. He still looks as though he might throw down his knife and fork in fury and demand answers.

Maggie smells of cigarettes and woodsmoke. Has she been camping?

"I'm fine, thanks." I nod overly enthusiastically, whispering loudly in the hope it will suggest that she should lower her voice.

"Any more weird men following you?" She is so loud.

"Ha, no—any more ice creams?"

"What?"

"Never mind."

The waitress brings her coffee in a takeaway cup and Maggie irritates her by drinking it with me instead. It's 15p more to drink in so technically Maggie is stealing from them. I will leave a tip to take this into account.

"So, what you doing today?" she asks after blowing on her drink.

"Just having a coffee, you know. Before I get stuck into work," I say.

"Sounds like you need a day off." She puts four cubes of white sugar in her coffee.

"I'm fine. And what are you doing?"

"Taking a day off." She smiles over the rim of her paper cup.

"What is it that you do?" If she told me in the car it hasn't stuck.

"I'm a witch." She says it simply and confidently and it is the single most irritating thing I've ever heard anyone say.

"Oh, really?" I try to think of what might be an acceptable follow-up question to ask. "Do you make money from that?"

She grimaces, swallowing her coffee. She has left a large smudge of lipstick on her cup but it doesn't seem to have affected the colour of her lips.

"Nah, I'm either unemployed or self-employed, depending on how you look at it. But what about you? How come you're procrastinating about a day off?"

"Oh, I wasn't, I have to work." I try to smile ruefully. Maggie laughs as though I have told a joke.

"So," she says, "what shall we do with our day off?"

"Really, I—"

"Listen," she says, "I'm planning on drinking this coffee and then walking up the Law and smoking a joint at the top. Then I'll get fish and chips down on the beach and feed the seagulls. And then I'm going to have a drink in the pub. I'm doing this because I'm tired and bored with myself. Hey now, baby," she says, pointing at me, "I could use just a little help." And she starts singing, not loudly, though other customers can hear; she sings directly at me, a competent voice, and I sit drinking my coffee too quickly so I don't have to think of what to do.

"This bum's for hire, even if we're just dancing in the park." She drains her coffee, yells "Hey, baby!," stands and offers me her hand as if I am a child and she is my mother.

I take it, because there really is no option not to.

We barely talk on the way up the hill, moving in single file: I wonder often what I am doing. I have not been fit in about seven years. Maggie strides ahead of me, smoking the whole time, her trouser legs rolled up so I can see the backs of her calves, which are muscled and have a thick covering of dark hair. She skips over the rocks like a mountain goat. I have blisters on my heels and one on my inner thigh, often I fall forwards, though the incline of the hill is such that there is not far to go. Wind whips through the gorse and peels seagulls away to the coast. When we reach the whalebone Maggie turns to me, her face shining, but not sweating. She says, "Do you feel it?"

"Feel what?"

A moment passes and I could swear the colours around us change like the earth is a cuttlefish, the sea in the distance becomes oil black, the trees go from green to blue to green again and the sky flickers yellow. Maggie's face, her eyes like opals. And then it is gone.

"The burn! The endorphin hit! When you're broke, you have to rely on your own body to get high." She smiles, and the split second of astonishment can only have been my blood settling after the exercise. She pulls out a bag of tobacco, and from it a joint.

"Luckily for us, I am not completely broke just now." She lights it, there is no breeze even this high up, and she doesn't cup her hands around it, just sucks it in and lets the smoke trail out of her mouth slowly, and the smoke goes straight up, white and pointed like a spear.

There is a moment in the evening when I see a line being drawn. Or is it a fork in the road? Whichever, I am ordering another bottle of wine at the bar, and Maggie is rolling us both cigarettes. I have told her that I don't really smoke any more, but this is of no interest to her, and she has handed me cigarette after cigarette all day. She takes off one of her shoes and places it on our table to keep it, even though there are just six men in the pub. She limps out into the street to smoke, beckoning me with one finger. I take the glasses and the wine and follow. She lights me a cigarette using hers. We are the only people on the street. It is freezing, Maggie has bare arms and stands with her chest thrust out, relaxed. I am as contracted as a cat's anus, my hands up my sleeves, my nose tucked into my coat, desperately breathing hot air down myself. The sky is clear and a big moon hangs overhead.

"No one does this any more," she says, taking the bottle from me and putting the cigarette into the corner of her mouth while she pours two large glasses. "I can't understand it."

"Everyone's healthier now," I say, "everyone wants to live a long time."

She blows a blue cloud of smoke right at me through a smile.

"Smoking has saved my arse a thousand times." She takes a long sip of wine, more of a drink for thirst than for pleasure. I don't ask, because what I have learned is that she doesn't need me to. She will tell me what she wants to tell me. She doesn't need conversation in that way—she has stuff to say in response to what you say, but they don't flit in and out of each other like with other people. It means she sometimes says things I do not like, for example, "I don't really do small talk," which offended me and made me think she is not someone I want to be hanging out with, but as the day went on, I understood: she is incapable of doing it, sometimes tries and fails.

After essentially the same conversation we had in the car the other night, I'm not really paying attention, there's a mural on the opposite wall, showing a puffin with a beakful of sprats, and it's making me hungry.

"I could write a list for you of places and situations I've got out of because I said I was going for a smoke. I could do you a line-up of men had me hogtied in the boot of their cars in their heads, but when they look for me I'm gone in a puff of smoke."

I look away from the sprats.

"You mean you use it as an excuse to leave?"

"Sometimes. Sometimes I use it to blind a guy." She smiles, and I assume she means with the smoke, but she holds up her lit end and makes a hissing noise.

"You've burnt someone? In the eye?" I feel I have not under-stood a joke, but she waves it off.

"You've gotta have a lot of methods, because they're some-times expecting one or two. You just have to be aware of all of the weaponry you've got on you, especially in a place like this where you can't carry a firearm. They're expecting the keys in your fist, because they've read the same articles you have. They know you're going to go for the nuts or gouge the eyes—if someone's planning something, they research it."

"Huh," I say. My mouth is dry and I think now that the last cigarette was not a good idea. Or the three coffees or the three bottles of wine. Somewhere in the day we ate, but I have trouble remembering what we had. I may have to sit down.

"You got a different experience that tells you otherwise, hen?" she asks. I swallow, get my composure back, but I'm not ready with an answer. She is rifling through her bag. She has a fold-out map of East Lothian. There are small crosses in different-coloured biro on it.

"See this?" she asks. "This year, starting from January. All of these are women." I look again at the map. It makes no further sense to me. "Dead women," she clarifies. "Murdered. In the same way."

I look again at the crosses. "A serial killer?"

"Yes—you have to do three to be a serial killer. There are twelve crosses on this map."

"I didn't know—"

She has already begun to answer my question before I've asked it. "The reason you haven't heard of this is because each murder gets called 'an isolated event with no wider threat to the public.'" I blink, unsure what to say next.

Maggie shakes the paper, points to a red cross in Dunbar. "This one, thirty-five-year-old woman executed with a knife by her boyfriend on Valentine's Day, described by the papers as a crime of passion. Whatever the fuck. Here"—she points to another cross—"sex worker bound and executed by suffocation—plastic bag over her head—here"—she points again—

"Wait."

Maggie looks up. It's as if she's forgotten I'm here.

"So it's different people? It's totally different people using different methods? That's not a serial killer then." The silence is thick.

"Listen to what you are saying." She speaks slowly. "Listen to how you're using the words they have given you."

"They?"

"The police say the murders are *isolated events with no wider threat to the public*," she says again.

"Yes, but surely if—but surely if that woman was killed by her boyfriend, they have the boyfriend and he's in jail and that crime was related entirely to their particular situation?"

Maggie looks at me. "The situation being: she was a woman and he is a man."

"But a serial killer—that's one person working alone and killing lots of people."

"Not true. What about Ottis Toole and Henry Lee Lucas? What about the Moors murderers? What about the Wests? Fuckin'—Yorkshire Ripper killed women with a hammer while his pals looked on, wondering what all the fuss was about. What about fuckin' Manson? It's one big black hole when you look into it."

"Look into what?"

"Life. Our lives. Our deaths."

There is a long pause. I could very probably vomit.

"Do you know the age range of women most often killed by men?"

"I do not."

"Thirty-six to forty-five. Know why that is?"

"I have no idea."

She moves close to my face; I can smell her breath, even past the wine and the smoke, something else, soured and old. "They've finished breeding with us, but we are still fuckable." She sits back again and watches for my reaction. I try not to give one. "Know what people mean by unfuckable? They mean disposable. They mean incineratable."

"Look, I have to go," I tell her, "I have to be up early in the morning."

"Sure," she says, no sign of offence taken, "let me get my shoe." And she is gone before I can tell her I wasn't asking her to come with me.

When she appears again, both shoes on, I say, "You really don't have to walk me back."

"Fuckit," she says, "I've just told you you're likely to get murdered, I can at least get you back to your house."

She walks a couple of steps behind me all the way, talking, not waiting for me to respond. It sobers me up listening to her. She sounds mad. She is rolling.

"It's about forgetting, it's about a vast and infinite amnesia. We forget the torture, the rape, the tit rippers, the scold's bridles, the loss one by one of our fingernails, then fingers. The death of our unborn children, the burning and tearing apart of our vulvas. There is no going home, no saving, there is no rest-of-your-life to get over it because what comes next is throttling and consumption by fire, sucked into the air, breathed in, pissed and shat out by men who make the money from our carbonised remains, as time moves on, ridiculed, turned into a holiday treat, a joke, a cute costume, a romcom, something to take the kids to on a bank holiday. A joke or, at best, something to harden the cocks of schoolboys and old nerds—*What's your thing? I like girls with a bit of an edge, you know, with a taste for darkness.* But do you want her tattered genitals, her nippleless breasts and her burned and scaled buttocks, her eyeless sockets? No. A push-up bra and black lipstick. A pointed hat and a cat's eye. You leave it alone until those ashes are not ashes any more, they are just the everyday air we breathe and it's all so different now, you say, that was barbarism, you say as you clip off our clits, as you burn the flesh from our faces and breasts with acid and maintain a slow, ponderous fuck of ownership up our arseholes and down our throats. Their desire to see their own cocks within us, watch our throats bulge with them, watch our small bellies swell as they go in. Seeing themselves reflected back, seeing how they would look in a woman's flesh? And if they kiss us afterwards on the mouth it is only to see how they taste."

Maggie is trancelike. "What would it take?" she says. "What if all the women that have been killed by men through history were visible to us, all at once? If we could see them lying there. What if you could project a hologram of the bodies in the places they were killed?"

"Well—look, we've all got to die sometime, isn't it?" I fall into step next to her. "History is bloody—there were wars, life was different." I don't feel like I am saying what I want to say. Maggie stops and looks at me. The silence grows, my feet twitch in their shoes.

"What is the correct amount of time at which someone's painful, terrifying death becomes unimportant, cosy? Before it becomes funny? Witches? Jack the Ripper? The wars? 1977?"

"I don't really understand what you mean."

She looks crestfallen in a way I couldn't have imagined her an hour ago.

"I know," she says. "I know, I know. I don't either—I can't articulate it, it's just a feeling I have all the time that I'm walking in and out of these deaths and I should at least notice. I should notice because I'm not dead yet, and there's no difference between these women and me, or you or your mother or the lady in the tea shop. We're just breezing in and out of the death zone. Wading through the dead. You know how sometimes you can smell it on a man, sometimes you just know—if he got you alone, if he had a rock . . . you know that thing when you feel it? Like your blood knows it. I try and take note, because it's all I have in my power, to witness it and store it away. To look at the crime-scene photographs and know it happened, and is happening and will happen in the future. The stains, the wounds. Your children."

We have arrived at the house and are standing on the dark path leading up to the front door. Maggie rubs her nose hard enough to make me wince. "Sorry," she says. "I might be a wee bit fucked." She looks about her, becoming aware suddenly that we have stopped.

"Wait," she says. "What the fuck—is this the house?"

"It's just where I'm staying. It's not mine."

She looks up at the dark windows on the top floor and smiles. "Does it have a sofa I can sleep on?"

II

The day of the winter picnic, four women arrived at the door. They had jumped on Ruth at the Pavilion the week before and offered their services in a way that made it impossible to say no.

Annabelle, Maura, Jayne and Janet were a full hour earlier than they had said they would be. Janet was their leader and she had brought with her a checklist.

"Please, do have a seat." Ruth had shown them into the drawing room where she had the sense they were inspecting the decor. She suspected Maura of straightening the fall of the curtain so that it was more to her liking. She held the tassel on the end of the rope that secured the curtains as though she were weighing it to determine its value. Once they were all seated, handbags primly on laps, toes together and to the side, heavily expectant faces, Ruth escaped to the kitchen, wary of overhearing whatever it was they might be saying about her and the house. Betty was already constructing a tray, the girl Bernadette was at the sink rinsing cutlery, and they exchanged smiles. She would have to put some time aside to get to know the girl a little—so far Betty had kept her so busy she hadn't seen her with an idle moment.

"Oh, thank you, Betty, I'm sorry, I didn't expect them quite so early."

Betty smiled grimly and laid napkins next to the shortbread rounds that were newly out of the oven.

"No bother at all, madam," she said. "I've encountered these women before."

Once the tea arrived, things softened. It was easier to navigate social difficulties if silences could be explained by full mouths and if it was possible to compliment something neutral, like the shortbread.

"I've always said that Betty makes the best shortbread in North Berwick," said Annabelle. "I'm sure her cooking is half the reason Reverend Jon Brown insists on the winter picnic being on your beach."

There was an awkward moment that Ruth couldn't ascertain the reason behind, until Jayne cleared it up for her. "Annabelle hosted last year, and it just didn't come together in the same way, did it?"

Annabelle put down her cup on her saucer gently.

"Anyway," Janet said, producing the checklist from her handbag. "Shall we get started? We'll do savouries first. Now, I understand Betty has organised sandwiches—fish paste and cucumber . . ." She looked up at Ruth and Ruth nodded. "If you could say yes, dearie, that'll save me looking up after every item, thank you. Now, pork and egg pies?"

"Yes." Ruth felt sternly reprimanded.

"Black bun?"

"Yes."

"Oatcakes and cheese."

"Yes."

"Good. And for sweet: gingerbread loaf, treacle tart."

"Yes."

Janet ticked enthusiastically at her paper.

"Now, costume, Ruth dearie."

"Costume?"

"I see nobody informed you."

"Yes, did nobody say?" asked Jayne.

"The women dress up," said Annabelle.

"It's all part and parcel of the game of hide-and-seek—such fun," said Maura.

"Oh, no I didn't know about that. Well, never mind, I'll know for next year."

Janet stood on a large inhale of breath. "Not to worry, I have spare items, let's dress in your room shall we? Ladies, why don't you change in the ballroom, provided that suits our host?"

"Of course, but—"

"Not to worry, they have their uniforms on underneath— nothing to scare the horses."

Annabelle, Maura and Jayne all looked a little put out by this comment.

Janet moved to the door and Ruth put down her cup of tea. "Come along," said Janet, and Ruth found herself obeying.

"I suppose you don't need showing where the ballroom is?" she asked the women who sat happily around their tray of biscuits.

"Ladies," said Janet firmly, "don't just sit there and fill your-selves." The women stood immediately and filed out and down the hall to the ballroom. "Honestly." Janet rolled her eyes and tutted for Ruth's benefit.

Ruth went quickly ahead up to her bedroom, because she did not want to be led there by Janet. The staircase creaked under them.

"Oh, look!" Janet said, stopping at the landing window. "You can see Reverend Brown and his boys have already set up the bonfire. How dear! They are working so hard!"

The bonfire was quite extraordinary, even unlit. It wasn't what Ruth had imagined when the reverend had talked of "bonfire potatoes." It was high, like a beacon.

"It's certainly impressive," she said, "they must've been working on it for hours, I should have sent the boys down to help."

"Oh, don't worry, they did," Janet said. "Reverend Brown came and got them just before dawn."

Janet carried on up the final set of steps and Ruth stayed on the landing with a very unpleasant feeling in her chest.

"I didn't know that. Nobody asked me about that." Since the week before when the boys had returned from school, she had felt a peculiar anxiousness about them, as though they had to start their relationships over again. She felt every small change in their personalities like a personal failure of hers— they were being shaped by someone or something else.

"Ah well, there's been a lot to organise." Janet was at the bedroom door and moving her head to beckon Ruth to hurry, and then she helped herself to the room, walked in with no sense at all that it wasn't hers to walk into. Ruth had a sudden horror that Peter might still be in bed, and she clambered the stairs three at a time, but he must have been already in his study, because by the time she got there, Janet was fussily making the bed. Ruth's rage was mitigated by a feeling of being lost. So lost that she wondered if she ought to feel grateful for Janet taking charge.

"Now then, take those off," she said, "and put these on." She pulled from her bag a long grey skirt and dark green flannel blouse.

"Thank you, but surely you need those for yourself. I'm sure I can find something—"

"No," she said rather crisply. "I brought these especially for you, it's tradition, really. We all dress in the same way." She laid out the clothes and turned her back on Ruth, unbuttoning her own blouse as she did so.

There seemed little for Ruth to do other than undress. She had a horror of the woman coming and helping her. She opened the wardrobe door in order to have something to shield behind, and it made Janet whip round, a look on her face Ruth could not read, before she smiled encouragingly. Ruth tried not to hold an arm over her chest, but even with the woman's back turned, she felt exposed. She stole glances at Janet's body as she transitioned between outfits. A peculiar mixture of thin and plump, her arms like wire, her hips doughy. She took off her stockings and revealed thin white legs. When Janet was dressed she turned round and inspected Ruth.

"You'll need your stockings off," she said.

"Oh, I'll keep them on, thank you—I'll freeze."

"As you wish," said Janet but her tone was such that Ruth found herself unclipping them while Janet sat at her dressing table. She tucked her hair into a thin black cowl, the kind of thing a nun wore under her habit, then she turned back to her bag and found one for Ruth.

"This will keep you warm; most body heat is lost through the head, after all."

Ruth pulled it on and tucked her hair under it. She felt like a frogman.

"What are we supposed to be?"

Janet handed Ruth a black half mask that finished just under the nose.

"We are supposed to all be the same."

When they went downstairs, Peter was standing in the hallway, looking with some confusion into the ballroom, where Ruth could hear the other ladies talking.

"Good morning, Mr. Hamilton," said Janet, gliding by as though she were the grand lady of the house.

"Yes," said Peter, "quite," and then he appeared to snap out of a dream. "Darling, what on earth are you wearing? You look like a medieval nun."

"It's a costume. Apparently it's part of the picnic."

"Right," he said. She had thought he might find it amusing, but there was something shadowy about him at that moment. He took her wrist and steered her into the dining room so the women couldn't hear, though Ruth noticed their chatter soften, and then silence.

"Did you know the boys were taken out of their beds last night?"

"Yes, I—"

"Do you think it might be possible to run that sort of lunacy by me before just sending them out in the freezing cold in the dark with a maniac?"

"I didn't know—"

"It just bloody beggars belief—you do know what killed their mother, don't you, you do know we moved here to protect their lungs, not to try and weaken them?" The words momentarily drowned her.

"I didn't know they were going to be woken up to help. It wasn't the middle of the night, it was just before dawn, really"— she heard herself defensive, even though it wasn't how she felt—"and there are other boys down there too."

"I don't care." The words were said with such finality, a blade coming down. He inhaled deeply and let it out, glanced at his watch. "Look, I have to go to the London office. Branning called and they can't do without me, it's the Howard file blowing up again. I'll catch the twenty past, which means I have to leave here in fifteen minutes."

He began to stride out of the room, folding his paper as he did.

"Peter." She said his name and wasn't sure what would follow. He stopped, looked at her over his glasses.

"Mmm?"

"The picnic. I . . ."

"Well, you all go on without me. I'm sure you'll have plenty of fun."

"But the boys—I mean, all of us—you're expected."

Peter took off his glasses and rubbed the bridge of his nose. "You have no concept of the workload I have to get through in order that you may frolic about on the beach in your fancy dress and picnic. Do as you're told and get on with it."

There was a feeling of the ground clawing up Ruth's legs and tethering her to the spot, a dead weight.

"Excuse me," she said, her voice calm but loud. "I am here because you brought me here, so that I can look after your children, while you carry on as if you haven't a family to speak of."

He moved slowly back towards her. She wondered for a moment if he would strike her, and she could see the thought race through him too; he moved his paper from one hand to the other. Suddenly it seemed like it might not be the worst thing.

"I'm not their fucking nanny," she said, her jaw clenched. The bad language echoed between them. She wondered if the ladies were listening and decided she didn't care.

"That," he said, "is patently obvious." He looked calmly at his watch again, then walked to the door, taking his briefcase, hat and coat in one movement.

The floor did not release Ruth for a long time. She wished she hadn't been wearing such a ridiculous outfit for the fight.

She tore the cowl off her head and stayed there, listening to the sound of his footsteps becoming fainter and fainter, heard rain drum against the window in a sudden gust of wind. His going to London felt so badly wrong. She went back into the kitchen and stood a moment, before picking up a heavy brown mixing bowl and smashing it on the floor.

"Fucking hell," she bellowed at it.

"Shit!" came a small voice, and she saw that Michael was standing in the pantry holding a sticky bun and looking at her. Neither of them knew what to do with their faces. Christopher appeared behind him.

"Yes," said Ruth. "Yes, shit, as well. Shit!" and they all smiled together in what may have been the first incidence of that kind.

III

"Good God, Jesus, hell," a man wails, and a scream sweeps down the runnels. We fly out of the house wrapped in our bedclothes, the Widow Clements included, though she has no business being in our home. You can smell it. The pig shed burns—the scream just an alchemy of pigs and fire.

A man staggers out, then another, both with their arms outstretched, appealing to the sky. Someone throws a bucket of water upon one, rolls him on the ground in the mud, but has no bucket for the second man. The second man drops to his knees and falls, flaming face down into stillness. He keeps burning, dead on the ground while the first man screams and screams and then is quiet and dead too. Smoke rises from them both. All of us stand, holding our bedclothes around us, unable to turn our attention to the blaze, because despite the abomination and the evil of what we have just seen, our stomachs turn with the smell of roasted flesh, and our mouths water. I say a prayer that pigs have also died in the blaze and this is what we are smelling.

"They will come for her, and they will come for us," says my father, turning his back on the fire and speaking in a low voice in case anyone should overhear. "Take only what you can carry," he says, "see the girl has boots to wear."

Sarah hasn't left her room, I know because I've been sitting outside it the whole of the night.

We enter the woods without speaking, Father in front, then the Widow Clements, Sarah, Cook and me at the end. We do not run, but we are on the very edge of it, we do not have a candle and we fall, often, planting our blind, outstretched hands into mud and leaves and bark. I take to moving in a hunched fashion, like I'm part animal. Cook's white calves glow in the dark, and I can see blood on them from a bramble scratch.

All of us carry what we can hold, which for Cook is a large pan and half a dozen cups and bowls. Their clanking and her coughing is the only sound above the crack and stir of bracken and the snort and rasp of our breath. I find that I have brought with me only a blunt knife wrapped in a short bit of sacking that Mother was teaching needlework to Agnes on before. I have slept with the sacking under my pillow since Mother died, because in the badly sewed lines of my sister and the straight economical stitches of my mother I see them by the fire and they are still mine.

Wolves have been reported on the edge of these woods. Agnes was found just beyond the boundary of the silver birches, where the light is snuffed out even at midday. You feel the wolves, or the ghosts of them, nearby, watching.

We fumble for what feels like hours on the forest floor, crawling over fallen logs, getting further and further from the village; there is not even the slightest glow any more from the fire, and the Widow Clements is trying to calm my father. "They will see we have gone and they will be glad of it. They won't come looking, surely. The girl is gone, the threat is no longer there. They will be putting out that fire until morning."

Our pace slows and within the hour we come upon a clearing. "No fire," Father says to Cook who has begun brushing a space to set one. It is cold and wet, and a fire would be welcome.

Cook and the widow lie down next to each other. Sarah sits against a tree, her arms wrapped around her knees. She shivers, and before I can offer my coat, Father has laid his over her shoulders. She looks up and smiles at him. Father I suppose cannot help but see Agnes in Sarah. Her small body that he took from the man who found her, and laid on the floor and covered with his coat so that Mother didn't see. I tuck myself underneath a fallen tree. It is no comfort, and yet I fall asleep almost instantly. I wake at a sound, a lowing, but it happens only once, and I tell myself it is just someone crying out in their sleep. I have to trust that everyone is still there, because the dark is full and thick. I try to stay awake, because I hope she will come and speak with me. For hours I think every noise in the night is her. The crying does not come again, just the sound of Cook's snore, which lulls me back to sleep.

II

The ladies had left by the time Ruth went back to the drawing room, and she heaved a sigh of relief while dreading the explanation she should offer. Let them wonder. She would not say a word on it. She would act as though nothing was out of the ordinary. This was what happened when you arrived at a person's house early and made them dress up like a goose.

The boys told her they had come back from the beach because they were hungry and so she returned to the kitchen to clear up the bowl and made both of them a cheese sandwich, blackening the bread on the boiling plate of the Aga.

"Why did you throw that bowl on the floor?" asked Michael once he had a mouthful of sandwich.

"It was a funny sort of accident," she said, wanting to move the conversation on as fast as possible. "Did you know that Reverend Jon Brown was going to come and wake you up this morning?"

"He said he might," said Christopher, "but that we weren't to tell anyone. He said it would spoil the surprise." Perhaps she would talk to Betty about locking the doors at night. For a moment she felt rather sick, but she breathed deeply through her nose. It was just a bad argument, they would settle things when he was back home.

"We had torches of our own to hold," said Michael, pleased.

Ruth studied their faces for signs of hurt. She regretted calling them *your children*. She found she didn't know what to look for, how a child's hurt presented. Perhaps it was completely fine. An overreaction. Perhaps next year they would look forward to the event. Still. She ate Michael's crusts. "Do you suppose we're ruining ourselves for the picnic?"

"I don't like picnics," said Christopher. "You have to eat in front of people and it's always pies."

"Will there be a cake?" asked Michael.

"There's a treacle tart that Betty made."

"Imagine the sand in it," said Christopher.

Ruth found some tablet in the pantry and shared it between them.

"Is Father not coming then?" said Christopher. She hadn't heard him call Peter "Father" before. It felt Victorian.

"He had to go to London."

"Is that why you broke the bowl?" asked Michael. "Because you wanted him to play the hide-and-seek game with you?"

Ruth smiled. "Between the three of us, I'm not particularly excited about hide-and-seek. I broke the bowl because I was being overdramatic, and I had a bothersome morning. And it looked like it would break in a satisfactory way."

"And did it?" asked Michael.

"Very much so. But we must tell Betty that it was an accident."

The boys nodded seriously.

On the way down, cowl in place, and carrying extra blankets and scarves from the laundry, they passed Betty and Bernadette walking back up to the house. Betty stopped when she recognised Ruth.

"Yes," said Ruth. "They made me dress up."

154

"So they did, madam." Betty looked very unhappy.

"Betty, won't you both be joining us?"

"Oh no, too much to do—I'll get behind."

"Well, let Bernadette come? We can get to know each other! I thought the whole point was so that the children can have a good time." The girl had been with them a month or so, and Betty had kept her so out of the way Ruth wasn't sure she'd be able to recognise her in a line-up.

"That's very kind, madam, but really, I couldn't impose."

"Nonsense, it's no trouble at all. I'm sure the boys would welcome the company."

Betty looked at Bernadette, who shifted from foot to foot.

Betty moved closer to Ruth, in an attempt to stop the children from hearing. The children were looking at each other shyly. It was clear Bernadette wanted to come.

"Madam, I just worry for the girl. She can't swim, and sometimes Reverend Jon Brown gets carried away."

"I'll keep an eye on her, and don't worry, I'm quite aware of how Reverend Jon Brown conducts himself." She smiled to reassure her. "I'll make sure she eats something, drinks something, plays cricket and is returned to you safe and well."

Betty turned to Bernadette who had laced her fingers together in front of her as though trying to tame them. Betty leaned down and said something firmly to the girl and the girl nodded and looked at the ground.

"I'm afraid she says she's not feeling too well," said Betty. All three children studied their shoes in the sand. "Another time. Maybe tomorrow she'll be feeling better."

"If you're sure." Perhaps it was some awful leftover Victorian feeling that staff shouldn't mix with their employers. Bernadette gave the boys a small wave and the boys waved back, and she started to move towards the house. Looking behind her at the house, Ruth noticed the shape of someone standing at her study window, and she wondered with annoyance if one of the women had gone around inspecting her home, but there was something not quite right about the shape of the person. Betty touched her arm and she jumped, and the figure was gone.

"And, madam," said Betty, "you watch out for yourself and the boys too."

Six large tartan rugs had been laid out at the base of a dune, where there might be a little shelter from the wind, which was, as ever, up. Two large trestle tables held the picnic, the food covered over with serving platters and dishcloths weighted down with cutlery and flasks.

Twenty or so people had already assembled by the time Ruth and the boys arrived. More than half were women dressed exactly as she was, while the men wore paper crowns with cut-outs of animal ears—hares and foxes, she thought.

"Your mask!" one of them shouted, and it made her start, the seriousness of the tone. She took her mask from her pocket and put it on. It wasn't comfortable, but at least she didn't have to try to look happy to be there. Someone handed her a glass of champagne and clinked glasses. Reverend Jon Brown appeared wearing a captain's hat and a neckerchief and put his arms around the boys' shoulders.

"Aha!" he said. "My prize helpers—come and we'll set up the cricket with the other boys and girls, there's some ginger ale in it for you." He steered them away to where a small band of children stood around a rowing boat pulled up onto the sand. A little way out to sea a beautiful schooner was moored. Reverend Jon Brown pulled a cricket bat from the rowing boat and began orchestrating a game. Without the boys, Ruth felt lost.

"Pleasure to see you," said a man, offering his hand. "My name's Aidan White, I'm the head of Carlekemp Priory."

Ruth opened her mouth to give her name, but was surprised by Aidan White putting a finger to her lips. She took a step back.

"Just to remind you not to tell us your name—we don't want to give the game away too quickly!" He was smiling, and another man behind him laughed and came forward, presented his hand.

"Richard Duggan," he said, "governor of Fort Augustus. Don't mind us, this must all seem very strange—"

Ruth could tell it was Janet that came up to intercept the group, she had a very particular walk, one arm always at a right angle and flush to her body, as though holding a phantom handbag.

"Are these men boring you, dearie?" Janet asked, brandishing a bottle of champagne. Both men laughed heartily.

Ruth smiled, it seemed the most peaceable thing to do. "I'm not sure I quite understand," she said. Janet topped up Ruth's already-empty glass. The discomfort was making her drink quickly.

"All it is, frankly, is a ridiculous tradition that certain people"—here she made out that at least two of those people stood before her—"have got rather carried away with. We all eat and drink, and then the women hide, and the men have to find us. It's completely stupid, but rather good fun."

"Why do we have to dress up to do that?"

"Once we catch you," said Duggan, "we have to guess who you are." He smiled broadly as he said it. Behind him came the sound of a ball being struck, and Ruth watched as

Christopher started to run. Other children's voices carried on the wind. She'd never seen him run fast before.

"The main thing is to forget about it, have a nice time and then have a giggle right at the end. And I know I'm not supposed to give away who you are, but frankly, these two can sniff out fresh blood a mile away—is Mr. Hamilton not well?"

It was perhaps a tactful thing for her to say, giving Ruth a way out.

"He's been unexpectedly called to London. I'm afraid," she added a beat too late.

"Come, come, dearie," said Janet and pulled her over to the picnic blankets where a small gathering of women sat drinking.

"Hello, everyone," Ruth said as she sat down; there was a friendly murmur back, some shifting up to make space. She turned to someone she thought was Janet, saying, "I thought there would be more children?"

The woman who answered had a thick Scottish accent. "Oh, d'you know, it's become less and less about the children—there just aren't that many here any more. They have a good time all the same though. That Jon Brown is a natural entertainer."

They looked over to the game of cricket, which had disintegrated into something like British Bulldog, with Reverend Jon Brown as the Bulldog. He snarled and crouched and chased and the children shrieked. Those he caught stood to the side, hands on knees, puffed and watching, cheering on their teammates. It seemed in the Scottish version of the game only Reverend Jon Brown was the catcher. Michael had been caught early on and had attached himself to an older girl, looking at her when she cheered and joining in. Ruth watched him pull a shell out of his pocket and hold it before offering it to the girl. The girl dropped out of cheering and examined the shell. She said something in Michael's ear and he smiled, and she gave it back.

Christopher was one of the last to be caught. It was more than a tag, Reverend Jon Brown had to physically *get* you, it seemed, and it took a long while of backwards and forwards to get Christopher. Long enough that some of his teammates lost interest and wandered down the beach. Someone touched Ruth's shoulder and she looked up to see Bernadette.

"Aunt Betty said I could come after all," she said.

"Oh," said Ruth, "smashing. How did you know it was me?"

Bernadette looked seriously at the other women and then said quietly to Ruth, "You don't look like the rest of them." It was extraordinarily pleasing to hear this, and Ruth wondered if she was a little drunk.

Reverend Jon Brown caught Christopher round the waist from behind, and he lifted him clear off the ground, holding him close before letting him go. Christopher spun round as though ready to fight, and Reverend Jon Brown pranced at him until the boy's body straightened and calmed, and the man threw an arm around the boy's shoulders and then let him go again. All was well.

"Would you like to go and join them, or do you want to sit with me a little and watch?"

Bernadette sat down and they watched a new game of cricket begin. "I don't know how to play cricket," said the girl.

"That's OK—I don't think they're taking themselves too seriously today. I'm sure they'd have you."

"I'll wait."

"How are you finding it here?"

Bernadette thought for a while. The thing that reminded you she was not Betty's child was her red hair like Mary's. She wore it scraped back and plaited so it was only when the sun shone directly on her that you saw how very red it was. "I like it better than Blyth, thank you."

"I am pleased."

"The house is bigger," she continued, "and it's nice we can have a fire on."

"Did you not have a fire in Blyth?"

"Uncle James didn't let us. Said if it was cold we had to put on all of our clothes, even when Aunt Betty gave them money for coal."

"That does sound miserable."

"And I like being able to see Mother a bit more."

It was a subject Ruth had no idea how to navigate, so she remained silent.

"Aunt Betty makes nicer food. Uncle James always wanted hogget and haggis."

"Oh dear. And how is school—is that man your head teacher?" Ruth pointed out the man she had talked to when she first arrived.

"Yes," said Bernadette. "Mr. Duggan." She turned back to face the cricket. "There's a little ghost, I think, in your house."

Ruth swallowed a mouthful of champagne, her glass now empty again. "Is there?"

A woman squatted down next to them to refill Ruth's glass and exclaimed, "And who's this pretty wee 'un?"

Bernadette looked wide-eyed at the woman.

"This is Bernadette. She's staying with us."

"You're not—are you the granddaughter of old Mrs. Whitekirk up at the house?"

"Yes," said Bernadette. It fell suddenly into place why Betty hadn't wanted to subject Bernadette to the picnic. Ruth hadn't thought that people would be so difficult, but, she supposed, they were a long way from London, or even Dummer. She bristled on Bernadette's behalf, but her brain felt very slow and mild after the drink.

The woman said, "My God, though, you're the spit of your father." She scurried away, and Ruth watched as the information passed through the group and all heads turned to the two of them.

"Maybe I shouldn't have come?" said Bernadette.

"I think that woman was both a little drunk and a bit stupid," Ruth said. "Really, don't pay attention to her." One of the mysteries of our times—wasn't that what Betty had said?

"Maybe I will go and join in with the other children."

"Of course, I expect it'll be lunch very soon," she said, and watched the child walk towards the others with the manner of a person entering cold water.

The men were now drinking whisky and smoking cigars, though not a single dish on the trestle tables had been touched. It would have been a very good idea to eat something, because really she was feeling rather drunk. She thought how she would tell Peter about the strange events of the day, and then remembered morosely they had fought, and she quickly felt anger at his absence. And she wondered exactly where he was and what he was doing, if he thought angrily or regretfully of her. She drained her glass again.

Janet appeared at her side. "Now," she said, "we didn't know that you had the girl staying with you. How long is she visiting for?"

"Bernadette? She's living with us. What on earth is the problem? That woman quite upset her."

"I know, and I did reprimand Megan—she has a very loud undistinguished mouth. But what you really ought to know is that one of our party today was married to Bernadette's father. If you catch my meaning. The husband had a love affair with your Betty's sister, and then the husband died. Leaving our member rather a wreck, I'm afraid. I just thought you ought to know. It might be something to talk to Betty about—presumably she didn't offer full disclosure to you taking on the child?"

"I haven't *taken on* Bernadette, she's just living with us. I don't see that it should make much difference."

"Well," said Janet, turning to look at the women huddled around one of their members, "it's gone and got his widow very upset." There was the hollow sound of crying and one of the women tucked a handkerchief up under her mask—the mask apparently more important than her grief. It was difficult to think of what to say. "Anyway, the children are off on the boat trip now, so hopefully she'll calm down."

At the water's edge, Reverend Jon Brown was helping the final child onto the rowing boat. He had his trousers rolled up high and he pushed them off the sand with surprising strength. Christopher manned the oars until the reverend swapped with him. There were nine of them altogether, and the boat sat low in the water. Ruth stood up.

"He didn't ask," she said to no one in particular.

"Didn't ask what, dearie?"

"He didn't ask if my boys could be taken out of bed in the middle of the night, and he didn't ask if he could take them out on the water—Bernadette can't swim."

"Well, he's not taking them swimming. You'll have to get used to him, he is rather eccentric, he does things his own way, but this is how things work here. You're much better off relaxing." Janet filled Ruth's glass again, even though Ruth tried to signal to her to stop. "And having a bit of fun."

If the children had not been on the boat, Ruth would have gone back to the house right then and had a hot bath. But in the end, when the men linked arms and closed their eyes, and began to count backwards from one hundred, and the women all scattered into the dunes, she felt she had no option but to hide too.

At first she considered somewhere easy to find, because then the game for her would be over, but as she ran, a feeling of self-preservation came over her. Something clicking its teeth just at her heel. It was the champagne. She found a hollowed drift-wood log just as she heard the call "We're coming to get you!" from the men. She scrambled inside, feeling some of the hyster-ical joy of hiding she remembered from childhood, laced with an unreasonable sense of dread. There were moments of silence, and then a scream went up and the sounds of men laughing.

Tell us your name.

NO.

Tell us your name.

NO.

Tell us!

And then screaming. The woman screamed and the men laughed and it went on like that until one of the men shouted, "We have her! We have Maura McDuff!"

And the same sounds could be heard up and down the beach, and Ruth could not think what was being done to those women.

She wasn't found for a long time; she heard footfall nearby, but none of it close enough for the men to spot her. She wondered how long until a truce was called, how much longer the children would be at sea. Someone pulled her roughly out of the log by her ankle. It was White, his moustache had collected sand, and he smelled strongly of whisky.

"I have her by the toe!" he shouted out, and Ruth tried to pull down her skirt, which had been dragged up, she tried to stand, but was pushed back down.

"My name is Ruth Hamilton," she said, but White sat on her hips, and pinned her arms down under his knees and commenced tickling her, his crown quivering as he moved. Immediately her breath was gone and the noise that came out of her was something like a wounded animal. No words formed, there was no time for them, he dug his fingertips into her ribs hard and deep, she felt her ribs separate, all the time he shouted in her face, laughing, *Tell me your name!* He dug into her armpit and over her breasts, and then another body was there, tickling her bare legs and working upwards, and with a sudden clasp of breath, she screamed *Ruth Hamilton*, so that others would surely hear, and the man tickling her legs—Duggan—stopped and he thumped White's shoulder to tell him to get off.

"Got to play by the rules, old man," he said amiably. White dismounted and Ruth rolled onto her side and coughed up sand. Her eyes and nose ran. She tore off her mask, and turned to the men but they had apparently thought nothing of it and were jogging back towards the picnic, Duggan with an arm over White's shoulders. Ruth sat in the sand and willed herself not to cry. She was sick instead, and she buried it in the sand, smoothed down her skirt. Back at the picnic, the other women chatted happily and shared plates of pie, their cowls removed. Someone lit the bonfire, and while it burned, Ruth went down to the water to wait for the boat. They had been gone too long.

I

In the morning I find an extra-large Post-it note on the kitchen sideboard.

> *Dear Viviane,*
>
> *As I've mentioned before, please do not use the mineral water fridge to store your own food. You left an open tin of something fishy in there and it smells bad. This is not the impression I am trying to give, and it would help me enormously if you could keep the place neat and tidy and as you would want prospective buyers to find it.*
>
> *Sincerely,*
> *Deborah, Evans & Walker*

I run water in the sink and watch it go down the plughole a while before it occurs to me to get a glass. I feel disgusting and ashamed. I spend a long time blowing my nose, imagining I am blowing out all the smoke from last night. I remember Maggie, and as I do, she enters the kitchen. She is wearing woollen socks, a bra, an open cardigan and nothing else.

We look at each other and she makes no move to cover herself.

"Whatsup?" she asks finally.

"What happened to your clothes?"

She looks down at herself. Her pubic hair draws the eye. I try not to let it.

"I don't sleep in pants—got to wear them today. And I sweat like a mutherfucker in my sleep so I took my T-shirt off." Maggie walks to the sink.

"Aren't you . . . cold?"

"I only ever get cold feet—pussy warms itself," she says lightly. She touches the kettle to see if it's warm, and her rings clack against it.

"You got coffee here?"

I open a cupboard and pass her the jar of instant. She wrinkles her nose but spoons some into a mug anyway.

"You got a washing machine?"

I point through to the pantry, the start of Bet's old quarters.

"Can I use it?"

I think of the note from Deborah. "I'm not supposed to use it during the day in case we get a buyer looking."

Maggie looks confused. "What. They don't like to think of you washing your clothes?"

"I think it's more the smell and the noise. The estate agent's pretty weird about it."

"You mustn't be afraid of the servants, Virginia," she says through her nose. "I'll put it on a short wash and we can turn it off if she comes over."

I shrug and she goes to fetch her rucksack, which is stuffed full of plastic bags with clothes in, the knots of which she undoes enthusiastically.

"Why do you have so many clothes with you?"

Maggie looks up at me.

"I'm not homeless, if that's what you think. I just choose right now not to have a home." There is an edge to her tone I haven't experienced yet.

"Are you sleeping out? In this weather?"

She pours soap into the barrel and closes the lid.

"Occasionally. Not often, but occasionally. I have an arrangement with a guy who's all right."

I am caught between extreme hangover, concern and a strong feeling of not wanting to get involved. She takes my silence as judgement.

"Listen, sex work is a completely sound way of making a way in the world. Like I said, this pussy warms itself."

"I wasn't trying to . . . look, all I meant was, I didn't know. When you're not with this guy, do you sleep on the beach?"

She sniffs, settles her shoulders a little. "Sand turns to concrete if you lie on it too long, the cold gets in your bones. Sometimes I find a bench in one of those golfing shelters, but the golfers are strange fuckers, and they kick me out. They're on the course at night with golf balls that glow in the dark, and that's not even a euphemism. I trust a man who golfs less than a man who pays for sex."

The kettle boils and clicks off.

"What about last night? What would you have done?"

"I make it a rule never to fall asleep drunk outside. I would have just walked. Does you good to keep moving." She brushes past me and pours hot water into her mug, then holds the kettle up at me in a question. I shake my head. She stirs her coffee, takes a sip, bares her teeth at the taste.

"Do you want to borrow some pants?"

She puts her mug down and places both hands on the counter. For a moment I think I might have upset her.

"You know what, I'd like that. Yes. Thank you."

*

After her coffee and now wearing my pants—with hers still going in the machine—Maggie says she has to go. "I have an appointment, I can't miss it."

"What about your clothes?"

"Can I come round and pick them up later?"

"Of course."

"Thanks, hen."

I see her to the door and she kisses me on the cheek like we are an established couple.

Vincent kissed me on the lips with a closed mouth last time we saw each other. It came back to me that morning, the memory hidden by drink. He called me *ducks*. It left me confused. If we're going to fuck, we should get on with it.

Do you call someone you want to sleep with *ducks*?

I am cross-legged on the floor of the ballroom, the light is fading quickly. I stand and go to the window; beyond the golf course the sea is a sheet of grey glass. I can't imagine myself out there. Maggie's clothes are hanging in the pantry, nearly dry, but she hasn't returned yet. I wonder whether she ever will, whether I could be the last person to see her.

I have a shoebox from the wardrobe in Mrs. Hamilton's room, and I sip whisky as I go through it, my hangover sufficiently tempered. A black-and-white photograph of a small boy in a Red Indian costume, half the size of a postcard. The boy frowns deeply, perhaps he is unhappy to be dressed up, but the more I look the more I understand he has taken on his role as an Indian Brave, and the serious expression is exactly what he means it to be. I turn it over and on the back, in pencil, *Michael 1949*. It makes me smile to see the adult there within the child's face, the same expression of gravity which he used to apply to skinning tomatoes for a pasta sauce.

Another photograph, older, of three children I don't recognise peering into a box. I think for a moment that it must be an advert on a postcard, because of how the kids' faces are treated—the lips defined, the skin perfect, and the expression of the boy in the middle, discovering something wonderful and glowing within the box. It could be an old advert for chocolate. The box is the one that Christopher sent me and that I broke when the spider ran up my neck. I turn it over: *Ruth, Antony, Alice* it says. Looking at the face of the smallest child I see the faintest memory of Mrs. Hamilton. I never knew she had siblings.

A bird flusters at the back window but has left behind only a smear on the glass by the time I get there. There is a creak from upstairs. The air in the house stiffens. In the last of the light I go outside and climb the wall and check my messages once more.

> *Hey, I have to move out of the flat. Can you help me? Dom has taken the car.*
> *Perhaps you aren't coming back for the weekend. Let me know soonest please.*
> *If plausible.*
> *K*
> *x*

Each line is sent an hour apart. It's the word *plausible* that makes me think I need to go back to London. Katherine reverts to a strange language when she's stressed. During her university exams I remember her telling me that my *request to borrow £20 was not actionable at this time.* Her computer brain takes over. I've always envied her computer brain.

*

Maggie knocks at the door at nine o'clock.

"Sorry I'm late," she says, but gives no explanation. She packs her clothes into her rucksack, smelling them with obvious enjoyment as she goes. She smiles happily. "Thanks for that."

"It's no problem."

I am surprised by how relieved I am to have her company.

"Look," I say, "I don't want to, you know. I just want you to know that—"

"Would it be OK if I had a bath?"

"Yes."

I find her a spare towel and there's some baby shampoo left under the sink. Bet used to wash her jumpers in it. I sit by the unlit fire, wishing there was no crow nesting. I can hear Maggie in her bath, the squeaks and thumps of her submerging and emerging from water. The low singing of a song I don't recognise. I've never known comfort this quickly with a person before. I feel a flinch of sadness for my sister.

She comes down wearing a man's shirt over yellow long johns with the towel on her head.

"Mint," she says.

"You can stay the night," I say.

"Double mint."

"You want a drink?" She smiles broadly and I go to the kitchen. I'm a little embarrassed by the assortment of snacks I bought during the day—honeyed almonds and wasabi peas. They are in bowls and I think it looks like I'm throwing some do, rather than persuading a homeless sex worker to stay with me because there might be a ghost. I bought bottled beer too, because how drunk can you get on beer? As I'm coming back into the room, bottle necks between my fingers, and the bowls of nuts and peas in the crook of my arm, I try out something she might do.

"Down there on the rocks," I say, not looking at her, "when I was a little kid, I found a dead woman. Her boyfriend killed her." I hand Maggie her drink, set down the bowls on the side table next to her. "Her boyfriend killed her with wire because he found out she was leaving. And he got her into a suitcase—cut bits off her so she fitted, hand-luggage-sized, really—and set fire to it, and then when that didn't work he threw her into the sea. And then she was in the rock pool."

I look up and Maggie has not touched her drink. Her mouth is open a small amount.

"I'm sorry," she says.

"Thanks," I say, like I deserve the sympathy.

She drinks and so do I.

"That makes a kind of sense," she says.

"Oh? How?"

"Because it explains to me who you are." She stands and comes and sits next to me. We chink bottles.

"Also," I say after we have drunk in silence a little longer, "also, I fucked my sister's husband."

"OK," she says. She gives me a shrug. "That shit happens."

"Katherine doesn't know."

"You sure?"

"Yes! Only Dom and I know. And he's not telling her."

"Are you going to tell her?"

"Do you think I should?"

"I don't know the situation."

"I feel bad for not telling her."

"You want to tell her?"

"No!"

"You're in love with him?"

"What, no. No. No—he's an arsehole. And he's fucking thick as well." I feel a bubble of panic in my chest talking about him. Maggie looks at me a speck longer. I should not have brought it up. Stupid to, now three people know. I scratch at my shin, dig my nail right in, can feel a dampness there. It feels so good to scratch it.

"What's that?" Maggie says, not pointing, but just looking to where I'm scratching.

"Oh, eczema. I've had it since I was a kid." I feel conscious of itching it and cross my legs so that my good leg is on top. There is some blood under my nails, which I tuck under my arm. Maggie gets an already rolled joint out of her pocket, opens it up and takes a pinch of the innards. She whispers something into her closed fist which I don't hear, then holds out the small tangle on her palm and spits into it, a long-drawn-out slaver into her hand. She closes her eyes and says something else.

"What?" I ask. She holds up a finger to silence me, rubs her spittle into the weed and then kneels down in front of me. She firmly uncrosses my ankles, and rolls up my trouser leg. She tuts at the wound there, which looks awful. Years of opening it up have left a shallow dent in my leg, it is scabbed over in places with a thick crust of black and in other places it glistens with new blood. It is not something I would ordinarily allow someone else to look at, but it occurs to me now that I don't often let myself look at it either.

Maggie rubs the contents of her hand into my shin. I don't flinch, I just watch her. She offers no explanation, rests her fingertips on the scar for a few seconds.

I have the impression she is somehow *having a word* with the wound, requesting that it behave itself. I remain very still. She returns to her chair, takes a long pull of her beer and says, "Don't suppose you've got any crisps? I'm allergic to nuts."

*

When I leave the next day, I give Maggie a key. "You'd be doing me a favour," I say, "if you stayed for a few nights. I'm supposed to be house-sitting."

She doesn't make a deal of it, just says "Sure," and hands me a cheese sandwich to eat on the drive home. "Don't go falling asleep."

Two and a half hours later I pull into a service station and sit very still for five minutes. What if she brings over this guy she has the arrangement with? Is she a confidence trickster? The kind who swindle old ladies out of their money? Am I the old lady? I imagine Deborah's face when she walks into the living room and finds Maggie in her socks with a naked man and a crack pipe. They'd bring in stray cats who would shit everywhere and give birth to kittens, they would call squatters rights. I rest my head on the steering wheel and try to imagine what I had been thinking. What would Katherine say? The phone is disconnected and Maggie and I have never exchanged numbers. The signal doesn't work unless you're on the wall anyway. Oh God. At the exit I hesitate. I could drive back and tell her I made a mistake and she has to leave. That's not something I will be able to do. I carry on to London, because I am a giant spoon. I will just stay at home the weekend to help Katherine and then I will come back and face Maggie.

I am late to meet Katherine, and she doesn't mention the evening we were supposed to spend together, and if we can get to the end of the month without it being brought up it will be filed in the disappointing sibling box and will only get mentioned if we have a proper falling-out.

We were supposed to have a coffee before going to the flat, during which she would no doubt recite her game plan, packing, leave of absence at work, deeply spiritual but educational holiday, rebirth. "Well," she says, flashing a smile, "you're late, so I suppose we should go straight to the flat and start."

She is polite as always, she has cut her hair and says she likes my boots. She walks faster than me, presumably to make up for the time I have lost us. We pass a newly refurbished pub—the kind that talk about brunch and bottomless prosecco, and an ironic quiz on a Tuesday.

"Shall we stop for a quick drink before? Might, you know. Chill you out a bit." I regret saying it as soon as it's out of my mouth.

Katherine turns to me, smiling again.

"I'm totally chill. What are you talking about?"

In her voice, *chill* sounds rather like when Dad used to say *groovy*. I shrug.

"Cool."

"Cool." Smile smile smile. "Anyway. It's a bit early, isn't it?"

"Oh, yes, but I was only joking," I say. The lie feels infantile.

"We can if you like? Sorry, Viv—is this a difficult thing to ask you to do?"

It is so like her to behave as though *I'm* the one having the drama. It's meant to highlight how absolutely good and selfless she is in the face of my shitness, and it puts me immediately into a funk.

"No, no, no—as I said, I was joking. I just meant, you know . . ." I change the subject. "I like your hair," I say.

She puts a hand up to it.

"Oh—it's just a bit easier like this."

I don't know what she means.

We walk in silence. It isn't far—there is the sound of traffic and of people playing football in the park and so the silence is not overwhelming. We have to walk in single file where the pathway narrows between the road and the park.

"He won't be there, will he?" I hadn't thought much past the logistics of parking near her flat and then parking near our mother's.

"He said not—but you never know," she says and smiles. It is a tight smile with something else behind it, something other than control, other than disappointment. She stops suddenly at the top of their road.

"Perhaps," she says, turning sideways, shifting her handbag from one shoulder to the other, "perhaps we should have a drink after all."

I watch her for signs of sarcasm but see none. She looks at me.

"Well?" She says it rather aggressively, and I nod and we turn back in the direction of the pub. "To be honest it's not that early now, because even though I told you to meet me at ten thirty it's now nearly eleven fifteen."

Inside is a collection of old cotton spools as a centrepiece above the booth we sit in. To our left children's shoes arranged around the head of a stag. Two small glasses of wine are £15.

"So! How have you been?" I ask in an over-the-top way. "Until now—until this?"

"Good!" she says. "Though not ideal, I suppose, just at the moment." As she takes a large swig of wine, something occurs to her. "I like my new hair," she says. "What about you? What's going on with you?"

I shrug. We are really acting out our exclamation marks.

"Mum says you're seeing someone?" says Katherine.

"What?"

"Says you've got that stoaty thing about you that you get."

"Stoaty?"

"You know. She said, like a . . . stoat in the snow—flicking about—like you might run up a trouser leg."

"Fuck's sake."

My sister smiles.

"Well? Is she right?"

"Not really. I mean she's wrong."

"How boring."

"A stoat?"

My sister runs her hand over her face, and as she does her expression changes.

"Oh God, Viv. I'm moving back in with Mum. What's going to happen to me?"

A bottle of wine is only £19, and so we get that next.

"Why are *you* moving out of the flat, and why does *he* have the car? Aren't both those things yours?"

"It's complicated."

"Does he know you're leaving?"

There is a long pause. She refills our glasses higher than she would ordinarily approve of. I remember, drunk, that I am driving. I concentrate on forgetting the fact.

"He ought to have understood the way things are by now," she says, which is meant to be inscrutable, but I understand from it that she is doing a runner.

At half-midday we blink into the bright sunshine and make our way down the road, a little unsteady.

Inside Katherine and Dom's flat, nothing much is out of place at first glance. I see her shoulders drop when there is no sound of Dom. We stand still in the hallway, looking. His overcoat, his briefcase full of notebooks waiting for him like a dog by the door. He takes it with him whenever he comes to family things and he rifles through it occasionally, as though there were a very important document he can't be separated from. I know, though, that it is full of fishing magazines and a notebook in which he writes poetry. I read a few of the poems once, Dom gave me a taster drunk. A stanza that sticks with me:

> Oh, the purple mountains of home,
> groaning with my absence,
> watch my blooming
> into the wild flowers of spring.

I remember him taking the book from my hands and saying, "It's about my ejaculate."

"You ever read his poems?" I ask Katherine. She gives me a look and I know that she has and finds none of this funny.

A voice from the bedroom makes her stiffen. The radio alarm, set to go off at six thirty each morning, has had nobody to silence it.

"He's in Swindon doing some kind of spoken-word event." She waves a hand in front of her face like she's describing something completely everyday. She sees to the radio and I wait in the hallway for instructions. An unsmoked roll-up in the ashtray and a half-drunk bottle of wine, with one glass, tinged with lees, on its side, broken at the stem on the occasional table by the sofa. The coffee table has snapped in half, as though someone has fallen on it.

In the kitchen, I open the fridge, curious about what they ate as a couple. The food in the fridge is spoiled, minced beef grey and sweating with mould, lettuce brown at the edges, tomatoes that have collapsed under the weight of their own skin. No one has eaten here in weeks. I close the door. A bowl of black plums withering on the table. Two tiny white shells picked out of a small ornamental bowl of others. These are

Katherine's and I pocket them, in case they get overlooked. Left in the bowl are small yellow sea-snail shells, pearlescent limpets and slate-black cockles. I run my thumb over the backs of the shells in my pocket. She was the collector when we were kids. She would spend hours combing the tideline with her fingertips, patiently examining every piece of shell debris for these white mouse-ears.

I am startled by the toilet flush. I am drunker than I thought, though exactly as drunk as I should be given how much wine I've had.

Katherine comes out of the toilet holding something.

"He left these." She holds up a pair of red knickers made out of some uncomfortable slippery fabric.

"They're not mine," she says, "he left them here for me to find." She looks lost, undone in a way I never expected from her. There are no tears—I sense all of these are in the past. What is left is salty bone dust lost at sea.

I move forward and put my hand on her arm. It is tensing and she shivers.

"Nobody would really wear those," I say, thinking that perhaps I'm right.

She lets the panties fall through her fingers; they heap on the floor, a small puddle of red.

Quietly she says, "I think that might be worse."

All she takes is a backpack full of clothes and a suitcase of books and photographs.

"What will happen now?" I ask once we are sitting in the car. "You can't just let him have the flat, and the car and everything."

"When some time has passed. When things are calmer."

I don't turn on the ignition. "Is it that he's fucking someone else?"

There's no response from Katherine. Slowly I reach for the keys and turn them.

"Fuck!" she shouts. I jump.

"What?"

"You're too drunk to drive." She says it quietly, puts her hands up to her face. I turn on the engine and we pull out into the afternoon traffic. She keeps her face covered the whole way to our mother's house.

There had been talk about the woman in the shepherd's hut, the girl had overheard her father and the fishermen.

"It was just a matter of time," she heard him say, and there was a murmur of agreement, until one of the men set his eyes on her and she was sent to collect her mother from the big house because the men were hungry.

Her mother wiped her hands on her apron, and handed the girl half a loaf of bread. "Tell him I'm not yet finished here. There's soup in the pot and there's herring in the pantry. Tell your father he can wait till later and I'll bring back mutton." Her mother gave her a coin for a jug of beer from the tavern. Her mother smoothed the hair down on the girl's head and kissed her on the crown. "There now—I need to get on or I'll not be back till midnight."

"Mother?"

Her mother already had the door half closed and opened it in irritation. "What is it?"

"What happened to the woman in the shepherd's hut?"

Her mother looked at her.

"What did you hear about that?"

The girl toed the dirt. "Father and the men were talking."

Her mother sighed, lowered her voice and stepped back out of the house, pulling the door so that no one inside would overhear.

"The woman in the hut was warned and she still didn't leave. That's all you need to know, and that you listen to your mother and your father—or at least your mother—and you stay away from the Law, and the hut, and you don't mention it to anyone.

If word gets to the Earl, there'll be a tell-about and a fuss, and no one can afford the stop in work, not right now. She knew that, and she still persisted, and now she has paid the price—just don't you go around making things worse than they already are, you hear?"

"What price did she pay?"

"Never you mind."

"But what did she persist in doing?"

"Never. You. Mind."

The girl went back home and delivered the bread and the beer, and some of the men had left but there were four of them to share the beer, the bread and the herring. They were not interested in the barley soup. "It churns my guts these days," said her father. The girl left the men to it and sat on the back step. From there she could see the hut, just a small shadow on the side of the Law, and above it birds circling, beyond it the water and then the silent black rock.

The Sow

I

Mum has invited our great-aunt and -uncle Pauline and John for dinner—they are in London *running some tests on John* as Mum puts it, as though he were a faulty dishwasher. Pauline and her loud husband Alistair lived in Edinburgh and used to take sugar mice to Dad and Christopher when they were at school. Dad blamed them for his addiction to sweets—he liked the cola bottles and the fizzy dummies. He laughed when the chemotherapy meant they burnt his tongue, but his laugh felt like seeing a dog kicked.

In return for the sugar mice, Mum insisted on having them over whenever they were in London, to repay the kindness.

"Not having a husband to look after is quite the most intelligent thing your sister has ever done," she says of me, to Katherine. "And quite the most exciting thing you've done for yourself in a very long time."

We both stand in silence waiting for the subject to be done with. Sometimes she can sound a little relieved to be widowed.

"I want you to look upon this move with enthusiasm, Katherine. And also, I want you to be here when Alistair and Pauline and John come over, because otherwise I'll have to talk to them." She points a chopstick at my sister. "Quite the most intelligent thing *you* did, within the highly stupid marriage thing,

185

was choose a man with no extended family. Good work, sweetheart."

My sister winces. "Mum, do you mind if I sit this one out? I don't really want to talk to anyone about it."

"My darling, John and Pauline barely noticed you got married in the first place. Dom's Canadian—it doesn't count to them." She bends down to rifle through a cupboard.

Katherine closes her eyes for longer than a blink. "It's not what I feel like doing. Why is it so important that I'm here?"

"They're old, they're bored, John's not well, and they're in London. And it's good manners, darling, to keep in touch with people from one's past."

Our mother passes Katherine a vase that she has filled with cheese straws.

"You put those on the table, then I'll make us martinis, and before you know it you'll be a bit drunk and everything will be better." She sticks her head into the fridge to get the olives, looks up to see Katherine still standing there with the vase. "Darling, get through the starter with us, and if you still feel wretched, you can slink away."

It is Mum's way of helping, we both know that. Her way of dealing with the weeks after Dad's death had been to keep busy, to fill the house with people and then to leave to walk the dog, sometimes up to four times a day, to avoid a bosomy embrace from some perfumed relative. She seemed to find it easier to become invisible among a large group of people, to provide them with food and drink and the reassurance that she was doing fine.

Katherine stomps into the dining room with her mouth a line and puts the cheese straws down heavily on the table. I watch her from the kitchen and she catches my eye. I give her a small shrug. In our forties we are still our mother's children. She goes into the front room and sits on the sofa with the dog, kisses the dog's ears. The dog stretches out her long legs and spreads her toes, groans with the weariness of a saint. It is strange to see Katherine like this—I am the one who sulks. It makes me anxious—she usually has Dad's ability to quietly make people feel at ease, to ask the right questions so that the conversation flows. He used to do it to me when I was a child, and being from hell. Like he knew everything about me and understood completely my reasons for not coming out of my tree, and even agreed with me that that was where I truly ought to be. His job was to make everyone understood, and everything understandable. He made sure people felt loved, he thought that was important. He remembered the sugar mice.

Katherine's face is turned towards the window, but I can see from the bones at her temple that she is clenching and unclenching her jaw, and her leg is doing that jiggling thing like she's being electrocuted.

When the three of them arrive, we sit around the dining table and Mum disappears almost immediately into the kitchen. Pauline wears a necklace of transparent crystal, cut into slithers through which you can see the undulations and shadows of her neck skin. My mother wears a black shift dress and biker boots. I've made an effort, never a good thing, and have on a light blue A-line dress.

"The waist's too high on that dress, isn't it?" says my mother, not intending to insult me, just to let me know.

"Is it?" I look down. I do resemble a clothes-peg doll. The sand shoes that I found whimsical when I tried them on now make me look like someone on the run from a mental institution.

"A little. It's OK—you look like a nurse." She hands me a bottle of wine in a cooler. "Go and administer this to the patients."

Katherine has tried very hard not to make an effort, but is still the most elegant-looking person at the table.

I pour wine while Pauline's husband Alistair talks about the route he has taken to get here, and how he'd once got a ticket for driving the wrong way up a one-way street. Everyone waits for him to finish.

"How's that ghastly old house then, Viviane? I understand from Christopher you're the caretaker there now," Pauline says and laughs loudly. Her hearing aid squeals. I'm not entirely sure which part she is laughing at—it is possibly the idea of me looking after anything.

"It's fine, it's good," I say, a little defensively.

"Never could understand why Ruth didn't sell up and live somewhere less ridiculous."

"Well, there were other people living there too," my mother says, putting bread and vinaigrette on the table, but she exits again before Pauline can reply to her.

"The thing about that woman was she was so stuck-up. And a terrible alcoholic with it too. She never could live up to Peter's first wife, you see, to our sister. But then who could?" She says it a little like it was a generous thing to say, and even raises her glass as though giving a toast. There is a long silence and everyone picks up their glasses and drinks to fill it. Alistair sits in the seat Dad would have been in. He liked to be close to the kitchen, he always did the clearing. He thought doing the washing-up was the best part of a dinner party, because he liked to listen to people talk without having to join in.

"I took Elinor to Clarke's on Sunday," John, Pauline's brother, says out of nowhere, like he's already been in conversation about Elinor or about Clarke's and has everyone's ear on the subject.

"*Did* you," says Pauline, in a manner that is a statement, rather than a question.

"Rather pricey, but very good—and Elinor eats very slowly. Anyway, we had a very good lobster salad, which I finished first, then Elinor had partridge breast, even though it's not quite the season, and I worried it would be tough, anyway, she said not at all so that was fine." I catch Katherine's eye. We share a flicker. "And I had some sort of fish if I remember, I think it was bass—samphire was a little over the top. Fish very good though. We both had the chocolate pot for pudding."

Pauline has long since turned her attention to her handbag, and when she finds what she is looking for—a light green handkerchief—she decides, on closer inspection, it is not fit for public use, and she puts it back and quickly dabs her nose with her napkin instead.

Alistair, who is a little deaf, had started talking over John at about the beginning of the description of Elinor's main course. Now he is saying loudly, "We're human beings, for God's sake, not robots. Nobody minds a pinch on the bottom really, they just like getting their knickers in a twist." And so it falls to me to behave as if I am the one being addressed by John. Our mother has absented herself, having deliberately planned the menu so that things have to be tended to as much as possible, flapping either of us away if we try to help.

"So all in all," says John, "I'd say it was a success. Yup."

"Good," I say. "It sounds very good."

Ordinarily my sister would, at this point, steer the conversation in a more universal direction. I look to her. But I'm surprised to see she is holding her head in her hands. When she glances up, her eyes are rimmed red. She stands and leaves the room quickly. If the extended Hamiltons have noticed, they hide it well by making no concession. Mum places a large earthenware bowl of artichokes on the table. She sees Katherine leave and sits down.

"Bernadette," says Pauline, drawing out the syllables, "do explain to me how on earth you cook artichoke—I never have been able to do it in a satisfactory way."

"Oh," says my mother, distracted, "I just steam them."

"Steam! That's where I go wrong, you see—I've always boiled. No wonder. And how long do you steam for?" My mother is looking at the empty doorway through which Katherine passed, her fingertips spiders on the table. She turns back to Pauline, manufactures a smile.

"About twenty-five minutes—depending on the size."

"I see, I see. You are so clever, and I've always said it."

My mother's eyes flick to mine and back to Pauline. John removes the leaves of his artichoke with his little finger high in the air, and his napkin tucked into his collar, as though the artichoke might squirt on him. He dips each leaf once in a ramekin of butter and applies it to his mouth, brings out the leaf again, dipping three times, inspecting each time to make sure he has taken all of the meat off it. The spent leaves he piles up on his side dish, wiping his mouth with his napkin when each leaf is done. I excuse myself. If he were here, Dad would have slipped out unnoticed and he would have sorted the whole thing without me having to get involved at all. I am not a good substitute.

Katherine is staying in her old bedroom. It has been converted into an office space, but some of her still remains. The lampshade shaped like a hot-air balloon. We shared a hamster that we used to put in the basket and it would jump

190

out onto the bed. The cat sticker on the light switch, the many grease marks on the ceiling from the time we both owned little jellified men that stuck to the walls or tumbled down windowpanes. Katherine is sitting on the floor with her back to the wall, leafing through a magazine.

"You OK?" I ask.

"I'll be fine. I just am not in the mood to listen to those people."

I have never heard her talk about anyone but me this way.

"They don't mean anything by anything." It's not a useful thing to say, but it's something. I feel a little excited, if I'm being honest, that Katherine has made a show of herself, even if no one noticed.

"I just don't want to try today. I just don't want to be sitting there saying the right thing. I want to go to sleep, is what I want."

I start to get ready to leave once the dishwasher has been filled, and Mum has asked for the third time if I know what's happened to Katherine.

"She's left her husband, Mum—she's sad about it."

"There's something else, don't you think?" She pours a whisky. "Will you have one?"

"I won't, I should be getting back." I feel pious all of a sudden, a picture of sobriety. There's a discomfort being in the house just the three of us. It loudens Dad's absence, but it also makes me feel like a child. I'd quite like to lie down with the dog in her bed and stay there, like he used to do. When my parents first got her she was a small mole-like puppy. I used to find him asleep on the sofa, the puppy tucked into his dressing gown.

"Taxi?"

"I'll let you know when I'm home."

"Careful."

We kiss, and on my way out, I stop and stand for a moment outside Katherine's room. There is no sound from inside, and no light under the door, so I leave.

I'm in that half-sleep place, my thoughts meandering stupidly, when I hear it.

There is a gentle tap tap tap sound and my brain has turned it into someone with a long fingernail tapping against the glass of the garden door.

I have never texted a man in the middle of the night, have never had the impulse to, have always been fearful of what it says about what you want from them.

Hey, are you awake?

I jump a little at the sound of the message being sent. A second later, the security light comes on. I sit up in bed. It is probably just a fox. Of course it's just a fox, it is always just a fox. It blinks out again. I should have got up and gone to the living room to check out the window while it was still on, just for peace of mind.

I am! What are you up to?

I already regret the text message. I don't want him to know I'm lying in bed wide awake imagining a psychopath at my window.

I bite my lip. *I'm fine. There was a noise downstairs that woke me up and now I can't get back to sleep.*

What was it?

Nothing. Just something tapping the glass.

Have you checked?

No but it seems to have stopped.

Want me to come over and check it out?

I pause, aware that there is no time for pausing, a pause looks like thought and this is not supposed to be a thought-out exchange.

I can be over in ten minutes. What's your address?

I feel for a second caught in a trap. But I'm being mad, of course, he is being kind.

Honestly, it's no problem, I'm putting my shoes on now.

Really no need, everything's fine.

I don't believe you, leaving now, will be there soon.

Seriously, don't, I'm fine.

I'm out the door. Text your address or I'll just stand outside the cheese shop and scream your name.

Get back in the door!

;)

Fuck.

How have I managed that? It was the pause. And now he will arrive at 2 a.m. and I will have to let him in, and not only that, he will probably have to stay the night, and what does that mean? Is this a sex thing?

Tap tap tap.

I turn on the light. My reflection in the mirror is the image of a woman who has not slept enough. At least I had a shower before bed. In the mirror I catch myself sniffing under an armpit. Christsake. The wound on my leg is itchy—in my sleep I'd scratched it hard and now the blood has dried and organised itself into a gnarled black scab.

I pull on jeans and a jumper. I brush my teeth and try to make myself look like I am not preparing for company. I put the kettle on and make some coffee, not because I plan on drinking any, but because it seems like the kind of thing a person in charge of their own life does. What would Deborah do? I stack some books that I've left on the floor, give the

193

table a wipe down, put the dirty glass and bowl next to the sofa in the sink, wonder how the place smells. I should have taken the bin out before I went to bed. I consider lighting a scented candle, but that might suggest I am trying to make things romantic. I use my foot to shuffle the spider's dressing gown into the bathroom and close the door on it. I open the door and check in the toilet bowl, put my ancient mooncup away in a drawer, close the door again. In the TV version of this moment, I would be tousle-haired and wearing a slouchy but clean marl-grey tracksuit, my tits would be braless and perky but not over the top. In my Foster's T-shirt they look like dogs' noses. I find a relatively clean bra and put it on.

The security light is on again, and has been for some time, I just haven't registered it. It's a cold light, and there's something stilling about it, like a photograph. I move slowly towards the back door, which looks onto the tiny garden. It has glass panels up and down to let light into the basement. A small fox stands in the spotlight, its nose pressed against the glass so that its teeth show. It licks the window. It would be funny if it was daylight. It's the kind of thing you see on the Internet. The fox either doesn't see me or is not bothered by my presence. It carries on licking. I walk slowly to the door, still he doesn't move, too fixated on what he is licking. I can see a residue, white and gluey. The fox stands over two large damp shoe prints on the decking. The prints are disappearing as I watch, and I look back at the residue on the window, the glassy eyes of the fox and into the dark back wall of my garden. I can't see the wall with the security light on, but I will be lit up and on display. I turn the kitchen light off, and take a large knife out of the block.

I stand in the hallway by the front door until I hear footsteps outside, and looking through the spyhole see that Vincent has arrived already. I don't think I could take the sound of the doorbell tonight.

The fox has gone by the time he comes in, so have the footprints. Vincent looks dubiously at the back door.

"So you're saying someone jizzed on your window?"

"I don't know what it was. But there were footprints there too."

"But a fox ate all of the jizz off your window?"

I don't reply.

"I'm sorry, look, that's obviously really horrible, it's just also a little bit funny?"

"I suppose so." It is possible I've imagined it, like those phantom breast lumps you find at 3 a.m. that are gone by the morning.

"Like, not to say that it's not a horrible thing to think about or anything." He looks at the fences on either side of the garden. "Be quite an effort to get in, don't you reckon?"

"I saw the footprints." I say it quietly, feeling very stupid.

"Of course, I'm not saying you imagined it. Just—trying to make you feel better. Hey, do you want to call the police?" He studies the grease mark on the window the fox has left. "They might be able to take DNA or something?"

"I'm not sure they do that just for people jizzing on windows. I feel like people jizz in worse places." We are silent for a while and then I surprise us both and laugh. As soon as I do everything feels better, Vincent starts too, we laugh until we both have tears in our eyes. It slows into a series of sighs and Vincent rubs at his nose.

"You know that you're holding a really big knife?"

I look down, I forgot it was there. I put it on the counter. "You want a coffee? I just made some."

He leans past me and pours us both a whisky.

*

We sit on the sofa and drink through the rest of the bottle. When my socked feet end up in his lap he puts an arm over them without pausing. We don't move from the sofa until the sun starts to show through the blinds of the kitchen window. There is a strange feeling of coming to. I have to get back to Scotland today. The drive will be deathly.

"I don't know what we talked about all night."

"Me neither," he says, and in a rare moment of seriousness, "but I really needed that. Thank you."

He stands and stretches, and I stand too.

"I should go." He looks at his phone. "I have work in three hours."

"Yeah." I smile, and at the door he kisses me. It is mousy warm. There is the thrill of being a person that another person would like to kiss. It erases the clumsy feeling of the first time— this is a different kind of drunk.

I take the bin out and watch him walk down the road. I stand for a long time, because he must have told me—it's the first thing you ask, the first thing you find out about a person. But I can't remember where he works or what he does.

196

II

Peter telephoned in the morning.

"Darling?" he said when she picked up.

"Oh, yes. Hello." Ruth had not slept well. She'd felt nauseous and worried, and had stayed too long in the bath, to try to calm the itch on her legs, the tickling bites of sandflies. From her bathroom she could hear Betty shouting at Bernadette, because of course Bernadette had not had permission to go to the picnic. And now Ruth had a cold, and on top of it, Betty was cooking bacon and the smell of it rested in Ruth's throat in a very unpleasant way.

"How was the picnic?"

She wanted to be able to say that it was a complete disaster because he had not shown up and it had been very embarrassing for her. The truth was not far off, but none of it was because of Peter's absence. She wouldn't let him know about the boat trip.

"Fine," she said, "strange, but fine." She wouldn't tell him that when the boat arrived back the children were wet and frozen and quiet. *Sea spray!* Reverend Jon Brown had said. *It was choppy, but we had fun, didn't we, boys?* He took no account of the three girls. The children had walked mutely back to the house with her, responding to her animated questions—*Did you see a seal?*—with shakes of their heads. She felt desperate

197

to know they were unharmed and to show that she was, too. They were so cold, Peter would have been horrified. As they neared the house, Betty, scarf off, black hair standing straight up, came running down the path towards them, her face white, and Ruth thought for a moment she might strike Bernadette, but instead she pulled her away and up the path at a trot without saying a word. Michael took hold of Ruth's hand. The one moment of the day that she tucked into her heart. She had stood outside their bedroom at points throughout the night, listening for evidence that she had killed them—a rattle in a breath. But other than the occasional sleeping murmur there was nothing but the husky warmth of children sleeping.

"Look," said Peter. "I'm awfully sorry I said those things to you. I think you're doing a sterling job with the boys. I was just taken aback rather by that mad vicar dragging them out of their beds in the middle of the night."

"That's all right, darling, I understand. When will you be home?"

Peter took a great inhalation of breath as though the very act of thinking about it exhausted him. "I'm looking at my diary now, and there's a Christmas lunch with one of the clients that I'll need to attend on the fourteenth, so it really makes no sense to come back until Wednesday. Will you cope without me?" She could hear a smile in his voice, and for that moment it felt so good to hear it, she resolved to respond to it. The winter picnic was over, and next year she would not attend or permit their beach to be used.

"Of course. We'll be just fine."

"And how is the girl settling in?"

"Well, Betty is keeping her busy." Ruth watched herself in the mirror as she spoke. Today it seemed a face not quite her own looked back.

"Good, good." He was distracted, probably reading a report while on the phone to her. She had seen him do this when Elspeth's mother called.

"Well, I'll let you go. Do drop in on Alice if you get lonely." The London office was in Holland Park and Alice was only at Kensington. For a moment she thought of the Christmas lights.

"Good idea—I'll see how she's fixed." He wouldn't, of course. They didn't understand each other in the slightest, and as for Mark, Peter thought him some sort of pervert because of his sculpture collection.

"Goodbye then, darling," she said.

"Sleep well," he said, despite it being just past nine thirty in the morning. He hung up. His attention was on something else. It would be terrific to have something to be engrossed in. As she hung up the receiver, there came the pound of footsteps on the stairs and down came the boys.

"Morning!" said Michael, just shy of a shout.

"Was that Dad on the telephone?" asked Christopher, more composed.

"It was, he'll be back on Wednesday. And then, hopefully he will stay put until after Christmas."

Betty had laid the table with her usual vigour. There was a loaf of bread, warm to the touch, and on the boys' plates two little bread ducks with currants for eyes. When she came in with tea, she seemed embarrassed.

"Have you been up all night baking, Betty?" It was supposed to be a joke but as she said it Ruth realised there was more than likely some truth to it.

"Just an early riser today," she said, and was gone again. While the boys ate breakfast, Ruth went to the kitchen, where she found Bernadette at the table with porridge and a comic in front of her, and Betty standing behind her, stroking the girl's hair. Bernadette appeared to be enduring rather than enjoying the attention. When Betty saw Ruth in the doorway, she walked down the steps and into the pantry. Ruth followed her.

"Everything all right, Betty?"

"Oh yes. I'm sorry about yesterday."

"No, I'm sorry, I thought she had your blessing."

"It was an overreaction on my part."

"No, if I'd known he was going to whip them all out into the sea for hours, I wouldn't have let her go. I wouldn't have let Christopher and Michael go, either. Reverend Jon Brown just sort of . . . took over."

"Aye. He'll do that," she said.

"And that game. To be honest the whole thing was a nightmare."

"Yes. I've always been grateful that my only part in the whole thing is to provide the pies. The reverend loves an event, and he's very good at getting people with too much time on their hands and too much money in their pockets to join in with him." Betty straightened herself and swept her hair back off her forehead. "When will I expect Mr. Hamilton back?"

"Not till Wednesday."

"He works hard, that man." There was something not altogether complimentary about how she said it.

"He does."

"And the boys are all right, are they?" said Betty, energetically wiping down a shelf. "After their boat trip?"

"They seem fine. They were very cold, which isn't ideal. Their mother had weak lungs."

Betty nodded. "Aye. The man likes the cold, that's true."

*

The weather was bad and the boys were content to stay indoors. She found them in the ballroom, Michael crouching on the floor drawing aeroplane after aeroplane and spreading the pictures out on the floor until he had a whole squadron, and Christopher propped up under the piano, with a cushion at his back so that he faced the French windows, holding a thick pile of comic books on his lap.

"Are you boys warm enough?" she asked, and they looked up at her, pale faces and dark eyes. They nodded.

"What are you drawing, Michael?"

"A squad."

"A squad?"

"He's drawing aeroplanes," explained Christopher, who was perhaps annoyed at being disturbed.

"Well, I'll be upstairs if you need me. Betty'll put lunch out at twelve, make sure you're clean and ready for it then."

She pulled the door shut, and listened outside for a few moments, but she heard nothing other than the scraping of Michael's pencil on the paper. Perhaps she had blown the whole thing out of proportion. She'd had at least five glasses of champagne, and had drunk them rather quickly. A childish game, ending in being tickled. The children simply went on an adventure in a boat and returned cold. And now there was Christmas to think about, nothing more, nothing more.

In her study, she settled into her chair. Christmas took planning. Especially since the children's grandparents were coming. Two lists, one of things that might be nice, including new outfits for the boys, getting the piano tuned and encouraging Peter to play carols. And a list of essentials: a goose, plum pudding, Peter's Christmas present (perhaps a new tweed), presents for the boys (who knew), a bonus for Betty, a book for Bernadette.

She sat back and looked out the window. The Bass Rock was completely obscured by mist, and large raindrops clung to the window. She ought to be happy. She ought to be. She thought of Alice in London. How she would, if she fancied some air, walk down Kensington Church Street and along to the park and sit by the pond or in the cafe, or visit the V&A, or meet a friend and just go and walk by the river. Going for air in North Berwick just at that moment meant having wind punched down your throat and rain slapped into your face. Ruth had the Pavilion, but she had no anonymity. Reverend Jon Brown, or Janet, or anyone at all might inform her that she had been spotted drinking a cup of tea, as though this was information to be wielded over her. How had she managed to get to her age and be somehow all alone? Her friends had dropped off after Antony died. It wasn't that no one had experienced the awkwardness of another's grief before—everyone knew of a lost boy in the war. It was the way that Ruth had responded to it that had made people stop calling round for her. Those days when she felt him so strongly in the air around her, in the birds especially, sometimes it was even like he had jumped into the dog. Wind thumped against the window, and a sharp draught made it through the glass.

Stupid. It was only tickling. It was childish, that was all. When she turned round the wardrobe door was open, and she hadn't recalled it being so before. She stood up and closed it, and as soon as it was shut three fast knocks came from the other side. She opened it again, thinking there must have been something hanging on the inside of the door, but there was nothing there, just the old wooden stool that had been there when they moved in.

She didn't join the boys for lunch, but checked on them and saw that they'd taken sandwiches into the ballroom in napkins and resumed their positions. The number of aeroplanes Michael had drawn had tripled and Bernadette was now in there helping him, by drawing, very carefully and rather well, some tanks. The two of them were talking quietly about their undertakings and Christopher was still sheltering under the piano.

"I thought we might get that seen to before Christmas," she said to him, "so that your father can bore us to death with some carols."

Christopher looked up at her and seemed to accept her joke. He smiled. "That would be fun."

"What are you reading?"

"It's the *Eagle*," he said. It was the same one he'd been looking at after breakfast, and she noted it was on the same page too— a fishy-looking monster with webbed fingers and the name "Doomlord" underneath him. Perhaps he had read it more than once through.

"Is it good?"

"I like it."

It wouldn't have been the right time to ask him if he was all right. He was all right. *Children don't bury things like adults do, you always know what a child is thinking*, was her mother's assessment of childhood. She hoped that it was true. It hadn't entirely been the case with her, but perhaps boys were more resilient.

She found Betty again in the kitchen, and set about making a cup of tea.

"Betty, this is awfully nosy of me."

Betty put down the knife with which she was cutting carrots. She took a seat at the table, appearing to know what Ruth was going to ask.

"Someone at the picnic said Bernadette is the spit of her father. And then there was a bit of drama. One of the women—"

"Mrs. Beech."

"Yes."

Betty dragged one leg up and rested the ankle on her knee like a fisherman. There was silence and Ruth sat down too. Betty let out a long breath.

"Mr. Beech interfered with Mary. From a young age. Our mother knew it, but rathered he interfered with Mary than me, because she saw Mary as already damaged, because of her fits." Betty picked up the paring knife she had been using and turned it in her hand.

"Oh good God. I'm sorry. That's terrible." These things happened in every girl's life at some point, of course—with Ruth it had been the curate, and he had only wrestled a fondle and a wet mouth out of her. But the hope was always that one's parents were oblivious and remained that way. What a dreadful thing for one sister to know about the other. And for the mother to let it continue. It was enough, certainly, to separate a family.

"And then Mrs. Beech walked in on them, and that was when Mary had to leave." The scene it must have caused. Briefly Ruth wondered how she would react on finding Peter on top of another woman.

"Reverend Jon Brown organised the spot for her at Landbrooke and Mr. Beech paid for it. We kept the pregnancy a secret, Mother being Catholic, because Mr. Beech would have forced her to get rid of it. When the Beeches found out, it was too late for them to get rid of Bernadette. Our mother retained her job on the condition Mary and Bernadette stayed away, and when Mr. Beech died Mrs. Beech sold up. That's the full scandal of the whole episode."

"Does she know? Bernadette?"

"No. She knows her mother lives in that place, and that's enough for any child to bear. We told her her father was a soldier and died in the war."

"I'm so sorry. Those stupid women at the picnic."

"They're not to blame. They're going by what they believe to be true. It's that Mr. Beech, and there's no one can reach him now. Men do these things and then they tick on with their lives as though it's all part and parcel." She placed the knife back on the table, laced her small fingers together and caged them over her knee.

"So now he's gone—who pays for Mary in the institution?"

"Since she became an adult, Reverend Jon Brown does. I chip in too, where I can, but the reverend has the ear of the board of governors and they give a reduced price. My hope is we'll get her out of there soon enough. We've been talking, the reverend and I, about putting a little away for a flat for Mary and Bernadette and me. I'd still work here, of course, if you'd have me—just wouldn't stay over."

Ruth put down her cup of tea. "Since she became an adult?"

"She was thirteen when all this happened. About Bernadette's age when he started on her. I used to hide her away at the top of the house when I could. There was a cupboard she'd fit in—in your study. During the day, when Mrs. Beech was out, I'd put her in there, but with her fits it became more and more a problem. It's a big enough house that a little girl can hide herself well, but the problem is so can a quiet man of bad intention. She had an episode in the wardrobe and when I pulled her out she was half dead and not the same again after that. They do all sorts of treatments at the hospital with the cold baths and that. None of it helps, but when she's left alone for long enough she'll come out of herself. I've seen it with Bernadette. Like our Mary's in there, hiding, and she only comes out when she knows she can trust a person."

Betty wiped a sleeve over her eyes, even though they were dry.

"Anyway. We've all got our things, haven't we? And there's a whole other life for her and that girl, we just need her to pass a few tests and she'll be let out."

"What kind of tests?"

"Well. There are people on the board who have to be convinced of certain things."

"Is she not free to go?"

"Not at the moment. There have been *several incidents* while she's been there." The woman's voice faltered a little.

"Betty."

Betty held her eyes very wide open and inhaled deeply and stood, to return to her carrots.

"As I say, everyone has their thing. But I am so grateful to you and Mr. Hamilton about Bernadette. I really am—it's half the battle won."

"If I can help?"

Betty nodded and smiled. It was there, just for a second, Betty's true age. Younger than Alice. Perhaps the same age as Ruth herself.

On the way back upstairs, carrying her cup of tea, she passed the door to Peter's study on the first floor, and then turned back and stood in front of it. She held her saucer in one hand and lifted the teacup to her lips while she looked at the closed door. She drank her tea like that, until it was gone, and then she opened the door. The room smelled of him— cloves and something antiseptic like peppermint. She placed her cup and saucer carefully on a coaster on the sideboard.

On the desk a pile of ledgers, a pile of papers and a magnifying glass. She switched on the desk lamp and sat down in Peter's chair. Out of his window a view of Craigleith. The sun shone brightly on it for a moment, illuminating the grass, and then a cloud passed over and the rain continued. Such wild weather. The rowing boat that Reverend Jon Brown had yet to return to the harbour after the picnic collected rainwater out of reach of the sea.

The first drawer held a disorder of items—pen nibs, bent paper clips, used typewriter ribbon, a compass with a cork on its point. It made her think of Michael's drawer of treasures and lost things. She felt a strange affection for Peter, like he was just another child, hurt by things that should not happen in childhood. It smelled strongly of tobacco. In the second drawer, a starting pistol, half a dozen shoehorns from various hotels, the letters sent by the boys from school, and several black-edged letters of condolence dated in the weeks after Elspeth's death. She didn't read them, it was too much like looking into the working strings and muscles of a living heart. Just holding the letters made her dislike herself very much. It seemed at moments illogical that she hadn't known the woman. This person so much a part of Peter and the boys' lives, whose death was the most significant moment any of them were likely to experience. And then along she had trotted, fresh from Kensington, and inserted herself into their lives. The moment that they had met at the interval at a showing of *All's Well That Ends Well*, which she hadn't been enjoying at all, and he'd bought her a gin and tonic. And from there had followed a series of motions, all with a feeling of being preordained, like it had already happened and all they had to do was follow their old footsteps. The visible relief on her mother's face that she would be married after all, and not remain some scarecrow spinster all her life. And these footsteps led her to this moment, alone in a vast house, distrusting her husband, and wishing for a link with his dead wife. Was this how it had been for Elspeth? How could it have been? She was too much alive for these things to happen to her. She surely didn't ever stand alone in a room and ask herself how she came to be there, or stare at her unknowable face in the mirror and wonder who she had come to be.

She pulled out a thick journal and placed it on the desk in front of her, brushed her hands over the leather, soft and warm, warmer than her own hands. She opened the third drawer, the deepest, and was rewarded with a bottle of whisky. She stood and poured a measure and slightly more into her teacup.

The notebook was not filled with writing about how Peter missed his dead wife. There were no descriptions of the ways in which Ruth had let him down and disappointed him and how their argument the day of the picnic had confirmed his worst thoughts of her. There were no words, only drawings. She hadn't known of this interest.

Pencil landscapes for the most part, some slight, some heavily worked, the pages brittle with lead. Just sketches, nothing too accomplished, but regular and practised all the same. She had never seen him sketch. He had never mentioned even a moment's interest in drawing, or art. After a few pages of seascapes of the Bass Rock and of the Lamb and Craigleith, there appeared in the sky the head and breast of a seabird, thick-beaked and straight-backed. It was cartoonish and nothing like the rest of the drawings, which had a seriousness about them. There was a feeling that had he drawn the rest of the bird, it would have been wearing lederhosen. It was perhaps an albatross, she thought, having known one from the cover of a copy of the *Ancient Mariner*. It was rather sweet. She wished he had wanted to show it to her. Further back in the book the drawings grew a little more proficient. The remains of Tantallon Castle, the black impression of the monkey puzzle tree from outside the house. The Law seen from the shoreline, and more cartoonish doodles above the horizon. A silhouette of a cat drawn as a child would: two stacked black circles and whiskers and a tail. A ladybird, a butterfly and a man sitting in a chair facing away. One almost empty landscape—a thin light line on which he had drawn a tree with no leaves, just reaching spiked branches. On the next page, the tree again, but a more focused drawing, as if Peter were bringing something forward in his memory. In the third tree drawing a figure appeared high up in the branches, a black shape, inexpertly drawn, clumsily posed. The next page, closer still, the man was missing his shoes and his feet were white blocks, like a duck's, and he leaned back in the tree, and when you really looked you could imagine that the man was dead with a branch thrust through his chest. After this drawing, the rest of the book was made up of the same image, of a man, sitting in a chair, facing away. She turned the pages becoming a little desperate. The drawings did not get better, or do anything, they just sat there, stuck, almost exactly the same. Two hundred, she guessed, or thereabouts.

Ruth pushed herself back from the desk, hands in lap. She rose from the seat and looked out of the window at the water, the same gunmetal grey as the dead shark. The whole landscape was a giant monster, the sky indifferent, the golf course a wasteland. She knelt and then lay on the floor, folded her hands over her chest. The ceiling dipped in and out of focus. She felt her heart rapping on the wood off the floor, through the back of her ribcage. One, two, three, four, five, six. It seemed that, instead of calming her, her heart's thud was becoming stronger and louder, knocking a tide of blood into her head, banging against the drums of her ears and she closed her eyes and felt the floor slope under her. Her body danced with prickles.

She sat up, hearing someone approaching, frightful to be caught on the floor of Peter's study, the whisky on the table. But the noise was gone, and once she collected herself, put everything back where she had found it, she checked on the boys and Bernadette and saw they were still engrossed in their activities in the ballroom, while Betty whisked eggs in a large bowl in the kitchen, like nothing had taken place, like no child had been stalked, like no man had been broken.

Long after Betty had instructed the children to wash, and the boys and Bernadette had gone to bed, Ruth turned in for the night. She had drunk too much while trying to read her book. She switched off the light in the drawing room and walked up the stairs to her bedroom, with her hand on the wall to be sure. She paused at the window on the landing and looked down into the raspberry bushes in the dark. Something moved, a cat or a fox; a black shadow streaked across the lawn and disappeared under the shadow the moon cast against the garden wall.

"Hello, night thing," Ruth said to it. "Where are you going?" She leaned her forehead against the cold glass.

III

In sleep, Sarah's skirt has pulled up and the skin of her leg holds perfectly round droplets of water. If you joined them up they would make a small flow. I have a fright when I see that she is no longer asleep and is watching me watching her. I look away, but back again quickly, and she has pulled down her skirt.

The morning air is thick with wet wood burning. No one has followed us from the village, though it did not stop me waking to every mouse shuffling through the undergrowth, or roosting bird refluffing their wings. Sarah now rests her head against her knees. Father watches.

The Widow Clements comes to stand beside my father, rests her hands on his shoulders and he touches her fingers. Sarah looks up at her. Her cut lip has healed into a sharp, thin line. Cook nudges me with a foot and hands me a tin of boiled water. I sit up and place it on the floor—it is too hot to hold. She administers her discouraging breakfast to everyone, and all sit and drink in silence. I try and forget the smell of the fire the night before, the crisp, hot sweetness of it.

"Right," says my father. "Our path is as follows. We head east to the coastline. That is where my people are from, before

211

we moved inland to preach. We will get to the coast and there we will not rely on the land to produce food for us, we will take fish from the sea. We will look for someone who remembers us. There will be someone there, and we can start again." Cook makes an approving noise. The Widow Clements dances her fingers over his shoulders. She is staking her claim to him. I look away. And if there is no one? They will all be dead, I am sure of it. People forget quickly when life is hard. I watch the Widow Clements brush something from Father's hair. She has forgotten her husband. Father has forgotten Mother. And what happens to us once we have fished, once our bellies are full? Will we look for work, disperse into different families, like Cook has? Or will we turn feral and live like this together among the wolves and badgers? I don't ask these questions. I am not brave enough to.

I have a memory, from before Agnes was born, when it was just my father and me, and we stood at a stream as he taught me to fish. I was only as high as his waist and he rolled up his breeks and waded in, stood still for the longest time, watching the fast-moving water. Then he squatted down slowly, put his hands in the water and all at once pulled out a trout, sparkling in the sunlight, thrashing in his hands. My father laughed and cried, "You see, Joe! If you listen quietly for long enough, He sends his messengers!" And, still laughing, he waded back to me, the fish frantic in his hands and he gave it to me to hold. It was huge and heavy in my small arms and it thrashed and thrashed and all of it was like a raw open heart beating, mouth gaping for something I could not give it. I was afraid of the fish. It stilled, alive but accepting of my grasp, the brown back of it holding the cold reflection of the trees and the sky.

"Will we take it home for Mother?" I asked.

"No," said my father. "I only wanted you to hold the beating heart of God for a moment, just so as you knew what to look for, always in life." He took the fish back from me and lowered it into the water, let it speed off underneath the glassy surface.

Father takes a leaf out of Sarah's hair. Sarah stares straight ahead, as if she has left her body.

Sarah walks ahead of me, and the fall of her dress on the backs of her knees takes my attention. She has to gather the dress, which is too large for her small frame, in two hands to stop from tripping over the cloth. It looks a little, when she high-steps over a bramble, like she dances.

We walk all day and find nothing. The woods feel endless, like when you lie on your back and look at the sky and begin to disappear into it. More than once, I spot an arrangement of weeds and saplings that I feel I have seen before.

Sometimes the woods are dark and dense and our footsteps are necessarily slow, no faster than the tramp of a cow's heart, and then out we will come onto a clearing. Here we will rest, or, if the day has been long enough, like today, we set up camp, and always, as we do this, the rain starts to fall and falls until morning. No one talks about the strange rhythms of the woods because to speak of it out loud will make it unavoidably real.

Sarah still talks very little. The main noise comes from the Widow Clements, who is full of good tidings and expects it all to be for the best, this new start.

"We will find a little village just close to the sea, and between us we will get such work that we can secure for ourselves a small house and set up and start again, and this time with fish and eel and whatever else lives in the water. I saw the sea once as a child, and I remember more than anything the smell—so fresh and clean. And water as far as you can see. An island, and a man to row you out to it, where you can find the eggs of seabirds and take a net for herring. Have you eaten herring?" she asks the group and no one replies. "Quite delicious, a little fish, strong and salty."

There is a long silence that a lesser talker would take as a mark to be quiet.

"You won't believe it, even to see it, quite remarkable, quite remarkable." The more she talks, the less Father responds. When we walk single file, he makes sure to put Cook behind him even though she coughs and spits often into the brambles, so that the Widow Clements has to talk her ramble at Cook's back instead. It is only fear, even I know this, but all of us are afraid and manage not to drive nails of irritation into each other.

That night I hear something move in our camp. I rest a hand on my blunt knife and wait, the hairs prick up on my arms. It is Sarah, and she comes and lies down facing me. I can see the wetness in her eyes. I would like to show her the sacking cloth in my pocket and explain its significance to her, I would like to tell her about everything from the past years and I would like to feel the cold soft flesh of her inner arm against my nose and mouth. Instead I stay very still, watching.

"I'm sorry for the trouble I've caused you," she whispers in her strange hoarse voice.

"We were not much liked any more in the village anyway," I say. Though in the dark you cannot see the brown of her eyes, I know it is there. My own eyes are open to their fullest as though more can be taken in that way.

"Still," she says, "I am grateful. I know something of not being liked."

My father calls out in his sleep. We are quiet until we can be sure no one has awoken.

"I have also lost my mother and sister." I feel a rush telling her, sure she will find a connection there.

"Yes, I know, your father has told me." I am deflated and ashamed at my deflation. I wanted it to be something we shared alone. How dare he use this to talk to the girl, it should be my sadness to tell. I do not know why I think this.

"Why did they say you were a witch?" I ask, because something needs to be said. I see her shrug in the dark.

"They caught me drinking milk from one of their sows. They were angry. They are men and I am a girl."

"Did you burn down their shed?"

"How did your sister die?" she asks instead of answering my question.

"I thought Father told you?"

"He told me the woods took her."

"She wandered away and something got her."

"The woods don't take people. There's nothing to be afraid of in the woods."

"Something tore out her throat."

She shook her head. "After. It would have been after."

"My mother died when she found out."

"Because she knew."

"What?"

"Because she knew what had happened. She knew what happened to her girl."

"I don't like this talk."

"We will stop then."

Sarah puts out her hand and touches mine, which is curled in a fist on the ground. I feel it hot through me. When she takes her hand away, I am left with the feeling of her paw, strong, boned and calloused, a hard-feeling hand that has lived around the edges of the woods.

When I wake it is to the watery green of new leaves and the sound of rain falling. Back home, had the crops not failed long ago, this shower of rain in early spring would have been looked upon with pleasure, fattening the corn ears, watering the cattle and their pasture. And though we are far from that place now, I still think of it, and wonder if it rains there too, if anyone sits affront our old cottage and weaves grasses together, watching the crow-coloured mud writhing and sighing under the touch of rain. Perhaps they have burnt it. It should not matter, there is no returning to that house.

Father is up, I hear him fart, then piss into the underbush. A trail of wet woodsmoke catches my nose, and I lean up to see Cook has, as she has nearly all the mornings of my life, lit a fire, and is heating water collected from the stream.

"Where is she?" I ask her, and Cook nods to the south end of the clearing, where Sarah sits, her dress pulled over her feet, her eyes sunken from lack of sleep.

The Widow Clements is always awake before us, and goes foraging. She returns as the water in the pan starts to boil, and she holds out to Cook the nettles she has picked with the shield of her pinafore. Cook looks them over and shrugs, drops them into the water. Father comes by and stands close.

"Careful—you'll get done for witchery," says my father. He means it as a joke. Everyone looks at him. Sarah starts laughing, and then everyone looks at her.

After we've eaten the nettles, which tasted good at first because of our hunger, but leave a strange fur on the roof of the mouth, we begin to gather our things. Cook likes to extinguish and hide the evidence of a fire, but Father puts his hand up and stills her before she can run it over with earth. He stands atop a fallen log, looking into the dark of the woods in the direction we arrived from. There is a strange gait to him, his chin thrust into the air, like he is trying to catch a scent, his hands in front of him, splayed, lost somewhere in the air in front of him.

He gets down off his log.

"We go now," he says quietly, "leave everything, someone's coming."

"But—" says Cook. Father takes her wrist and gives her a wrench in the direction we are headed. She wheezes, covers her mouth with the hem of her dress and coughs pathetically into it.

"We go now," he hisses, scoops a hand under Sarah's armpit to make her stand. The widow fusses with her skirts as she runs. To see Father afraid is unsettling. I catch the mumble of other voices on the air. We run.

II

Ruth sat on the edge of the bed as Peter folded two shirts into his overnight case. It was to be, he assured her, the very last bit of work that needed tidying up before the New Year. There was a softness between them. Earlier that morning, Ruth's dream of being followed by a creature with silent feet had bled out into the bedroom. He had woken her with an arm around her waist, a look of concern on his face, and she had been so grateful to wake up that way, that they had made love almost immediately. He packed his good weekend slip-ons but no undergarments. Their conversation continued very nicely.

"I don't suppose it matters very much whether or not one rode as a child, because by now all of those muscles have quite passed on. I'm not sure I could manage even a rising trot in an easy chair."

Peter laughed. "I should like to see that." He turned to look at her. "I think you'd make a very fine sight on the back of a horse—quite striking."

There was a flattering lightness of spirit to him that Ruth had noticed on the day they met, and for a moment, leaning back on the bed, she wondered if he might make love to her again. But instead he zipped his case closed and moved around to kiss her chastely on the cheek.

"It would be a very good idea to learn a new skill—something to keep busy with." He straightened. "Who knows, if the boys took to it, we could even think of renting a stable." They stayed like that a few moments, Ruth smiling up at her husband, him smiling down at her.

"Darling, why haven't you packed any underwear?" It came out quite unexpectedly.

"What?" he asked still smiling, though she may have witnessed a flicker in his eye.

"I just wondered—you have a couple of shirts but no underwear—no spare trousers either, in fact."

"I keep some at the office."

Ruth continued smiling. "Well, that's that mystery solved then."

"Ha, yes—perhaps you really ought to see about this horse riding, rather than playing underwear detective." But something had passed between them. If she could have slowed the moment down, she would have captured the look. His eyes, asking her to drop it, telling her not to notice. And her eyes telling him back, *I cannot un-know this.*

But the moment lasted only a grain of salt.

They walked downstairs together in silence. In the hallway, as he dressed in his coat and hat, she remembered Betty had made lunch for him.

"Betty left sandwiches for your journey."

"Oh really, how beastly, some sort of ham and piccalilli disaster no doubt. There's a perfectly good dining car."

"I know, but at least take them with you." She ducked into the kitchen, where Bernadette sat doing her homework at the table. She looked up and Ruth smiled.

"Just getting Mr. Hamilton's sandwiches for him," she said.

"They're ham and piccalilli," said Bernadette dutifully.

219

"Oh, he *will* be pleased," she said as earnestly as she could.

The sandwiches were wrapped in wax paper and tied with string.

"There you are, darling," she said, handing them over while Peter stood in the open doorway looking at his watch. "Don't put them in the station bin, because if she goes into town Betty stands at that end of the platform." Peter made a drama of having to hold both his case and the sandwiches.

"Righto," he said, "see you in a few days, must dash." Another peck and he was off.

Was it not an unusual thing, to keep underwear at your office? Where in your office? Perhaps they had a special dispensation for their employees who stayed over. It seemed very unlikely. And it wasn't as if he kept a room at a hotel in London. The sound of his footsteps faded. Ruth wandered back to the kitchen, where Bernadette appeared to have been waiting for her.

She smiled again, went to open her mouth to ask what she was working on, or some other platitudinal observation, but instead she said, "Can you tell Betty that I've gone to see my sister? There's a small emergency I need to attend to. I'll return tomorrow, hopefully not late." She'd already started to back out of the door, Bernadette nodding seriously.

What she needed was her coat, her hat, her purse; all hung by the door, and she shrugged into her coat and stumbled out, searching her bag as she walked—for her chequebook, for money—and then breaking into a run on the balls of her feet so that her steps wouldn't echo in the empty street.

She got to the platform in time to see Peter board the first-class carriage, which was good, as it kept the dining car between them. She stepped up into the coach and closed the door behind her feeling her heart hammering in time with the pistons. Before they departed the platform she noticed Peter's sandwiches resting at the top of the full station bin, visible to all.

Her carriage was mercifully empty and she breathed deeply, tried to become calm. Then she began to laugh—what a ridiculous thing to do, stalk your husband because of his underwear habits. For a while she smiled and shook her head at herself, even considered getting up and moving to first class, she could surprise him and then stay at the hotel waiting for him to finish work. Why had she never thought to do that while the boys were at school? It seemed something a wife might do. She tried hard to imagine a look on his face that might be pleasing, but somehow the picture escaped her. He would more likely feel ruffled at being surprised, and it was a work trip, so he was probably sitting there working right now. Better to wait and see, and perhaps talk it through with Alice. Alice, she was fairly sure, understood this sort of thing. Mark, after all, was a member of a lunch club.

They drew into Edinburgh and a man boarded her carriage. He smelled strongly of tobacco and whisky, and the smell put her in mind of the notebook in Peter's drawer. It would have been better not to have seen it. She wouldn't like Peter to have access to her inner thoughts, wouldn't dream of writing them down. The man cleared his throat in a greeting, and she smiled, looked at her shoes and then focused her eyes out the window, just as the train started to move. The man produced a paper and made a fuss of opening it, flipping through the pages and sighing contentedly when he found the article he was looking for.

A woman with an open green wool coat and a tight yellow jumper ran down the platform, moving at the same speed as the train for a few moments. It was funny, Ruth thought, how sometimes you knew exactly how things were going to go in the moments before they happened. The woman was smiling and had red lipstick on and thick eyeliner. She was easily five years younger than Ruth, barely an adult. The man coming to meet her was Peter, and he wrapped an arm around her waist and buried his head in her neck. And then the picture was gone and left on the platform, and the conductor came to take her money.

"Where to, madam?" he asked.

"I don't know," she said very quietly, and the man with the paper looked up. To be done with the transaction, she said, "London."

There had been the slightest suggestion of a bump in the front of the woman's skirt. Ruth held her ticket in both hands, kept both feet flat on the floor for the entire journey.

"Shall we go out to eat? Or should you prefer to stay in?"

Alice had greeted her as though they had made prior plans, without surprise, and told her maid to make up the spare room. The maid looked quite unhappy at the request.

"I hope I'm not arriving at a bad time," Ruth said once the maid had gone.

"A bad time?"

"I mean just showing up like this without warning."

Alice put a hand up to her chest. "Oh, thank God. Honestly, I assumed I'd forgotten we'd arranged something—that makes me feel so much better. I'm delighted you're here. Rebecca is just annoyed because we've had a few unplanned late nights recently. In fact, what serendipity, I was just thinking it time for a drink, and Rebecca looks flatly revolted when I drink alone." Ruth smiled. "So are we going out? Or will we stay in?"

"I'm not sure I have the clothes to go out."

"You didn't bring a scrap with you?" Alice looked Ruth up and down. "I'd offer you something of mine but you're awfully long, aren't you? Come on. We'll stay in—I can mix a passable martini and make a rather efficient little sandwich—we won't involve Rebecca, she'll only pull a face."

They went into the drawing room and Ruth sat on the sofa while Alice opened the drinks cabinet. The room hadn't been in service when last she'd visited—the couple had moved in shortly after they married, but Alice had insisted on doing the interiors herself, something that had never occurred to Ruth to want to undertake. She wondered if she ought to make more of an effort with the Berwick house to make it feel like her own home.

Alice's sofa was dark red and very deep. If she leaned against its back, Ruth's feet would dangle off the end like a child's, so she perched instead and watched Alice pour one and then two drinks, the light from the window behind her cold and white. There was a wicker chair suspended from the ceiling, like a child's swing. She wondered if it was for show or if it held a person's weight. Books covered the walls in a way she couldn't imagine their mother approving of. Many of them were large books with names of artists on the spine, she guessed, though she had not heard of most of them. On a glass-topped coffee table, a statue of a man on a horse, with a large member. The horse's buttocks were more defined than they needed to be. Ruth found herself looking away from it, not because it disgusted her but because it made her feel so prudish to have noticed it in the first place. Alice saw her turn away.

"Is it a bit much?" she asked. "Mark's very into that sort of thing—he likes to buy young artists, likes to think he's giving them a helping hand. But in all honesty, I'm not sure he knows as much as he thinks he does about art."

"It's a lovely room."

"We don't let Mother in here, if that's what you're thinking— this is *our* living room. We have quite a plain ordinary room with nice kind willow print for when Mother and Father come. Mark's so lucky—his are dead." Alice handed the drink over and sat in the wicker chair to drink hers. She dislodged her feet from her shoes and curled them up underneath her. From somewhere a blue cat came and settled itself on her lap. They swayed gently together. "Darling, do relax, kick off your shoes, won't you? And tell me why, after all this time, you've finally decided to visit?"

If it was a barbed remark, it felt soft and already forgiven. She'd had no intention of telling Alice anything, but there was, after the first few sips of her drink, an overwhelming need to. She bent down and slipped her feet from her shoes. They were blistered—she hadn't thought about changing her shoes before running to get the train, and then she had walked to Alice's house, looking at the Christmas lights and trying to balance her thoughts, make sense of what she had seen in Edinburgh. She held the drink in one hand and shifted herself deep into the sofa. This room was so unlike their own drawing room, which had the puffed-out cushions, pale blue and cream stripes she had been used to in her parents' house. But Alice's house was not at all tasteful, it was something else that Ruth felt outside of. It was the kind of decor a young fashionable beautiful woman had control of. She wondered what the girl in the yellow jumper's drawing room looked like.

"I've come to understand, recently," she said, taking her time to place the words correctly, and then sipping from her drink to make sure it was all quite what she meant to say, "that Peter has another girl."

"Swine!" Alice said and her voice peeped a little. "Absolute swine, darling. When did you find out? *How* did you find out?"

"This morning. I saw them. And I have a suspicion she may be pregnant."

"Oh for God's sake." She shooed the cat off herself and came to join Ruth on the sofa. They sat at opposite ends, their feet touching.

"And what are you going to do about this? Are we thinking divorce? Mark has a great man, he'll get you sorted, and Peter's loaded, you'll come and live down here close to me, get yourself a pad, I'll introduce you to—"

"No—I, I don't think so, Alice. I don't think. I don't know."

"Have you confronted him?"

"No."

"A child. I mean Mark's no angel, but if he had children with someone else . . ."

"Has Mark had other girls? After you?"

"Oh, darling." Alice shifted herself around a little. "Well, yes, but—he's never got anyone pregnant. Men are so . . . driven by their blood. I mean if Mark didn't occasionally have a—an interlude with another woman, I wouldn't get anything done, ever. I view it as a lessening of the load, but if he did get someone else pregnant, I don't know. I would expect him to take care of it. Before I found out."

"By which you mean get rid of it?"

"By which I absolutely mean get rid of it. And you must speak to him about that. You tell him things are absolutely not allowed to progress." She leaned over and caught a nearly empty bottle of sherry that was on the sideboard with her fingertips. She motioned for Ruth to finish up her martini, which she did, and Alice poured for Ruth and for herself.

"Honestly. If I'd have known men were going to be such hard work, I'd have moved to France and found myself a lesbian."

"I suddenly feel like he had this plan all along. Like he would get me and put me in Scotland, so the boys have somewhere to retreat to. Like when they're back from school, we do this dance of being a family. Sometimes it really feels very good. And now I wonder if the whole time he's been elsewhere in his head."

"Darling Puss. Darling Puss, men just are, that's the truth of it. They are made differently, they want different things. And in order to be able to enjoy your life there are certain things that one has to accept. It's not being deluded, I won't have that—it's seeing things for what they really are, and buggering on until eventually the penny drops and you find yourself living a very fruitful life partly with them but partly with yourself. And the great thing is, they almost always die first."

Ruth thought of the path down to the sand dunes, the wind, the black lumps of tar that stuck to her boots on a walk, her jumper sleeves wet and sandy from reaching into rock pools. The quiet sigh of the house as she came home, as she saw it, and smelled it. The feeling of danger in the water. Betty's kitchen table and all its history. Cigarettes in the back garden. Perhaps it had crept into her bones and become home without her noticing.

Her drink was empty again and so was Alice's. Alice stood, took their glasses and kicked the cat out of the way, went to the drinks cabinet and brought over a new bottle of sherry and two new, more appropriate glasses. She poured uneven quantities into both and left the bottle within reach.

They sat quietly for a moment, then Alice moved forwards and took Ruth's glass from her, and set it on the floor. She held both of Ruth's hands and positioned herself so that she had to look her in the face.

"If it's more than that, it can be taken care of. I know a man who can get proof and you can move down here with us until you find something for yourself. I have two friends who are divorced and they live very happily."

It was the quiet in Alice's voice that made Ruth's eyes fill up. It was the pity. She imagined her mother's face. She imagined Michael's face, Christopher's, Betty's, even Bernadette's. She imagined the woman in the yellow jumper in her house with those people. Peter's face did not make an appearance in her thoughts, though she did find herself thinking of that ham and piccalilli sandwich, all neatly tied in its wax paper and sitting in the bin while the rain fell on it.

Alice sat back. "Well, my darling, I don't know what else to say. Those are your options. What would Antony have said to you?" On the mantelpiece was a framed black-and-white photograph of Alice's wedding day. Ludwig on his back on Alice's trail, which pooled in the foreground. Mark next to her, heels together like a penguin. Their parents to the left, her mother as proud as Ruth remembered her, her father a man on the edge of fat. Her own face and her long frightfulness a step back from the rest of them. A gap left that Antony ought to have filled, but

EVIE WYLD

of course he had been four years dead already. The distant and now even further-away dead. If he had been present, the photographer would have taken a shot of the three of them, and Antony would have draped his arms over their shoulders.

I

I take the train because I need to sleep. I want the bad coffee and packaged sandwich and the time to rest, but instead I sit upright and alert, my feet hot in their shoes as though I might have to spring from my seat at any moment. I know this feeling, of the wolfman catching up. By the time I arrive in North Berwick, I have convinced myself something is very wrong. I have this heat, a heavy heat in my body, and I scan it constantly to locate the cause of the feeling. Nothing is clear. Yes, I am sad for my sister, but I would be lying if I said there wasn't a tiny thrill that something in her life was not going to plan. Perhaps the heat came from the guilt of feeling that thrill. Then the worry that I would enter the house and find that Maggie'd turned it into a sex house with sex people.

The police have cordoned off the alleyway that is my shortcut down to the promenade. Four police cars and two vans line the street beyond it, and policemen and women stand at regular intervals down the road. I struggle to think if I've even seen one policeman before in the town. They could be here for any number of reasons.

I see a man dressed in a visi-vest sprinkling white powder onto a dark patch of the ground. I've seen that at a car accident, the powder for soaking up the blood. I think of cake.

There is a small white tent and a lady's shoe on its side at the entrance to the alleyway. I only see it for half a second, between the navy legs of the police officers who guard it, but it has a white chalk circle around it and a little paper marker by it with the number 3 on. Which could mean anything. It could be a car accident.

The shoe is brown and round-toed. The heel, a wooden blocky thing. It would have made a clopping noise as the woman walked. And then the clopping would have stopped. Along the seafront the sky begins to darken; there is a slice of sunlight left on the Bass Rock. It is golden and yellow and makes me sad.

At the house, I close the door behind me and I don't take my coat off, or even unsling my bag from my shoulder. I am tired. I sit down in the kitchen with the lights off and stay there, looking at a damp patch where the wall meets the ceiling, and thinking of nothing I can put a name to.

"Maggie?" I call out. No reply. She is gone. I sit until I am hungry and then I get up and take a slice of bread out of the bag on the kitchen counter and spread on some peanut butter. I struggle out of one half of my coat, recognise the urge to pee but ignore it and sit back down with my shoed feet on the table to eat my dinner. Something has followed me. Some feeling of certainty that my life is a series of boring mistakes or fortunate accidents that will amount to nothing more than a puck of flesh-coloured cake, blood soaked up by flour.

I don't get up again until the need to pee overtakes me. I shed my coat and leave it in the hallway. I sit too long on the toilet so that when I stand up I have pins and needles in my thighs. I stare at the toothbrush on the edge of the basin, cannot imagine where the energy would come from to use it.

I scratch at my scab to feel a reassuring wetness on the tips of my fingers, but it doesn't yield tonight. I have started to put lights on around the house when the doorbell rings. It has just turned 10 p.m. It is Maggie, and she is drunk.

"I left you a key," I say.

"Can you feel it?" she asks, grabbing for my hands as she enters, looking glassily into my eyes and letting me take an inhalation of her beery breath.

"Feel what?" She doesn't answer but pushes past me down the hall to the bathroom. She pulls her tights down and sits on the toilet, and I try to walk past without looking but she calls me back once her flow has started.

"Viv. Viviane. Don't you feel it?"

"Feel what?" I say again, on the verge of anger. I feel sure I was just about to get going on my evening—the computer is only sleeping.

"That your life is a meaningless lump of shit and you can die and no one will give one single dry fuck."

She comes out of the bathroom pulling up her tights—she yanks them over her dress and does not correct the problem. She goes to the kitchen window, looks out, drags down the blind, then she goes to the fridge but finds nothing relevant to her needs, just the green bottles. She starts opening cupboards.

"Where do you keep the drink?"

"I don't have any left." That's a lie.

"Seriously?"

She looks at me like I've disappointed her dreadfully. The silence deepens between us. If I am passive and silent and give her nothing to grab hold of, she may still go quietly to bed. I'd like to be alone, I'd like not to drink, I'd like to sleep to get the feeling off me, have the day finished.

"You *do* feel it. I see it on you. I bet you didn't even take your coat off, you just sat right down and waited, didn't you?" She is smiling because she knows she is correct. The pattering murmur of my heart, a toothpick-sized spear of ice on the back of my neck.

"You felt so mutherfucking hopeless—no hope." She holds up her index finger to me, to bring home her point, and says again, "No. Mother. Fucking. Hope. You've got to fight it, Viv. You've got to acknowledge it, and then—" her voice now not much more than a croak—"you've got to pick yourself up, and fucking down something until the feeling goes. You've got to have an end point in sight—your job tonight is to get your body drunk—you have to believe that there's worth in that. You have to."

"You're not making any sense."

"You," she says, with complete confidence, "know that what I am saying makes perfect sense." I wonder if she is only drunk, or on something else as well. There's a flicker of danger, something manic about her. "That smell—all the fuckin' pigs, and flowers and the fire, and all the holes in the ground, everything clogged with the mud." She looks at me, her eyes glassed over; she rocks a little, not unbalanced, just like the blood pumps through her strongly, like it wants to get out.

I go to the drawing room and take the whisky from the drinks cabinet. Back in the kitchen, I take two mugs and pour large measures. Maggie says nothing but fixes on my eyes as she takes her drink from me. We stand with eyes locked, drinking. Inside I am repeating, *She's right, she's right*, but I don't know what about. My scanner is picking up nothing. I don't know anything other than once the glasses are empty they are refilled and we drink again, and only after the second mugful do I realise I have yet to turn the light on in the kitchen and we are standing in the dark.

There is a knock at the door, steady thudding. One, two, three, four, five. We both jump, then Maggie holds her finger up and mouths, "Don't move."

The wolfman.

After a pause the thudding returns, faster and louder. I go to look out of the blinds to see who is there, but she holds my arm and shakes her head. When the thudding stops and several minutes have passed she takes the bottle from me and pours again, but this time her hand is shaking.

I wake in the night on the sofa, hearing the back door close. My coat is over my head. I find Maggie necking a pint of water at the kitchen sink.

She is holding her phone, staring at it in disbelief. "Listen to this," she says. "*You taste like peaches.*"

She turns and looks at me, eyes round and ringed by mascara.

"I do not fucking taste like peaches." She raises her arms up like she is soliloquising to an audience. "I taste of soil and salt and the mutherfucking ocean. The fucking depths of the darkest parts of the ocean with the oil slicks and the scaled fish and the mutherfucking sea scorpions. That's what I taste of. And sometimes, beetroot."

She smacks the phone down hard on the table and rolls a cigarette. She is still drunk. I don't have it in me to ask her to go back outside to smoke. I open the window instead.

"Do you ever scare yourself?" she says as she moistens the edge of her paper. "Do you ever look at yourself in the mirror for such a long time that you start to see something else? Like there's someone else under the skin. Have you ever looked in the mirror and deliberately made an ugly face, bared your teeth, growled and snarled and become suddenly aware that there is something else inside of you that you're not letting out? Like we're the wolves, and that's why we're hunted."

She leans back on the sofa and lights up, takes in one long draw and lets the smoke curl out of her. I know I am not expected to give an answer.

"It's the same as when you lie in bed thinking bad thoughts—those thoughts are in your head. None of this 'it's all a dream' bullshit. Where do you think the dreams come from? When you're looking at yourself, growling, flecking spit on the mirror, that's just as much you as when you're grocery shopping or sucking a cock, or cooking a Christmas fucking ham."

"I need some air," I say. It occurs to me that Maggie is not well.

We go outside in the dark and climb the wall to look at the sea with the moon striped on it. It is cold but not oppressively so. Maggie is quiet now. The cigarette lights her face. She looks divinely sad.

My phone buzzes. *Hey, let me know when you're back from Scotland. Had a really good time yesterday.*

"Who's that?" Maggie asks. It irritates me, this presumption that my life is something to be made available to her, that it is something with which to pass the time. I think of lying, but it would be one inconsequential piece of information exchanged for another.

"Just some guy I'm seeing." I am not seeing Vincent. Not in the way Maggie will interpret it. But I like how it sounds—casual—like maybe we're having sex, like maybe Vincent is some dark and attractive man person who comes and stands at my window at night, who is interested maybe even beguiled by me.

"Some guy you've been seeing?" A long pause, while she looks at me like she can't gather her thoughts in her head. "What the fuck?" She puts out her cigarette on the wall. "Who?"

"Why is that so hard to believe?"

Maggie shifts in her seat. "Just. I didn't think you had anyone."

I shrug, but I feel a quiet, deep satisfaction that I have surprised her.

"It's nothing serious," I say, like I'm brushing her off. Secrets—the careful drip-feeding of your life to make it seem tantalising.

"What does he say?" Not, Who is he? Not, What is his name? Not, Where did you meet? I don't reply.

She looks up, awaiting an answer.

"Wait—have you fucked?"

"Jesus, Maggie, it's none of your business." She holds eye contact, trying to read me.

"Just. What is he? A wolf? Or a fox?"

"What?"

"Oh, I don't fuckin' know. I don't know."

I go to bed, leaving Maggie out on the wall as the sun starts to come up and the first birds begin to sing.

I wake feeling worse than before. I must stop drinking. I think about the times in the past week where I have drunk too much and eaten badly and I imagine being able to go back and pluck them out of my past so that by now I am clean and healthy. I wish I was a female detective from the telly who deals with her feelings by running and running until she doubles over and sobs or vomits up the feeling. I would probably vomit before I even made it to the beach.

Maggie has left a note saying she has gone to work. I wonder when she left it. I put on a green woollen hat and my coat and I go down to the sea to clear my head. I can't see to the far end of the bay where the police were yesterday, but I walk slowly in that direction. The tide is out and I find myself heading towards the rock pools. The spot is one I have visited often since I was a little girl. The place is always just the same, the limpets I could swear dot the rocks in just the same pattern as they did when I was a kid, the waves roll in the same rhythm, a gull cawing, the bark of the dog, the rake of the wind on my face. It is always precisely as I remember it, not a detail out of place, and I search the rock pools for some scar of what has been there, but there's never anything to give it away. Nothing. The rock is indifferent.

A girl walks by me, I see her from the corner of my eye, but I can't move my eyes from the space in front of me. She goes onto the edge where the waves send white spray high into the air and stands looking out at the Bass Rock. When I look up, she is gone, and my heart races because she must have gone over the edge, where the sea is roughest, but when I reach the spot, there is nothing there, only the shallow foam of the retreated water, and a hollowness in my stomach.

Back at the house, Christopher is waiting on the doorstep.

"Hello, old thing," he says and kisses me lightly on the cheek.

"Oh, hello—sorry, I didn't know you were coming. You don't have your key?"

"I suppose I do, yes, but I didn't want to alarm you. I don't like to just turn up unannounced, but you know—the signal here is no good at all. Is it OK that I've come?"

I open the door and smile. "Has Deborah been in touch?"

236

"What? Oh. No, poor Deborah. I don't imagine this place'll sell for some time—do you?" There is something disarming about the way he asks my opinion, like I might have insight.

I shrug.

"No, really, I was in Edinburgh, and I had some news, and I sort of came here on a whim, I hope you don't mind—are you in the middle of something? Because I can go, I don't want to interrupt your day." He has started to back down the steps and I find myself reaching out and holding his arm, which embarrasses us both.

"No, come in. Good news? Or bad news? Would you like a coffee?" I let us into the hallway and Christopher closes the front door quietly.

"Please," he says to the coffee and we start towards the kitchen. "Yes, well. It's not good news really, it's a friend of mine from school, one of the few I'm still in touch with—he died yesterday."

He has his hat in his hand, his coat still on.

"Oh. Oh, I'm sorry." And then I can think of nothing to say.

"Yes," he says, turning the hat, smiling. "Yes, it is rather tragic, I'm afraid. And anyway, I just thought I'd like to talk to someone, silly really, and as I say I don't want to be a nuisance, and I've always rather admired you. I hope you don't mind me saying that."

I let out an inappropriate snort. "Me?"

"You're just so like your mother."

He hangs his hat on the valet and begins to shrug out of his coat. I leave my coat in a lump on the floor. I've never thought of myself as being like Mum. Mum is capable and organised and contained. She can make me feel like an old sock.

"Yes," he says, answering an unasked question.

In the kitchen I fill the kettle. He puts his hands in his pockets and watches as I put it back into its dock and flip the switch. The noise of it is welcome. "Shall we have a drink?" he says. "I have brought a bottle of whisky with me." I turn off the kettle.

"Yes," I say, "let's." We go into the dining room and I take two crystal glasses positioned by Deborah so that morning light passes through them and onto the breakfast table on which she has done what she called *a minimal lay* with a coffee pot and silver toast rack. There are two silver partridges in the middle of the table, *to add amusement*.

As Christopher pours, the clock in the hallway chimes eleven. I think *Could be worse, could be before ten.*

"The world does conspire to make one feel guilty, doesn't it?" he says, and then briefly clinks his glass with mine before throwing the drink back. I sip my drink, my stomach not yet settled from the night before. It occurs to me that perhaps he'd rather not drink alone, and I was just the person closest when he got the news.

"Who was he? Your friend?" We sit opposite each other on the window seat.

"Wally. Kind, sensitive chap. We used to share a bunk sometimes, in winter. He came here once or twice in fact—after Dad was installed at Edinburgh, and Deborah was born." Here he seems to stumble a little at the memory. "We have to give poor old Deborah a chance. I always feel rather bad I don't know her better, and she had a terrible time, I gather, with Dad and her mad mother." He puts down his glass for a moment and rubs his legs vigorously as though trying to get the blood flowing there. I know the tic, I recognise it—the urge to tear off the skin. "We'd row out to the Bass Rock and smoke dope, Wally and I, after your mother had gone to London."

238

"Was he sick?"

"No, not that I know of. Unless you mean depressed, which I expect he was. He's not the first of them though."

"Oh?"

Christopher pours another large measure. He looks away for a moment. He is looking at the Bass Rock, which today is far in the distance. A rust of seaweed surrounds it like a frill.

"It must take enormous strength to hang oneself, don't you think?"

"Oh. Did Wally?"

"He did. He did."

There is a gap where I know I should speak, but I don't.

"Him and me and your dad shared this thing we used to call the Wolfman—a sort of dread feeling—like one's being chased by something. Silly really, rather childish, but truth be told I do still get it sometimes."

I blink. Perhaps Dad told me about the Wolfman. Perhaps that's how I know exactly the feeling and exactly the beast.

"It's close to the feeling of homesickness. The only thing for it is distraction, and I came down last night and called Wally's phone from the station and got his daughter, poor thing." There is a long silence. I can think of nothing to say. "Of course, Michael and I used to recognise it in each other, we used to know when it was coming and be able to head it off at the pass sometimes.

I make an unintentional sound—it was supposed to be a contemplative *hmm*, but what comes out sounds more like a yelp.

He reaches over and squeezes my hand realising too late that none of us are hand squeezers in the family. The squeeze which started out natural becomes confusing and he pats my hand twice and stands to look out of the window. There is a suggestion in his breath of great emotion. After a moment's composure, he turns and says, "Do you know I almost killed a man a few years ago?" He looks happy.

"I didn't know that, no." My stomach feels burned, but I can see there will be no getting out of this sober. I refill my glass.

"I'd gone on a little holiday on my own. It was springtime, and I wanted to walk the Tennyson Trail—have you done that one?" I shake my head. "Very lovely, and only one golf course. I didn't take the car, because, and you won't believe this—it's cheaper to rent a car on the island and buy a train ticket than to drive and take the car over. Appalling what those people get away with—and to think some islanders commute every day. They have to take their cars. Quite frightful."

There is something forlorn in his digression. I wonder if he had already started drinking before he came to see me, and then I feel stupid, because of course he had.

"Anyway, had a lovely walk, was feeling very pleased with myself and, back on the mainland, I got the train from the ferry—they still have the old trains on that line, the ones you open and close yourself. No locks on them, you just pull down the window and open them from the outside."

"Oh yes?"

Christopher swirls the whisky in his glass. Outside the sound of seagulls. The rubbish truck making its rounds, I hear the beeps as it reverses.

"And I look over, and there was this old man sitting there, and I thought fuck and shit. My old housemaster. I recognised him at once. Charles Fucking Lahore. And I thought, if I go and sit opposite him and I calmly open the window and then the door, I can just push him out." He chuckles to himself. "I put on my gloves so that they wouldn't find my prints on the door handle. I could feel it, like I'd already done it, like when you're walking and you see the point you're heading towards and you can feel it drawing you to it. It was a straight-forward task that I would carry out, and perhaps no one would miss him. And even if they did, I thought, if I got caught, I imagined all those boys—all of us old men now—and I thought of those of us left opening up their papers at the breakfast table and reading about it, and the comfort of that, and I was sitting there smiling to myself about that.

"I hadn't noticed we'd come into Brockenhurst and that he was trying to get off the train. And I'd missed my chance. He couldn't do it, though, he couldn't get the handle up. I sat there and I watched him struggle—he was very old and very weak, just a bundle of sticks really. He turned to me with this smile, a *Can you help an old man, dear boy* smile, and I smiled back. I got up and I opened the door for him, and he wobbled out and I passed him his briefcase, which had his initials on. And he said to me, *Thank you so much, dear boy*, and I said, *You're quite welcome*. And then I said, *Have a good day, sir*. And he gave me a little look then, when I said *Sir*, but not much of one. And I didn't say or do anything else." Christopher keeps his eyes on the water all the time he speaks. There is a very light tremble in his voice.

"What did he do to you?" I didn't expect to ask the question, but when it falls out of me, he does not flinch.

"There was one time I got caught smoking. That was what gave me away, he'd seen the smoke from across the pitch—I was also drinking—one started rather young in those days—not like now of course. I can't recall if that was better or worse than smoking at the time. There was this beech tree at the edge of the cricket pitch and I kept a bottle of brandy in there, for sensible moments, and suddenly he was there. And he said, *I'm not going to punish you now. You're not going to know when I'm going to punish you, but when I call you, then you'll know.* And after a week or two I forgot about it. I thought he had forgotten about it. My brandy was still in the tree, he hadn't confiscated anything. I think there was even a home visit, and then when we went back, there was some kind of masters' dinner, midway through term, and I got sent for in the middle of the night. I go down in my pyjamas and there he is, drunk as anything, in his gown and his mortarboard, and his cane, and he's pacing up and down his room, swishing it about, like he's either excited or furious. Of course now, looking back, I'm quite sure it was cocaine. He had a cigar going. He made me stand in front of his desk. And he said, *Hamilton, strip.*"

My big toes point straight upwards pressing against the tops of my boots. Horror is a physical thing. I regret asking the question.

"And he thrashed me for some time, taking breathers, having a drink here and there, pausing to look out the window and hum a tune, puff on his cigar. Broke my nose rather badly, which is why it has this rather attractive bump in it." He touches the bridge of his nose, where it's skewed slightly. "And then when he was tired, and I should think I was getting too bloody to keep in his room, he ordered me back to bed. He said, *There's something you won't forget in a hurry.* And he was so pleased with himself."

There is a silence, in which both of us look at the floor.

"Anyway," he says with a chuckle. "Really I ought to have killed the bastard, it would have been absolutely worth it. I could have shouted *There's something you won't forget in a hurry* as he tumbled out of the train—it would have been glorious."

"How old were you?"

"I expect I was fourteen."

"Couldn't you tell anyone?"

Christopher looks up at me and for the first time since he started talking we have eye contact.

"Who? I'm afraid our father had his attention elsewhere—and dear old Ruth, you know. It was hard to tell what she was thinking. Your father and I only started calling her Mum in our twenties, because we sensed she needed it. She wasn't our mother. And you know, even if Mother had been alive, I just don't know. You didn't report these things. It was all part of life, we were led to believe. And honestly there was much worse that went on. Your poor father had a beastly time. He was a dreamy sort of person, and very pretty."

Christopher seems to snap a little out of his thoughts, perhaps remembering who I am to that pretty boy.

"In actual fact, there was a time just after all that went on that I considered saying something. I thought up a way of talking to Ruth about it—I'd run it past your mother actually. I was going to talk to Ruth and tell her. I was going to ask if she could convince our father to take us out. I rehearsed it and everything, went down on those rocks right there—" he points with his glass out of the window—"and practised it into the wind. There was this vicar here at the time, he was a real creep, he was all connected with the schoolmasters, had this thing about the cold—he encouraged them to turn off the heating and make us have cold showers in term time, said it brought us closer to God. Anyway, he found me out there, and I don't know if he heard anything, but he just had this way about him that implied he knew whatever you were thinking. Ghastly man, so convinced he was sitting on the right hand of God. Do you believe in God, Viv?"

It takes me by surprise. "I—no. No, I suppose I don't."

243

"Not many of your generation do, do you? It was rather built into us. Not your mother, though."

"Mum believes in ghosts."

"Yes, well, those she has seen with her own eyes. But anyway, like a strike from God, before I quite had the courage there was an accident and Ruth lost her baby, and after that I really couldn't bring it up. It was too much. And she was quite different after that. Dear old Ruth. I expect she was quite terrifying when you were small."

"I didn't know she had a baby."

"No, well, she went out walking on the rocks or something, and she was quite far along, and something happened, and anyway, she lost the baby. Rather horrible for her, and for our father, though he was away. And Dad, rather hideously of him, left quite soon after."

"A catastrophe."

"Yes! Yes I suppose it was." He laughs, pours again. "Funny how things all meet at once like that sometimes."

"I'm so sorry all that happened." It is an awkward thing to say, it is just like the hand squeeze, but I have to say something. Christopher gallantly doesn't let it fall flat. He refills my glass, though it already has a large measure in it.

"Well, you know, I was lucky in many ways. I'm still alive. They were beastly non-stop to"—there is a pause which I interpret as *your father*—"a lot of the other boys. And I suppose you might have heard about the drama when they looked into it however long ago."

"Didn't your housemaster get into trouble, even then?"

"Oh no. What he was doing was thought of as rather quotidian for the time. As I said, there were worse things going on."

Beastly.

"I do so wish I had thrown him from the train."

"Yes."

"Well," says Christopher, "to my friend Wally."

"Wally," I say, and we clink glasses again.

When I was eleven, I stayed over at a friend's house and woke in the night knowing something dreadful was coming. I stayed still for the longest time, whispered my friend's name, but she didn't stir. I crawled out of bed and went down the hallway to find the telephone, called home at 4 a.m. Dad answered, and before I'd spoken three words he said *I'm on my way, just hang tight*, and he collected me with a blanket from the front step, posted a note through the letterbox and drove me home in silence, the orange street lights streaking the wet pavement.

It is not fully dark but the promenade has a ghostly feel. The girl is late. The parcel has a little moisture seeping out, it has left a small stain on her dress where she was not careful. The way back is cut in half by crossing through the woods. The seep from the stewing steak is growing.

The truth is the girl met her friend and they had sat back to back on a bench at the shore, and watched the gannets rise and fall off the rock, sharing a bottle of cider her friend had stolen off her father's farm. The friend produced in the girl a warmth of feeling that no one else did. It was not just the cider that kept them talking, it was a need to tell her, to know her and the peculiar feeling of her friend's shoulder blades pressed against hers, interlocking wings. She thought of the other girl's hair, washed in hard soap and pinned up on the top of her head with leaves of it snaking down her dark neck.

Entering the woods she is distracted for a moment again by the leak of her package—the cook will complain the meat has been fed with water, and the girl will have to hide the hem of her dress, or pretend her monthlies have surprised her.

She sees ahead of her the master's oldest son, and keeps her head down. Close up a smell of flowers. He touches his brim at her, doesn't slow his step, "Evening," he says and she dips her head but says nothing. She glances behind her twice afterwards, but he has gone.

She did not tell her friend she had allowed the footman to do what he wanted in the hope that the feeling about her friend would be replaced with something more in keeping with nature. The footman had quietly toiled away, and she had felt nothing other than a blistering from his dirty hands.

When she hears the twigs breaking behind her, she feels something rolling over in her stomach, and knows she has made an error. There is such a sharp scratch suddenly in the air that she drops her package and begins to run, doubts herself only a second, thinks of the fury of Cook when she comes home late and empty-handed, but there is the master's son, his hat and coat gone, his stick raised above his head, running fast and silent at her.

She scrambles off the path, an animal part of her tries to hide among the dead leaves and bracken, the damp black soil, and he pauses, catches sight of her white hand glowing in the dark and is on her, and no scream comes from her, the best she can hope for is that nobody finds out, she shouldn't have leaned up against her friend, she shouldn't have drunk the cider, and been late, she shouldn't have taken the shortcut, he pushes his thumbs into the soft dip in her throat like he is pushing through the thick skin of an orange.

The Law

I

In London the sky outside my window is white and the tree-tops black against it; they sway with the first winds of a storm we've been promised. I have a cold glass of water and it rests on my belly. I drink from it whenever the silence feels too deliberate. We are lying in the crumpled remains of my bed. The previous twenty-five minutes of sex have been loud and . . . I am trying to find the correct adjective to describe them. Urgent? No, Vincent had not seemed urgent, he had seemed confident the sex would happen. Passionate? Still wrong—we're not young enough for that to be the right word. It was not slow but it was hard. Animal? That's closer. But it was not as erotic as that sounds. Unhurried but hard. That's as close as I get.

At any rate we have ended up between the sheet and the mattress protector. I am glad of the mattress protector—a Christmas present from Katherine long ago—she had felt it would lead me in the right direction.

"What," Vincent says, "is your favourite food?"

I put down the glass and pull the sheet up to cover my front. He pulls the cover back off and rests his hand on my belly.

"I like seafood."

"Which one?"

"I eat a lot of clams."

"I don't know if that's sexy or not," he says.

"Probably not, they're mostly tinned. What about you?"

"Hmmm?"

"What do you like to eat? Don't say something disgusting about clams, I won't laugh."

"Er." He is nuzzling my shoulder. "I like the flesh of a freshly fucked woman." His teeth catch a little on my skin.

"Tickling." I flinch. "I hate being tickled, which is not an invitation." This is always a stupid thing to say, it is always received as an invitation.

Vincent sits upright in bed and makes little bunny ears with his fingers, fixing me with a peculiar look, his teeth bared.

"What are you supposed to be, the fucking Easter bunny?"

He carries on staring, moving closer, begins sort of purring or growling. I have missed something. He straddles my chest and his thighs clamp tight around me. He bends down close to my face. I remain smiling, because there is a joke I'm not getting and that is all it is.

"I am the thing that watches you through your window at night," he whispers. There is a moment, just a pulse, like when you step out into the road and a car sweeps by close enough that you feel it as a wind on your face, and you feel it to the tips of your fingers, but then it's gone and what remains is anger.

"Can you get off me please? You're heavy."

Vincent takes down his bunny ears, and I think he will dismount but instead he begins to tickle me.

"Oh fuck off!" I go to roll him off, expecting him to allow me but he does not, so I slap at his chest, "Get off me," but he keeps going, digging at my ribs, that awful feeling coming on me, the loss of breath, the loss of control, and I hit him hard in a panic, make contact with his ear, and he grabs my wrists and holds me down and the panic worsens. "What the fuck?" I hear myself say over and over again, because no other words will come, and the breath is gone. He lowers his face so that his nose touches mine and he sits staring into my eyes, close up, squeezing hard with his thighs and his hands on my wrists, breathing through his nose like a bull, and I say, "What the fuck are you doing?" tears in my voice but he remains silent, his head pushing down on mine.

It feels like it goes on for a long time. And then he sits up and gets off me and walks to the loo without saying anything, closes the door. I lie in bed for a moment then I get up and pull on my jeans and a T-shirt, am fumbling for my bag when he comes back in, brushing his teeth with my toothbrush.

"What the fuck you doing?" he asks through a mouthful of foam.

"What the fuck am *I* doing?" is all I can think to say.

"Yeah," he says. "What the fuck are you doing? Why are you dressed? I was going to make some clams or something."

"Vincent—what the hell was that?"

He casts his eyes about the room. "What? How'd you mean—is there a spider?"

"What you just did."

He holds out the toothbrush and looks at it. "Are you angry I used your toothbrush?"

"No—what, I don't understand what that was, just now, in bed."

"What are you saying?" A look of horror comes over him. He swallows as much of the foam as he can.

"The tickling."

He exhales. "Jesus," he says and smiles. "Fuck, for a minute I thought you were going to say I raped you or something."

"The tickling, it was not OK."

"The tickling?"

"Yes, the fucking tickling." The more I speak the more stupid I feel. "You made that face and then you tickled me."

He narrows one eye. "You're angry I tickled you?" He sounds so very confused. I feel so very stupid. "Sorry, did I miss something?"

"I told you I hate being tickled."

"Yeah, but so does everyone—and anyway, you knew the moment you said that, you knew that you were going to get tickled. That's how it works. It's an invitation. Fuck, you want me to apologise to you because after fucking you, I *tickled* you? Jesus Christ, I'm so sorry." He turns round and walks back into the bathroom, slamming the door. I sit on the edge of the bed, embarrassed.

I meet Katherine at the Southbank and we have coffee. She is disordered. Her face is puffy, like she's been sleeping too much. When she takes a tissue out of her coat pocket, an unwrapped tampon comes with it as well as half a dozen old receipts.

"Shit," she says.

"How is it at Mum's?" She blows her nose on the tissue. We are in the unlikely position where I know I have a pristine pack of tissues in my bag, and Katherine is blowing her nose on some rough loo roll that has twisted and come apart in her pocket. It leaves fluff on her nose. I don't offer her one of my balsam-covered ones. It would be unkind.

"It's fine. Mum's giving me space. She tries to make me do the puzzles in the paper with her in the morning, but that's it."

"Do you want to talk about what's going on?"

"No," she says. We sit for a moment in the quiet. We both drink our coffees. Next to us a woman wrangles a baby on her lap while trying to get a forkful of quiche into her mouth. She is only just successful. Katherine watches her without trying to disguise it. The woman colours a little and sits back, unlacing the baby's fingers from her hair.

"I had an abortion about six weeks ago," Katherine says.

I nod. "It was the right thing to do."

"Yes. It was."

"I'm sorry, though. Was it awful?"

"Not really. I just wondered if it had something to do with why I feel so . . . unhinged. The hormones."

We sit with our coffees, drinking them slowly. What we will do once the coffee is gone is a concern.

"Do you want another one?" I ask.

"A baby?"

"A coffee."

"Oh. But then what?" she says. She puts her hands over her face and pushes. I hear the wet noise of pressure on her eyeballs. She sniffs and looks up like she's risen from a deep sleep.

"He just won't stop calling. And texting."

"Turn your phone off."

"I'm scared to. It just sits there collecting his . . . pain. He sent one last night saying he was outside Mum's and if I didn't come out he was going to *do something*."

"What does that mean?"

She shrugs.

"Find a good therapist?"

Katherine smiles; it is a rarity to be able to make her smile and I am caught unawares by the warm feeling that floods through me.

"He's just so lost and hurt," she says. "I didn't expect him to react this way, but I think maybe he really does love me."

I pick aggressively at the quick of my thumbnail and then start to bite it. His hand on my back, his mouth on mine. What would a good person do at this point? Tell her it doesn't matter if he does love her—it only matters that she does not love him? Admit to her we kissed, so that she can see him as the creep he is? Admit to myself we fucked once or in reality twice, but the second time I quit it halfway through, if you count a whole fuck to be from penetration to ejaculation. I stand up, and she looks at me.

"What are you doing?"

I sit down, and scratch vigorously at my leg.

"Nothing."

"Are you all right? You don't look all right."

"Please stop that."

"Stop what?"

"I'm not the one that's not OK this time. Stop trying to be extra good by being kind to me while you're falling apart."

Ordinarily, this kind of snipe would spark decades-old bickering between us, which would end in a silence of a fortnight until she suggests a drink or dinner with Mum and then we carry on like nothing has happened. If I'm honest, that is what I'm hoping for. Instead she makes a face I do not recognise. She opens her mouth wide and silently, I think for a second she's going to be sick, but she's crying. I don't recall ever seeing that. The reddening of eyes, at Dad's funeral, a flick away of a tear, nothing more than an irritant greenfly—but this is the picture of physical pain. She covers her face quickly when she sees my look of alarm. I take out my fancy tissues.

"Hey, sorry," I say, "here." I push one into her clenched fist. Her hand is cold. The woman with the baby leaves her half-eaten quiche and takes herself and her child away from us.

Katherine makes no sound in her crying, but she cries for a long time, hiding her face. She doesn't get up to go to the toilets because I can see she is not capable of moving. I chew my thumb, taste the blood, scratch and scratch at my leg but frustratingly it will not bleed.

She holds the tissue to her face and whispers, "Thank you. Thank you."

I can't be the bad person to her right now. Even if it might help her to know Dom was as bad as we all suspected. I'm too afraid of what I did and who I am and what it means that I did that.

Katherine sniffs deeply. She shakes herself down like a horse after a long run.

"Did Dad ever talk to you about Dom?" she asks.

"About Dom?"

"Yeah—he would never tell me what he really thought. Did he like him? Did he think he was a good man?"

I pause.

"I believe his exact words were, *He'll make Katherine a perfectly decent first husband.*"

For a moment I think Katherine is crying again, but she's laughing. She rests her forehead on the table and hiccups a little.

"What an absolute bitch," she says. "I miss him."

II

Christmas was to be just the children's maternal grandparents, Peter's being dead, and Ruth's being not inclined to make the journey when the grandchildren weren't, as Ruth's mother had put it in a voice imploring to be understood, *anything to do with us*. The wedding had been a situation they did not want to repeat, Elspeth's mother Judith sobbing openly during the vows, Ruth's own mother with not a shred of sympathy—she had lost her only son after all, which was surely worse than losing a daughter—kept her mouth a line and muttered audibly about Americans to her father. Even Peter, who had the ability to drift above awkward social moments, had sweated as he placed the ring on her finger. Elspeth's younger sister Pauline loudly proclaiming to guests how their sister would have livened things up at the wedding breakfast, her brother John recounting the foods that had been served at *Peter's last wedding*.

Since her trip to London, as Ruth made herself think about it, she'd been noticing the urge to break things. Like she had with Betty's mixing bowl, though she couldn't just go around smashing the crockery. Instead she had crept into Peter's study while he was out and snapped three of his pencils in half, and at another time, she tore all of the pages out of her school copy of *Pride and Prejudice*. There was a pair of very stupid

258

brown-and-white Staffordshire dogs on the mantelpiece that she had her eye on, but she hadn't quite worked out the best course of action with those. They were, she knew, rather expensive, and had been a wedding gift from Pauline. To break both at once would look rather suspicious.

The Sandlings arrived with the same fanfare they always did. So loud, so obnoxiously fun. Mrs. Sandling wore a hat with a large drooping white feather in it which she immediately forced the boys to stroke, telling them it was ostrich, from Africa, and all about the ostrich egg the size of Michael's head. Ruth's mother would have been unable not to flinch at the vulgarity of it, but Ruth managed to smile and take the coats that were handed to her and accept the cheek kiss from Denis Sandling whose moustache smelled of old tobacco. He held her by the arms and looked into her face. "How are you, old lady?" he asked, and moved her out of the way of the children before she could answer. At the children he sang:

> There was a young lady called Hart
> Who felt that she needed to fart
> She stepped outside
> And to her surprise
> Blew over a horse and a cart.

"Denis," said Judith Sandling sharply, "will you please not swear in front of the children?"

"They love it, and anyway, that's not proper swearing—we'll get on to that after lunch, won't we, chaps?"

Both boys smiled dutifully. It was confusing for them, she supposed. They must associate their grandparents with losing their mother, but their grandparents always acted like clowns when the boys were around, and the moment they stepped out of the room, Judith howled like a wounded animal, at a volume that the children could no doubt hear. Denis blew a loud raspberry that finally tipped them over the edge and they giggled. He then pulled a coin out from behind both boys' ears and while they each held them in their palms, he ruffled their hair so that the partings Ruth had so mindfully combed in that morning were ruined. It didn't matter of course. It was important the partings had been there for the Sandlings to see. It was up to them to ruffle them or not. She had done her part, upheld her side of the bargain.

Ruth hung the coats and went to fetch the tray of drinks she had laid out. Betty was up at Landbrooke with Bernadette, and Ruth both missed her and was relieved not to have more witnesses as she failed to deliver the Christmas the Sandlings expected.

Pinned to the glassware cupboard she had written out a list.

11:45–12:15 Arrival
12:15–1:45 Drinks and canapés

She took a pencil and put a line through the first item, as if she had achieved something already. The jug of snowball had separated a little as they had arrived closer to 12:15, so she stirred it with a wooden spoon, checked its temperature and poured. Judith of course refused her glass, Denis looked confused by the bright red cherry.

"They're snowballs," Ruth explained, "for Christmas." She had thought they would have been all the rage in America. "Not that—that's a maraschino cherry." She had had Alice send her a jar up from London specially.

260

"And what's in the drink?" asked Denis, sniffing it and failing to disguise his mistrust.

"Lemonade, brandy and egg white."

"Egg?"

"Yes, but that's just for texture."

"Do you have perhaps just a simple glass of sherry?" Judith asked.

"*Egg*. You don't say," Denis said quietly to himself and took a sip. He pulled a face that was not entirely wretched. "You know what—that's not too bad." He smacked his lips together as if considering the taste, then set the glass down on the occasional table next to him. "Try it, Judy, you'll surprise yourself."

"I'm just not such a fan of eggs."

"It doesn't taste of egg, really, honey."

"Still. It's the thought of it that turns my stomach."

"I'm sure Ruth can find you a sherry, Judith," Peter said and looked at Ruth expectantly.

Back in the kitchen Ruth opened a new bottle of sherry and looked at the mutinous devilled eggs she had made. Was it worse to serve them or to pretend she hadn't made appetisers? The book had described devilled eggs as *a guaranteed crowd-pleaser*. But now it seemed an altogether disgusting idea.

She tipped the contents of the plate into the bin and poured Judith's sherry. She fought the urge to dip one of the binned eggs into the glass. Then she poured some for herself and drank it standing at the bin. She'd had her first drink of the day just after nine o'clock, a teacup of brandy. "A breakfast drink," she had said out loud to herself.

She listened for a moment outside the door of the drawing room.

"So, boys," said Judith, "what did Santa Claus bring you?"

"I got a potato gun," said Michael. Judith made a noise as though she had been told something offensive again.

"And Christopher, what did he bring for you?"

"A Swiss army knife."

"A knife? A knife and a gun."

Ruth entered with the sherry.

At lunch, the goose, *perhaps a touch overdone*, and the potatoes, *not hasselbacks, like we had in Sweden that one time*, the Sandlings sat together facing the children. They had given Peter the gift of a silver-framed photograph of their daughter, and one each to the boys, smaller—the same gifts as the previous year, the same as they would get for birthdays. And it would no doubt continue until their deaths. The house was lousy with images of Elspeth that Peter put up before a visit. "You understand, it's for them?" he had asked and she realised he assumed she was jealous.

"Leave them up if it makes you feel better about anything," she'd said, and he'd frowned at her but said nothing further.

After the goose came the wretched steamed pudding, which, as Judith remarked, was purchased rather than hand-made, and the boys were excused and Peter opened the brandy she had bought for him. "I suppose," Ruth said, "someone made the pudding with their own hands. It didn't just form itself out of goodwill." She smiled. She had perhaps had a little too much sherry and she held her tongue between her teeth hoping to still it. Denis laughed loudly and Peter proposed a toast to those present and departed very quickly afterwards, as though Ruth had said something highly inappropriate. She felt his foot on her ankle, and skittered her leg away from him.

With the boys out of the room, Judith finally and inevitably felt comfortable enough to collapse into tears. Ruth cleared the plates and brought her a glass of water.

"For God's sake, girl, I'm not choking!" the woman sobbed into her napkin. Her husband patted her back and Ruth went to see to something in the kitchen. Betty kept a bottle of gin under the sink, and she poured herself a large measure of it. She felt better. She pulled on the washing-up gloves, frowning at the texture of damp rubber on the tips of her fingers. Betty had told her she would return in the evening to take care of the washing up, but Ruth felt grateful for it. She wondered at the Christmas happening in London with Alice and her parents. No doubt they would have kept staff on to prepare lunch—Alice was even less of a cook than she was. And Betty and Bernadette up at the home. What ordeal were they being put through?

She could hear that conversation had started up again next door—the woman was evidently able to pull herself together as long as Ruth stayed out of the way. Peter was speaking about a business trip he would take to Frankfurt in the spring. It was the first Ruth had heard of it, but she shook that off and poured another drink. Suds slid down the green bottle.

The kitchen door opened and Denis stood, uncomfortable in his moustache.

"Could you use a hand?" he asked. She was going to say no, but before she could he spotted the bottle.

"Aha," he said. "Glass?" She pointed to the cupboard and he took another glass, refilled hers and then filled his. "There's no tonic, I suppose?"

"There's none—this is Betty's secret stash."

"Well." He handed her the glass. "By way of apology. Cheers. Judith does not mean to . . . well, yes, she does mean to, but, what I—"

"It's all right," said Ruth, "you really don't have to."

"Thank you," he said and drank his gin, grimacing afterwards. "Good God. The things you people drink." He filled his glass from the tap to wash it down.

"Elspeth was no better. Hers was cherry brandy. Disgusting muck."

There was stale air between them, which Ruth did not feel inclined to dissipate. Eventually Denis spoke.

"I've been wondering about you here in this old house." And she knew as soon as he'd said it what was going to happen. She stilled her hands underneath the suds, girded herself in anticipation of a blow. "It's a funny old thing, grief. Can do strange things to a person—to a man. What with the war and one thing or another, I expect there's rather a feeling that those of us left behind are . . . indestructible. But . . ." he struggled for the words, "the flow of emotion—the size of it, you know. It doesn't sit well—inside the body. What I'm getting at is we all cope in various ways, and the important thing in all of this, of course, is the children." She felt him curl a stray thread of her hair around her ear, sending an unwanted feeling down her back. Her job, she knew, was to stay still and be petted. Instead she turned round and faced Denis, put her gloved hands either side of his face and kissed him. It was a long and dangerous kiss, and both kept their eyes wide open. Ruth pressed against him, felt his body twitch into action.

"Go on," she whispered, staring him dead in the eye, "go on."

His hands went to his belt and she could see him weighing things up. He put his hand under her skirt instead and clutched at her. His breath in her face was loud, wettening. Eventually he stepped away. Ruth turned back and carried on with the washing-up. That, she thought, ought to confound him.

"Ah," he said. "Another drink?"

"No, thank you, Denis, I really ought to get on with this."

"Good," he said, "good." She did not look at him, just scrubbed in the sink. "I'll just," he said, and left the room.

Once she had finished the washing-up, she went into the drawing room, took one of the Staffordshire dogs off the mantelpiece and carefully snapped its head off by cracking it like an egg on the hearthstone. It made a satisfying noise, but nothing loud enough to arouse suspicion next door, and she took the two pieces and wrapped them in a bit of old newsprint from the coal box, placed it on the hearth and stamped on it with the heel of her shoe.

"There we are," she said and brushed the coal off her fingertips. She felt someone looking at her from the corner of the room, and turned in alarm, having no excuse at the ready. There was just the face of the ticking carriage clock, and once she had shaken off her unease, she thought about how she might, at a later date, go about scrambling the insides of it.

Once the Sandlings had gone, and the boys were quiet in their room, Ruth went to bed, leaving Peter standing with an expectant face in the drawing room. She took off her shoes, her stockings and dress, and got into bed in her slip, make-up still on. Her mother would have had a conniption fit. She lay awake listening to the house contract and expand around her, the sound of Betty coming home with Bernadette and wishing Peter a happy Christmas. Booey in the garden barked three times before being silenced by a hush. A seagull, the waves, the creak of the stairs. She closed her eyes when Peter came to bed, pretended to be asleep, felt his side of the bed depress and spring up as he removed his watch, and settled in.

"You awake, old girl?" he whispered. She didn't answer and he ran a hand from her thigh to her shoulder. She felt deeply that she wanted to hurt him, physically. How dare he ask if she was awake, receive the information that she was not, and then seek to wake her. It felt at that moment like the very most callous thing he could do.

"Denis kissed me in the kitchen."

His hand stopped. There was no spear of vindication.

Peter sat up and his light went on. "What on earth are you on about?" He was angry. Not confused in the slightest, and that, she supposed, was the difference.

"You know."

"I absolutely do not. What is it that you thought happened?"

"He kissed me. He put his hand up my skirt."

There was a silence in which a decision was made by both of them.

"Well, I don't know who you think you are. Whatever ridiculous idea you've got in your head is entirely of your own making. Quite honestly—" his voice was rising in volume and pitch—"your level of self-regard is what disturbs me most. That and your recent drinking problem."

"I don't have a drinking problem."

"You made an absolute show of yourself tonight. I only put up with it because I didn't want to worry Denis and Judith, but what on earth were you doing behaving like that? I don't want to have to explain it to my children. All this nonsense springs from drinking too much—I just hope you realise that." He turned out the light. They lay in silence.

"Do you kiss other men's wives?"

"That's it," he said. "I won't put up with this poisonous nonsense." He removed himself from the bed and crossed the room to the door. "If I were you, I'd think very carefully about how you behaved tonight."

He left the room and Ruth listened to the sound of his footsteps moving down the hall to his study. The door opened and closed.

Three thumps came from the corner of the bedroom—one, two, three—and this time Ruth felt none of the dread of her nightmares, just a vague satisfaction that the scene had been witnessed by a third party.

On days when the weather was not absolutely unmanageable, Ruth strode inland, leaving Peter alone in his study, bent over his desk, and the boys and Bernadette nearly always gone either down to the sea or into town for pikelets straight after breakfast. She made her way to the foot of the Law, which gave one a feeling of vertigo until you were close up to it, when it seemed to shrink right down. On her first outing, she had imagined a walk to the whalebones would take half the day, but as she reached the initial steep incline, two runners in white singlet vests and shorts appeared from behind her and overtook her, running straight up. They nodded a good-morning to her and flung themselves upwards, scrambling over rocks and sending a small landslide in their wake. She chose a gentler path but they passed her on their way back down not fifteen minutes later.

Today she was comfortably alone. The light rain that had started when she left home had hardened somewhat, though the drops were not too concentrated. Recently she had found herself less and less comfortable in the house with Peter. In the long quiet days between Christmas and Hogmanay they had stepped around their argument without quite addressing it, one or the other or both had said *Christmas can be a stressful time*, and though Peter still kissed her on the cheek and called her *old girl* something had been cleaved apart, the vital tendons separated. It was only movement that felt correct. If she sat in the drawing room and tried to read a book, it was like the house was on fire and she needed to take action.

When she reached the top of the Law, her hair flipping into her eyes, her coat not tight enough around her to stop the wind finding its way down the back of her neck, she noticed a swimmer bobbing in the shallows. What they could have been doing in the cold escaped her. She sniffed deeply and felt a burn down her throat—perhaps the flu on its way. She lit a cigarette in her cupped hands and smoked it, leaning on the whalebones. Such an unnatural thing to have up there, decayed white beauty.

The Bass Rock's colour looked, from where she stood, as white as the bones. She thought of the birds on its pate unsettling and landing again. Movement to her left caught her eye, a wren in the gorse. It hopped from one branch to another, cocked its head at her. She felt a tremor in her mouth, a belt of great emotion, which she stilled. It was not fair on Christopher and Michael to have one mother die and another let go to insanity.

She finished her cigarette and turned to make her way back down, and nearly walked straight into a pony. It stood just a couple of feet away, walnut brown and barrel-like. The surprise made her stumble and she held her hands up in front of her, expecting the creature to start and run away, but it stood and looked at her with its long-lashed eyes. Its nose was patterned with a cream-velvet heart. She took a careful step forwards and still it did not move, reached out her hand towards its nose. It let out a snort, coming white from its coaly nostrils, but accepted her touch. The muzzle was cold and smooth. The pony's forelock was muddled through with burrs, it smelled of her father's potting shed. It lifted its lip a little, its teeth large and tea-stained. The air was still.

"Hello, Antony," she said. It blinked, and in its eye, she saw the whalebones reflected behind her, the figure of a girl standing in front of them; she turned, afraid, but no one was there, and there was nothing now in the pony's eye, it was clouded with age.

As the pathway wound downwards around the hill, Ruth looked again for the swimmer but did not see him. She passed by the derelict shepherd's hut and a large crow flew up from it—she could just make out the ribs of some dead animal sheltered by the remaining wall—and the wind blew its scent onto her—that rot again, from the boys' school, something long-ago dead.

With the path flattening out, and not ready to return home just yet, Ruth found herself back on the coastal track, winding towards the rocks. There was a kind of waxy residue on her hands from the pony—she wondered if they produced lanolin, like sheep did. The Bass Rock looked not unlike the pony, in its stillness, its disregard for the weather. A fishing boat blinked by the side of it, and it was that which drew her attention to the change in the weather. The clouds had dropped down low and the sky turned a dark yellow, suggesting snow. It was certainly cold enough. The water blackened, and quickened, sending sharp little waves with white at their blades towards the shore. It was quite beautiful and, in a moment of romance, Ruth climbed over the rocks towards the beach to get a better view, imagined herself with a shawl and a lantern a hundred years ago, watching for a ship. She stopped when she saw a figure alone on the beach and had to refocus her eyes. A naked man stood facing the water: the swimmer, his arms held high above him as though he were beckoning something down, as though he were conducting the storm.

He turned his face to greet the rain and wind from the north, confirming that this was of course Reverend Jon Brown, his white buttocks clenched in rapture, his hair sticking up on his head and on his shoulders too, like an old dog spat out of the sea. The wind carried a few notes of what he called into it, but none of the sense of it, if there was any.

Ruth crawled backwards until she could properly get her footing, and made her way towards the house, smiling and then laughing. The man really was a lunatic. She felt an excitement about telling Peter, and then a thread of disquiet. She wouldn't risk it. She would talk to Betty. Betty would laugh.

III

Sarah sings as she walks, a tune I can never quite catch. She has gathered up her hair on top of her head to keep it out of the way and the stray hairs are thick like red straw. I catch glimpses of her neck as she moves ahead of me, and while all of our faces and arms and legs are coated in the dirt thrown up by the rain, her neck is milk white. And the rain worsens. It rains through the night and all day, but it is not cold. The air is heavy, in the early parts of the morning, like a blanket weighing on us. The loud patter of drops on leaves and the way it moves the scrub around us, jumping off the spring-green growth, weighing down branches, makes me think of us moving across the belly of a gigantic scaled beast, warmed by its blood. It is true that ten days' walk from home the seasons appear to have changed; where in our village the mud makes all black and anything that stands out against it pale and dead, the thick green of the woods here is a different country.

We come to a break in the path where the roots of a large oak have churned the earth enough to make room for us to sit close to each other and rest against the trunk and receive some shelter. Cook is laboured in her breathing, she coughs less now, but when she does you can hear things coming up. Sarah watches her and winds the stalk of some leaf around her thumb over and over.

Father closes his eyes and the Widow Clements is silent and sits with her arms folded across her chest. She stares hard into the woods.

Sarah stands and moves beyond the clearing. "I will be back," she says, disappearing into the darkness. She is gone before anyone can object, though Father's eyes open and he sits up straighter.

"She will have gone for a piss," my father says. The Widow Clements turns away from him and leans her head against the tree roots, like it pains her.

Sarah has been gone a long time. Cook holds her head in her hands. "We should go," says the Widow Clements. "She has run off."

"No," I say and everyone looks at me.

Father nods. "We wait. Perhaps she is lost." Cook stands and bellows, "Sarah," into the woods, but Father hushes her. The shouting has exhausted her, and she sits back down unsteadily.

But Sarah does return. Nobody speaks when she does. We are tired and I am grateful that her absence has meant we have not moved. If the voices come again, I would rather hide than run. I would make myself and Sarah a shallow grave and sink down in it.

She has the roots of some plant gathered in her pinafore, and she digs a hole in the earth and quietly and slowly prepares a small fire, using a flint and some twine she has managed to keep dry. Watching her work builds a comfort in me. Her white hands move quietly and efficiently, with a certainty that shows how many times before she has done this. I feel embarrassed about our efforts to light a fire in the rain, which she must have watched in frustration these past days. Father's face also betrays a look of discomfort. In this moment he must feel a child is taking charge, and I feel pride on her behalf. *There, Father*, I think in a voice I don't recognise, *she is not for you*. The Widow Clements looks away. Cook is delighted by the fire, and keeps making little noises of approval, like a sitting hen.

"How did you find anything dry enough to act as kindling?" Cook asks.

"A mouse nest in a hollow log."

The Widow Clements clucks in disgust.

"The fire will see to the droppings," says Sarah, but the widow is not appeased. We move closer to the flames.

"Well, now we have fire, I will go and find something to eat—there may be some mushrooms or perhaps fish in the stream," my father says, starting to rise.

"No," says Sarah, not looking up, "the mushrooms here are all poison and the stream has gone underground." Father stays half risen, that look again, that he is the child. Something dark crosses his face. He remains on the floor.

"But," she says, "I found some salsify and nettle." She takes several roots from her pinafore and nestles them deep in the flames. While they blacken, she asks us all for our tins and places them in the stream of water coming off the leaves of the tree. The smell of the roots is good, like potatoes done in the embers. Why one of us did not think earlier of collecting rainwater in our tins, I can't say. I feel stupid in light of her shrewdness. For how long has she lived on nothing but roots and vines? I think, allowing myself a shred of pity, which feels better than the embarrassment of inaction. It is not the life I would give her. I would find meat for her, I would make money to buy bread. I wallow a moment in the image of us, our small children at my feet, my hand on her knee. But then out of her pinafore she takes a dead hare, and Cook gurgles with delight. It is like some magic trick.

"I found her in the same log with the mice," she says, "sheltering from the rain." There is a small smile of triumph on her face, she knows she has surprised us, perhaps she knows that she has saved us, when we thought we were saving her. I have such a feeling of admiration, and underneath that the wish that it had been me that had provided the hare. But after a moment, Father smiles, then laughs, and everyone, even the Widow Clements, softens at the idea of roasted hare. Sarah holds out her hand to me, and I pass my knife. She skins and cleans the animal with her careful hands, and there is a quiet reverence from the rest of us, the moment the flesh is shown to be deep scarlet, and the smell is only of blood and grass. We have passed out of reach of the rot. Once the thing is speared through with a sapling branch, and resting on the embers with the salsify, she squats down by the entrails and looks at them closely, pawing through them with a stick.

"What are you doing?" I ask. She looks up quickly, as though she has forgotten I am there. She looks to see if anyone else has noticed, but they are concerning themselves with turning the hare, and drying their boots out by the fire. Everyone's mood is lifted at the smell of the meat and Father and the Widow Clements exchange soft words.

"I am just checking the health of the animal," she says.

There is a pause and then I start laughing. "I'd say it's not doing well."

Sarah smiles, sweeps dirt up around the entrails and wraps them round the end of her stick so that she can pick them up.

"When we've eaten, we'll burn them," she says, "so nothing comes scavenging." She leans the stick against a tree, and collects the tins of rainwater, which she places in the hot earth next to the fire. She drops in the nettles, pinching hard with her forefinger and thumb to avoid the sting. After they have soaked a little, she goes around again and pinches them out, throws the leaves into the fire where they hiss. She takes each of us our tin, and if there is any distrust of what she has given us, she lays it to rest by telling Cook, "If you just let them soak a little moment, then take out the leaf, it doesn't fur your tongue." Cook nods and takes a sip of her warm drink.

"It is good," she says. "Thank you, Sarah."

Sarah collects the salsify from the fire, lays the roots on four broad leaves, and rolls them until their black skins come off. The leaves steam with rainwater. She wraps one around the base of each root and distributes them among us. It smells sweet and woody and Sarah breaks another one in two, not using a leaf to shield her fingers from the heat, then she puts half in her mouth, and chews, letting the steam cloud out of her. It tastes like sweet chestnut, and it is the best thing I have eaten in two years. Sarah sucks the taste off her fingers, and then sees to the hare. She takes it off the stick, using my knife to slide it onto more leaves. Then she takes the head off, and the rest she cuts down the backbone with a sharp crack and across the ribs so it is in four equal parts. She hands these out, and keeps the head for herself.

"You should have more of the meat," I say, offering her back my hindquarter, which I badly want to eat.

"No," she says, "I prefer the head," and she demonstrates by chewing on the ear, which crackles and then comes away from the tiny skull. She looks up at me smiling.

"Thank you," I say.

If the roots were the best thing I have eaten in two years, the hare is the most beautiful thing I have eaten in the entirety

275

of my life. I am struck dumb by the chew of it, the sweetness of it. I could eat five hares this way in one sitting. I try not to show my amazement, and watch how Sarah slips the teeth of the hare's head into her pocket.

"It seems we are always sleeping here," Sarah says. The others have fallen hard into slumber. For myself, I have a quickened heartbeat, and a tension in my body that makes me feel I could walk another ten miles in the dark. I want to speak, I want to climb a tree.

"They are tired," I say. "They are old and we have walked a long way."

"Imagine," she says, "how far we could get without them." She says it so lightly that it sounds not the slightest bit cruel— it sounds like just a thought.

"I feel I could make the coast and back before they wake."

Sarah smiles. "I bet you could," she says. She moves next to me so that our legs touch. She takes from her pocket a small wooden box and the teeth from earlier. She drops them one by one into the box so that they make a light hollow noise, like rain does when you are inside and warm and dry. She blows on the open box, as though the teeth are hot, and then she carefully closes the lid.

"What is that?" I ask.

"It was my mother's—she made it."

"What is it for?"

"It's for me."

"I do not understand."

Her teeth are white in the dark. "What is your bit of cloth for?"

"To remember."

"But when your sister and mother sewed it, why were they sewing it?"

"To practise, to teach my sister how to."

"Show me," Sarah says. I find the swatch in my pocket and hand it to her. She turns it, looking at it from the last of the firelight.

"See," she says, holding it up, "there is creation in this—the stars they have sewn, the coloured threads. There's story here, they talked this into life."

"I don't know what you mean." But I see a little of what she means. Agnes is living in the line of thread that leads from the centre of the little black starburst, in her movements, my mother in the cross-hatching next to it, the moment held in the making.

"It's a woman's thing, creation," she says, moving a hand down to her belly, "you can see how they felt in each stitch, you can hear the words they spoke to each other and into the cloth."

I look at the piece of sacking, and for a moment I see it, but it hurts to look.

"What do you keep in your box?" I ask, to move the talk a little from me.

"That's my secret." She does not say it unkindly, but I suddenly want nothing more than to open it and see what is in there.

"I liked watching you make the fire and cook the food," I say instead. My eyes feel large and my body is very warm. It is the effect of having eaten well, and the tingle of the nettle tea in my gullet.

"I liked cooking for you," says Sarah.

"Tell me, what did you see in the hare guts?"

"Nothing," she says, "they are just guts." But she says it with a tremor in her smile, and looks away.

She gets up and walks to where the guts are leaning against the tree, takes the stick and places it on the fire.

"I was only thinking," she says, coming back and sitting next to me, the fire flaring a little around the entrails. "I was thinking about what happens next."

"Were you asking them?"

She looks at me, as though we are sharing a joke, but she sees my face is serious and she takes a moment.

"I don't care if you were. I'm only interested. I'm interested to know what you saw."

She looks at me a long time. In silence I can hear my heart beat.

"Only blood," she says. She crawls forwards and upwards onto my body. The feeling I have is so strange. I am not alarmed. I am something else. The darkness behind her moves like water. Every hair on my skin stands and throngs and is made of fire. Sarah kisses me and moves against me, and even as it's happening, I am not sure that it is.

When I wake in the night, I am unsure of what took place. Sarah is no longer next to me, and someone vomits in the darkness. I hear it again and again, the turning out of a stomach, Cook, I think, from her deep gasps. I do not move to help her. There is a dread on me. I wish I could take Sarah and leave, that we would make the sea journey alone. Another sound in the dark, a deep moan. Someone else sick too.

II

On a morning in March when the boys had long been back at school and a gale blew outside, Betty answered the door. Ruth hadn't heard the bell, the wind was so loud, rattling the windows and gripping over the chimney. But she heard his voice and sank lower in her chair, before getting up to receive him.

"Mrs. Hamilton," said Reverend Jon Brown, "we haven't seen you in church for quite some time now." He leaned and kissed her on the cheek, which surprised her, though she tried to look as though it hadn't. He smelled of the sea and his cheek was so cold it felt wet.

"We've been busy," she said, trying to muster the degree of friendliness that might not offend but might also have the reverend on his way sooner rather than later.

"I'll fetch some tea," said Betty and the two women waited hopefully for it to be refused, but Reverend Jon Brown said, "Splendid," and showed himself into the drawing room. Betty and Ruth exchanged a look.

In the drawing room, the Reverend added a log to the fire and sat in the armchair.

"I thought you liked it cold, Reverend."

"Oh, I do, in matters of God. In personal matters, though, I like to be as cosy as the next person."

"Personal matters, Reverend?"

"Yes. Is Mr. Hamilton here by any chance? Not on one of his trips again?" The way he said *trips* suggested to Ruth that he knew something about what those trips involved. It made her hate them both.

"He is home, but he's working. Do I need to disturb him?"

"Well," he said, adjusting the cushion behind him, "it's about young Christopher and so really I'd prefer to talk to you both."

"Has something happened?"

"Nothing to worry about, just some issues I thought might be well brought up with you both before Christopher returns."

"What issues?"

"Mrs. Hamilton, I'd really rather Mr. Hamilton were here too. They are his boys after all."

Betty brought in a tray and set it on the occasional table. She eyed the two of them, wondering no doubt what she had walked in on.

There was a game of chess going on, but Ruth didn't know the rules.

Ruth would have fetched Peter herself, enabling a moment of connection between them, against Reverend Jon Brown. But she didn't want to leave the man alone in her home, she felt like he might pocket something.

"Betty," she said, without taking her eyes off him, "would you call Mr. Hamilton down for me?"

Ruth sat on the sofa while they waited. There was a long silence through which the reverend smiled.

"What happened to your other dog?" he asked, without looking at the mantelpiece.

"I don't know. It disappeared a while ago."

"A thief?"

"I don't think so, no."

"Do you think perhaps the girl broke it and is hiding it?" His eyes narrowed a little.

"I think it's best all round if we don't talk about it, Reverend."

He smiled again, nodded. "Right you are, Mrs. Hamilton."

Ruth shifted on the sofa and tried to examine the top corner of the room as though there was something important hanging there.

When Peter arrived, in his slippers and a hurriedly thrown-on jumper—he'd most likely been wearing his dressing gown in his study—he peered into the room as though he expected it to be on fire. Or like a boy entering the head's office, Ruth thought. The reverend stood, shook hands with him.

"Is everything all right?" he asked, looking from one to the other.

"Quite all right, as I was saying to Mrs. Hamilton, nothing in the slightest to worry about. I just did want to flag a few things before the boys return—something I do for all the parents of boys at Fort Gregory, I just find it's useful to know a little about how a term has gone before they arrive home. Something other than academic progress and manners, something more about their *psychology*." He said the word as though they might be impressed that he knew something of it.

Peter sat down on the sofa next to Ruth so that once again it felt as though Reverend Jon Brown was the owner of the house and they his guests.

"As you may or may not know, I have an interest in child psychology, and I make it my business to get to know the children of North Berwick. I like to know what's going on, what makes them tick, and so I have a special relationship with St. Augustus, Fort Gregory and Carlekemp Priory where I am the chaplain. Now, nothing to worry about, as I said, but both your boys have struggled in the past term. This is not uncommon—there are changes coming about in Christopher, he's becoming a young man, and for Michael, he's had a great deal of upheaval, and I rather feel that, given the death of their mother, these things have been . . . magnified. So this all comes together to create behaviour which you may find a little . . . uncomfortable."

"What do you mean?" Ruth asked. Peter was sitting forward in his seat, as though trying hard to understand something.

"Well. Christopher has been in more than one fist fight this term."

"Fighting? But that seems so unlike him," said Ruth. She'd never seen the boy so much as raise his voice even at Michael. "Has he been hurt?"

"Oh, nothing serious, I assure you. A few bruises. An out-of-place nose, but you should have seen the other boy!"

"His nose is broken?"

"Really—" the reverend held his hands up as though Ruth was being hysterical—"don't get yourself upset."

"I just—" She looked at Peter, who remained silent. "Peter, are you going to say something?" He appeared to be deep in thought or memory.

Eventually he said, "It's just all part of growing up and becoming a man." Once he had said this he looked much more convincing. "Really they've been very sheltered since their mother died. I suppose it's good to toughen them up. It can't all be picnics and boat rides."

The reverend nodded, pleased.

"But he's only just fourteen." Her chest felt hot. "Michael isn't fighting too, is he?"

"Not so much, no, but he is telling a lot of tall tales. Again, to be expected."

"He's lying about things? What things?"

"He's making up stories, some of them just a bit of fun I think, something to scare the other boys in the dorm. Wolfmen at the windows and that sort of thing. But I'm afraid some of his other stories have been focused on the masters themselves, and that's where we really need to take a stand."

"What has he said?"

"Really it doesn't matter. Children know the value of an adult's name, and Michael is just trying to win favour with his peers by tarnishing the names of his teachers."

"What does he say they've done?" An unnamed panic in the base of her stomach.

Peter stood, a fist of nervous energy Ruth hadn't seen on him before. "Really, darling, the details are not important. What's important is that he understands that this sort of behaviour is not tolerated in a man. And Christopher needs to get whatever this is out of his system and fight, if he must, but in the ring." It was as though a different person spoke through Peter. Ruth imagined a hand thrust into his back making his mouth move, like a puppet.

"As I say," Reverend Jon Brown spoke up, smiling, "this is not to urge you into any sort of discipline with your boys, that's the job of the school. It's more to warn you of how they might be a little changed. Adulthood comes in leaps and bounds, and more than a few tumbles."

Ruth did not listen to the winding up of the conversation. What, she thought, was happening? She felt as though her life were a picture made of sand and someone was blowing through a straw at it. Each thing she held to be true—Peter's love for her; the boys healing after their mother's death; her desire for her own child.

And then the reverend was leaving and shaking their hands, and Peter showed him out. Ruth waited for her husband to return to the drawing room, and when he did she stood up.

"Well, what shall we do about this?" she said.

"Do?"

"There's a day school in Musselburgh. We can—"

"My God, what are you proposing? You can't send boys to a day school. We don't need them back here working the farm."

"But they're not happy. That's what he came here to say—something's wrong, they don't like it."

"You're not meant to like it." Peter's voice had an edge to it, and he pinched the bridge of his nose, as though she were a silly little girl throwing a tantrum. "You're meant to transform into a man, and that is what's happening to them. They might not like it now, but in time they will hold affection for the place."

"Don't you care?"

"OF COURSE I CARE." This he shouted as though all of his strength and soul went into it. His whole head and neck were red with the power of it; he wiped spit from his lips with the back of his hand.

He was a person changed. Danger was in the room. Ruth sat back down. She felt compelled to look away from him as one would an angry dog. They remained in silence a while longer until Peter's colour had returned to normal.

"You assume that just because I send them there that I don't think of them."

"No, not at all, I—"

"You think I had an easy time at school, that I don't know the hardships of being a boarder? I don't do it for my good, I do it for theirs. I'm not having them here with you and Betty and the girl turning into poofs who watercolour and collect seashells. There's violence in the world that they will have to face up to, and it is my job as their father, their remaining parent, to prepare them for that." He nodded to himself. He kept nodding. He was convincing himself. "Because that's what you do, that's what was done to me, and it didn't do me any harm! Look at me now, I survived a war, I survived the death of my wife. I survived you!" The jab was dark and low, and before she knew it she had returned it.

"And will you send your new baby to the same school? Or will she stop you?"

"What are you talking about?"

Ruth stood up, moved a step closer to him.

"Will you send the baby you're having with your girl to boarding school to be torn apart or is that an honour you reserve only for your legitimate children?"

Peter struck her hard across the face and for a moment there was nothing in the room but the ringing sound it made. It didn't hurt so much as it tasted—she had bitten her cheek. Peter looked startled, and turned his back on her.

"You hit me," she said redundantly.

He ran his hands over his head back and forth, back and forth.

"You need to get control of yourself, Ruth. These fantasies are fast becoming tiresome."

Her face was warm—his hand had been open. The small seep of blood from the corner of her mouth was quickly extinguished by her tongue.

"I know about the girl," Ruth said. "You can't deny me that." The words were out now and what would happen?

Peter sniffed, rubbed at his nose, leaned on one hip. His body held a strange energy, something new beneath the skin.

"The girl?"

"The girl in Edinburgh. Don't make me spell it out for you, Peter, it's too humiliating," she said. She felt she too might have an outburst and hit him. Perhaps this was the time in which outbursts were allowed.

"I have absolutely no sense of what you're talking about."

"Stop it."

He sat down as though exhausted, and looked at her. His face softened. His voice was gentle.

"I'm sorry, my darling, I can't think what you're talking about."

"I followed you, I saw you on the platform at Edinburgh."

"You saw . . . ? I'm worried, quite frankly. Are you feeling unwell?" Peter stood, put a hand to her forehead. She leaned away.

"The girl, and I saw her . . . I saw that she had a baby on the way."

"Ruth, darling, you're scaring me."

"Don't you 'Ruth darling' me."

"I'm afraid you've made a mistake." His softness was awful. His hurt at what she was suggesting. "And I made a mistake just now. I'm sorry, I was afraid for you, you were becoming hysterical."

She pulled the dog brooch from her jumper. "This," she said, throwing it on the floor between them.

"I knew you didn't like it," he said.

"This is Greyfriars Bobby, from *Edinburgh*." He looked at the brooch there on the floor for a long while. "You didn't find it in London at all." In time, he looked up at her.

"All right. I admit, my secretary shopped for it. I just had too much work on. I told her you liked dogs."

Some moment of understanding passed through her.

"You sent the girl, didn't you? She chose a present for your wife." She knew she was correct. She didn't know what told her, but she was certain.

"You're talking like a madwoman," he said. His tone was a little changed, it had an edge again. "I know you're angry that I've been away a lot but I have been working my fingers to the bone so that we can—"

She cut him off. "My God, we moved up here *because* of her, didn't we?"

Ruth saw for one second the face of a caught man, and then it was gone, replaced with rage.

"How dare you accuse me of these things. How *dare* you." He stood and, as he did, he picked up the brooch. "I shall have my secretary return the brooch and send you a cheque, shall I?" He moved towards the door with it, then turned. "You know, we were talking about the boys—did you feel you weren't getting enough attention?" His voice dripped with disappointment. He walked from the room.

Ruth caught her reflection in the mirror, and saw the other face staring back at her, younger, thinner, frightened. And then she settled, and saw that that was all she was, young, angular and afraid.

I

As our train pulls into Blackfriars I recognise Dom on the next platform.

"Hey." Katherine looks up. "Hey, look, it's Dom."

I immediately regret speaking. Katherine's face does not crumple, but something far and deep within her withers, I can see it in the tightening of her lips and the way she pulls her hands close to herself, as if to hide them.

Dom, like he has heard me speak, looks up, but the reflection of the sun on the window must be hiding us—his face does not alter, he doesn't raise a hand to wave. Another second passes and then a tension comes into his body.

A beat. We have slowed to a stop but the doors are yet to open. Dom turns on his heel and begins to run. We watch him pelt down the stairs, nearly knocking over an elderly man, not stopping to right him again. The man clings onto the handrail and shakes his head.

He's coming for me.

"Shit," Katherine says, and the doors chime open.

"What's going on?" I ask. "What's he doing?"

"I don't know. I don't know."

"Should we pull the emergency cord?"

"I don't know."

I look up at the departure sign. We have ten seconds until we are due to leave. We can't look away from the staircase to our left where Dom will appear. I am counting down—eight, seven, and he is there at the bottom of the staircase and his face is not the face of a man, who was once a boy, and who has loved my sister, and comforted her, laughed with her, made love and a thousand pasta dinners with her to eat in front of the television. He is not the man who, after the first time we had sex, held me very tightly and let me cry on him, told me my loathing should be for him only and not for myself. Who brought me a box of worry dolls one year for Christmas and watched me open them, and later held my cheek in the hallway as I tried hard not to tear up, kissed my forehead and said, *I'm so very sorry*. He is changed. He roars up the stairs, three, two, one, and the doors chime and begin to close, lock, and he slams his body against them, puts his fingers into the crack and tries to prise them open, but they are fast, and we sit looking at him and he is shouting something that I cannot make out, and his spit flecks the windows, his eyes show white all around the blue centres, his mouth is dark red and deep, his teeth are sharp. He looks like an ape, and he bangs on the glass one last time with both fists as the train starts to move; he stands back so he is by our window and for five or so seconds he keeps time with the moving train, his forehead pushing against the glass, looking into Katherine's eyes, an inch away from her, saying nothing with his mouth, but his message is clear and dreadful.

He doesn't see me.

When the train picks up speed, he pulls back and I watch him standing, his arms by his sides, his fists clenched. He becomes smaller and is gone, we are out in the sunshine and on our way. My sister is white and there are tears in her eyes. When she opens her mouth, her front left tooth is bloody.

"What should I do?" she asks.

"Come home with me," I say. "We'll think of something." I move to sit next to her, and in doing so find that my legs are shaking. I put my hand on her knee and she takes it and holds it in hers. Her hand is very cold, and it vibrates with fear.

At home I ring our mother and tell her not to let Dom know that Katherine is staying with me.

"Don't you think he'll assume that anyway?" she says. "What happened?" Then she whispers down the phone, "Do we need to call the police?"

Katherine is behind me during the call, drinking a black coffee, having refused to join me in a glass of wine, because she is not rattled, because it is not yet even midday. She says loudly, "Everything's fine, Mum, Dom's just being a bit of a pain, that's all."

While Katherine is out of earshot I say, "Don't answer the door to him."

My mother takes this in.

"Viviane. This sounds serious."

"It's probably nothing—we're just being cautious."

In the mirror, I see Katherine pouring whisky into her coffee, looking over her shoulder like a child stealing a biscuit.

The girl is looking out through a crack in the wardrobe door. The glow from the lighthouse on the Bass Rock comes into the room like a ghost and then leaves again. She was midway through dressing for the trip they were to take when he had burst in. The maid had been told to leave, which she did, making those large eyes at the girl as she closed the door. Poor thing, there was nothing to be done.

He had taken her by the hair, which the maid had only just finished pinning, and he had laid her on the bed, and when he could not at first find his way under her corset, he had punished her for it, and then ordered her to turn over. He took the grape scissors from her dressing table and cut the laces. She had remained very still, and even so, he had made several cuts upon the skin of her back. There was nothing to be said, it was only a question of weathering the storm, and in any case he was careful, in his way, because he never caused destruction to her face. In order to weather the storm, it was important, she had found, to think of one's head and one's body as separate. The body was more robust and could deal with the force he visited upon it. She was always grateful that the gentle bones of her face and hands remained intact. Though wearing her corset would be uncomfortable, and she may have to feign other ailments instead. He did not understand the great problem of the corset. She had reduced too much in the past months, which he did not like, but also she had had that corset specially made for her new smaller frame. Perhaps the maid could cleverly unlace one of the old ones, and rethread it.

After he had finished, he had tidied himself in the mirror for a moment, and she made the mistake of moving too soon, and had been shocked to tears by the feeling in her ribs, causing him to take her once more by the hair and shut her in the wardrobe. He expected her to sit on the stool he kept in there for her, her hands neatly folded on her lap—he had explained this in detail the first time it had happened. The repercussions of leaving the wardrobe, which was not locked, were great, she knew this, there were still ridges on the backs of her legs from the first time when she had with some indignation come out to use the chamber pot.

He had left the room humming a tune to himself. She was not to go on the trip after all.

Sometime later the maid enters the room and lights the lamp. She has a tray with her, and upon it a lit candle, a glass of water and two boiled eggs with bread. The girl sees through a crack in the door as the maid sets the candle down on the side table and creeps to the wardrobe.

"Miss, Sir's gone—he's not back till the day after tomorrow. Will you come out and have something to eat?"

"No. Thank you, Jane. I am quite content in here."

"Please."

"I said no." There is a pause, and the maid looks about. The poor thing is new and is distressed.

"Can I pass through some supper then, Miss? A blanket?"

"Jane, he will know."

"But you can't stay there all night."

"Please leave." The maid stands unsure. "Leave." She uses her strongest, most angry voice; she hasn't heard it herself in several years. It hurts her ribs. The maid starts, and hurries from the room. There is a small tinkle outside, the water unbalancing on the tray. The maid is gone, but she neglected to put out the lamp on the side table, and the girl breaks the rules and leans her forehead on the door and stares at it, willing it to go out. The lighthouse makes her bedroom glow again, for just a moment, and then leaves darkness.

Fidra

I

I can't sleep.

I'm thinking about how we just sat and waited for him. If the train hadn't left on time, what would have happened? If it had been even a second late to close its doors, if he hadn't been minutely slowed by bumping into the old man. Why did we just sit there? We knew something bad was coming. We could have hidden in the toilets, or got off the train and run to the lifts, we could have pulled the emergency cord, we could have called the police. But we waited, just in case we were wrong. What would Dom have done if he had got those doors open? I think Katherine knows. And then I think of the embrace he gave me at Dad's funeral, how it had felt like the first deep inhalation of breath. I reach down to scratch at my shin, and find the scar has completely gone. When I look there's nothing more than a light tea stain on the skin. I stare at it a moment. I wonder if I go at it with my nails if I can get it back.

Vincent has sent a message.

Are you ignoring me?

It is the fifth in two days.

There is a clear and easy version of my life, I can see it. Text him back. It was only a tickle. What does it feel like to like someone? *Does it matter?—he likes you.* I can see how he

297

would fit into my life. I can see us caravanning, driving to France. I can see us maybe getting married. *How did you two meet? She was buying wine and I was buying cheese.* I can see it all. A geriatric pregnancy. Some direction. Respond to the text message, always. *You owe him.*

I get out of bed and pack clothes for us both, though I can't imagine Katherine wearing anything I have to offer. If we leave now, we will make it by dawn. Katherine is awake on the sofa, her knees pulled up to her chest. She has been crying.

"We're going to Scotland," I say, and she doesn't reply, just nods and moves to pull on her socks and shoes.

In the car she sleeps. A feeling, leaving London, of intense relief, similar to the one we felt as the train left the station. Wolves chase us all the way. Past Leeds I pull into a service station. Katherine is heavily asleep and I don't wake her, I go inside and eat a blueberry muffin and drink a large, bad coffee. Two more messages from Vincent. One hurt, one angry. It is ending without my input. I turn off my phone and go to wash my face in the toilets. I stare a long time at my face in the mirror. I stare long enough that the different parts start to float away from each other. I am willing a plan to appear, but nothing comes. I should have picked up Mum, too. As long as she doesn't answer the door to him. I'll call her in the morning, suggest she comes. They were friends once, her and Dom. He would buy her Christmas presents from him alone, not shared ones with Katherine. I liked that about him. The drip of the tap slows to a steady, calm beat. I whisper, "It's OK it's OK it's OK," but I don't know who I am comforting. I pull up my trouser leg and look again at my healed skin. There's a quiet knocking from one of the stalls behind me, and it breaks me out of my dream. The knocking becomes louder.

"Hello?" I say. The knocking ceases. Just the pipes. I leave the toilets, pick up an almond croissant for Katherine as well as a milky coffee. I know she finds almond croissants and milk revolting, and I know that my failure will be a comfort to her. The bright lights of the service station feel safe. This place is a constant, a limbo, somewhere no one would think to look for you. A family with a six- or seven-year-old child enters, she is in her pyjamas and is slung over the father's shoulder, deep in slumber. I shouldn't have left my sister on her own. If she wakes, how will she find me? I go back to her and she only stirs when I start the engine.

She blinks. "I dropped off," she says, perplexed.

"That's OK." I hand her the coffee and croissant. She looks at them a while, still confused and in the grip of sleep.

"Sorry," she says, "I've been asleep a long time, haven't I?"

"You could argue we all have," I say and it sounds trite and quippy and I'm embarrassed, like I think I'm in a play, but to my surprise Katherine takes the lid off her coffee and nods, blowing on the surface of it.

By the time the sun has started to come up, we can see Tantallon Castle silhouetted against the sea. Katherine has neatly pulled apart her croissant and laid it out in strips on the paper bag on her lap.

II

The slap had only made a very temporary mark, and three days later, the nick in Ruth's mouth had healed, though she found herself worrying the spot with her tongue often. She felt that perhaps she had not been made like other women, and perhaps her true ambition in life was to be alone. It did not seem frightening to be alone. If Peter left her, there would be logistical difficulties, of course. What of the house? What of the boys? But ultimately these things would be resolved, and she would not mind no longer having to live to the tides of another person's will. She would become a hermit, she would find a cave and settle in it, begin something there that was not a family, or sewing or planning a picnic. She would eat bread and cheese, she would grow fat and squat and strong, drink whisky and wear gumboots. She would learn to smoke a pipe, and wear a woollen hat so she didn't have to pin her hair in the wind. Perhaps she could learn to fish off the rocks. The idea appealed to her so much that on her walk she found herself scanning the gullies and clifftops for the ideal place to build a hovel. There was the old shepherd's hut on the Law that looked over the town—no roof and the wild ponies sheltered there. It amused her very much to think of her mother coming to stay with her divorced fat childless daughter in a derelict sheep house. She would serve sardines in their tins and tea from a bowl.

It was a particularly bright morning that she decided to go and find the well. She had read about it in a slim volume in among the few books and maps on sale at the grocer's. It was called *Holy Wells of Scotland*, and the description of the one at North Berwick read simply "small and oval." It sounded so boring that she had convinced herself there was more to it, and had bought the book which had a line map of where she could find it. She gathered a flask of tea and some cheese and an apple and set out. The air smelled of flint. She walked first along the coast, where she saw the boys and Bernadette eating hot pikelets on the bench overlooking the rocks. They were huddled against the wind.

"What are you fellows going to do today?"

"We're going to the castle," said Bernadette.

"And have a picnic in the ruins," said Michael.

"We've got apples for the ponies," said Christopher. There was something a little too wholesome about it all. But she smiled just the same and wished them a good time. When she looked back, she saw Christopher gingerly take a lit cigarette out of his pocket and pass it to Bernadette. *Ought I to feel outraged?* she wondered. She found it bothered her not a bit. Christopher was only a year off what she had been when she had her first cigarette, rolled by Antony, and she hadn't boarding school and a dead mother to contend with. Bernadette, sat in the middle, offered the cigarette to Michael, but he shook his head. *Well. There we are, that's all right then. The children are policing themselves to an extent*, she thought. Bernadette passed it back to Christopher and then she stretched out her arms so that they went around the shoulders of both boys and the boys moved in a little to her. Strange and rather beautiful. She walked on, heading inland towards the church-yard. She had felt lightly hysterical when the boys returned for Easter break, she had expected to see such misery from them. But other than Christopher's nose, which now had a bump on its bridge, they seemed, if anything, more content. The three of them went off all day, apples in their pockets, returned at suppertime with roses in their cheeks, smelling of rock pools and bonfires. She had caught Betty staring out the window at them as they crossed the golf course, ignoring the rules. They walked three abreast and you could hear their voices even through the glass. "I hope it's not a worry to you, madam," Betty had said, "your boys hanging around with Bernadette? I think she's been lonely for a brother or sister."

"I think it's a good thing, Betty," she'd said. "Everyone needs someone."

"Mr. Hamilton doesn't mind?"

"Mr. Hamilton does not mind." Mr. Hamilton more likely had not noticed.

About half an hour into her walk, sheltered from the sea wind by trees and houses, she turned inland and started across a field. The map in her hand marked the well as somewhere in that same field, but there was no obvious place. A light sleet began to fall, and now she saw that, other than a narrow plank of wood leading to a stile, the field was deeply mudded, with cow prints and pats and water seeping up through the turf. She climbed the stile and as she swung her leg over, her gumboot slipped on the bright green lichen and both legs went out from under her. She fell inelegantly, cracking her back on the second step of the stile.

"Buggering fuck!" she whispered loudly, and she stayed still for a moment to make sure she was not truly broken. When she rolled over, she discovered that she had fallen into bog water—a leaking cow trough had made a smelly brown pool over which danced a herd of orange flies. From her lower back to her shoulder she was very wet, and now, very cold. She made several angry noises trying to stand up, and her apple rolled out into the mud. This was the thing that made her want to cry most, she discovered, because it seemed suddenly such a sweet and childish thing to have set out for an adventure with a picnic and to have fallen over in the mud. *Everybody needs someone.*

A pain in her shoulder brought back how Peter had looked at her with such disappointment, such disgust, how she had not been the person he was expecting her to be, and now he was saddled with her, and how marrying her had been a decision he regretted. It was that more than the slap that she'd found herself replaying often since the fight. She wanted to do more than slap herself, she wished she had fallen harder on the stile, and it ran through her suddenly that she would feel a great satisfaction if she slammed her head into the fence post.

She sat down on the stile and collected herself. It wouldn't do to become actually mad. She held her own hand and stroked it, felt sorry for the little hand, all mudded and cold. She took a deep breath and held on for a moment longer, then felt a touch better. She still had her flask of tea and so she poured herself a cupful, and drank it, horrid, but it became rather amusing, as though she had planned this as her picnic spot all along. The sleet continued. She threw half of the tea into the stinking bog water, and the flies rose up. She screwed the lid of the flask back on. "Well," she said out loud. She might as well continue until she got too cold. She stood and took a step, but her boot had become stuck and her socked foot came out and before she could stop herself she had stepped forward, full weight on top, into the mud. She stood, startled by how uncompromising the mud was. She didn't laugh or cry, but when she tried hard to think of a reaction other than those none came to her. After she had pulled out the stuck boot, she put her wet and filthy foot back inside it and limped home, the dirty boot making a revolting noise the whole way.

She opened the back door and stopped halfway out of her coat. The smell of cigarette smoke and the sound of voices that ceased abruptly at the thud of the door closing. She used the scraper to help her get the offending boot off and the stench hit her nose as it did. Peter appeared from the drawing room.

"Oh, hello, darling. That was a quick walk." He looked rather ruddy. He stood in the doorway as though guarding something. Her heart beat slowly. "You look a little worse for wear."

"I stepped in mud. I fell over." She wanted him to come and help her, to be kind the way he would have been just a few months earlier, but also, she wanted him to stay away. There was the smell coming from her foot.

"Ah. Oh dear. And are you all right?"

"Quite all right. Just hurt pride. Do we have a visitor?" A terrible thought struck her. Surely he wouldn't have invited her here? She walked slowly towards the drawing room, one dirty boot still on, a far dirtier sock squelching on the carpet.

Peter looked at her in a kind of horror. "Good God, what is that smell? You're quite ruining the carpet."

She finished taking off her soiled coat and handed it to him, and he was forced to take it. "My boot came off and I fell in cow shit." A feeling of walking through tar. She heard the sofa complain as someone got up from it, and Peter had no option but to allow her into the room, his wrist shielding his nose from the smell. Reverend Jon Brown was standing with a cigarette and a glass of whisky in one hand.

"My dear Mrs. Hamilton!" he said. The two of them were a little drunk she realised. "Goodness me, you appear to have done yourself quite a mischief!" The fire roared.

"Reverend," she said. It made very little sense. "I see you're not here on God's work." She nodded to the fire. Reverend Jon Brown laughed loudly and for too long.

She turned to Peter, who sprang into action. "The reverend just popped over to talk about the boys."

"Yes," the reverend backed him up.

To accuse them both of lying would have gained her nothing.

"Oh. Again? And is everything all right?"

"Oh, quite all right, yes—we were just drinking to how all right things are."

"Were you."

"Yes," said Peter. There was a long silence which neither man tried to fill.

"Well. Perhaps I shall go and find Betty."

"Oh, she's gone out to find the girl."

"Bernadette, Reverend, her name is Bernadette."

"Yes, of course."

There was something disturbing about the way both of them conceded to her. She stood a moment longer in the doorway feeling foolish.

"Well. I shall change out of my wet clothes, I think."

"Right you are, darling."

"Reverend." She turned to go and behind her Peter closed the door. Their conversation did not start up again. She climbed the stairs slowly, thinking she might hear them rattling on, but all was silent. She had the distinct feeling they were whispering. She poured a large glass of whisky and took it into the bath and stayed there a long time. Afterwards she examined the beginnings of the long purple bruise across her back. She found she still had mud outlining her toenails and nothing could be done to get rid of it.

Peter came to bed late that night. For some time after Reverend Jon Brown had left, he had locked himself away in his study, and though she had stood outside his door, she felt unwelcome—and something else. She felt a little afraid, like some giant wheel had been set in motion and whatever she did to try and take control would only speed the thing up. She would wait until he came to her. She stayed up with the light on, but it was only after she turned it off that he entered the room. He came in already undressed and slipped under the covers so as not to wake her.

"What was Reverend Jon Brown doing here?"

She felt him hold his breath.

"I thought you were asleep."

"Well, I'm not. What was he here for?"

"To talk about the boys." He smelled strongly of whisky. It felt like an advantage she had over him.

"Why was it such a secret?"

"It wasn't a secret. I suppose we felt rather naughty being caught drinking before three."

"And what's the problem?"

He rolled over and sighed loudly. "What problem?"

"With the boys."

"Oh. Nothing really."

"What did you talk about all that time then?"

"Am I getting interrogated?"

"You said you thought him a lunatic."

"Well, maybe I was wrong. He's actually quite an interesting man if you spend the time to talk to him properly."

"Peter. What is going on?" She sat up and turned on the light. "What is happening? I demand to know."

He placed his hands over his face in frustration.

"Oh for God's sake."

"What is it?"

"Look." He propped himself up on his elbows. "Look. Would you agree that we haven't been getting along all that well recently?"

"Were you talking to him about me?"

"I was asking his advice."

"And what would he know?"

"He's a man who's lived a life. He—he has connections all over the place."

"What does that mean?"

"I just. Look, I think you've felt under some sort of pressure—maybe to live up to being a mother—and looking at how your sister carries on . . . I feel like that's been difficult for you, and perhaps what you need is a break."

"What on earth can you be talking about?"

"I'm talking about . . . I'm talking about these ideas you get in your head, about which you are totally unshakeable."

"About your girl in Edinburgh?"

"I'll have no more of that." His voice built suddenly and echoed in their room.

"Is that what you were talking about?"

"I was enquiring about the possibility of a voluntary short stay at a health spa. A couple of weeks."

"A spa? Why would I need to voluntarily stay at a spa? Aren't all spa visits voluntary?"

There was a pause in which she could sense him trying to arrange his words so that he remained in control.

"Are you trying to have me admitted to an asylum?"

Peter laughed loudly. "Dear God, woman. I just think a break is what you need—a holiday, and there's a nice place not too far from here. I'm trying to help you. You see, it's this paranoia that everyone's out to get you. The reverend told me about the picnic—that you blew a gasket because you lost a game of hide-and-seek. It's not the best way of making friends, is it?"

"That is not what happened."

"Well, either way, I don't think you're very happy the way things are, are you?"

She turned to him. "Are you?"

"Frankly, no."

"Well. You're the one with the heavy workload. Why don't you go off for a couple of weeks to this spa? Voluntarily. I dare say it would be as good for you as it would be for me."

He looked at her with his mouth a little open. Then he shook his head, smiled a smile of utter disbelief.

"I don't know what has happened to you in the past few months, but you've very little to do with the girl I thought I was marrying." He swung his legs out from under the covers and stood, taking his dressing gown from the chair. "And to be honest, I have to wonder where the behaviour problems that Christopher is experiencing at school have come from."

He left the room. Ruth sat there. She didn't feel how she expected to feel. There it was out in the open. In order to hide his affair, her husband was willing to have her committed to an insane asylum. She felt the thought form and looked at it, and did not feel afraid, just tense and poised. She heard him banging about down the hall in his study, the clink of the top of the whisky decanter being put back too strongly. She heard him marching about. Soon he would settle on the chaise longue and sleep there, she thought, and long after that she would fall asleep and in the morning they would find a way around it again. Instead she heard his study door open, and his heavy footsteps. He was coming back to argue more. Ruth quickly turned off the light and pretended to sleep.

"Right," he said loudly, as though something had been decided between them, "come on then." He grabbed her by the ankles and pulled her sharply.

"Peter."

"Shut up," he said, and yanked up her nightdress, and when she tried to turn away, knelt painfully on her and proceeded anyway. She stopped moving and played dead for the rest of it, because the absolute worst thing she could think of was the children hearing, and once he was finished he rolled over.

"See," he said, "there you are, you're still my wife." And it all seemed to make perfect sense to him, because he was suddenly calm and able to fall into a sleep from which he did not wake until late morning.

III

In the night, a familiar smell creeps into our camp. Sarah crawls towards my sleeping space.

"It's just a stinkhorn," she says with assurance, and she strokes my face, which has become, in the last weeks, covered in a light beard.

But I can't sleep for the memory that the smell brings with it, the first days of rot, the feeling of a ball of tallow nesting above my heart after Mother's funeral. The other three sleep, the sniffs and snores of Father and the women; the two of us are silent.

I see my mother's face in the dark canopy above us.

It is not crying, but the tears run out of me all the same. Sarah takes my hand in the dark. Before I can decide what to do about it, the warmth of her hand has softened the feeling in my chest and has me breathing easy again. All attention in my body is in that hand. I feel her heart beat through it, this live thing, like God. I move it underneath my shirt so that it rests on my chest, and she can feel my heart too. I sleep, I suppose, because the next I know, cold light shows the spiderwebs between leaves and grasses in the dark, which have caught nothing but dew water. The smell of the stinkhorn is lessened in the morning or I am used to it. There is the sound through the rain of running water. Sarah is gone. Perhaps, I think, she is relieving herself or foraging.

I leave the clearing and the sleeping bodies. The morning is unseasonably warm, and my throat pricked with thirst. The river is not far at all from our camp, I find it in minutes. I will wash my face and look for fish to catch. I daydream of returning to the clearing with three large trout, how Cook will place them over the fire and blacken their skin, when I see that Sarah is in the river. She wears nothing except for her shawl, which is wrapped around her and clings to her when she stands, billows up like wings when she floats. She is singing to herself, something I don't know. *He'll give up all his comfort and sleep out in the rain.* It is slow and serious like a wail of abandonment. Her belly, I see, is rounded in a way that tells of a child tucked away in there. I did not see this weeks ago, in the pig shed. But then I don't know how long it has been since that moment. It may be months rather than weeks.

My father shouts from the clearing. Sarah turns and she sees me, clutches her shawl to herself and makes towards the bank, but I am gone before she gets there.

The Widow Clements has gone in the night. Her coat lies like a body on the ground. Cook has a fever and her stomach makes sounds we can hear if nobody talks.

"Charlotte!" my father calls into the forest. "Charlotte, where are you? Come back! I'm sorry!"

We spread out and search to the river and the same depth of forest all around. There is nothing. We wait in the glade. I want to point out that the widow was for leaving Sarah when she was just gone a few moments finding us food, but I don't. Father looks afraid. Cook's eyes bulge, she is silent. The sun glides briskly overhead, shadows move and dance in the rain, and we build up the fire and leave Cook curled next to it, and set out and search again.

"She's gone," Sarah says, when we are far enough behind Father that he can't hear us. "And we should go too."

"Father isn't going to want to leave without her."

"Don't be so sure of that," she says, but when I ask her what she means, she shakes her head.

"We must keep moving."

"What are you talking about?"

But she turns to me, takes my hand and puts it under her dress to the tight drum of her stomach. My skin prickles and my mouth waters as though she is hare. She stands on the tips of her toes to reach my face and gives me a kiss; inside her mouth is hot, the rain finds its way between our lips, I taste salt. When she comes away, I am thudding to leave with her, my groin aches. We will leave together now and I will fuck her again, and all will be well.

"I cannot abandon my father."

"He abandoned you."

I decide not to hear her.

"What were you singing in the river?" I ask.

"It's a mourning song. I think I made it up."

"Is it a spell?"

"It's just a song."

"What were you doing in the river?"

"Washing."

"And . . ." I say, but am not sure how to continue.

"My belly," she says simply. "I would not have chosen it, but there it is. It is not the first time. It will not be the last."

My face burns with heroic thoughts. Though we are both young, when we get to where we are going I will help her, we can be together with the child, we can pretend it is mine. I can have her to keep, and her red hair and her white skin. The children at my feet, my hand on her knee.

We stop walking.

In front of us the forest floor has been rucked up, dead leaves and moss, freshly upturned earthworms and black beetles, the carcass of some animal, its ribs reaching out of the ground, the meat on them still red. There is the smell again, the stinkhorn, strong. Wolves. Sarah takes my arm and we turn round and make back for the clearing without speaking.

More time than we realised has passed when we get back. Father sits with his face in his hands and stands up quickly as we arrive.

"You're back."

"Yes."

"Nothing?"

I feel Sarah looking at me. "Nothing."

Cook is curled around the fire and does not wake. Her skin has a greenish colour, the sound of her breath like a broom sweeping a wooden floor. The next morning she is dead. All of us heard her last breaths in the night, and pretended we did not.

II

Bernadette sat with Michael by the fire. They missed each other in term time, and now the long summer holidays were on them, and they were thick with secrets. That was how Ruth thought about it now, not that she missed the children but that Bernadette was lonely without them. She saw a cleverness in the girl that scared her. It would be impossible for her to be happy in North Berwick once she was a young woman, when Christopher and Michael had left—and if an attraction should grow between the boys and the girl, Peter may insist upon her leaving. Betty was teaching Bernadette to cook, and without intervention the girl would leave school and be in service within a few years.

Ruth heard them laughing and wanted to see what it was about but feared disturbing them, it would have been terrible to interrupt. Instead she walked stealthily to the door of the drawing room and peered through the crack. They were whispering, smiling. Michael put a hand up and smote Bernadette with an imaginary weapon. She writhed on the floor calling, "You've done it now, you old witch!" The pair collapsed in laughter, and Ruth retreated to the kitchen to make tea. The play was still so innocent. The baby twitched against her pelvis.

She had not seen Christopher since lunchtime, when he took his net and set off for the rock pools at Milsey. Ordinarily the others would have gone too, but today they kept their distance. He was older suddenly, after the last term. He needed space. The boyishness had been siphoned off and replaced with something else. She would give it until two o'clock and then go looking for him.

She poured a cup without using a saucer, and some of the tea dribbled down the spout. She had not the knack. She wiped this away, located the biscuit tin. She was not hungry, just wanted something to occupy herself with, and Peter had been on at her that she needed more weight on *for the baby's sake*. He had threatened her with the health spa if she did not keep the weight up. But he had meant it kindly this time. He had made sure also to be at home more frequently, only away for one night here and there, and the odd day like today. If she inhaled deeply and thought about it just in the right way, she could see how she may have been wrong about things. Or at least she could see how her pregnancy changed things for Peter and that was where she made her thinking stop. *In order to be happy, one must think happy thoughts*. This was the advice of her mother during the terrible first months of the pregnancy, when Ruth had felt like she was adrift on a rough sea and had to lie with a damp cloth over her eyes and sip lemonade. It was only once the sick months had passed that she thought about this advice and how her mother had assumed it was put on out of unhappiness. And then again, she wondered, was it?

There was a knobbled flapjack which she placed on the saucer she ought to have used for her cup and she carried it into the dining room so that she could view the sea without disturbing the children. There was to be a cricket game on Sunday, and she had been asked to provide a savoury sandwich filling, and she was not quite clear on how much she was expected to make—Janet had said, "Oh, no need to go mad." An irritating answer. She would go mad if she pleased. She would ask Betty, though be firm that she was not asking her to carry out the task, which Betty would doubtlessly undertake to do anyway. The afternoon held a deep yellow light, and a warmth. Her thoughts at times felt not her own. A hamper had arrived, sent by Peter apparently, from Fortnum & Mason. The card reminded her to eat. The hamper sat unopened on the dining table. She knew what was inside—proof that he was in London. As though one couldn't arrange such a thing over the telephone. As though just because one was in London, one was automatically alone. Ruth blinked the thought away and took a cigarette from her pocket. The tea and flapjack sat untouched on the table and she smoked and looked out the window.

The sun reflected upon the water softly, not its usual sharp blinding light. The waves frothy at the water's edge, the shadows thrown by seaweed and rocks sharply defined and black. She thought of Christopher and his fishing net over in the next bay. How lovely to spend hours poring over the shapes and colours of those pools, alone, undisturbed, to be safe on the rocks and not to hear afterwards from one of the ladies in a cheery voice that you had been spotted tottering around, endangering yourself and the baby. The ripples that ebbed outwards as you poured sand into a pool, the urchins hiding in their turtlenecks. Perhaps she would take a net out, gambol like a child in the shallows. She didn't have to climb the rocks.

Ruth looked towards the rocks and saw Christopher was not in fact at Milsey but closer, on an outcrop that usually had a fisherman posted to it. He must have stopped on his way back, and was now one of the black shapes upon the black rocks. No doubt he was smoking. He looked out to sea as the waves splashed gently around him. On another day, this would have been dangerous, but the day was so calm.

The baby moved inside her. She wanted to stand in quiet reverence of the ocean with Christopher, name the birds, test the direction of the wind, break open the empty husk of a crab shell and watch it float away on the wind. Another shape emerged from the rocks—Reverend Jon Brown, and she wondered how long he had been there, if he had in fact been with Christopher all along. There was a lurch in her stomach, a tincture of alarm that made her look down, expecting to see an elbow poking out of her dress. She watched the man put his arm around Christopher's shoulders and move close to his face. It took a while for Ruth to understand Reverend Jon Brown was lighting his cigarette for him. He then walked away from the boy, who remained still and fixed on the horizon, and he walked with practised ease, like a man on holiday. Perhaps the reverend found that by giving Christopher a cigarette, the boy would trust him, and tell him the things that were troubling him. She tried hard to think happy thoughts, but what she found was that a familiar seasickness began to churn through her.

Reverend Jon Brown walked slowly to the mid-point of the bay, and the wind picked up. It was only evident in the way his hair danced straight upwards, like he hung upside down, and how his coat billowed out behind him. He turned to face the sea and he opened out his arms, as though beckoning down the sun. Another figure appeared quite suddenly at the dunes—unmistakable: it was Betty, not walking or running, but loping, as though she carried a great weight. Ruth picked up her cup. Betty's scarf blew off her head and her hair came loose around her. She must have called Jon

Brown's name because he turned towards her, but in a matter of seconds she had taken a mallet from beneath her coat and brought it down between his neck and shoulder, as though trying to strike his head off his body. He went down and Ruth could see his black open mouth, surprised, and Betty raised the mallet again, this time perhaps making contact with his head. Ruth could not say for sure; all she could see were Reverend Jon Brown's boots cycling pathetically in the sand. Betty raised up the mallet again and again brought it down, and the boots then were still. Ruth dropped her cup and held both hands over her mouth. From the drawing room, laughter.

She ran out the back door, through the garden gate and onto the empty golf course before she recognised she was barefoot, but carried on; the mild day turned suddenly very cold, the gust of wind that played in Reverend Jon Brown's hair moments ago had brought with it ice from the north. She searched the black rocks for Christopher, but couldn't see him. She reached the sand, where things were bad. Betty sitting in the sand keening, wailing. The water licked at her ankles and Reverend Jon Brown's head. Jon Brown, dead. His ears the same, his hairline the same, but his face gone, just an empty basket of bone and pulp. The mallet lay next to him in the water. The sand around them a cake of pink, but the water by Jon Brown's head, black.

"What did you do?" Ruth said into the wind. She held her fingers over her mouth in case she might breathe in some airborne pulp.

Betty looked up at her, black hair plastered all over her face, catching in her eyelashes. "He took my Mary's brain. He had them burn it out of her."

*

318

There was barely a moment of hesitation, and Ruth found it hard to understand her strength as she pulled the rowing boat down to the water's edge.

"Help me lift him," she said and Betty looked up as if she had forgotten Ruth was there. The woman's face was far away and white. She stood slowly, wiped her hands down her coat, and took Jon Brown's shoulders. She looked directly into the cave of his face.

"Don't look at it." Ruth took the scarf that had blown off Betty's head and covered the face.

She took his ankles. He was so heavy, the water was seeping into him, even just a leg felt impossible.

"On three. One, two—"

They heaved and scrabbled, Betty sinking into the waterline, Ruth feeling herself bearing down, like she might birth there and then.

"One, two—" Again, they half lifted, half pushed Jon Brown into the small boat, where he tumbled, leaden, into the hull, landing face down, making the water in the bottom of the boat turn brilliant crimson, then, quickly, black. Betty hurled in the mallet and it gonged like a church bell.

I

"Now look," I say as we pull up outside the house. The sky is just lightening, it has rained in North Berwick recently, the road is sodden. "I have a friend staying."

My sister looks at me. "Is this the guy you're seeing?"

"No. Her name is Maggie."

"Oh. Oh—are you seeing Maggie?"

"No. She's a friend."

"A friend."

"Yes. Look, I'm only saying because she can come across a bit strange. I don't want you to freak out about her."

"What is there to freak out about?"

"Well, she sometimes, and not all the time, just sometimes when things are slow and she's broke, I think—she sometimes does a bit of sex work. I wouldn't have said anything, except she's the sort of person who might just bring it up at any moment like she's talking about the weather, and I just don't want you to get offended and then . . ."

I look at my sister, expecting a face of horror.

"Viv. It's really none of my business." She has never seemed less herself, with morning light in her unbrushed hair and improperly removed eyeliner. She is a smudged version of my sister.

"Cool then," I say.

"I got paid to fuck someone once," she says. I have taken the keys out of the ignition, and I put them back in to have something to do with my hands. "And to be honest I don't feel strange about that. Sex has bought me a lot worse things than money." She looks at me. I am holding the steering wheel. "Do you disapprove?" she asks.

"No. I just didn't know." But that's not it. "I feel bad I didn't know that about you. No one has ever offered to pay to have sex with me."

Katherine smiles. She lightly thumps my arm. "I bet if you took up yoga and drank some water someone would pay to have sex with you."

Inside, we find Maggie in the dining room. She has put a bunch of carnations in a vase on the table and she's sitting with her legs crossed on the window seat looking out towards the sea. From her earphones comes a tinny version of "When a Man Loves a Woman." Maggie is sniffing. She hasn't noticed us, so I knock hard on the open door. Her head whips round and she takes us in like a predator, recognises me and softens. She rips the earphones out.

"Hey," she says and gets up and gives me an unexpected hug. "This is your sister?"

"Yes, this is Katherine. Katherine, this is Maggie."

"You look the same."

I snort as though I'm eight years old. Maggie wraps her arms around Katherine and hugs her.

"Hi," she says through a squeeze. Tentatively Katherine puts her arms around Maggie, sends me an uncertain look.

"Nice to meet you," she says.

Maggie releases Katherine and turns to me. Sniffs. "You know there's a ghost here, right?"

To my surprise Katherine answers, "The girl with the hair?"

Maggie looks at her. "She's so sad."

"Excuse me," I say, but I have no further thoughts on what to say next.

"I thought no one else saw her," says Katherine. "You never saw her, did you, Viv?"

"Well, no."

Maggie and Katherine look at each other.

Pathetically, I feel left out.

Katherine is straddling the garden wall, talking to Mum on the phone.

"So what's the deal with Katherine?" Maggie asks. She takes a long sip from her coffee, which I notice she has upgraded to cafetière coffee in my absence.

"I guess her husband might be more of an arsehole than I thought."

"Oh?"

"Hey," I say—I don't want to talk about Dom, and have to remind myself that he is not mine to talk about, "when we came in, you seemed like maybe you were crying?"

"I *was* crying."

"Is everything OK?" Maggie puts down her cup.

"Sometimes things are just really sad."

"Which things?"

Maggie sighs. "I was thinking about work. How we work for money, to have nicer things—and that's all fair enough until you think about what those things are." She talks slowly, like she's very tired. "A pair of shoes, a nicer chair to sit in, a phone that you can use to look at pictures of other people's nice lives. Fancier salmon on your bread, mint humbugs from Marks & Spencer, a lovely imported tomato."

Her voice is brittle in the way it gets when she's lost in herself. Her hands are flat on the table, and she focuses on the old clock above the door.

"And it seems mad that you'd do that shit job you hate just so you can have a nice tomato which will be gone in two minutes."

I watch Katherine sign off from Mum, and sit for a moment looking out at the sky. A seagull gambols in the updraught. Katherine swings her leg over the wall and slides down onto the bench.

"And it's the same with men and women. The reason men want women is to fuck them, ultimately, right? And sometimes, once they've fucked them, they kill them because they weren't allowed to fuck them and they don't want to get in trouble. And always it's about property, it's about being clear that this is your tomato that you worked hard for and it should do the thing you expect of a tomato, it should sit on your plate until you cut it open and sprinkle on the salt." Maggie leans forward. "Am I talking shit?"

"I don't know."

"It's just, how does it make sense? Why would a person throw another person away like that? That's the question. And what I realise is there's no answer—it doesn't matter if there's a reason for it. That person doesn't like redheads, they feel rejected, their mother used to dress them up in sailor suits."

The last message from Vincent: *Don't forget I know where you live. You can't just disappear.*

Katherine is standing in the doorway.

"John's dead," she says.

"What?"

I stand and sit down again. Maggie stands and takes the whisky out of the cupboard.

323

"Who is John?" she asks.

"Our great-uncle. He was old and sick."

Katherine sits down and Maggie pours the drinks, just for Katherine and me. I don't know why it feels momentous, but it does.

It is a surprise when Katherine starts to cry. I put my hand over her cold one.

"Sorry," says Katherine. "I was horrible to him when he came to Mum's. I think he saw me rolling my eyes when he was talking about partridge."

"It's OK—he didn't notice. I promise you."

She sniffs. "Anyway, the funeral will be here in a week so Pauline doesn't have to travel far. Uncle Christopher is sorting it. Mum's coming up."

"Hey," says Maggie. She takes hold of my hand and of Katherine's. "Close your eyes."

There is no other point in our lives when either of us would follow these instructions, but I see Katherine close her eyes without hesitating and it feels good to follow orders. When my eyes are closed, Maggie starts humming and then chanting. I am surprised that I'm not embarrassed.

> *Diana, goddess of the moon, light the light*
> *Pan, horned god of the wild earth, light the light.*

She squeezes our hands and we join in, and we just say these sentences over and over, and there's the feeling that you get when you're crying and shouting in the car on the motorway, but also later a feeling of elation, and all there is, is the rosy black of my closed eyes and the sounds reverberating in my teeth and it feels good, I am just my hands joined to my sister's and my eyeballs safe in their sockets, my tongue and my spine all the way down to my base. I don't know how long we chant for, but it is like I'm a bat or a whale, and I can see that there are people in the kitchen with us, there are children and women, all holding hands like us, and I wonder, is this the ghost everyone sees, is it in fact a hundred thousand different ghosts? It's only possible to focus on one at a time. They spill out of the doorway, and I see through the wall that they fill the house top to bottom, they are locked in wardrobes, they are under the floorboards, they crowd out of the back door and into the garden, they are on the golf course and on the beach and their heads bob out of the sea, and when we walk, we are walking right through them. The birds on the Bass Rock, they fill it, they are replaced by more, their numbers do not diminish with time, they nest on the bones of the dead.

"What in tarnation is happening here?" Deborah stands in the doorway, a plastic file clutched to her breast.

"Hello, Deborah," I say, and I feel for some reason elated. Deborah looks behind my head at something and the colour drains from her face. She drops her plastic folder and leaves and her footsteps echo down the corridor and the door slams behind her.

"That's her," says Katherine, who is facing me and can see behind. Maggie does not open her eyes. I don't turn round but I can smell the woods, the earth and the rain.

The opening chords of a song play loudly in the master bedroom, a man, dark-haired, wiry, stands legs apart in the middle of the room testing the swing of his golf club. He is wearing yellow trousers that flare out at the ankle, and no shirt. He mimes along to the song.

When a man loves a woman, swinging the golf club, enjoying himself. He raises it above his head like someone who has won a prize, as horns sound. He sings loudly over the top of the music. If she's a bitch, he can't see it and applies his gaze to the corner of the room. His poise changes, as if he is being lifted by the nape of the neck, and he squares his shoulders and stalks leisurely in time with the music to the corner of the room, where a woman is crouched. He uses the golf club as a microphone. He'll give up all his comforts, and go and sleep in a drain, then swings the club in the air above the woman's head, she cowers, and then scrambles across the floor to the doorway. As she stands he manages to hook the club under her ankle and she falls, hard. He moves calmly, everything is slow as if he has watched the scene play out before and knows what will happen, everything is choreographed in time with the song. She pulls herself up on the door jamb, and her face is mottled with blood, her nose has burst, the area around her throat is purple-red and she is having trouble standing. She moves out of the room, unsteady, and the man follows at a leisurely pace, golf club strung across the back of his neck with his wrists draped over. He disappears from the room. Baby, please don't treat me bad. Even through the volume of the record, there is an audible thump and then another. He reappears, the woman crawling on all fours as he holds a large clump of her hair, as though it were the neck scruff of a dog. He hoists her up onto the bed. She is not much conscious, only following orders, they are the only thing she can connect with. He stands at the foot of the bed, windmills his arm like Elvis Presley. When a man loves a woman. Deep down in her hole. She brings him such misery.

He jumps up on the bed, smiling, calm excitement. He straddles the woman, pushes his club up under her chin, and rests his weight on it. He stops singing, he stops miming, the music is gone from him, he bares his teeth, applies all of his pressure on the club. There is blood on the mattress, but where it comes from is unclear. It could be from so many places. A tugboat sounds its horn at the lighthouse keeper as it passes the Bass Rock.

The Cave

I

Mum has brought with her three bottles of wine, which is better than whisky. "I would have brought more," Mum says as we head to the kitchen. "But I couldn't carry them on the train and look after that old cow." The dog is rattled by her train journey and nods to everyone through squinted eyes and curls up in the easy chair by the unlit fire. She hides her nose with her tail, eyeballs us, and switches herself off.

We haven't talked about what happened in the kitchen; instead we have spent the past few days getting the house ready for the wake. I wouldn't say I'm not afraid of what I felt behind me at the kitchen table. But she felt so like the rock out there in the sea, an immovable observer, unchanged and calm.

Maggie is sitting at the kitchen table and she smiles shyly at Mum.

"Mum, this is Maggie." Maggie hugs our mother in a way neither of us would. Mum is surprised but in the end she closes her arms around Maggie and returns the squeeze.

"It's very good to meet you," Maggie says.

"Yes," says Mum, and she wipes her eyes. "I'm sorry, I don't know who you are. But you do seem very nice."

Maggie beams.

"Nothing changes, does it?" says Mum, glancing about the room.

She takes a small bowl from a cupboard. She opens a bag of pistachios and there is the sound of her pouring them into the white bone-china bowl. She puts the nuts on the table along with a pale green mug.

"Shells," she says, indicating the mug.

One after another we pick out a handful of nuts and begin the process of shelling and eating. The sound of the shells in the mug. The tick of the clock, wine glasses on the kitchen table.

"My mother underwent a lumbar puncture on this table." Our mother says this as though it will brighten the mood.

"So there's that," says Katherine.

Mum lets a handful of shells fall in single file into the green mug. She never talks about her mother.

"When she was a child, she lived here, just like me."

Maggie picks up her cigarettes. "I've got to go and check my messages on the wall," she says, and stands up using my shoulder to balance on. She squeezes it lightly before picking up her wine glass. I don't know what she has sensed. Once she is gone, Mum refills our glasses and sighs.

"I still chat to your father, you know. I still ask him what we're going to eat for dinner, and I still argue with him about the same boring stuff. But John—and I know he was very old. And I know it comes to us all. But all of his memories and thoughts. All of his routines. All of John's secrets, whatever they were. That's it, because no one is left behind talking to him." Our mother's eyes have filled. I have never seen her cry, it is deeply unnerving.

"Mum," says Katherine.

The morning it happened, Katherine had stayed over. She called me at seven and said, *Dad's died. Take your time.*

And I did take my time, I showered and dressed and then I sat in the car listening to *Graceland* for close to an hour.

For that hour he was still alive, because Katherine may have lied. And then I drove to Mum's and was met by Dom, who had tears streaking down his face. He hugged me and breathed into my hair, then he held my face and said *He's gone, he's gone.*

I stroked the wiry hair at his sideburn all the way down to his jawline. *People do go*, I said, and it sounded like I spoke a foreign language. He went for a walk to clear his head.

In the kitchen, Mum and Katherine were as tearless as me, but the dog was worried by something, she kept offering her head to us as we sat. All of us embraced—that was the correct word for it—comfortless squeezes that ended quickly so that we might all carry on. We drank a whisky at 9:30, and then Mum said, *You should go up and see him. It's important.* And I realised I had forgotten there was anything to see. I stood outside the kitchen for a moment, wondering if I would just pretend to see him, but Mum had said *it's important*, and so I followed her advice, and in their room, he lay with a counterpane over him, tucked in up to his chest, his arms neatly laid over the top, hairless and yellow with large still hands. His head and feet large too, his body just as flat as the counterpane. I watched closely for breath. His mouth was open just enough to see the outline of one ruined tooth. His eyes were open too. I watched closely for breath. He looked to be concentrating on skinning a tomato. I did the thing that people do in films and passed my hand over his eyelids to shut them, but it didn't work and so I just stroked his face, and drew my hand away like it had been burned and had the impulse to wash it immediately. I watched closely for breath. I wanted to have a thought, but I felt like I was in the presence of a stranger. I went to the window and opened it. Across the street, Dom was sitting on the wall of the house opposite, writing in a notebook. He looked up when the window opened and when he saw who it was he blew me a kiss.

She lets out a long exhale.

Katherine looks at the table on which our grandmother underwent her lumbar puncture.

Mum takes a handkerchief from out of her sleeve and blows her nose longer than any human can possibly need to. "Oh dear," she says. Katherine pats her hand and Mum withdraws hers quickly. "I'm fine, just a bit tired."

"Christopher should be arriving tomorrow morning," I say to have something to say. "He's bringing some sandwiches and some wine."

Mum, now completely in control again, says, "Did I ever tell you girls that Christopher and me were together before your father?"

Katherine picks up her wine glass and moves it a foot away from herself, then moves it back. "No. No, Mum, you didn't mention that."

"Well," says Mum.

"What are we supposed to do with that?" she asks. Mum shrugs. The tears are a distant memory.

"He didn't want kids." She shrugs again.

I excuse myself and get up and leave the room. I go into the ballroom and stand for a moment. I watch Maggie outside smoking on the wall. Katherine comes and stands next to me. Mum appears in the garden, to top up Maggie's drink, Maggie hands her the roll-up she is halfway through and Mum smokes. I've never seen her smoke before. I watch her mouth the smoke expertly.

"Right," I say. "I fucked Dom." It is out of my mouth. She looks at me.

"Yes. I know."

"You know?"

We stand like that looking at each other for the longest time.

"How long have you known?"

"Long enough." She sniffs deep and hard. My fingers go up to my head and down again. "And honestly, I wanted to tell you—I wanted to say, hey! Thanks! You've ruined my marriage!" She makes not quite a laughing sound. "But you were too ill. And fragile. I didn't want it to be my fault that you got sick again."

I lean against the wall and slide down it. *Now what? Now what?* squeaks the voice.

The hospital hadn't been about Dad. It was all I talked about in there. His illness, my memories of fights we'd had we hadn't ever settled. The touch of his dead skin.

But what I had thought about was that Dom had wanted me, more than he wanted Katherine. The kiss blown at the window.

"There's too much to think about." It is so typical of my sister to do that—forgive.

"Look," she says, in the tone I have heard her use for travel agents and shop assistants. "Dom and I weren't going to last. He's a fuckwit. Which doesn't make it all right that you did what you did, but I don't want you going around thinking you were the only element that ended us."

"Should I have told you?"

Katherine shrugs. "It doesn't matter. This is how it is."

I dig my back into the wall and we both look out at the deserted golf course.

"I can't settle on what to think about."

My inner squeak is silent.

I pull up my knees and rest my forehead on them.

Katherine places her hand on my knee and moves it in circles. It is the kindest thing. The dog wanders in and lies underneath the piano.

In the night I spy on Katherine in the bed next to me—the bed Dad or Christopher would have slept in as children. Two sisters sleeping in the beds of two brothers. It's like a riddle where the answer is something annoying like *Romeo is a goldfish* or *they were killed with an icicle*. I wonder if Christopher ever spied on Dad to make sure he was breathing. In the moonlight I see Katherine as stiff as a mannequin, thin fingers laced over her stomach, eyes open to the night air. In the morning she will be pristine, competent.

The funeral is at St. Baldred's, a strange little church with a large monkey puzzle tree outside, bearing a plaque to a vicar lost long ago to the sea. Inside, they have an empty coffin for show—John's ashes are in the boot room at the house—Pauline asked that we look after them. They came in the purple plastic container, which Mum has put in a supermarket Bag for Life, a confusing message. The church is small and half filled, the only people I know are Pauline and Alistair, but I recognise a number of faces from town, mostly very old. John was eighty-three by two months. There are photographs of him up in the church; in one he is a child and stands with Pauline and his other sister Elspeth, Dad and Christopher's mother, who died young from bad lungs. I get that creepy feeling— the one where you look at a long-dead woman and know that she has the requisite materials of creation within her to make your existence possible.

*

Christopher missed us at the house, and it's not until we're all settled in the church that he appears in the doorway. He and my mother kiss and then there is a moment of shyness from both of them. I wonder if it has been there all along.

He sits next to Mum and the backs of their hands touch on the bench. I catch Katherine's eye and she raises an eyebrow, shrugs.

Maggie has come. She is sitting in the front row, even. She has been implanted within our family, and though, when I think about it too hard, it seems strange and unnatural, in general it seems correct. She is excellent at talking to Pauline, I can hear Pauline going on at her in front of me.

"Alistair may go golfing later on this afternoon—" she pronounces golfing to rhyme with coughing—"and then we've booked supper at the marina. We had Nigel's wedding there—aeons ago now."

"Who is Nigel?" Maggie asks, and it occurs to me Maggie is actually interested. They bow their heads closer to her. For them too she has slotted in.

"Oh, our son," says Pauline, and with pride she adds, "a solicitor."

Alistair arrives having parked the car; he lumbers somewhat. Maggie stands to shake his hand.

"Trouble is parking around these parts now," he says loudly, over his deafness. He doesn't let go of her hand, though he can have absolutely no idea who she is.

"Oh, I know," says Maggie. "Did you try the seabird centre? They don't check their pay and display tickets."

"Good tip," Alistair says, touching his finger to his forehead. These people I try hard to avoid are kind. I know that I will continue to avoid them. But there it is, they are nice. I think of them taking Dad and Christopher their sugar mice, so long ago. Something in a sea of nothing.

The vicar fluffs up by talking about Lazarus. Mum whispers, "Idiot," loud enough that I can hear and Christopher smiles. When the vicar has wrapped up his part by inviting us all to take a leaflet about the Alpha course after the ceremony, Christopher gets up and talks. I don't hear any of what he says; instead I play back the speech he gave at Dad's funeral.

"*My little brother,*" he said. "*The wild man of south London.*" *There was a murmur of amusement.*

"*Oh yes,*" *Pauline had confirmed.*

"*Quite,*" *John had agreed.*

"*I remember the day Michael was born. I remember our mother, Elspeth, lying in a hospital bed, and she said, 'Look what I've brought you.' And really at the time I would have preferred a copy of the* Eagle, *or a Dinky Toy.*" *Another rumble of approval.* "*But then after she had left us, I came to see what it meant to have a brother. It was he who at seven years old suggested we might ride the pigs in the neighbouring farm in Dummer, and he who saved me a thrashing from the farmer, making him laugh by falling face first in the mud. We had some delicate explaining to do when we arrived home. Nanny was not pleased.*" *Pauline had clapped her hands together.* "*And then later, he came to board with me at Fort Gregory, and though one would not call our years there happy exactly, they were always entertaining times with Michael. One rather feels this is not the time to bring up how he set Matron's skirts alight, nor how he became a legendary thief, collecting cigars, measures of brandy and once the housemaster's switch, which we ritually burned together.*"

"*Mmmm,*" *Alistair had said, as though being told of the specials at a restaurant.*

"A little further on he was a boy full of secrets. He weathered all kinds of contraband searches by making a false bottom to a can of fizzy pop. In there he hid at least an ounce of weed, and he was always good for cigarettes and of course his prized high-quality LSD."

Christopher spoke with a smile. The vicar had laughed loudly and uncomfortably as Pauline, John and Alistair had nodded and mumbled agreeably.

"Of course later in life he set his eyes on the birds, and never really took his eyes off them. His affection for the gannets of the Bass Rock, the white ghosts." Here Christopher had looked at Mum. There was something unknown to me there that explained the whole lot of us.

Christopher had straightened himself, wiped his eye with a red-spotted handkerchief.

"And I like to think, although you will have to allow me a certain amount of sentimentality here, I like to think our mother has simply come to take back what she brought me that day in the hospital." There was a gust of emotion from someone behind me but I didn't look. *"My little brother Michael was a kind soul. He was a little broken from life's eccentricities, but he was deeply humane and quietly funny, and I feel the loss of his presence in the world. I shall always think of him fishing in the rock pools at North Berwick with a net, a small bear, Wilfred, tucked in his coat pocket."* There was a small movement to my left, which I took to be a cat streaking by, but when I looked I saw Mrs. Hamilton, her face of bone and paper, a red handkerchief held up to her mouth.

There are drinks and what Aunt Bet would have called "a spread put on" back at the house, but there are not many of us after Alistair has gone for his golf and Pauline for a lie-down. What is missing is John's commentary on the buffet. Maggie takes around platters of vol-au-vents and disgusting curried eggs, and makes sure everyone's glass is topped up. It's as if she has become the good daughter and it means that Katherine can sit quietly and not fix anything. I find it hard to take my eyes off Mum and Christopher. I wonder if there was ever a possibility of a three-parent family. Whenever one of them has to talk to someone else, it is with effort they drag their eyes from each other. Christopher has the same eyes as Dad, as me. Mum leaves the room for a moment, and Christopher comes and sits next to me and seems as though he will say something profound. He is searching for the words. "Deborah quit," he says.

"Oh—oh God, I'm sorry, was it—"

"It's absolutely fine, there are more estate agents than houses. I just had to give her a try, you know—she had such a rough go of it, what with Dad going off and leaving them." He draws breath to speak, but from the direction of the front door someone is calling my sister's name. Bellowing it. The small party of us grow silent. Katherine is glued to the grey sofa. Dom stands in the open doorway.

"Oh dear," says someone, like a child has spilled a glass of water.

In one hand Dom holds a hammer. When he sees me he smashes it against the wall, and the plaster falls onto the floor.

"Dom," I say, but he doesn't hear me, calls Katherine's name again.

"You WILL talk to me," he bellows. I feel my heart beat through my spine. He does not see me. He sees Katherine, she is small and dark on the sofa. He begins to stride towards her. Christopher stands, and my mother comes out of the kitchen. She moves to intercept him, Christopher moves to stand with her. Mum holds a knife.

Maggie walks quietly and calmly past us all, towards Dom. Too late I make a grab for her and she puts her hands on Dom's shoulders and whispers something into his ear, and as she does it she takes the hammer from him. I can see she is speaking quickly, and Dom's face changes, the colour drains from it, he is almost like a boy again, not an ape, and when Maggie pulls away, a light smile on her lips, he looks around him like he is seeing something for the first time, and he backs away, terror on his face. At the garden gate he starts to run. Maggie places the hammer on the tallboy, and on her way to the kitchen, picks up a spent tray of sandwiches.

"What did you say to him?" Katherine asks from behind me. Her face is white.

Maggie shrugs. "Just said it's not the time or place." She winks at me. Through my tights I rub at the spot where my scab used to be.

II

Those first months after Antony died, and the birds came thick and fast to her window, Ruth had felt certain. She had known what she was there for, she was there to interpret the birds, just like the Pope was there as the mouthpiece to God. She had known this, and yet she had also known it wasn't for her mother or father or even for Alice that Antony spoke through the birds, it was for her alone. She was the way in which his elements remained in the world. If she had a baby one day, it would be a boy and she would call him Antony, and then he would speak through the baby. In fact, it had become an urgent worry to her, almost as soon as he died, to have a baby, to create a life, to whisper into the growing child all the secrets of who he was and how they had been together. And one day the child would be able to answer back and would answer back in the voice of her brother. She felt certain of it. She was left with his secrets, told to her alone, and with him gone, they threatened to disintegrate like ash. She had tried first with the curate, who had when she was younger expressed an interest. But when she went to him at eighteen and suggested a union, he turned red, said, "Get away from me, I don't know what you're talking about, don't come here again." Which had left her confused. She suspected he had been scared off by her boldness. Girls were supposed to be shy and retiring.

For a while she had tried to summon a baby within herself without a man. She sat and thought about Antony and about how the grains of his bones existed somewhere in the world and how they might blow into the sea, and be taken up into the clouds and rained back down, and all of it felt like a magic spell. When nothing happened, her belly sat there, skinny and white and silent, she took herself off to a country fair and met a young man with dark hair who manned the tombola. She picked a ticket out of the box and asked when he finished work.

"Now, if you're asking," he said, and took her to the hayloft in the next field. Having little idea of how it happened in nature, only that a man was required, Ruth put her hands palm down on the straw and tried to tell just by his touch what was going on.

"Does it hurt?" he kept asking, in a hoarse voice.

"Not in the slightest," she said and noted her voice was flat. Perhaps it ought to mimic his a little more, but she found herself very tired, and so just let him do what he would. He seemed not to mind.

Afterwards, he asked, "Have you done this much?"

"Just this once," she replied, and he nodded gravely.

"Well, you'll want to move about a bit more if you're going to have a future."

Perhaps it was a joke, but it didn't particularly matter to her. She went home and waited. And nothing at all happened.

At the hospital in Edinburgh, in the weeks after the incident on the beach, the walls of her room were duck-egg blue. There was a dressing table, in case she should want to have a sit-down and a long look at herself. It was a different one from the room in which the baby had come out and made no noise, that terrible quiet. She had asked Peter to bring her a drink and he had misunderstood and sent for tea.

"Can you bring me a bottle of sherry?" she had asked, and the nurse had overheard, and said, "Not with your bleeding."

A silver kidney dish by her bedside, in case of nausea. Next to that a framed photograph of her and Peter on their wedding day. Peter had brought it in to make the room more homely, he said. He came once a day, stayed until he could bear it no longer—she could see it on his face. And it was convenient to be in Edinburgh, she supposed. If all had gone well for her, the other baby would be a couple of months old now. She felt at times a genuine misery for Peter.

There was a grey television on a brass stand. Two dark blue lamps standing in diagonally opposite corners of the room. The one nearest her lit a framed oval photograph of a young woman in Victorian dress. Who she was wasn't clear, perhaps that was what Florence Nightingale looked like. Ruth had never seen a picture of her. The image was small but the frame ornate. The table it sat on was covered with a white crochet, seemingly designed specifically for the table, and the table itself was there just to house the framed portrait and its crochet.

On another table, which would be wheeled around and slotted over her when time came to eat, was a squat yellow jug and a vase of chrysanthemums. The jug had hairline cracks in the glaze. There were two chairs in the room, one a pale pink easy chair, the kind that would not have looked out of place in their drawing room. It had, she suspected, a reclining back and also a footstool. The other chair was a modern blocky orange thing, rather more austere and less comfortable. When her parents had visited, her father was able to feel useful by insisting her mother sit in the pale pink, resigning himself to discomfort in the modern chair. Her mother had wept in that chair—weeping was the correct word for it. It made the noise, *weep weep weep*. And then later as her mother had screwed up her handkerchief, she was able not to weep, but ask instead, *What on earth were you thinking, out on those rocks in your condition?* and her father had shushed her mother gently. Her mother had left a light mark on the fabric, a weeping stain, where her tear-soaked handkerchief had bled into the grain of the material. Alice had come without Mark and used the modern chair as a surface on which to lay the hamper she had brought from Harrods, inside of it apparently a great list of delicacies, all of which turned Ruth's stomach to such an extent she had to ask the matron to distribute it among the nurses after Alice had left. Alice had chatted a lot and then she was quiet a long time and held Ruth's hand and said, *It wasn't meant to be, was it, Puss?* When Betty came, she did not use the chairs. She bribed the night sister and came after dark with port and they talked it through, Betty standing at the side of her. They didn't talk once of Jon Brown, and in fact neither did they talk of the baby.

Betty said, "When you're ready to be at home again, I'll give you all the help you need," and then she read out letters from Christopher, Michael and Bernadette, wishing her well, and hoping she would be home soon. She stayed long enough for two glasses of port and then she hid the bottle and Ruth's glass in her bedside cabinet.

III

When I find them, Sarah is on top of Father so that I can only see the back of her head. She does not struggle. I wish she would struggle. Father's eyes are closed. Something more than disgust wells up in me, something else. Disappointment run through with nails. I understood that he saw Agnes in her, but she has made him see Mother too.

We were to wed, to have children of our own. To keep Father in his dotage in a room off the parlour, like we had kept Cook. Sarah to pack his pipe for him in the evenings, a child sat on his knee by the fire, a pot steaming with good things to eat. I am ashamed to have had these thoughts, to have held her hand and thought she had them too. The softness of the skin of her cold arm. It is so like a witch to make a man fall in love.

The rain it patters off the leaves. The sky above the trees is lightening with dawn. Still I stand behind them undetected. The stick I hold in my hands is heavy and thick, the kind sawn down to make gateposts. I don't recall where I found it. A small disgusting noise comes from them. Sarah moans.

The sound the stick makes when it comes down on her head is the sound of digging a spade into thick mud. She is torn off him, and with his eyes open wide in confusion, he scrambles to cover himself, to get away from what is happening.

Sarah looks up at me from where she crouches in the dirt and leaves of the forest floor. A white puckering of her skin at her temple, and then blood flows out, redder even than her hair. She keeps her eyes on mine, but they are not seeing me.

"If she had lived she would have been just like you," she says, in a voice not quite her own. She keeps herself away from the ground, on all fours like she knows to lie down is to die, she sways there, as though in a body of water. I wonder how long she would live, left in this way—if she has some root or tincture she can apply to her poor broken head, some pleading, some suckling with the Devil.

I strike her again across the forehead, and she flips onto her back, surely she is done, but her chest rises and falls fast like a sick animal. Her hands find her belly and her lips move, her eyes as dead as a baitfish. I kneel next to her and put my ear close to her face, to hear the last breaths. All is clear now, I understand what the Brownings had seen in the pig shed. The breath hisses out of her in short bursts, and with the last of them she says, "Look. Look, it's a baby." And then her face stills and her hand falls from her belly. I have set free the souls of countless men. I take the small wooden box containing the hare's teeth from her pocket. When I open it there are the teeth, nothing more special than that, but I keep it, because I must be reminded of empty promises.

Father is white. I look at him. He has tears in his eyes.

"It wasn't her," I tell him. I get up and crouch next to him, help him to cover himself, place a hand on his back. "She was only wearing Mother's dress to trick you. She made herself into the image of Agnes to bewitch you. You were bewitched." And I hadn't known these words would come out of me, but as I say them, I see that they are true and there is such a thing as evil in the world.

"All will be well now, Father," I say and he sniffs back tears, wipes his eyes and breathes out of his nose. He pats my arm.

"Thank you, son. Thank you so much." And my disappointment is replaced with pride.

II

It was nice that the boys and Bernadette still thought of the place as home. It was though rather ridiculous that she still thought of them as *the boys*. Ruth watched out of the top bedroom as Michael and Bernadette arrived, Michael carrying the baby, Bernadette swinging her arms like a child. Her hair had turned a deeper red in adulthood, and Ruth could never be sure if it was coloured or if Bernadette's life really was as carefree and as simple as she made it seem. No bra, she noted.

As she heard the doorbell chime, she saw Christopher arrive behind them. He stood hidden a moment, perhaps to let the baby be introduced to its great-aunt, or to finish off his cigarette in peace. It was only the matter of half a minute, and then he rounded the garden wall and flashed a smile in greeting. She could hear his practised loud friendly voice, heard him cooing to either the dog or the baby, the murmur of Michael's softer voice and Bernadette laughing in the way that she did, the way that Betty had described as *a laugh like a drunk sailor*. There was a feeling in the bones of the house when all visited at once, everything fused back together, the marrow of the house became dewy again, a warmth, like it rolled over in its sleep and opened one eye and smiled.

*

The girl had started to appear in a more or less regular way. It could quite easily be the first showings of a habit with gin, that would be no great surprise. She would see a fleeting movement out of the corner of her eye, look up expecting the dog, and instead see, just for a moment, a girl with a shawl wrapped around her shoulders. She disappeared if looked at straight on, but just now she stood in the corner of the room, picking at the quicks of her fingernails. She would stay there as long as Ruth continued to look at her own hands, clasped on the dressing table. She had wondered at first what the girl meant—that death was near? She had been near and getting closer for some years now, and it had stopped being frightening. It was just a third person in the household to take into account, a silent fixture which had meant that when the opportunity had arisen to sell the house, she had not. For a long while she had awaited a message from the girl. But the girl did not speak.

Ruth pinched her cheeks and tucked her hair behind her ears, took the stairs carefully, and found them all in the drawing room, the baby wrapped in a blanket and very much asleep in Christopher's arms.

All looked up.

"Darling," she said to Bernadette, and Bernadette smiled and moved towards her. They exchanged kisses on the cheek, Bernadette's pleasantly cool.

Michael stood and kissed her too. Christopher remained seated, unable to move in case the baby woke.

"Are you quite well?" Ruth asked Bernadette.

"Oh, I'm fine," she said. "Grateful to be out of London."

Ruth's hands were laced in front of her, and she couldn't for the life of her remember where they usually put themselves.

"Well," she said from afar, peering at the child, "she certainly looks very well too. And have you a name yet?"

"Viviane," said Bernadette, and Ruth tried to look like she thought it a pretty name.

"It means *lively*," said Michael, perhaps noting a look of uncertainty on Ruth's face.

"Yes," said Bernadette, "she's a wriggler."

"Well, I'm sure," said Ruth and smiled. She was, she realised, afraid of the baby.

Christopher's hands looked enormous next to it and rough. He held her like she was a bowl filled to the brim of water and he mustn't spill her. He was conspicuously quiet, and Ruth noticed with alarm that his eyes were wet.

"So!" she said loudly, hoping to take attention away from Christopher and also from herself. "I wonder where Betty has disappeared to—she's been baking God knows what for several hours. Let me get you all a drink—what will it be?" Unusually she clapped her hands together and then felt hot dread run through her—*Don't wake it. Don't be the one responsible for waking it.*

"I tell you what," said Bernadette, "I am absolutely desperate for a cigarette. Christopher, do you have a spare? Michael's gone and given up."

On Christopher's face, a giant and over-performed smile.

"Why yes I do," he said and cleared his throat.

"I'm going to get our bags in," said Michael, "and then I'd love a Scotch, Mum, if you've got it—I've brought a bottle with me just in case." He left the room and Christopher patted down his jacket pocket to locate his cigarettes. Bernadette took the sleeping baby from him, with an ease that looked precarious. Christopher found his tobacco.

"Join me?" Bernadette asked. He nodded and suddenly Bernadette was holding the baby very close to Ruth, and before she knew it, it had been handed over. "Do you mind, just for a second? I'm absolutely dying for a smoke, and apparently it's not great for babies. She's perfectly unsmelly at the moment." And just like that Ruth found herself holding the sleeping child. She had never held a baby before. For a few weeks after she had lost her own, she had woken at night feeling a weight in her arms like she had been holding something tightly to her in her sleep, but her own baby had never materialised. She had woken and time had passed and very little was said other than *you can try again*.

Her blood remembered the leaping-salmon feeling when the baby had repositioned itself inside of her.

None of that.

The baby did not wake up even in her dangerous arms. The rain that had been threatening since the early morning released, and somewhere through an open window came the smell of it like old stone. Ruth shushed the baby and gently jigged her up and down, not because she needed comfort but because that was what she had seen mothers do, and because Ruth felt afraid for the pink creature, at a loss of how to help it. She wished to be the sort of person who could comfortably sing to take away the silence and the heavy feeling the child gave her. There was lightning but for the moment no thunder, the rain fell harder, making the rose heads in the garden shudder. She could see it out on the Bass Rock, the rain coming down like a lace veil that made the edges blend into the clouds.

If she had lived she would have been just like you. She didn't think it, but the words sounded in her head as if they had been injected there with a thick syringe.

352

Behind the piano, the girl appeared, picking as she always did at her fingers.

Look, Ruth thought loudly. *Look, it's a baby.*

The girl stayed where she was, flickered a little as thunder rolled over the water, as though she was startled by it. There was a feeling that in the drawing room there was more than just the girl, like the hammering of rain on the windows had summoned a host of others. The baby twitched in her sleep, her lips moving like she fed in her dream.

I

Katherine has taken a sabbatical and will stay on with Maggie and me at the house until it sells. Christopher has decided to keep Mum company a while in London. No one questions anything. No one mentions Dom. We walk Mum and Christopher and the dog over the golf course and down to the beach, we pass the rocks, we pass the skeleton of the rowing boat, upside down, holes in the hull. Mum and Christopher stop. They look at the ribs of the boat, their hands join. The dog pees next to it.

We are at times a line linked at the elbow. When we come to the site of the old outdoor swimming pool, now a seabird centre, and the auld kirk, we kiss each other goodbye. The two of them carry on up the ramp—it feels correct to leave us on the beach. Mum's hair, standing up on end and to the side like a wind-altered blackthorn tree, Christopher holding on to her elbow. They are not young.

Katherine, Maggie and I walk back, no longer linking arms, but talking. When we get to the turn-off to the golf course, I say, "I'm going to carry on for a bit—do you mind?"

"We'll make something to eat," Maggie says and pulls Katherine up towards the house, which I am grateful for. I want just a few moments alone. I wind up the track through the rough to the remaining trees of the little wood. The wind blows the sound of the train whistle through the trees, likely it is the Edinburgh train. There is such stillness in that small wood where my grandmother died that it catches my breath, I feel I am looking up into space or into a deep high-ceilinged crevasse. "Hello!" I call, just to hear if my voice echoes back. It does, three times.

On the bed, the girl's largest suitcase. It is not big enough to move a whole life, but it will have to do. More than half the clothes are for the child, she will grow out of them quickly, but she can't bring herself to leave them behind. She can't believe they have come to this place.

When they met, the girl was still in uniform at school. And he insisted they wait. That is how she knew the difference.

Her nan and her mum kept telling her "Don't be in such a hurry to grow up," like they'd forgotten how it was. Like there was a choice. She'd seen it in the other girls in her class, even some the year below who hadn't even any tits yet. It arrived in the night, this weight. One day you're putting on a load of washing to help your mum, and the next you're picking up your brother's filthy pants off his floor, opening a window so the smell goes. First you're preheating the oven so your mum can put the dinner on when she gets in after work, the next you're doing the cooking every other night, your dad and brothers sat in front of the TV, shooting prostitutes or Afghanis, and they don't answer you when you tell them tea's ready, and you roll your eyes, but feel a little warmth of satisfaction alongside the annoyance. You have been accepted into womanhood by the boyhood.

I don't know why I bother, you say.

The girl rings a taxi, asks it to come in fifteen, remembers the toothbrushes, and baby shampoo. In the bathroom, she puts on a little more cover-up—she doesn't want people talking, she hates how embarrassing it all is. You have to put something with a hint of green in on first to properly cover up a deep bruise, but there's not time. She checks out the bathroom window, the street is still empty, the sea slate grey and the rock looks white today against thunderclouds.

The night they did it, at his bedsit, the night she turned sixteen, she had teased him that she'd been born in the early hours of the morning, so technically he was still a rapist, and he had become angry. "Don't even joke about that shit," he'd said steamily. "You have no idea what it's like, the panic that one of these is lying about her age—you're not lying, are you? Are you?"

Men, she'd thought with affection. *What are they like?* His concern was endearing, she decided, and they did it again so she knew she was forgiven.

He came a few weeks later and met the family. He popped in before they went to the pictures. She wore a full-length dress, heavy eyebrows and make-up to hollow in cheekbones that would be there once her puppy fat had bled out. He was in clean work overalls, which she was pleased about—it showed her father and brothers he was a grafter, and that he could take care of her. He held his van keys in his hand, anxious to get going, but the girl's father offered him a beer and they sat awkwardly in the front room, a quiz on the telly. He was quiet but polite to her father, ignored her brothers until one of them turned on the shooting game, and he sat forward on his seat, asked about it. Before long he was one of them, and her father told her, *Bring the lad another beer*, and she could feel her lipstick drying on her mouth.

"If we go now we can still make the film—won't get the adverts, though," she'd said, and he'd looked at her, disappointment on his face.

As they left her father squeezed her arm, a sign he liked her choice. He didn't speak much on the drive to the cinema and was a little surly after the film. She shouldn't have forced him to leave when he was having a good time. When she got back late, one of her brothers was still up, she saw the back of his head.

"That bloke's all right," he said. "You bringing him round again?"

And a funny thing happened when she got pregnant, that he was already part of her family, and although she was only seventeen, no one minded, and if she did she tucked it behind herself with the other things she couldn't be sure of. It is important to be sure. Always.

He was there every Sunday as she and her mum and her nan served up the roast, he even made a small speech at her nan's funeral, which everyone clapped him on the back for. When her waters broke in the middle of a row about the amount of money she spent on brand cleaning products, he rang her mum and spoke on her behalf, told her no one was wanted at the hospital, they'd call when the baby came.

A girl, another.

There was an infection and they stayed in the hospital a few days, he had to finish a job he was under contract for. When she complained about being left alone, he broke her finger. He was so sorry. He was just under so much pressure and the girl knew how to push his buttons. The nurse who splinted her finger asked how it happened. *Caught it in the door*, she said.

The suitcase is not yet closed, but it is full. She will take only her daughter's one favourite soft toy. That will have to be enough. She is due to pick her up in the next hour from her mum's then she will go on to stay with her friend, it is all planned. She catches her fingernail on a loose thread and it feels raw, like how she feels on the inside. Her fingernails are painted red, she did it last night to try to calm herself down, but her hands had shook and it had taken a long while to clean up the mess she'd made of them. She imagines herself and her daughter five years from now, sees them on a tropical island for some reason. Anything is possible.

She takes the cuddly toy, a long-eared rabbit, from her daughter's room and lays it on top of the pile of clothes in the suitcase. She closes the top over and sits on it to squash everything down, begins to tug at the zipper. It starts to give. The taxi will arrive in just a few minutes. She stops and stands very still. Downstairs the soft closing of the door.

Acknowledgements

The quotation on page 64 is from "You Can Call Me Al," with lyrics by Paul Simon. The quotation on page 128 is from "When a Man Loves a Woman," with lyrics by Calvin Lewis and Andrew Wright.

Thanks to:

Mum, Dad, Scout, Juno, Hebe, Speedy, Tom, Emma, Flynn, Jack, Matilda.

The Wylds, for being unfazed by my prying. I hope in among the carnage you recognise my affection for you all.

Everyone at Jonathan Cape, who, like always, provided exactly what I needed, especially Ana Fletcher, Michal Shavit and Joe Pickering. Diana Miller at Knopf and Nikki Christer at PRH Australia.

All at Watson Little, but most of all Laetitia Rutherford.

Sherele Moody, who I've never met but whose Australian Femicide and Child Death Map feels like the baseline of what I think about.

ACKNOWLEDGEMENTS

Karen Kilgariff and Georgia Hardstark, Kiri Pritchard-McLean and Rachel Fairburn for their fantastic podcasts and for making women feel less shifty about themselves.

Friends who helped in all sorts of ways, Karen and Minnie, Gwen and Ross, Joe, Sian, Claire, Lizzie, Katia, Roz, Ruth, Alex, Ary, Max.

David and Johanna, Dylan and Blake for playing with Jamie and Buddy on the weekends while I finished the book.

Jamie, I wouldn't write anything without your support, you can have half of whatever.

And Buddy, I wrote much of this book with one hand while you held on to my fingers in your sleep, thanks for the company.